# THE STONE LION

# THE STONE LION

## WILLIAM EISNER

THE PERMANENT PRESS
*Sag Harbor, NY 11963*

For information, address:
  The Permanent Press
  4170 Noyac Road
  Sag Harbor, NY 11963
  www.thepermanentpress.com

*Library of Congress Cataloging-in-Publication Data*

Eisner, William—
    The stone lion / William Eisner.
        pages cm
    ISBN 978-1-57962-312-8
        1. Businessmen—Fiction. 2. Corporate culture—Fiction.
    3. Fathers and daughters—Fiction. 4. Man-woman
    relationships—Fiction. I. Title.

PS3555.I89S87 2013
813'.54—dc23                                    2012039507

Printed in the United States of America

*There is no greater sorrow*
*than thinking back upon a happy time*
*in misery . . .*

—*The Divine Comedy: Inferno,* Canto V
Dante Alighieri (*c.* 1265–1321)

# ONE

On a sun-drenched May morning, after twenty-two years with the same company, George Breal left his office at United Electric for the last time. He shook hands with his staff, noticed that few looked him in the eye, and drove home over the Pennsylvania back roads and past the budding trees and white farmhouses protected by hex signs on the barns. The landscape had taken on an unfamiliar look, as though seen for the first time. His possessions, the detritus of almost a decade in the same office—engineering texts, photographs of his wife, three daughters and grandson Matthew, Philadelphia Phillies coffee cup, notepads printed with his name—rattled in a cardboard box in the trunk of his Buick.

Breal turned at a bullet-pocked sign: "READING 3." As he approached his house, nestled in a grove of trees and now spangled with sunlight, the sense that all was new, never before seen, intensified. He had the impression that this vision of his home—where he and his family had lived for the past nine years and on which he had lavished so much care—still and out of time like a painting, would stay with him; and as the years went by would remain the most precious image of an era soon to be gone. Breal was out of work for the first time in his life.

When he bitterly told his wife what she already knew—how he had given years of sixty-hour weeks to the company—Susan Breal, her large-boned face and hazel eyes showing annoyance, cut him short. "Your best bet now," she said, "while the company is loaded with guilt, is to extract as much money as possible from them as you leave."

Breal composed his résumé, and tried to make the haphazard turns of his career appear an orderly and planned progression. He puffed up his responsibilities, tried to quantify his accomplishments, was tempted to lie but thought better of it, and, when it was done, observed to his wife that this bloodless description was only distantly related to his actual life. Finally, he wrote a cover letter asking for an interview.

Breal searched the Reading public library, found the *Dun and Bradstreet Million Dollar Directory*, and listed on three-by-five cards the name, address, and president of every electronic controls company in the Northeast. He then mass-mailed the letter and résumé to the president of each company, praying that in the current recession someone still needed a general manager.

In about ten days he started to receive replies—attractive envelopes printed with company logos—containing a form letter from the personnel office saying no in the most gracious terms. Others sent complex employment applications which Breal dutifully filled out and returned, though he felt his résumé should have sufficed.

He studied the ads in the *Wall Street Journal* and responded to anything that remotely fit. He interviewed with a company outside of Philadelphia that made electronic proximity fuses for artillery shells. He could tell by the expression on the personnel director's face that the job was lost when he said that he had never dealt with military customers. Weeks passed. He broadened his net to include companies in the Midwest and South, and finally California. Most never bothered to reply.

Breal concentrated his energies on the house; he scrubbed the brick exterior, painted the wood fence, pruned encroaching branches, mowed the grass, ripped crabgrass from the lawn, changed the filter in the furnace, planted a vegetable garden. The spring rains were heavy that year and he experienced a bad allergy season. He glared at the newly sprung grass and flowering trees as if they were enemies and sighed, a man done in by innocent things.

As the days lengthened to summer, Breal crouched for hours under the bright sun weeding his garden, then rested in the puddle of shade under a tree. He thought the neighbors avoided him as he worked around the house week after week. He painted the back porch while his wife performed the unaccustomed task of preparing his lunch; he learned that at midday she grimly limited herself to salads.

"It's hand-to-hand combat, George," she said, "and you fight it out every day at every meal."

Breal had to admire Susan's tenacity in the uneven struggle against her Pennsylvania Dutch heritage that insidiously fastened weight upon her robust body. Breal had no such problem.

He interviewed with a manufacturer of high-speed computer printers in Tulsa. Breal knew as he spoke to the president that his accent was wrong for the job. He interviewed with a company in Lansing that made automotive electronics, but he had no experience with production lines that output a million units a year. He found that at the third interview his speech had taken on a whining tone, the voice of a supplicant. He interviewed twice more, once with a headhunter who was recruiting for an electronic instruments company in San Jose, then with an ITT vice president who arranged to meet him at the Admirals Club in the Philadelphia airport, and who was continually distracted by women passersby. Breal became conscious of his age.

He watched his wife's apprehension rise as the months passed and his severance pay was eaten up in mortgage payments and the costs inherent in staying alive. They no longer ate out, and for the first time Susan cut money-saving coupons from the papers. Unemployment insurance amounted to little and they were now depleting their savings. Time had become hostile. Susan found a job in a day care center and while she never complained, Breal saw her frustration in the hardened lines of her face and her irritation over trivial things. He mildly suggested she search for something other than spending the day with squalling brats.

"Like what?" Susan said, short-tempered now. "There's a recession in the land. Remember?" Then she went on, "Maybe you should lower your sights. Forget about management. Get back into engineering. You won't make as much but it beats not working."

Breal did not answer. Some internal map had grown blurry, where he had been, where he was going.

The summer passed; frost came early and he raked leaves in the cold morning air. Unreality cloaked his movements. He had a slippery sensation, the world gliding by—he left behind, somehow fluid, insubstantial. He stared at his face in the mirror, had difficulty recognizing himself, saw a face disfigured by the loss of hope. Fear lapped at him.


ONE EVENING, the Tuesday after Columbus Day, as he sat brooding before the TV, he received a phone call from a Miss Krane, secretary to Dr. John Lowell, president of Electronic Technologies, in Cambridge, Massachusetts. Was he still available? Did he have experience in electronic production? Would he amplify on his letter and detail his manufacturing background? In an inspired moment, Breal asked Miss Krane if she would send him by Express Mail the company's annual report and proxy statement.

Breal studied the annual report: Electronic Technologies was a medium-size company, had been in business for forty-two years and was still run by its founder, John Elliott Lowell, who was chairman and president. The company had shown little growth over the past ten years. Its shares were traded on the American Stock Exchange under the symbol ETI. He learned from the proxy statement that Lowell owned forty percent of the stock. Breal proceeded to build his letter around the manufacturing technology of the company, cribbing several phrases from the annual report. A week later Miss Krane called inviting him to Cambridge for an interview with Dr. Lowell. "I wouldn't mind living in Boston," Susan said. "In fact, I wouldn't mind living at the South Pole as long as you were working."

BREAL WAS shown into Lowell's office by Miss Krane, a hunched sunken-faced woman with a scarecrow body and worried eyes, clothing moth-colored. He walked at least fifty feet before reaching the president's desk. Set back against the wall and flanking the massive desk were an American flag to the left and a light blue flag to the right. The office resembled an old English men's club: paneled walls, couch and chairs upholstered in maroon leather, a circular coffee table with a thick variegated marble top; and an elliptical conference table in dark wood encircled by six chairs, also upholstered in maroon leather, sat in a far corner of the room near the entrance.

Lowell rose from his wing-back executive chair and, moving quickly, came out from behind his desk, a liver-spotted hand thrust forward. He was short but broad-shouldered, bald, with a perfectly trimmed white beard. His head seemed meant for a larger body. A Titian-red handkerchief in his breast pocket matched the silk of his tie. He conveyed the impression of old-world elegance, a Rothschild or a DuPont. Lowell sat on the couch and motioned Breal to take a place on the other side of the marble table. The large windows behind Lowell gave out on the Boston skyline and the Charles where three sailboats now broke the expanse of sun-brightened water.

"Are you working now?" Lowell asked

"No. I was general manager of the Electronic Controls Division of United Electric. They sold the division to a British company who appointed one of their own to run the place."

"Nobody lets a good man go. If you're any good why didn't they find something else for you to do?" Lowell's jacket was open; a Phi Beta Kappa key dangled from a gold chain that hung in an arc across his vest.

"United Electric is a twelve billion dollar enterprise. It's a huge impersonal machine. I was caught between austerity at United and the British who wanted someone from London to run the show. I was just plain unfortunate. Wrong place at the wrong time."

"I can't tell the unfortunate from the incompetent," Lowell said. His voice also seemed meant for a larger body. He leaned back, contemplated Breal, then said, "What have you accomplished in your life? What are you most proud of?"

Breal stared at Lowell: bald head reflecting the light from the windows, eyes intelligent, hard, about him a sheen of wealth and power. The room itself had an air of superiority. What was he proud of? Certainly not his family. His father who asked too many questions, who in fact questioned everything Breal did; he was always faintly accusatory, drank too much and could never keep a job. His mother, a frightened resentful woman who suffered terrible nightmares all her life, who saw disaster around every corner, whose greatest need was to be needed. All events for her embodied an important law, but she could not say what that law was.

He had made his way through the electrical engineering program at Temple while running a forklift truck nights and weekends at the John Wanamaker warehouse—but then many others had done similar things. He escaped from home while still in college and married a girl from Harrisburg, an English Lit major at Temple. They lived in Philadelphia during the early years and that's where their children were born, then Pittsburgh and finally Reading. "Any place that can produce a Wallace Stevens and a John Updike can't be all bad," his wife said when Breal told her that he had been offered the chief engineer's job in Reading. His daughters were all safely married now and the oldest had a baby boy who was two years old. But becoming a grandfather was something that in the course of time just happened. On reflection, he wasn't proud of much of anything.

Breal remembered that manufacturing was Lowell's primary interest. "I came to the Controls Division nine years ago as chief engineer. Four years later I was appointed general manager. I made the place a major cash generator and all the emphasis was on efficient manufacturing. I sliced overhead, doubled our return on assets, grew sales through increased market share, and grew profits twice as fast as sales."

"Why did they sell the division?"

"It didn't fit United Electric's strategy. They're only interested in high-growth businesses. We were very profitable, but in a low-growth market."

"Why did the other fellow buy it?"

"The British company wanted our distribution channel for their own products. It's much easier and a lot less risky to buy an established distribution network than try to build one from scratch."

As Breal spoke, Lowell's eyes stayed locked on him with the intensity of a mind reader. "I understand what makes a company work and what makes a manufacturing unit effective," Breal said to Lowell's unblinking stare. "If you can deliver a quality product to the loading dock on schedule and within the target cost then you've done your job."

In response to further questioning, Breal summarized his career in engineering and general management, emphasized his work with manufacturing, tried not to ramble, to keep his presentation crisp, orderly, interesting.

Lowell continued his scrutiny of Breal as if he were deciphering his DNA. "Tell me," he said, "why are manhole covers round?"

Breal thought he had misheard. He was about to ask Lowell to repeat the question when Lowell went on, "Why aren't manhole covers square, or hexagonal? Why round?" Lowell's eyes, stony as a snake's, were without humor. It was a serious question.

Breal searched for an answer, could think of no reason why a manhole cover couldn't be any arbitrary shape. He was about to say that it was easier for a foundry to cast something round rather than square since there were no stress corners. But he sensed this was not the right answer. It had something to do with application. Lowell continued to stare at him and in that stare Breal saw all the interrogators in his life: his father, teachers, other bosses. . . . He learned early to dislike those who interrogated. Lowell's eyes were unwavering; Breal thought of twin spiders, motionless, waiting for prey. The room appeared to have grown larger, filled with a bright tyrannical light, he shrunken. Then Breal felt the jab of intuition: an answer came to him, simple, possibly right. "No matter how you turn it," he said, "a round cover can't fall into the hole. Any other shape could."

Lowell, unmoving as a monument, gave no sign whether Breal's answer was right or not. "What are your weaknesses?" Lowell asked.

Breal considered this an unfair question, a confessional kind of question, and decided to offer as a negative something Lowell could construe as a positive. "I work too hard," Breal said. "Maybe I give too much of myself to the job. But that's the way I'm put together." Again, no response from Lowell. Then Breal decided that instead of passively waiting for questions, being proactive was a better strategy. "What specific job am I interviewing for, Dr. Lowell?"

"We'll get to that," Lowell answered. "Or maybe we won't. . . . What do you consider the world's most beautiful object?"

Breal was tempted to leave, as if he were there by mistake and should be elsewhere. What did manhole covers and beautiful objects have to do with manufacturing? Plus, the man struck him as one who in other times would sit on the Inquisition's interrogating tribunal, one who happily condemned heretics to burn at the stake. But long months of idleness, the recession, and his wife's bitterness caused humility to fill Breal's soul. The world's most beautiful object. . . . He decided there was no use trying to guess an answer that would please Lowell. He was debating between flowers in a garden and the naked body of a woman when Lowell's telephone buzzed.

"Excuse me a moment," Lowell said.

Breal closed the door behind him, and waited in the antechamber where Miss Krane was hunched over a mound of letters. "That's a lot of mail," Breal remarked.

Miss Krane gave Breal a tunneled look. "It should be," she finally answered. "It's the mail for the whole company."

"The whole company? Do you route the mail for the whole company?"

"Not exactly," she answered, staring at Breal obliquely as if sensing a trap. "Dr. Lowell reads all the mail, then parcels it out."

Breal, his interest aroused, noticed a pile of forms next to Miss Krane's typewriter. "What are all those orange papers?" he asked.

"Purchase requisitions. Nobody at ETI including the vice presidents can spend any money without Dr. Lowell's signature." She uttered the phrase as if it were dogma, as if the rule were ordered by papal decree.

Breal was about to observe that Lowell certainly had a hands-on management style when Miss Krane's phone buzzed.

"Dr. Lowell is free," she said, face blank as a window shade.

Breal reentered Lowell's office and returned to his chair; the sun had shifted and now shone directly in his face. Breal squinted, turned his head.

Lowell rose to adjust the blinds, "Neither the sun nor death can be looked at steadily," he said and smiled.

Breal had the feeling the smile should be accompanied by a sound—that of an ice field cracking. Then the smile sank into his face, disappeared. He wondered whether Lowell had ever felt anything deeply, either pain or pleasure.

The world's most beautiful object apparently forgotten, Lowell asked, "What do you want out of life?"

What Breal wanted, and wanted desperately, was a job. And what he wanted to talk about was his job qualifications; but Lowell was obviously into psychologically oriented questioning, and so Breal answered, "The health and happiness of my family."

"Surely you want more than that," Lowell said, waving an impatient hand. "What about professionally?"

It occurred to Breal that Lowell was testing his level of ambition. "To contribute to the company I'm with," Breal answered. "To make a difference."

Lowell brushed the air before him as if waving away a gnat; he did not seem satisfied. "Whom do you most admire?"

Recognizing that Lowell had founded the company, Breal answered, "Entrepreneurs, those who start from nothing and build an enterprise. That's not easy. It takes vision, drive, staying power, persuasion skills. Qualities you don't often find in one man." Again, no reaction.

In response to further questioning—feeling Lowell's gaze as a steady pressure on his face—Breal skewed his answers toward his career in engineering and general management, again emphasizing his work in manufacturing.

Then Lowell, who apparently had stopped listening, rose, stood at a sunlit window, spoke toward the river and the city beyond. "ETI needs renewing," he said. "And the place to start is manufacturing. That's where the profits are made or lost." He elaborated on this theme, resting against a wall; Breal had the impression that the wall, the building itself, all weak and dependent, leaned against Lowell for support. "I need a top-notch manufacturing man. Maybe you're that man. But I'm not at all sure."

Lowell returned to his seat opposite Breal—returned to his observation of him—and his questioning changed character: "Is there any superstition in your life—what is it, and does it work? Looking back, is there anything you did *not* do but wish you had? Is it okay sometimes to lie? If you could recreate yourself, what would you choose to be? Were you ever really amazed at anything? Why does time only move forward? Why does religion exist? If you could change the world in one way, in what way would that be? What is the purpose of your life? Why do we die?"

Breal sensed that Lowell was fishing for something deep within him, some weakness or hidden shame that Breal himself was not aware of. As the questioning went on and on, the room itself seemed to be interrogating him, relentlessly, and Lowell himself appeared barbarous and feral.

As Breal stumbled through answers—feeling he was being stripped bare and detesting Lowell more by the minute— Lowell became something other than human. He seemed assembled of alien parts: reptilian organs, acid blood, stainless steel bones.


THEY WERE joined for lunch by Dick Miles, ETI's treasurer and chief financial officer, a spectral man who, Lowell remarked in passing, had had the job for the past thirty years. Lunch was at a private club in Boston. The maître d' escorted them past the paneled walls hung with illuminated paintings of old English hunting scenes, to a table adjacent to a huge casement window that gave out onto a boulevard where trees, now russet, cast leafy shadows on the central swath of grass that divided the avenue. As Breal took a place opposite Lowell and Miles, he caught a glimpse of the Hancock building silhouetted blue-green against a now clouding sky. But he was not focused on the landscape but inward: how to persuade Lowell that he was a top-notch manufacturing man, though his own hands-on manufacturing experience wasn't much.

"Dick, ask Mr. Breal some questions," Lowell said.

Miles turned a pinched face toward Breal—he resembled a discouraged Stan Laurel—and asked, "What is your production background?"

Breal, not yet recovered from Lowell's interrogation but pleased to get away from metaphysics, once again reviewed his years at United Electric, stressing manufacturing, directing his reply to Miles though intending it for Lowell. While Miles asked and Breal responded, Lowell heavily salted a filet mignon, rare, which he washed down with a Tanqueray martini; he seemed to pay no attention to Miles' questions or Breal's replies. Rather he interrupted Breal in midsentence with a statement unrelated to the topic they were discussing.

"Tell him how I started the company," Lowell said as he flicked a crumb from his sleeve.

"Dr. Lowell was a pioneer in the use of electronics for the control of factory machinery." Miles said his boss' name with a certain awe, as though it were magic. "He built the company's first products on his kitchen table, and taught electrical engineering simultaneously at MIT and Boston University to raise the working capital for the company." Miles recounted this in a steady drone, as if he were reciting the rosary. "Dr. Lowell would go to Detroit, make a sale, design and build the unit, then deliver it in two weeks." Breal sensed he was listening to the recitation of legend.

"It was a hard sell in those days," Lowell chimed in. "A plant foreman once said to me, 'You mean you're going to use a *radio* instead of *people* to control this here machine?'"

"Nobody before Dr. Lowell had ever thought of using electronics to control factory machinery," Miles added.

WHEN THE three returned to ETI, they took the elevator to the executive floor. As they stepped out onto their floor, Lowell stopped abruptly and stared down at the carpet. He pointed with his toe at a small yellow object on the rug. *"What is that?"* he cried. Breal was startled by the volume of Lowell's voice; Miles jumped as though he'd been shot.

There was a long silence. Miles now seemed paralyzed. No one moved. Breal imagined the scene as a video placed on pause: Lowell resting on one foot, an immaculately shined shoe pointing to the mysterious object; Miles, thin and stooped, staring downward. To Breal, the nature of the offending object was perfectly clear.

"I believe, sir, that it's a French fried potato," Miles finally said.

"I have told people time and again to limit their eating to the cafeteria!" Lowell boomed with medieval ferocity. "This has got to stop! Get someone to clean this up before it gets stepped on and mashed into the carpet."

"Yes, sir," Miles said, looking like a man thinking of hanging himself; then he bent, picked up the sliver of potato between thumb and forefinger, held it as though it were a dead mouse, and stood staring into remote space, apparently waiting for further instructions.

Lowell seemed not to notice. "And draft a memo for my signature. If I catch anybody bringing food to the executive floor, he is gone. I mean *gone*! Right then and right there!" Lowell dismissed Miles and the French fried potato, and invited Breal on a tour of the plant.


As LOWELL strode through the factory, people in his path scattered like pigeons and the air seemed to part before him. Breal, observing the long production lines chock-a-block with women on high stools bent over moving belts and assembling printed circuit boards, was struck by the antiquated nature of the facilities and equipment. Many operations were done by hand that could be done more efficiently by machine. He was astonished to see that ETI manufactured its own relays and transformers, specialized parts sold by many competent vendors who produced these devices in far larger quantity than ETI and at much lower cost. United Electric purchased small relays from Japan, of superb quality and at less than a dollar apiece. Looking around at the archaic assembly lines, Breal concluded that it must cost ETI ten times that to produce the same product. It occurred to him that perhaps Lowell knew this but refused to buy cheaper, perfectly acceptable components on the outside for the same reason that he read everyone's mail and signed off on every penny of expenditure.

With a flourish Lowell opened a door and Breal saw ten-thousand square feet of modern production space. He recognized the machinery as that used to make miniature electronic circuits. "We've invested two million dollars in new equipment," Lowell said, "not to mention another million in renovating the space—special air conditioning, special lights. . . . The one thing it all has in common is that it's expensive. This place makes parts for the M-90."

Breal scanned the operation, was surprised that none of the workers wore lint-free gowns or caps.

"Have you had experience with this kind of manufacturing?" Lowell asked.

"Yes, sir, I have," Breal said. "We used this process at United."

"How does this place look to you?" Lowell's hand moved in a sweeping arc to encompass all before him.

Lowell's gesture and expectant expression admitted only one response. "It's impressive," Breal said.

Lowell stopped to watch a woman take a completed circuit board, carry it to a table where there was a microscope and an electronic instrument, place the board on a tray, then return.

"Why is that table against the wall?" Lowell asked the supervisor. His voice had the growling intensity that Breal recognized from the French fried potato incident.

"That's an inspection station," the man replied, but carefully as one would answer a hostile prosecuting attorney.

Lowell stared at the man. "That table is at least twelve feet from the end of the line. The girl has to walk twenty-four feet every time she takes a circuit board to the table." Lowell's voice was rising in volume; it now reached a full-throated roar. "If that inspection station were in New Jersey and the girl had to take an airplane to get there every time a board was produced, it might occur to you that the table is too far away!"

The supervisor's expression was that of a man who had spotted a T-Rex bearing down upon him. Everyone turned, peered first at Lowell then at the table, then back to the safety of their work. Lowell stood rigid facing the supervisor; his face and bald head had a purplish cast under the fluorescent lights. A droplet of spittle hung in his beard. "That table is where the moving men put it when they brought it into the room!"

A pink purse lay on a bench; Lowell stared at it as if it were a dead rat. Then with a great swipe launched it into a wall; a tube of lipstick, a circular mirror, coins and safety pins scattered from the purse. "This is a place of business, not a checkroom!" he bellowed in a voice loud enough to command a regiment. All now huddled over their work as if a tornado were approaching and they were deep in prayer that it would pass them by.

Lowell aimed a finger at the supervisor. "Move that table! Clean up the inspection layout. I mean now!" He waved a hand, seeming to encompass not only the production line but the world. "Wasted motion! Did it ever occur to you what that costs?" Breal had seen angry bosses before but never like this. In that explosion of rage Lowell seemed to take on mythological proportions, some ancient god gone berserk. Lowell gave the supervisor and the table one last withering glance, then stormed out. All eyes watched him go.

Back at his office, Lowell, who seemed refreshed by his outburst, said, "My intuition is the one thing I trust. My intuition does not clearly tell me you can do the job. I'm not sure you have the vision. Isaiah says, 'Where there is no vision the people perish.' Well, where there is no vision companies perish also." Then Lowell's face and voice seemed to soften.

"I'll be in touch," he said, and in that instant Breal had a premonition of calamity.


As Breal waited outside for a cab, the sky now pewter gray and the wind shivering the surface of the river, he recalled Lowell's expression when he said, "I'll be in touch." Breal was sure he had detected a glimmer of sympathy and promise. A glimmer of hope. But as he thought of the weird man who had interrogated him and the business that had not grown in ten years, thought of the eunuch-like Miles, the scene in the ancient factory, he knew that being part of that world was not what he wanted.

Breal recounted the interview to his wife as she eagerly listened. "He wasn't sure I had vision," Breal said. "He quoted Isaiah, 'Where there's no vision the people perish.'"

"That's not Isaiah," Susan said. "That's from Proverbs. . . . Does he have a job for you?"

"It figures that he got the source of the quote wrong," Breal said. "It's a nice example of how he strikes me: a man often in error but never in doubt. Not to say crazy."

"How did he leave it?"

"That he'd be in touch. . . . But he's a strange duck: reading everybody's mail, throwing a fit over a French fried potato on the rug, going bonkers over a misplaced table in the factory, asking nutty questions. Is that the kind of person I want to work for? I mean, if someone sees little green men running around on his hand, can that be the only thing wrong with him?"

Susan's face had settled into a hard mask. "You can't always pick and choose," she said. "I work now and I've worked before. One way or another, to work for someone means to take shit. That's how things are. And these are bad times. . . . Aren't you sick of staying home?"

Breal's voice grew resentful, of one embittered by the injustice of the world. "Sure I'm sick of staying home. And

I'm not sure I can handle another interview, assuming I ever get one. I feel belittled sitting there, having them ask me idiotic questions while they count the wrinkles around my eyes. But this guy . . . a crazy little Napoleon is what he is."

"So what if he overreacts sometimes," Susan said. "Maybe he *is* paranoid. Maybe he's a little nuts. So what? That's a real business he's got there and if he wants you to help him run it, why not take the job? Anyway, if he wasn't interested why did he take you to lunch, or bother having that guy tell you how the big man founded the company, or give you a plant tour?"

"We'll talk about it if he ever makes me an offer," Breal said. He thought back to that final look on Lowell's face, that glimmer of hope. Had he only imagined it? And the more he thought of Lowell and Miles and Miss Krane, and the factory supervisor and the crazy questions, the more he prayed that the look was his own imagining. And so Breal humbly followed up on more help wanted ads as he waited for Lowell's call, hoping this strange man would not call—because if he did, Breal knew he could not refuse the offer.

In the wasteland of a sleepless night, Breal recalled Lowell's interrogation, question after question, the man's reptilian gaze, the light reflecting off his marble-like head, the scene in the factory. The possibility of working for Lowell, being subject to his will day after day, settled in Breal's joints like the start of the flu.

## TWO

I have even given the scene a name: The Banishment. The black and white image is grainy, soundless, gestures exaggerated, faces congested. Catherine's legs are apart as she tries to hold her ground while I shout, then finally point toward the door, arm extended like a nineteenth-century villain. We're in the Great Hall—it seems more vast than it is, like those enormous European railroad stations, Frankfurt or Milan—a stage that in retrospect strikes me as far too large for the scene. I have lost the words I hurled at her, if indeed I ever remembered them. Do you, does anyone, remember words shouted in anger? But the intent was brutally clear: if you marry that fool, then you will never again enter this house, never again see me, nor ever touch a cent of mine.

Catherine, brave and beautiful, her pale face at that moment resembling her mother when *she* left, does not cry, does not plead. I remember (or think I remember) what she said: "I am a grown woman, father, and we are not in the middle ages. You cannot dictate whom I marry." Even got the grammar right—or have I, in recollecting, unconsciously corrected it? Ah, how trite are the pivotal scenes of life! She turns, head high, strides to the door. A child ripened into ingratitude. Yet never have I loved her so much. Come back, for heaven's sake, come back! . . . How many years ago was that? It all glides away, doesn't it? Dead leaves on a slow stream.

Only now do I replay The Banishment with any regularity. It has taken on the look of those old-time movies where one turned a crank and watched the hero drive away the villain and rescue the girl. It must have to do with age and regret, this slow review of your life, your failures, the mess you made of so many things. Bad to look back, though, useless really. But then who of us would not want his life before him? Who would not want to begin again?

JOHN LOWELL'S legs ached. He called it show fatigue—his theory was that it was caused by the cement floor, being on your feet all day, never walking in a straight line. "It's the crowds," he recalled, once remarking to his ex-wife, "you're always sidestepping people. You're not used to spending a day walking sideways." That was toward the end, she behind a gray curtain of indifference, face hardened, a goddess grown remote. But Lowell had not been on his feet for a day or even an hour. He dropped into a canvas chair, surveyed his company's booth. The displays demonstrated photoelectric devices in action in response to rotating wheels, sliding bars. A fish tank sat in the center of the booth, goldfish swimming about. Four M-90 photoelectric controls, each about the size of a cigarette pack, his company's newest product and on which three years of effort and virtually his entire engineering budget had been expended, hung by their electrical cables, immersed in the water, each connected to a red light. Each time a fish swam in front of a control a light flashed.

Andre Tergelen, Lowell's head of marketing, must have seen him staring at the tank. "We got tired of hearing customers complain that the M-90 failed in washdown. We wanted to show that we've fixed it so it's now watertight," Tergelen said, with a determined expression.

"We should have gotten it right in the first place," Lowell grumbled. "Nothing worse than a new product getting off to a bad start. Upsets your customers." Lowell frowned, "By the way, where *are* the customers? I see our salesmen sitting around, and lots of people in the aisles, but only a couple of pack rat brochure collectors in our booth."

"It's still early," Tergelen said, as his determined expression abruptly collapsed.

Lowell picked up a show directory from the table beside him. On the cover, in bold square-edged type, were the words International Packaging Week, McCormick Place, Chicago, IL, October 1980. Lowell riffled the pages, found his company's entry: "Automatic sensors for industry. Advanced photoelectric controls. Fiber optics." He shut the book, vaguely dissatisfied: an awfully thin summary of forty years of labor. It read like an epitaph. He got to his feet. "Let's have a look around," Lowell said to Tergelen. "See what the competition is up to."

The two men zigzagged through the crowded aisles. Lowell observed with distaste the strategies exhibitors used to gain the customer's attention. A British company, one of Lowell's competitors, resorted to a magic show with a pitchman in a tuxedo. Another company had placed a gold bar on a metal plate above a hole in the center of a table, and the visitor was invited to grasp the bar. As his hand moved toward the golden object, a photoelectric device that sensed the motion activated a hydraulic arm which, in turn, yanked the metal plate and bar through the hole. It was a great favorite and drew many people to the booth. Lowell watched: no one succeeded in getting close to the gold bar. He found the whole contrivance Kafkaesque and the scene a gloomy metaphor for life itself. Lowell's gaze was continually caught by young women dressed in reds and golds who handed out brochures and plastic shopping bags imprinted with the company name. There was an air of conviviality among the salesmen at the booths. It had the festive air of a sporting event or a company outing; and selling—rather than the desperate business Lowell knew it was—took on a carnival atmosphere that cloaked the seriousness of the enterprise.

Lowell noted that many of the shopping bags people carried were yellow, with a name in bold black on the plastic. He stopped at one booth where the photoelectric devices on the machines were bright yellow and of astonishingly small size—controls he had never seen before. "Who makes those?" he asked Tergelen, pointing to one of the miniature devices.

Tergelen approached a salesmen at the booth and indicated the yellow device. "Mühlmann, a German company," the man said. "They've got a booth on the main aisle."

Lowell tensed as he visualized another competitor entering his market. "Goddamn it, Andre! How come I have to find these things out at a trade show?"

"This is news to me," Tergelen said gloomily.

"Let's go see," Lowell said.

On the way, Tergelen paused at the booth of Opticon, a small U.S. manufacturer of photoelectrics. "Hi, Emil," Tergelen said to a young man, and then introduced Lowell to Emil Rostov, Opticon's Chief Engineer. "If you want shock," Rostov said, "go see the Mühlmann display."

"He's a Russian émigré," Tergelen said after they left Opticon, "and a very smart man."

"That smart man says we're in for a shock," Lowell said. "Why do I have to hear that from a competitor?"

At the Mühlmann booth, as at Lowell's, there were no costumes and no women on display. The salesmen wore oversized badges with the name Mühlmann in square black letters on a yellow background. They were all dressed in identical dark blue suits and bright yellow ties, each with a cluster of customers before him. A neat pile of yellow plastic shopping bags, the name Mühlmann printed on the side of each bag, was lying on a circular table in front of the booth.

What first struck Lowell about the Mühlmann controls, other than their yellow color, was their size. They were not much larger than a match box, about a quarter the volume of his company's newest product. He scanned a Mühlmann brochure, then studied it more carefully.

"Good Lord, Andre," Lowell said, "if you have tears prepare to shed them now. Their sales literature says this thing's performance is superior to the M-90."

Tergelen stared at the brochure, squinted at it as if it were written in Cyrillic. Lowell then pointed at the Mühlmann controls arranged on a display table. "How do they make them so goddamn small?" he asked.

"Integrated circuit, probably," Tergelen said. "All the control functions on a single chip."

"Why did our engineering department say that wasn't economical?"

But Lowell did not listen to Tergelen's mumbled reply as he stared at the bright yellow objects. They seemed otherworldly, something from another civilization, another planet. A thought, hard-edged, crystallized: Lowell experienced an instant of panic. "Ask them what they're selling these things for," he said.

"Their price is about half ours," Tergelen said when he returned, his expression that of a man with a toothache.

Lowell once again stared at the Mühlmann controls, had the impression of staring into an abyss, the order of his world shifting. Lowell, mouth a compressed line, pulled Tergelen to a corner of the booth. "Where in hell have you been?" he hissed. "There you stand, wrapped in ignorance, while all this is happening around you." He stared at Tergelen, face turned to concrete. "As I understand it, marketing intelligence is part of your job. That means not spending all your time tinkering with our distribution, but devoting a couple of days a year to tracking what the competition is doing."

"They don't have the distribution to sell it," Tergelen said, quietly but decisively.

"Lay not that flattering unction to your soul!" Lowell cried. "Buy a dozen of these things. Have Reliability check them out. Test hell out of them." But as he said this, Lowell knew what the answer would be. His new product, the M-90, on which so much precious time and budget had been expended, was obsolete before it came to market. Lowell stared further at the yellow rectangles—they imposed themselves like a bad odor—then looked around the Mühlmann booth: the air itself seemed ominous, the dawn of battle. Still, Tergelen was right: they didn't have ETI's distribution.

# THREE

Catherine walked through her department, Young Women's Wear, toward her office, noticed that the cable knit sweater dresses had hardly budged and the Leslie Fay plaid wraparound kilts hadn't moved at all. Maybe she should have gone for the giant hound's-tooth checks. Christ, who knew what the kids wanted? The tailored outfit—tweed blazer and tapered jeans—had sold out. And she'd bought only a half dozen of those and that after a whole morning of agonizing.

"The big boss was looking for you," the girl at the register said. "She didn't look too happy." The girl gave Catherine a rubbery smile, seemed pleased, as though her own life had suddenly become more interesting.

Catherine sat before her new boss. The woman, thin as a ripsaw, couldn't be much over thirty, makeup artfully applied to emphasize aggressive cheekbones, hard mouth. A month ago there had been a shakeup at the top that in the ensuing weeks rattled down to the bottom. Catherine's boss of fifteen years, the head of all women's wear retailing, had suddenly taken early retirement, replaced by this woman, recruited from Robinson's in Los Angeles. Not only had Catherine's old boss disappeared, but his solid mahogany desk, leather-covered chairs, potted plants and beige rug spotted with Coke stains had disappeared as well, replaced in days by a wall covering in French blue, a cobalt-colored rug and sleek Danish-modern furniture.

On her first day, the woman had called a meeting of all buyers, and stood in front of them, sharp-boned in a perfectly fitting no-nonsense blue-gray dress. (Catherine figured the dress, a straight line gabardine, was made by Adolfo or Louis Féraud; but whoever made it, Catherine had to admit, it was the real McCoy.) "We want clothes with an exciting story line," the woman said, "clothes that fire the customer's imagination. She can accomplish anything—from coaxing the man of her dreams into bed to getting that big promotion—when she's wearing those clothes." She then lectured on the importance of inventory turns and sales per unit floor space. The woman maintained eye contact throughout her talk, her oversized gold loop earrings flashing as she moved her head from face to face. "Are there any questions?" she finished. There were no questions, all faces quiet and blank as though waiting for a pain to subside.

The woman raised her eyes from the papers on her desk. She now wore miniature pearl earrings and large-framed glasses that made her narrow face appear wider. Catherine caught the distant scent of her perfume, something sweet and expensive, like Joy or Je Reviens. "Sales in your department are twenty percent below average and the sales per square foot *thirty* percent below average." She stared at Catherine with nailhead eyes. "We won't talk about profit. Young Women's Wear is always running a sale. You know what that means?" She paused as though expecting an answer, then went on before Catherine could speak. "I'll tell you what that means. The shit isn't moving. That's what it means. Clothes that move don't need sales. We're a full price house, not Filene's basement or K-Mart."

"We need more saleswomen in the department," Catherine said. "High quality, high priced clothes don't sell themselves."

The woman waved an impatient hand. "Nonsense! We want clothes that shriek, Buy Me! Your shit just hangs there. Mute. Dumb. For example, have you ever thought about body hugging denim jumpsuits? They give a terrific lean look. Or a leaf-print jumpsuit with jacket to match. Or in silk— that's got sex written all over it. It yells Fuck Me! Screams it out. And color. Forget that tartan. We're not in Scotland. How about hot pink, apple green, rugby stripes?" She glared at Catherine as if her life depended on the answer, then the new boss pointed an immaculately manicured finger. "Look, I want you to get out there. Look around. Talk to designers. See what's hot, what women on the make are wearing. Get some data."

"Sure, if that's what you want," Catherine said in a calm voice, feeling that she must speak soothingly, placate the hysteria that flickered in the woman's face.

The woman seemed not to have heard. She leaned back, touched her fingertips, scrutinized Catherine like an object. "I have a feeling that the clothes you're buying, you're subconsciously buying for yourself. Matronly things. Can you *relate* to young women, Catherine?"

"Of course I can," Catherine said and had a sudden sense of her own vulnerability.

"Show me, Catherine. That's all I'm asking. Show me."


CATHERINE STUDIED and restudied the menu, sipped her Pinot Grigio, munched grissini, and kept glancing toward the entrance. She experienced relief when he came through the door—fear of being stood up always lurked at the bottom of her heart—hair disarranged, scarf outside his jacket, looking about—then his neatly cut features lit. He bent toward her, his lips carrying the October chill.

"Sorry to keep you waiting," he said as he laid his scarf on an adjacent chair and plopped opposite her.

"Just don't make it a habit, darling," she said as she reopened her menu.

They ordered their dinner. Catherine reflected on her new boss—a madwoman pretending to be sane—and was tempted to tell him of their conversation, but thought better of it. One lamented to an older person not a younger one, particularly a much younger one. "Tell me, Kent," she said, "what do young women wear these days?"

He gave her a rakish look, the look she knew was his trademark. "Why are you asking *me*? That's your line of work . . ."

"Think of it as a market survey. I figure women will wear what men will most notice them wearing."

"Well, I notice a lot of stuff that clings to their ass."

Catherine thought of her own ass, which was flattening, then of silk jumpsuits, tight-fitting. Maybe jumpsuits weren't such a dumb idea after all. "I'm talking about women with enough money to shop at our store."

"Same answer. Maybe they buy better material, a better fit, maybe more subtlety, but the stuff still clings to their ass."

She thought of her own view of clothes: tight enough to show you're a woman, but loose enough to show you're a lady. Where had she learned that? From her mother probably. All wrong now.

"Did you get that assignment on the homeless?" Catherine asked.

"No. The guys at the *Globe* say nobody is interested in the homeless. They just want them to disappear. I'm trying to sell the paper an article on car theft in Boston. Did you know our town is the car theft capital of America?"

Catherine's thoughts had again shifted to her boss, pitiless eyes staring at her through those oversized frames, about the same age as the man before her. Maybe that bundle of nerves was right, maybe she could no longer relate to young women. Other than in bed, could she relate to Kent? "No, I didn't know that," she said as their food arrived.

They strolled toward his efficiency apartment on Beacon Street. Kent had made vague motions toward the check, but she had picked it up as she always did.

"Gin and tonic okay?" he said while fixing their drinks, then he stopped. "Is something bothering you, Kate? You've been, I don't know, sort of absent all evening."

"I'm okay. Just worried about sales of the fall and winter lines." She gave him a vague sidelong smile.

"You're a worrier," Kent said. He looked at her mischievously. "Maybe that's why you're successful." He set down their glasses, sat beside her.

Catherine closed her eyes, tried to lose herself in lovemaking, escape time; but a sense of impending disaster ran through her, that she could never satisfy those nailhead eyes, that like her old boss' mahogany desk she had been targeted for destruction.

CATHERINE HEARD the music in the hall, recognized the electronic sound of Luciano Berio that her son played over and over. "Turn that down!" she called as she opened the door. "Do you know what time it is? Think of the neighbors, for god's sake . . . What are you doing up, anyway?"

Her son Michael appeared in the doorway to his room, a skinny seventeen-year-old, unfortunately no taller than she, not at all like his older brother, a husky six-footer. "Studying for a math exam," he said.

"How can you study with all that racket?"

"Helps me concentrate."

Catherine knew she shouldn't complain because whatever the boy was doing worked. His grades were excellent—had been throughout high school—and now, starting his senior year, he had a chance at a scholarship.

Unlike his brother Tom, who had dropped out after one year at U Mass and now drove a cab on the night shift. "You get bigger tips at night," he said. "People are grateful, looser. Then you meet all sorts of weird and interesting characters."

The older boy—for boy is how she still thought of him though he had just turned twenty-one—aspired to be a writer. He had edited the school paper in high school and had a short story published in an obscure magazine. "Isn't the night shift dangerous?" she asked. "Greatly exaggerated, Mom," he answered.

Tom shared an apartment on Worcester Street, near the Boston City Hospital, with another driver, a black man with large solemn eyes who was usually mumbling in a foreign language over a thick book when she visited. "He's a Dante scholar," her son said. When they'd first met the man said, "My name is Ishmael," but a bit sadly as if he were the last in a long line of Ishmaels. Their apartment was in a decaying brownstone and always a mess. Sometimes she was tempted to clean at least Tom's room and the minute kitchen, which was stained with spaghetti sauce and substances not identifiable, but always decided not to. She would not be a maid, not even to her own son. The place broke her heart. "This is the sort of room where great novels are written," Tom said, gesturing at the faded and spotted wallpaper.

Michael, with the encouragement of his teachers and guidance counselor, had opted for engineering and applied to three prestige schools: MIT, Carnegie-Mellon, and Cal Tech. Catherine had checked their tuition fees plus the room and board were he to leave Boston, and was appalled at the numbers. She had no idea how she would handle those expenses if he didn't win a scholarship, especially since his father, long remarried, had new children and wanted nothing to do with his old life.

Catherine gave her son's arm a motherly touch. "You look tired," she said. "Maybe a good night's sleep would do you more good than last-minute cramming."

"You look tired yourself, Mom," Michael said. "Can I fix you a cup of tea?"

Once the tea was poured, they sat together at the kitchen table.

"Been with Kent?" Michael asked, looking at her across his tea cup.

"Yes." Catherine caught the altered tone of her son's voice. "You don't much like him, do you?"

"You know I don't. I think he uses you, and I'm not sure he's good for you."

Catherine shrugged. "You might be right. But then maybe we use each other."

The boy said nothing more but his face had hardened into an accusatory expression. At that moment Catherine had a vague sense of recognition. The expression was not new to her, came from somewhere else, from a distant past. As they rose to leave the kitchen, the boy's short stature and large round head before her, she recalled the expression. It was the boy's grandfather, her own father who he'd resembled. But then, why not? He resembled his grandfather physically and in his aptitude for math and science; the same genes could put his grandfather's expression on the boy's face.

Catherine, the recognition fresh in her mind, lay in bed and thought of her father, something she rarely did. After he had thrown her out of the house, banished her from his life, her own life had taken over, and by degrees she had forgotten him as though he had died. Occasionally, she saw his photograph in the financial pages of the *Globe* (did she, she wondered, turn to those pages unconsciously, searching for him, for, after all, what conceivable interest did she have in the financial pages?), always the same flattering photograph. Surely he would look much older now. Then she remembered another photograph, taken perhaps forty years ago, stark black and white, he in a paterfamilias pose, her mother, jaunty in a cloche hat, at his side; she, Catherine, small, black-haired, smiling, her younger brother Eric sullen, unhappy to be there, now long dead.

How old would her father be now? Born in 1908, would make him seventy-two. Next month, in fact, was his birthday. She passed his company every day, on Memorial Drive in Cambridge, at the foot of the Longfellow Bridge, on her way to work. But she no longer thought of the place as his company, him striding about his stadium-sized office, stubborn as stone, no doubt browbeating someone—all conversation with him an exercise in the use of power—for to be in his iron shadow was to be an instrument of his will. Now his headquarters was just another building to her, old and a bit seedy. Why, she asked herself, was she thinking of her father now? It served no useful purpose. An old wound that throbbed in changing weather. She held her pillow, thought of Kent, jumpsuits, college tuition, her own life.

TWO DAYS after his interview, Breal received a phone call from Miss Krane to appear in Lowell's office at nine the following morning. And so Breal left for Boston, Susan's words of encouragement trailing after him. But Breal had the feeling that he was now in the clutch of an unstoppable black tide, swept along toward a destiny beyond his control.

"ETI needs modernizing, renewal," Lowell said. "And manufacturing is the key. That's where you win or lose." He elaborated on this theme, then, as he went on, he seemed to tighten, to gaze more intently at Breal. "We have a new product going into the market. It costs too much. I need a good man, someone with a fresh eye, who can spearhead driving its cost down." Lowell turned a sidelong glance toward Breal. "Can you do that?"

"Yes, sir, I can," Breal responded, trying to overcome his own reluctance, searching for the right words, for a positive response. "But to do it effectively, I'd have to analyze product design, production, purchasing . . . I would need the cooperation of your staff."

"That's no problem," Lowell said. "You'd report to me, as vice president and assistant to the president, and would have the authority of my office. Your initial assignment will be to address the cost of our new product, the M-90. I'm prepared to offer you a starting salary ten percent higher than your old company paid you. My intuition, a bit hesitantly I have to admit, tells me you can do the job, and my intuition is the one thing I trust. The job is yours if you want it. You can start this Monday."

Breal babbled gratitude. "I'm delighted to work on cost reduction, Dr. Lowell. I'm also delighted to share your vision for ETI."

"We shall see," Lowell said. His gaze drifted to the papers on his desk. "We shall see," he repeated.

Breal left the building, then turned: the structure reminded him of an old tire plant in Akron. On a pedestal to the left of the entryway a stone lion sat like a sentinel, mouth turned down, its massive head and mane blurred, probably eroded by wind and weather, and no doubt by time itself. Breal looked around further: at the gray granite of MIT next door, the river, the Boston skyline, the new construction to the east. As he stepped into his cab, he asked himself what in the world was the company doing running those ancient assembly lines in that location. And the new microcircuit operation: that didn't look too sharp either. There must be a hundred things wrong with ETI, not only where and how they manufactured, but the way they sold their products or did their engineering.

As the taxi rode along the Charles toward the Callahan tunnel and Logan airport, Breal stared out at the river sparkling like mica in the sun and concluded, despite himself, that ETI was filled with opportunity. He was working again: that's all that mattered, it was the only thing that mattered.


"But others must have seen that," Susan Breal said, "and tried to change things and came up against The Great Man. Maybe he really doesn't want to change anything. Didn't you say he was in his seventies? We're talking about new tricks and a very old dog. Be careful, George. Very careful."

"He gave me a pitch about renewal and modernizing the company. I've got to believe he means it."

"Let's hope he does."

Breal sighed a long sigh, hunted for something positive he could say about John Lowell. Then he repeated, though without much conviction, what Susan had said after he related the details of his initial interview. "Yeah, the guy overreacts. Yeah, he's paranoid. But that's a real company he's got there and he wants me to help him run it. This is the first and only job that's come along in half a year, though it seems like a millennium. I'll give it all I've got."

Susan contemplated her husband. She had thought him handsome since the day she'd first seen him hurrying across the Temple campus, books and slide rule under his arm, and had marked him for her own. And now, graying hair and stubborn jaw, she thought him handsome still. From the beginning she'd sensed a penumbra of misfortune about George Breal, and in her Shakespeare course, when young Susan pictured the melancholy prince of Denmark, it was her future husband who came to mind. Her intuition had not been wrong: he had always gravitated toward jobs that were difficult, that placed him in conflict, that caused him to work long frustrating hours. She now sensed he was once again being sucked into a maelstrom and her own life, ordered and fixed for so many years, would now shift—in directions and ways she could not predict.

"Let's not rush into moving to Boston," Susan Breal said. "If the job doesn't work out, you can leave and we won't be any worse off than we are now."

# FOUR

All men are mortal. Aristotle is a man. Therefore Aristotle is mortal. I, John Lowell am a man and therefore I, John Lowell, am mortal. Depressing thought! We all owe God a death. Hopefully, he's not in a rush to collect. "The soldier's pole is fallen: young boys and girls are level now with men." Who said that? Was it Cleopatra over the dying Antony, or Antony's friend Enobarbus? Memory: the woven patchwork moth-eaten, frayed edges, unaccountable blanks. Things fly out of your life like scattering birds, a flutter of wings and they're gone. One day *I'll* be gone. Time's up. Poof. Gone. Buried in darkness. Who will weep for me and what difference does it make? A disembodied name on a university building or above a library door, a bust in the lobby. Who was this Lowell guy? No idea. Probably the dude that gave the money. I'm mortal but ETI can go on forever. My lengthened shadow. Small comfort. Who will run the place? Look at these men. Faithful hounds. That new fellow has a lean and hungry look. Good. Where there is no vision the people perish. Biblical wisdom. Easy to say.

"Gentlemen, we have two tasks before us this morning." Lowell sat in a throne-like chair at one truncated end of a boat-shaped conference table, its dark wood, unmarred by stains or blemishes, reflecting as ghosts the faces of Lowell's staff seated around it. "The first task is to discuss production costs of the M-90. The second is how to react to a competitive threat. And the two tie together." All faces concentrated on him, intent, serious. What actors they are! Learned long

~ 40 ~

ago to humor me. Avoid discomfort. Get through the day. Lowell turned to his head of marketing. "Andre, show everyone the new Kraut photoelectric."

Tergelen laid three yellow rectangles, each about the size of a cigarette lighter, on the mahogany surface. At that instant Lowell recalled that his ex-wife had a horror of yellow, never wore the color—associated it with knavery, disease, venomous wasps, senility—and yet when she left for the last time she wore a yellow hat. Lowell, for a moment, stared along with everyone else at the yellow rectangles. They seemed so innocuous. Of course, so does a stick of dynamite. "These were demonstrated at Pack Expo in Chicago . . . What's the name of the company, Andre?"

"Mühlmann."

"They claim these things have performance superior to the M-90." Lowell laid an M-90 beside the yellow rectangles. He thought it looked like a ponderous truck beside a sleek racing car. "They're selling these—taking orders right now—at half our price." Lowell waited for this thought to sink in. He glanced around: everyone continued to gaze at the Mühlmann control, expressions unchanged. Look at them: they might as well be staring at a wedge of apple pie. They all look alike, don't they? Sleek, well-fed—hadn't noticed that before. Lowell turned to Warren Slater, his chief engineer. "I assume Andre has asked you to test hell out of these things." Slater nodded. "They must use a custom integrated circuit to make these things so small," he said to Slater. "Why are we stuck with discrete components on the M-90?"

Slater cleared his throat. "If you recall, Dr. Lowell, we did a tradeoff analysis on the two approaches. A custom chip just wasn't economical at our production levels."

"Why is it economical for the Germans?"

"They don't offer the complete line we do."

Lowell shrugged this off. "Let's start an M-90 follow-on project using a dedicated chip," he said. "Start it right now." Lowell scanned the room. "Where's Craig Holloway? Get him in here. In the meantime let's talk about cost. If the M-90 is going to compete we've got to get its cost down. I've brought in Mr. Breal here to analyze the M-90 and lead a project to drive its cost down. He'll report to me. Unless we can lower the cost, the M-90 is dead on arrival."

Holloway, a slight man with a high sloping forehead and blond hair gone sparse and grayish-white, entered the room, looked about as though searching for shelter, then took the chair furthest from Lowell. "Can you redo the M-90 as a single integrated circuit?" Lowell asked.

"With all the variations?" Lowell waited while Holloway's stammer struggled through "variations." "Is that economical?"

"There's an eighty-twenty rule in all of life," Lowell answered. "Twenty percent of the people at a cocktail party drink eighty percent of the liquor. Twenty percent of the people in the world do eighty percent of the work. By the same logic, twenty percent of our products account for eighty percent of our sales. Let's look at converting just those."

Tergelen shifted uneasily in his chair. "Our strength is a complete product line," he said. "That's what appeals to our distributors, keeps them loyal to ETI. They know that whatever sensor problem their customers have, we've got the photoelectric to solve it."

Lowell shook his head. "You don't understand," he said. "That's not what I'm saying at all. We'll *always* offer a complete line. But a customer can't have the smallest cheapest control in order to solve an oddball, one-shot problem." He squinted at Tergelen. "Is that clear?"

Tergelen's face was now blank, his answer a faint nod.

"Good. Now, Andre, you identify the proper twenty percent of our products and Craig, you investigate an integrated circuit design for those products."

Craig Holloway appeared to concentrate on something above Lowell's head. His boss, the chief engineer, peered at the table as though a minute alien insect were traversing it. No one spoke. Look at them, will you, marinating in unhurried time. They all look as though they could use an enema. Not exactly greyhounds in the slip, straining upon the start. Long ago, they mastered the art of making themselves invisible.

"Any other questions this group should address?"

Silence.

"Good. This meeting is adjourned. Mr. Breal, I'd like to discuss cost reduction actions with you in depth, but among the burdens I carry is being a trustee of the Museum of Fine Arts. I'll be at a meeting there for most of the day. Are you available this evening? Perhaps you can come out to Burlington, to Lowell House, and we can discuss it at our leisure over cocktails and dinner . . . Shall we say at six?"


Elwood "Buck" Clawson, ETI's vice president of manufacturing, motioned Breal to a seat while he continued on the phone. Breal dropped into the cracked leather chair in front of Clawson's desk. He noticed on the desk a huge lead-colored metal affair with isolated scabs of green paint, the rest worn to the base metal, amidst a jumble of paper, plastic parts and circuit boards, greenish-colored objects, about the size and thickness of a slice of chewing gum. In the muddy light from the streaked window Breal recognized the microcircuit, made of tiny electrical components placed on a ceramic wafer, the heart of the M-90. Breal, who had used the same technology at his old company, knew how tricky the manufacturing process was, and the months of difficulty he'd had before finally mastering it. And what he'd seen on his interview tour with Lowell had not given him confidence that ETI had the process under control.

"Do you have a few minutes to show me through the microcircuit facility?" Breal asked when Clawson had hung up the phone.

Clawson held up a letter, writing scrawled along the top. "You never have to bother telling the old man about a letter you got because he always saw it before you did. The mail net—that's the most efficient operation around here."

"The mail net?"

"Yeah. That's Dr. Lowell trapping everybody's mail." He tossed the letter back on his desk and got to his feet: a heavy man with broad shoulders, round head, small shrewd eyes, and gray hair, crew cut, Marine fashion. The lower button of his shirt was gone and the fabric, stretched taut against his gut, pulled the shirt open to reveal gray underwear.

Clawson introduced Breal to Doug Reith, the microcircuit supervisor. Reith, who sported a British aviator mustache, was round-shouldered and wore a white smock with a platoon of pencils, pens and small tools in the breast pocket; as he ambled about the room describing the operation, He reminded Breal of a floor walker he had known at John Wanamaker. The mustache did not fit his face—it looked like a disguise.

Reith outlined the production process. While he was speaking, Breal noticed that the woman handling the microcircuit used her bare fingers. "Isn't there a risk that the oils and acids from her hand might contaminate the ceramic wafer?" he asked Reith.

Reith gave Breal a slack uneasy smile. "I don't think so," he answered.

"But it isn't a question of opinion," Breal said. "You've got to know."

"The manufacturer told us special handling wasn't necessary," Clawson said.

Breal discerned that there was much tweaking of components on what should have been a completed wafer. He decided to no longer question the details but go directly to the end result. "What's the yield at final test?" he asked. Reith's face momentarily creased; he seemed to be visualizing Breal's words as if they were an encrypted message, then he peered at something far away. Breal tried again. "How many good ones do you get at the end of the line?"

"About twenty percent of the units pass at the final test station."

"Then what?"

"We try to rework them. After that, about forty percent are good ones."

Breal looked around: here and there, lying like small dead animals in a pile, were heaps of rejected microcircuits. He decided to be incredulous. "Are you telling me that you throw out six of ten microcircuits? That sixty percent of your production—all the invested material and labor and over-head—goes into the trash? Is that correct?"

Reith stared at Breal: he looked like a man caught cheating at cards. "The test equipment has problems too," he said. His mind seemed to move in a narrow circle of problem and blame.

"Design problems plus lousy test equipment," Buck Clawson said. "They don't add up to high production yield."

Reith nodded agreement and the droop of his mustache appeared to increase.

Breal then visited with Warren Slater. The chief engineer, while staring at the two dusty potted plants that flanked his doorway like sentinels, placed the blame for poor yield squarely on sloppy manufacturing practices.

EARLIER THAT afternoon, Breal had wanted to discuss field problems with Tergelen, but Tergelen was traveling so Breal searched out Miles instead. On his way to Miles' office, Breal paused before an enlarged photograph that dominated one wall in the executive hallway. All the figures, Lowell at the center, were bent in concentration over a drawing spread on the great conference table. Breal recognized a much younger Miles, Tergelen, Clawson, and Holloway. They appeared more hopeful than now. The other men were unknown to him, probably long gone. Like portraits of ancestors, there was something sad and remote about the images.

Miles told Breal that he was completely nontechnical, knew little of field problems, but said that the poor performance of the first M-90s had upset ETI's distributors and that doubly upset Tergelen. Alone with Breal, Miles appeared open, his long-suffering face relaxed. "Tergelen loves our distributors," Miles said, "loves them more than his own children. That's where he spends most of his time. On the road, stroking the distributors."

Then Breal said, "Tell me, Dick, you've been here a long time. What's the key to longevity in this place?"

Miles stared at Breal, brow drawn together, eyes brown and sorrowful like a setter. "People tend to hide things from Dr. Lowell," he finally replied. "They send him too many letters. Dr. Lowell is an impatient man. He gets irritated if he has to wade through a long report. He likes to be kept informed on a face-to-face basis. And he hates surprises."

Breal, discouraged, called his wife, told her of the pending dinner, then grumbled that at ETI all problems were the other guy's fault. "The ETI logo," he said, "should be crossed arms with index fingers pointing in opposite directions."

"I'm sure there's a good reason for that," Susan Breal said. "The penalty for being wrong at ETI may well be the guillotine. There's not much point in confessing your sins in that kind of environment. Those who did are probably no longer there."

When Breal left the building that evening, the image he retained of the day was of the heaps of rejected microcircuits piled like sad little cairns, mournful memorials to ETI's inefficiency. He despaired that the place could ever be fixed. Breal paused at the entryway and he and the stone lion stared at each other. The turned-down mouth of the lion was both regal and scornful: he was above questions of blame, he was above everything.

As Breal prepared to leave for Lowell House, he thought of the furnished apartment that in a burst of impatience he had rented the previous weekend. The second floor one-bedroom unit was on Pinkney Street in Beacon Hill, and the narrow street precluded any sun from ever entering. The place was dank, anonymous. On entering, Breal always switched on all the lights. Above a green sofa was a faded Remington print portraying pioneers in covered wagons drawn by oxen fording a stream while under attack by Indians. A man's hat floated on the water. It didn't look too promising for the pioneers.

THE DOOR to Tom's apartment was open. When Catherine walked in, Ishmael, wearing a black t-shirt frayed at the neckline, was bent over a rolltop desk. His shoulders were narrow, ribs and vertebrae outlined by the clinging shirt; he seemed frail, gave Catherine the impression of a starving student. She cleared her throat and the man turned large solemn eyes toward her.

"Ciao," he said.

"Is Tom around?"

He stared at her as though she had asked a profound question, and then seemed to return from a distant place. She noticed a handwritten sign on the wall above his desk: IN LA SUA VOLONTADE È NOSTRA PACE. "He just stepped out. I'm sure he'll be right back." His speech was clear, his voice deeper than she would have expected, unaccented.

"What's that sign over your desk say?" she asked, uncomfortable, though for no reason she could discern.

"It means 'In His will is our peace.'"

"Sounds Arabic. Muslim . . . Is it from the Koran?"

"It's from Dante's *Divine Comedy.*" He leaned back, looked directly at her, seemed to be weighing whether she was worthy of a detailed answer, then said, "The line sums up the faith on which Dante rested his soul. He's saying where God is, there is heaven, and without submission to God's will there's only sorrow and confusion." He seemed embarrassed by his explanation. "I change the sign whenever I find a line I particularly like."

"What line did you like before this one?"

"'I cried not, so of stone grew I within.'"

~ 47 ~

He said this in a non-poetic way, his face marked by gentleness, and this caused Catherine to relax, feel less uncomfortable. "Tom tells me you're a Dante scholar."

"I'm translating his work into English. I don't know if that qualifies me as a Dante scholar."

He continued to look at her, waited, as though he expected her to ask about Dante, his translation. She felt she had come upon something important, but the moment carried an intimacy that troubled her, so she said, "How's Tom doing?"

He hesitated an instant, seemed reluctant to switch subjects, then rubbed his eyes with his knuckles, like a child. "I'd say Tom is struggling, stuck somewhere in the middle of his book. Maybe he's pressing too hard."

"Hi, Mom." Tom came into the room carrying a bag of groceries. He kissed her cheek, his face and clothes carrying the outdoor chill. "Do you want to have dinner here or eat out?" he asked.

Catherine tore her gaze away from the roommate's large questioning eyes. "Let's eat out."


THEY SAT in a coffee shop under fluorescent lights; Catherine ate her chicken salad, watched her son attack a hamburger and fries and wash it all down with a Coke. "Your roommate tells me you're stuck in your book," Catherine said.

"You mean Ishmael actually talked to you? He must like you . . . I've been stuck for a while, but I can see my way out now. You've got to bleed a little, you know. Leave some of your blood on the page. Otherwise it's not much of a book."

"Is the book about us, our family?"

"Sort of." He looked uncomfortable for a moment then said, "You look stuck yourself, Mom. I mean worried, uncertain kind of . . ."

"My new boss tells me I'm out of touch. Buying the wrong stuff."

"Is she right?"

"Maybe. I don't know. Fashion—the big designers in Paris, Milan, New York, they decide what's in and that trickles down. But fashion is like most things—it has to be sold. It doesn't just happen, like mushrooms on a lawn . . . The store doesn't advertise enough or have competent saleswomen."

"But doesn't every department have that problem? Why pick on you?"

"My stuff is high priced. It needs more advertising, better selling." Catherine was suddenly tired. She sighed, turned her gaze toward the entrance—the line of coats hung on hooks resembled ghosts—then went on. "I've always tried to spot what'll become a lasting trend, not just a fad—clothes that are attractive, practical." She gave her son a half-smile. "Clothes that make you feel good."

"Sounds okay to me," Tom said, then chomped into his burger.

"But it isn't okay with the new boss. She likes extravagant looks, like built-up Samurai shoulders or deep décolleté. I always figured you were better off giving a hint of what's underneath rather than exposing it."

Her son nodded, jarred ketchup onto his fries. She wasn't sure he was listening but continued anyway. "I look around now and to tell the truth I'm not sure I understand why young women wear what they do. Fashion is only as good as it looks on you. But some of the stuff young women are wearing looks awful."

Tom speared a couple of fries. "Why don't you get into mature women's wear?" he said.

"We've got buyers there. Successful ones. No opening."

Tom wolfed the last of his burger, gurgled his Coke.

"I've tried bows," Catherine said, "French cuffs on blouses, dropped-waist velvet dresses with lace collars for women who want to dress like their grandmothers, tiered skirts, suits with giant herringbone patterns . . . even tried jumpsuits. Just can't get it right."

"What does Kent say?"

"We don't talk about it."

"What *do* you talk about?"

"His problems mostly." She finished her salad, looked up at her son, now leaning back against the maroon plastic of the booth. "You're like Michael. He doesn't much like Kent either."

Tom made a small motion with his hands. "It's your life, Mom." His brow wrinkled. "What is it that you want?"

Catherine experienced a sudden sense of hopelessness and loss. "To tell the truth, I'm sick of buying clothes. I think that's my problem. But maybe it's deeper. Maybe I'm on the brink of menopause and dissatisfied with everything. Permanent depression. That's what my life is going to be like." Catherine felt a lump rise in her throat. She took her son's hand. "I've never said that before, Thomas. Not to anyone. Not even to myself."

"Jesus, Mom, don't cry. Everything will be all right."

She took a handkerchief from her purse, dried her eyes, looked at the mascara-stained fabric, and wiped her eyes further. "You know what I'd like?" she said. "Maybe you'll think I'm crazy, but I'd like to be a lawyer, like my mother, your grandmother, was. There couldn't have been more than a dozen women lawyers in all of Boston, maybe in all of Massachusetts, in her day. But she did it."

"Maybe you can too, Mom. Go to law school nights . . . you can do that."

"Sure, maybe. But right now the most important thing I can do is buy dresses that shriek, Buy Me! Have you ever seen clothes that shrieked, Buy Me?"

"No, I never did."

"I never did either." Catherine shrugged and at that moment Ishmael's voice entered her head, clear and matter-of-fact, as it said, "I cried not, so of stone grew I within."

# FIVE

Lowell's directions were confusing. He had given them
to Breal quickly and Breal did not think it appropriate to
ask Lowell to draw him a map. He had difficulty finding
the house in the hidden turnings of the Burlington suburb.
Finally, on a narrow wooded road, he found the wrought-
iron plaque with the initials JEL nailed to a huge oak, and
below it another plaque, CAUTION SENTRY DOGS. As Breal drove
through a thicket of trees, Lowell House suddenly appeared
before him.

Breal had given no thought to Lowell's dwelling but had
concentrated on finding it. He now realized he had expected
a rambling mansion of gables and eaves and tall windows,
covered with ivy and topped with gray slate. Instead, a composition of pure horizontal lines rising in tiers was before him.
In the silver dusk, the overhanging planes of the roof, thin-
edged, hovered like protective wings over the dark interlock-
ing spaces below, the windows great panes of silver directly
beneath the rooflines. The house was surrounded by maples
and oaks; stone paths drifted through the rolling lawns and
into the adjoining woods and the twilight. The entire house
seemed to have grown out of the landscape itself, like some
geological formation. The structure was so perfectly matched
to its surroundings that it took Breal a moment to grasp its
full size and extent.

Breal pulled into a parking area beside a garage and was
met by a uniformed guard. "You're Mr. Breal? You can leave
your car right here. The colonel is expecting you."

Breal heard the deep barking of dogs; and through the slats of a thick wood fence he saw the heads and wild eyes of two angry shepherds as they alternately barked and clawed at the wood of the fence.

"Not very friendly, are they?"

"They're not supposed to be," the guard answered.

Lowell met Breal at the door, probably alerted by the barking. "I was admiring your house as I drove up," Breal said. "Though 'house' is a feeble word to describe it."

"I'll give you a tour after dinner," Lowell said. "I gather the directions were adequate."

"They were perfect," Breal said. He noticed the place had an odd odor, of closed space never aired, of a museum rarely visited as Lowell led Breal up a single step, through an entryway and into a study dominated by an oil painting of two red boats under sail on the dappled blue of a lake. In the lower right hand corner, in an imperious script, was the artist's signature: Claude Monet.

"This is the Great Hall," Lowell said as they stepped through an archway. The room was at least a hundred feet in length and half that in width, and the ceiling climbed in slanted beams to a peak perhaps fifty feet above the floor. But the roofline was not uniform; rather it rose out of horizontal planes and broke the room into differing spaces, all flowing together: low and intimate near the massive fireplace, and low at the south wall where the volume spilled outward through sheets of glass to a stone veranda and the woods beyond, and high and spacious in the center. Organ pipes were embedded in one wall. The room was sparsely furnished: a grouping of stuffed chairs and a coffee table near the fireplace, two other groupings where the ceiling ran low, and then a closed cabinet against a wall. A sand-colored rug covered the floor and an oriental rug defined a space around the fireplace. Lowell threw a log on the fire as Breal continued to survey the room.

Breal's attention was drawn to a painting on one wall. It took Breal a moment to recognize the Lowell of an earlier epoch: he had no beard and his face was fuller, but the similarity was evident around the eyes and the shape of the large bald head.

"What would you like to drink?" Lowell asked, as they were joined by a woman with small features in a round face, black hair pulled back in a bun. She wore no makeup or jewelry, her dress dove-colored, white ruffles at the neck and sleeves. Her manner as well as her attire gave Breal the impression he was in the presence of a nun.

"This is Miss Edna Graham, my chief of staff," Lowell said. She smiled at Breal, teeth surprisingly small, as though she had retained her baby teeth.

"Welcome to Lowell House, Mr. Breal," she said. "Are you getting situated in Boston?"

As Breal started to answer, she suddenly turned her head as if she'd heard someone call her name and hurried off. She returned shortly with a tray containing small squares of smoked salmon on crackers which she placed on the coffee table in front of the fireplace. She then settled into a chair and watched Lowell as though waiting for a cue. Breal noticed her pointed patent leather shoes: they seemed rigid, as if cast in metal, and too tight.

The martini in Lowell's glass disappeared as he spoke of the growth of the business and penetrating overseas markets. Then he said, "Our problem with the M-90, and all our products, is inspection. Our inspectors aren't tough enough. Bad units get out the door, customers complain, then we waste a lot of time and money trying to fix things. You should look into that part of our operation. From what you've seen, wouldn't you agree that's a problem?"

Breal had learned through hard experience that you could not inspect quality into a product. It was either built there in the first place, through a robust design and careful manufacturing, or there were problems forever. To depend on inspection for quality was like depending solely on the police to maintain order: if the citizenry didn't believe in it, there would never be order. Breal felt the Great Hall around him, its hushed church-like presence, the logs burning in the huge fireplace; he looked at Lowell's face bent toward him and decided to wait before disagreeing with his new boss.

"A competent inspection organization would improve quality," Breal said and finished his Cutty Sark and water.

"That's a consummation devoutly to be wished," Lowell said.

As Lowell mixed them both a second drink, Breal, irritated with himself over his inspection answer, decided he had not been hired to be a yes-man. "We had a microcircuit facility at United Electric," Breal said when Lowell handed him his drink. "It was a clean-room operation where the women were dressed like nurses in an operating room. Microcircuits rolled off the line like cookies in a bakery and at least ninety-eight percent of them passed the final test."

"How well do we do?"

"Our first pass yield is only twenty percent, and forty percent after expensive rework."

"What does Clawson say?"

"He said the new generation of equipment made a clean-room environment unnecessary."

"I gather you don't believe that."

"No, I don't," Breal said, feeling better now.

"Holloway sold me on microcircuits as the leading edge of technology, but it looks more like the bleeding edge." Lowell sighed, seemed a man somehow betrayed. He stared at his glass, appeared to be consulting his martini. "What do you recommend?"

"The obvious: review every aspect of microcircuit fabrication, find out what's wrong and fix it."

Breal was about to make a further recommendation when Lowell looked about, tossed back his drink, and stared at Edna Graham. He seemed to have lost interest in microcircuits."What's holding up dinner?" he said.

"I'll check," she said as she jumped to her feet.

"Well, to quote W. C. Fields," Lowell said, "a man's got to believe in something. I believe I'll have another drink. How about you, George?"

That was now a problem question for Breal. He felt shrunken in the Great Hall while Lowell seemed to grow larger. Another drink—it would be his third—appealed to him. But liquor always made him think of his father, sloppy with alcohol, and aroused in him a feeling of disgust. Besides, it would be best to keep his wits about him. "I'll pass, Dr. Lowell, thank you," he answered.

On the dining room wall hung a portrait in oil of a handsome young military officer, a part buried like a path in his thick black hair, eyes sparkling, looking happy to be alive. As Breal paused before the painting, Lowell said, "Me as a dashing soldier during the war." He stopped for a moment to contemplate the painting. "Yes," he said in response to nothing and appeared suddenly gloomy.

The dining room table, glittering with silver candelabra and crystal, occupied much of the room and was surrounded by open-backed barrel-shaped chairs. Dinner was served by an elderly Chinese couple, perpetual smiles fixed on their faces. There was white wine which Lowell occasionally sipped, but he continued to toss down martinis throughout the meal. The drinks were brought to him by the smiling Chinese butler who magically appeared with a full glass when the previous one was empty.

Breal decided to press on with his microcircuit observations and cost reduction, which after all was the reason for the dinner invitation. "At United we used a consultant, a very knowledgeable man from GE, to help us sort through our problems. I'd suggest I find him and make use of his services at ETI."

"Let's you and I visit the place first thing tomorrow morning and see if we can sort out for ourselves what's wrong," Lowell said. "I'll give you a call when I come in."

Edna Graham chose that moment to ask Breal if he liked the halibut. "Yes, it's fine," he said, then observed that she was frowning at his plate. She must have noticed that he was just picking at the fish. He wasn't much of a fish eater and found this one gummy. "I'm a slow eater," he explained.

"Edna, the unexamined fish is not worth eating," Lowell said, then continued. "Let's fix the damned thing quickly and get these problems behind us." Lowell drained his latest martini. "How long do you think it'll take to fix?"

Breal thought that without someone knowledgeable, like the GE consultant, the problems would never be fixed. "About six months," he replied.

Other than her fish question, Edna Graham had said nothing throughout the dinner; she concentrated on Lowell, plucked at his words as if trying to memorize them. Her face now struck Breal as innocent, open to attack. When a course was completed she signaled with a small buzzer, set in jade-green stone, on the table. The Chinese couple then slid into the room with the unobtrusiveness of cats, removed the plates, and brought the next course. "Mr. Breal, were you thinking of living in Boston or the suburbs?" she asked with a dim smile.

"Well, our children are grown. We thought we'd try a condominium in town."

"You might consider Beacon Hill or Back Bay," Edna Graham said. "I see houses on Mount Vernon Street and Marlborough Street being redone into condominiums every day. Those neighborhoods are near the Common and the Public Garden and are delightful old Boston—"

Lowell absently studied Miss Graham as though she were a household pet, then stood up. "Let me give you a tour of the premises," he said, and swayed slightly as if jostled by an imaginary crowd, then recovered his equilibrium. He stopped before an oil portrait of a young woman: black hair pinned up in Victorian fashion and dark eyes in an unsmiling face.

The background lighting glowed like a halo giving her the appearance of a Madonna in a Renaissance painting.

"That's my grandmother," he said reverentially. "She raised me after my mother died."

"She was a handsome woman," Breal said.

"She was a saint," Lowell said. He dropped into a reverie as he gazed at the painting. Breal waited respectfully beside the lost Lowell, until he turned away from the painting and swept a hand at the walls. "This place was designed by Frank Lloyd Wright. The old house my grandmother left me was a wreck, so I decided to just tear it down and start over. That was in 1957. Wright was eighty-nine at the time and living in Phoenix. He never came out to look at the place but sent his son Lloyd, who was a spry sixty then. He took a lot of photographs of the landscape and drew site plans and that's what Wright used to do the design. I think you would agree that The Master Builder did quite well, though in the early days the roof leaked. I still have the original drawings signed by Wright. They're beautifully done. He was a meticulous worker, a man who believed, as I do, that God is in the details. His son supervised the construction and did the landscaping."

Lowell then led Breal to a library and stopped before a photograph of two men in uniform in front of a tank, one slender, the other taller, heavier, steel-rod straight, wearing a pistol at his belt. VERITAS was stenciled on the turret of the tank. In the lower right hand corner were the handwritten words, "To John Lowell, one of the great tank commanders of the mighty Third Army. George S. Patton, Jr., Commanding General."

"I gather the man with the pistol is Patton," Breal said.

"Yes, that's Patton all right. I served under him from the beach at Normandy all across Europe to the gates of Prague. I have few heroes in this life and George Patton is one of them. He was a throwback, you know—to the Teutonic knights, the Saracen, the Crusaders—the greatest combat general since the Civil War, maybe the greatest American general ever."

Lowell gazed at the photograph. "Uncanny is what he was. He had a battle sense, a sixth sense, and could foresee things before anyone. He was up front every day. Like Napoleon on the bridge at Lodi, he was always at the head of his men. Duty, Honor, Country—those words ruled his life."

"That was your tank?" Breal asked.

"Yes, that's *Veritas*. Patton liked the name. I ran part of the 4th Armored Division. Hell on Wheels we were called . . . We were really kids then . . . funny how you forget the suffering. I remember those times now as the high summer of my life, those days of pursuit across a continent with Roaring George."

Breal vaguely recollected an oddity about Lowell's hero. "Didn't Patton believe in reincarnation?"

Lowell shrugged. "Patton was a great actor . . . But maybe he really did believe, as he said, that he had fought on the plains of Troy and with Caesar's murderous Tenth Legion in Gaul. Who's to say he was wrong?"

As Breal took his leave, Lowell and Edna Graham accompanied him to the door. Lowell stumbled on the single step after the entryway and Miss Graham grabbed his arm. "Be careful, John," she said.

At the door, she said, "I'm looking forward to meeting Mrs. Breal. Please have her call me when she comes to Boston. We can lunch together and I would be delighted to introduce her to the city."

Lowell, his speech slurred now and overly deliberate, said he found these one-on-one discussions—where one could relax over a drink and dinner—very useful, and hoped that Breal would be available to have them periodically. Breal assured him that he would.


WHEN BREAL returned to his apartment, he phoned his wife. "How was your evening?" she asked. "How does The Great Man live?"

"Well, it's like nothing I've ever seen. Would you believe that Frank Lloyd Wright designed his house? If I said the place was magnificent, that wouldn't dent the surface." Breal then went on to describe Lowell House and finished with, "and besides all that, he's got an original Monet hanging in the library."

"You're not being terribly coherent," Susan said.

"That's because I'm still overwhelmed."

"What did you have for dinner?"

"Halibut with the consistency of chewing gum. When I was picking at it Lowell said, 'The unexamined fish is not worth eating.'"

"That's quite clever," Susan said. "Who else was at dinner?"

"This woman whom he introduced as his chief of staff."

"What does she look like?"

"Hard to say. Sort of a forty-something Mother Teresa."

"That's not very helpful."

"You'll get a chance to find out for yourself. She said when you come to Boston, she'd be pleased to show you around."

"What does she do?"

"I'd guess she runs the household. She seems to be in charge of two inscrutable Chinese servants. But I suppose there must be other servants."

"She's not his wife, is she?"

"No, no. He introduced her as *Miss* Edna Graham."

"Do you think she, ah . . . provides other services?"

"For God's sake, Susan, the guy is seventy-two years old!"

"Well . . ." she said, clearly not convinced.

"Anyway," concluded Breal, "Lowell is a man of many parts: successful businessman, soldier—"

"You sound infatuated with him."

When Breal hung up he remembered that he had forgotten to mention that Lowell had also been a tank commander under Patton. Nor had he mentioned that Lowell could hold his liquor better than anyone he'd ever met. Nor had his evening yet coalesced into a single impression; this came later, as he lay in bed thinking of nothing at all: that Lowell was a man who had spent his life being waited on by slaves.

# SIX

When Breal came in the following day he called Clawson to alert him to Lowell's impending microcircuit visit, then waited for Lowell to show up or call, but neither happened. Late in the morning Breal stuck his head in Lowell's office and mentioned the microcircuit facility tour. Lowell appeared befuddled for an instant, then said, "I haven't forgotten. Be with you in ten minutes."

Clawson met Breal and Lowell when they arrived. Breal glanced around the two million dollar facility: it occurred to him that Mühlmann, using integrated circuit technology, had leapfrogged ETI's investment before the company had derived any benefit from it. Breal wondered when that thought would occur to Lowell. They were joined by Doug Reith, the supervisor that Lowell had chewed out during Breal's initial visit, a man whom he now knew would have to be replaced.

Before the group could start their tour, a woman tiptoed toward Lowell and whispered, "There's a Mr. David Ramsey to see you, Dr. Lowell."

"Our lawyer is here," Clawson said.

"What lawyer?" Lowell asked.

"The attorney who's defending us in the age discrimination suit."

At Lowell's blank look, Clawson went on. "She claims age discrimination, but we let her go because she couldn't do the job. Lousy manual dexterity."

"How long was she employed?" Lowell asked, glaring at Clawson.

"About eight months."

"Why did it take so long to figure out she was butter-fingered?"

"The supervisor thought he had to build a case against her."

"The idiot!" Lowell exclaimed. "Who was the supervisor?"

Clawson hesitated a heartbeat, then nodded toward the man beside him. "Doug Reith," he said.

Getting rid of Reith, Breal saw, would not be difficult.

"Come along, George," Lowell said. "We'll all talk to the barrister."

Ramsey was a man in his fifties, with thick glasses and a professional air. They sat in Lowell's office as Ramsey went through the case. "I believe your company has a reasonable chance of winning since your supervisor, Mr. Reith, has a well documented file." Ramsey spoke in a ceremonial way, paused, arranged his hands in a steeple that just touched the tip of his nose. "However, the length of time it took to discover that the employee in question lacked certain basic motor skills is troublesome."

"Mr. Ramsey," said Lowell with a sigh, "can you win this thing or not?"

Breal concluded that Lowell saw the world in black and white; there were no shades of gray.

Ramsey's magnified eyes appraised Lowell. "Yes, I'm confident we can win this case. The most compelling reason is that I know the plaintiff's attorney and he's incompetent." Ramsey smiled dimly and took on a satisfied look as he shared his judgment of the opposing lawyer.

Lowell stared at Ramsey as though he were a newly discovered stain on the executive floor carpet. "Incompetent?" he cried. "The more reason to be wary! If you were the greatest swordsman in the world and were up against the second greatest swordsman in the world, you wouldn't have much to worry about. But if you were up against someone who had never held a sword in his life, you would have a great deal to worry about. He might stand twenty feet away and throw the damned thing and skewer you with it!" Lowell's look was one of impatient astonishment at the stupidity of the world.

Clawson left to show Ramsey out, the lawyer looking like an apprehensive schoolboy concerned about his grade.

Lowell turned to Breal. The November sun slanted through the windows and illuminated his face and beard with a golden radiance, giving him a saintly appearance. "What did you think of the lawyer?" Breal asked.

Lowell seemed not to hear. He took the Mühlmann control that was on his desk, turned the small yellow object around in his hand, contemplated it, hefted it, and then said, "They've vaulted over us. That whole facility downstairs is obsolete." He set the object down. "At least they don't have our distribution channel. Thank heaven for that." He gave Breal a friendly smile. "How about lunch?"

Breal had the impression that Mühlmann, like a prism, would reveal the full range of Lowell's possibilities.

When they left the building, Breal commented, "I like your lion."

Lowell turned toward the statue. "Leo? Think of him as the building's amulet. Wards off evil spirits. He was here when I bought the building. It bothered me that there wasn't a second one on the other side. These fellows usually come in pairs, like bookends. But we make do with one." He contemplated the stone lion with evident affection. "Leo is getting a bit ragged, but he's still imposing. Wouldn't you agree?"


CATHERINE DECIDED not to take the T but to walk home. She had an urge to keep moving, not to stop until fatigue caused her to drop, as though physical motion could reverse events. She turned up her collar against the November chill and headed westward toward Beacon Hill. The sun was down but it was not yet night, the sky a cloudless darkening blue. She passed the T entrance—the wall gave off the ammonia smell of long-standing urine. Two homeless men on a bench by the Boston Common, one about her age, watched her pass. The younger man held out a hand, palm cupped, in a mechanical way, and the gesture filled her with disgust. The older man took an astonishingly long drag of a cigarette as though the smoke was some essential gas he needed to stay alive, then scratched his crotch. She hurried by, down Beacon Street and past the State House, its golden dome reflecting the remaining light, then climbed into the labyrinth of streets that was Beacon Hill.

Dead leaves scuttled across the sidewalks. She sidestepped a dog turd on the pavement, thought it a hieroglyph of disorder and ruin. She had been marked for destruction from the onset, her demise a symbol of the new order. What, after all, was a new boss if she did not sweep clean? The nailhead eyes had not informed her; it was personnel, Harry Smith no less, who for years had tried to take her to bed, who delivered the message. His eyes had darted about the room as though following the movements of a fly, never landing on her. His manner was apologetic though his little speech was remote, impersonal. Underneath, unspoken, were the words, I'm just doing my job. But severance had been generous: she was safe for six months. Then what? What was she good for? What could she do? She peered downward as she hurried along, as if the answer were findable, like a lost penny, on the dark asphalt of Mt. Vernon Street.

Catherine, perspiring now despite the cold, turned on Cambridge Street toward the Longfellow Bridge and her apartment in Somerville. On the bridge she thrust her hands deep in her pockets, hunched against the needle-like wind blowing across the Charles. A train passed, its clatter born away by the wind, disembodied faces gazed out: ghosts in the dark night, they seemed embarked on some solemn journey. She stared across the bridge: atop a six-story building the sign, ELECTRONIC TECHNOLOGIES, INC., illuminated in blue light, stared back. Beside it, a circle enclosed the letters ETI; a blue lightning bolt ran diagonally across the circle and flashed on and off. Her father's company. She had seen the sign so often that it had ceased to have meaning, like the CITGO sign in Kenmore Square; but now it seemed to be beckoning, as though her walk and this special encounter with the sign had been preordained.

She stepped aside on the narrow walkway to allow a lunatic jogger in shorts and a t-shirt to pass, then returned her gaze to the sign. She recalled her father, hard-surfaced, sharp-tongued, quick-witted, a man armed for combat. What had their differences been about? His need to dominate, control the lives of those around him? (For he always knew better than they what was best for them.) But that was twenty-some years ago. He was now in his seventies, surely not the same man. Her thoughts returned to her own needs, her home, her son Michael, his schooling . . . She felt an abyss around her, cold and black like the river flowing below. The idea came to her at first without weight, then took on substance. What was there to lose? Pride that no longer mattered? If there ever was a time, it was now. She started to compose a letter.

Dear Father—no, Dear father; he wasn't God:
I have given much thought to the circumstances that parted us. They have long passed and for me at least have lost their meaning. The man you objected to I divorced years ago.
Before it is too late, I wish to enjoy the pleasure of your company and would like my sons to know their grandfather.
Can we meet, just briefly, say for coffee, to get to know each other again and discuss what separates us?
My phone number . . .
Your daughter,

Catherine looked up at the sign: it seemed to have retreated, the words shrunken to the bottom line of an eye chart. She worked and reworked the letter all during the long march home.

EDNA GRAHAM gave special orders to the servants to polish the silver and dust everything and everywhere, even the draperies, for that evening Dr. Lowell was hosting a dinner for his fellow MIT trustees. She never understood his love for this faceless thing that was his alma mater, his eagerness to attend their reunions, the seriousness with which he discussed their affairs. Why did it matter so? Lately, she noticed, he was endowing monuments: a chair in molecular biology, the John Elliott Lowell Electronic Sciences Building. She thought of tombstones, sensed some dim connection.

At eleven o'clock, as Edna reviewed the dinner menu with the cook, she heard the barking of the dogs and knew it was the day's mail. The bell rang: she went to the door, took the mail from the guard—a youngish man who had long since stopped smiling at her—and dropped the packet on the credenza. She checked the firewood (for Dr. Lowell enjoyed a roaring fire), liquor cabinet, hors d'oeuvres ingredients, made a list for shopping that afternoon, then toured the house with a servant, indicating areas that needed attention. She insisted the organ be carefully dusted, for Dr. Lowell would have an organ recital as part of the evening's entertainment. Edna had the cook fix her a ham and cheese sandwich, permitted herself a small glass of Dry Sack, and thought she would take a nap before shopping. First, though, she would peruse the mail. She set aside the bills, her paycheck from ETI, tossed the junk mail, and took Lowell's correspondence and technical reviews to his study.

One letter caught Edna's eye. It was the only one addressed by hand. The name in the upper left hand corner caused her heart to leap. She held the letter, stared at it as though it were a hostile presence, then took the stainless steel letter opener from Lowell's desk, carefully pried open the envelope and read the handwritten contents. For a moment thought was impossible as though her brain had been short-circuited. Something Lowell had once said as they sat in the Great Hall—he soggy with martinis—emerged from some hidden recess of her mind: "If you can't be near the girl you love, you can love the girl you're near." She stared at the letter a moment longer, and with abrupt savagery ripped it in half, then in half again three more times. She hurried to the kitchen and buried the sixteen pieces deep in the trash.

# SEVEN

"You seem elsewhere," Kent said, ignoring the white slip of paper lying face down on the black tray. "Something bothering you?"

Catherine debated whether to tell him that she was now out of work. She stared at the white slip. "I think we're going to have to split that," she said, nodding toward the check.

"Ah, money problems," Kent said and gave her a veiled smile.

"I lost my job."

"Jesus! What happened?"

"The new broom at the office didn't like my taste in clothes. She thought I was out of touch." Catherine shrugged. "For all I know she's right."

"Welcome to the ranks of the unemployed," Kent said. "It's really not that bad." He made a face. "I'm sorry." Catherine did not think he looked particularly sorry. "What now?"

Catherine was tempted to speak of the letter to her father, but she had never mentioned him to Kent and decided against it now. "I'm thinking about it. But splitting the tab is a start."

"Sure," Kent said; he made an inconclusive gesture. "I understand."

She could not believe he had not offered to pay the whole thing. On her way to the restaurant, Catherine thought she would mention her desire to return to school, imagined Kent encouraging, helpful. Now she found that she had nothing to say to him, and was asking herself why she had taken up with this man at all. Viewing him now, dispassionately, she decided there was a touch of stupidity in his face.

"Women will keep wearing clothes," Kent said as they prepared to leave. "Off and on you might say. Stores will keep selling them and there'll always be buyers. You'll have no trouble finding something."

Catherine found his reassurance irritating, patronizing. "How do you know I'll find something? There're only a handful of department stores in Boston and they've all got buyers." Her voice had risen and she noticed heads turned towards her. The restaurant itself now seemed an enemy. She rose, twirled on her forest green cape—she liked the color, thought it set off the green of her eyes, her finest feature—realizing it was a theatrical gesture, an act of confused defiance toward those around her, and strode to the door. On the street, Kent hesitated; his face tensed, a familiar look traveled across it. Before he could invite her to his apartment, Catherine said, "Why don't we just say goodnight?"

Kent seemed relieved, pecked her cheek, said he would call, and disappeared. Catherine had a sudden desire to see her eldest son. It was still early: his night shift hadn't started yet. The urge for physical movement returned. She hurried through the cold and empty streets, and looked around— snow had been forecast. As she thought about Kent, he took on the aspect of a burnt-out fire, one that had flared quickly and conveniently, provided momentary warmth, filled a momentary need. Insight grazed the edge of her mind: whatever Kent had ever accomplished, ever obtained, had been through a woman.

When Catherine entered Tom's apartment, Ishmael looked up from his desk, stared at her for a moment, and as usual seemed to emerge from some remote world. "Ciao," he finally said. *"Donna m'apparve, sotto verde manto, / vestita di color di fiamma viva."*

"What in the world are you saying?"

"A woman appeared in green mantle clad, / her robe the color of the living flame . . . It's from the Purgatory."

"You memorize all that?"

He made a small gesture. "Driving a cab doesn't exactly engage your intellect. Fighting Boston traffic, I run through verses in my head and work out the best translation."

She wanted to keep talking to Ishmael but remembered the purpose of her visit. Before she could speak, Ishmael said, "Tom's not around. He had a date." He fixed her with a somber look. "Can I make you some coffee? I only drink decaf. Is that okay?"

He went to the kitchen, his shirt, faded denim, had the words "Abandon all hope ye who enter" printed on the back.

"Do you always wear clothing adorned with pessimistic words?" she asked.

"I was going through a bad time about a year ago," he called to her. "I bought the shirt second hand at a swap meet. The woman who sold it to me said it had belonged to a guy who committed suicide. A real nice guy, she said, and hoped I wasn't superstitious. The Dante quote matched my mood at the time."

They drank their coffee by his rolltop desk. "What got you interested in Dante?" she asked.

"I was an English Lit major at U Mass, and got into a state where I decided it was all useless. I chucked the whole thing and joined the Air Force to be a pilot. Wild blue yonder and all that. I flunked out of flight school—I'm not the most coordinated guy in the world—and wound up as a Clerk, Second Class, at Aviano Air Base in Aviano, Italy, and stayed there for two-and-a-half years. The place is only fifty miles from Venice and sometimes I'd go there on weekends, or I'd go to Verona or Florence. Those were the best years I ever had. I loved Italy, the only time in my life when I can say I was happy. I learned Italian—it turns out to be an easy language to learn—had an Italian girlfriend, actually a Somali girl who had been raised in Italy. She was surprised at how prickly I was about being black. She was right. I never felt black in Italy, at least not usually."

"How did that get you into Dante?"

"My English instructor at U Mass gave me a letter of introduction to a professor of languages at the University of Florence. He was a *dantista*, and urged me to read the master in Italian. Dante is very difficult, but as I got into it I was blown away by the man. The professor said Dante was the greatest poet who ever lived and he's probably right. When I ran into trouble with the Italian, I read an English translation. It wasn't very good so I tried another, then another. You wouldn't believe this, but there are about a hundred English translations of *The Divine Comedy*."

"Why are you working on another?"

"If one of those translations were any good, why would we need the other ninety-nine?"

She liked the quiet way he spoke. She did not find him at all handsome—his nose flared across his face, lips too fleshy. But his eyes claimed her attention: heavy-lidded, gentle, melancholy. He stood and cleared the coffee cups, shoulders narrow, body too thin.

"There's a portrait of Dante in the Duomo in Florence. I stared at it for half an hour, trying to understand the man who could create *The Divine Comedy*. It was the saddest face I'd ever seen. Never could penetrate the mystery. Like your son Tom says, you can't tell much about a man just by looking at him."

Catherine sensed that it was time to leave. Yet here with Ishmael she felt a sheltering warmth, of one who wanted nothing from her. He continued to look at her, and the look touched her as though he had laid his hand upon hers.

"Please tell Tom I was here," she said as she stood and twirled on her cape. "It was nice chatting with you and hearing about Dante."

"Sure, any time." He smiled, a surprisingly innocent smile, his teeth even and unstained. She had the impression that before her was a man who had never lied.

Outside, light flakes were now falling, the first snow of the season, creating white halos around the streetlamps. It felt welcoming and, for no accountable reason, made her light-hearted. She did the little dance step from the *Wizard of Oz* on her way to the T, childishly avoiding the cracks in the pavement.

As the winter deepened, it became more difficult for Breal to commute to Pennsylvania on weekends because of flight delays. Susan now spent most of her time in Boston. She accepted Edna's luncheon invitation and they continued to meet: at the Cafe Budapest or the Parker House for lunch, at the Athenaeum, and sometimes they shopped together. Breal discussed the idea with his wife of making a final commitment to ETI and moving to Boston. Susan counseled that they wait a while longer.

Breal, knowing that cost reduction on the M-90 depended critically on the microcircuit operation, obtained Lowell's approval to hire the retired GE engineer as a consultant. The man—deliberate and meticulous—presented Breal and Clawson with a ten page list of recommendations after a week of digging into ETI's microcircuit facility. Then, in private conversation, he offered his judgment on Doug Reith: "I don't think the supervisor you've got in there is worth a shit."

In painstaking detail, the list spelled out over one hundred items that needed fixing. None of the fixes were particularly difficult, but it was the sheer number and variety of them that overwhelmed Breal. As he studied the list, a feeling of impotence and despair took possession of him. The items, piled like boulders one on top of the next, seemed to lead across a vast mountain range, a journey he feared would be impossible with the existing ETI staff—or, at best, would take forever. Clawson seemed befuddled by the extent and sweep of the list. When Breal showed it to Lowell, the old man's brows drew together as he turned the pages. "They're all trifles," he observed. "Every last one of them."

Breal did not agree with Lowell's characterization of the fixes. "They add up, Dr. Lowell," Breal said. "They all add up. Together, they fix all the inefficiency and lost production we're saddled with now."

Lowell sighed. "You're right," he said. "They do add up. Trifles make perfection but perfection is no trifle . . ." He tossed the pages back to Beal. "Let's get this done in the next week."

"We'll need someone more dynamic than the current supervisor to do this," Breal said.

"Make it a special assignment for Clawson," Lowell answered, then returned his attention to a letter on his desk.

It was evident to Breal that Clawson was not overjoyed with the assignment and considered Lowell's timetable ridiculous. To this Breal could only make sympathetic noises.


BREAL STUDIED the shop and talked with the production supervisors, became aware of the high level of absenteeism, was astonished at the number of pending union grievances, and listened to Clawson gripe about the union's unresponsiveness. Engineering issued a report on reliability testing of the Mühlmann control. Its performance was superior to ETI's M-90. Breal saw a copy of the report in a black folder on Lowell's desk, but the old man never mentioned it and one day it was gone. Lowell was now deep into a manuscript that lay before him, which Breal learned was ETI's annual report to shareholders. Lowell pored over it as though it were a sacred text, and barely looked up. Once, Breal commented on the poor state of personnel relations and Lowell, without raising his head, said, "Why don't we have personnel report to you? Prepare an organization announcement for my signature."

At odd moments, while Lowell was at a meeting or at work on ETI's annual report, the image of the Mühlmann control appeared before him. The small yellow object, a single black wire trailing from it, crept across his mind like some alien rodent. Lowell checked sales figures, which appeared unaffected, queried Tergelen, who seemed unconcerned, placing his faith in the unshakeable structure of ETI's distribution system. Yet the rodent always reappeared. Lowell knew the answer was straightforward: ETI needed a control superior to Mühlmann and at a competitive price. And quickly, before Mühlmann made inroads into ETI's market.

Lowell visited Craig Holloway who, he was gratified to see, was starting work on a breadboard layout of the new control. "First we'll get it to work in discrete components," Holloway said as he fiddled with some wires, "then we'll reduce it to chip form." For thirty years Lowell had observed the slight, self-effacing Holloway—the engineering genius who had placed ETI at the forefront of photoelectric design—but now he sensed something new and disquieting. There was a hesitancy in Holloway, an increase in his stammer, an uncertainty beyond his usual diffidence.

"Can you do this, Craig?" Lowell asked.

"I think so," Holloway replied and looked over Lowell's shoulder as he said this, as if someone he feared was approaching. Lowell had hoped for a simple yes.

Lowell ordered Tergelen to find out all he could about Mühlmann. The Marketing head reported back that the German company's main products were computers for factory automation. But over the past several years they had broadened their product line to the sensors that fed their computers: mechanical and electronic switches, and now photoelectrics.

Their annual sales were $400 million, about ten times that of ETI. "A big fish," Tergelen concluded.

Lowell did not care for the implication in Tergelen's last remark. "Andre," Lowell said, "it's not the big fish that swallow the little fish. It's the fast fish that eat the slow ones."

WHEN BREAL and Buck Clawson joined Wilbur Scott, ETI's personnel director, in his office, two men dressed in work clothes were sitting in front of Scott's desk. Scott, a lumpy pear-shaped man in a knit suit, introduced one as Jerry Sullivan, the union president, a man with wiry red hair and a narrow string of a mouth, and the other as Jim Scadlock, the shop steward, a black man with a severely flattened nose and scars on his eyebrows.

"I asked to meet with you gentlemen so we can get acquainted," Breal said. "I assume Mr. Scott is taking good care of you."

"No, he's not, but maybe *you* can help," Sullivan said, and in the slant of the man's body and the set of his mouth, Breal sensed before him someone perpetually wound tight.

"I'm not here to set personnel policy," Breal said, trying to be amiable, "but I'm certainly willing to listen." He smelled the grease from their clothing, their perspiration, the odor of cigarette smoke, and instinctively pushed his chair back.

"I've been union president for over a year," Sullivan said, his hard gray eyes targeting Breal. "All the presidents before me had a reserved parking spot and a company phone. I don't have either and complaining to Mr. Scott hasn't gotten me anywhere." Sullivan took a cigarette out of a pack of Marlboros from his shirt pocket, and lit up.

Breal turned to Scott, who was scrawling on a yellow pad. "I'll discuss it with Mr. Scott," he said.

"Another thing," said Scadlock. "We've got over a hundred grievances pending, but we can't get Mr. Scott off his rear end to schedule grievance hearings."

Scott looked up, earnest-faced, wounded. "We schedule hearings whenever we can, Jim," he said, his voice that of a man bent on appeasement. "But it's a five-step process, and if a grievance goes all the way to the last step—and most of them do—that takes time. We're trying to get these open issues settled."

"You have to get Mr. Scott to try harder," Sullivan said to Breal.

"While we're airing our complaints, gentlemen," Breal said, "let me share a couple with you. The absentee rate for this plant is nine percent. The average for our industry is four. Doesn't that lead you to suspect that people are abusing the system?"

"Nobody is abusing anything, Mr. Breal," Scadlock said. "We got a lot of older employees. They get sick more often."

"That's a nice theory, Mr. Scadlock. Unfortunately the data doesn't support it. We analyzed absenteeism by age group and it's the younger people, those under thirty-five, that account for most of the absences."

"A lot of them are working mothers," Scadlock said. "When their kids get sick they have to stay home."

"Whatever the reason, Mr. Scadlock—and I notice it changes depending on what I say—if absenteeism continues at this level we'll have to ask for a doctor's proof of illness for anybody out more than a day."

Sullivan sucked up a draft of smoke, gave his head a rapid shake. "No way you can do that," he said. "It's not in the union contract."

Breal glanced at Clawson who was studying his watch as if he had just learned to tell time. "Let me register another complaint while we're at it," Breal said. "The productivity of this plant is a low eighty percent. The industry average is over ninety. It's a cold, competitive world out there, gentlemen. If the troops want the company to give them pay raises and more benefits, then they're going to have to do their part."

"Before you blame us, Mr. Breal, you might want to look around and see how your guys screw up productivity," Sullivan said, taking a drag on his Marlboro before setting the cigarette on Scott's ashtray. "Take a look at shipping. We've only got one forklift but there's work for three. We spend most of our time standing around waiting. That doesn't help productivity, does it?" Sullivan, words punctuated by cigarette smoke, leaned forward, pointed at Breal, his finger amber with nicotine. "Have you been down to the punch presses, in the basement? Those guys stand on a cement floor all day. They've asked for floor mats for years. A concrete floor is tough to stand on for a whole shift. The men get tired. That doesn't help productivity either. One guy brought in his own floor mat, not to help the company but to save his feet."

"And I'll tell you something else," Scadlock chimed in. "There's always a big rush to get production out at the end of the month. Then the first week after that everybody stands around like waiters while the supervisors scrounge for parts."

Breal again turned to Clawson who was now staring at the ceiling, head tilted back as if he were in a dentist's chair.

"There's lots more," Sullivan said, moving to the edge of his seat, a man warming to his task and enjoying it. "The girls on the production lines have dull cutting tools so sometimes they have to try two and three times to clip a wire."

Breal again looked toward Clawson, then Scott: no help was forthcoming.

"Another thing," Scadlock said, crossing his arms like a genie. "You've got old production equipment. The machines keep breaking down. Don't blame the troops. We try to keep this place running. We know which side our bread is buttered on. We're not stupid. Get Lowell to shake loose some money for maintenance. That's the best way to up productivity."

Breal sighed. "Anything else we can do for you, Mr. Sullivan?"

"Yeah," Sullivan said. "If you really want to improve things, you ought to know that the plant is unsafe." He paused, presumably for dramatic effect, and shifted his hard gray stare from the furiously scribbling Scott to the Buddha-like Clawson, and back to Breal. "If this place ever had a fire nobody would be able to get to the extinguishers because there's junk piled around them. When you say something to the supervisor, he turns down his hearing aid. And another thing, talking about safety, the guarding on a lot of the machines don't work. OSHA could come in here and shut this place down." Sullivan settled back in his chair, took a last drag on his Marlboro before crushing it in the ashtray. His face split into a grin showing an exaggerated expanse of nicotine-stained teeth. "You can call me Jerry," he said to Breal.

"And you can call me Jim," Scadlock said.

"Okay . . . Jerry, Jim . . . anything else?"

"Yeah," Scadlock said. He got to his feet and in a macho gesture hoisted his pants and tightened his belt. "Get Mr. Scott to shake loose those grievances." Amusement flickered in his eyes.

When Sullivan and Scadlock were gone, Breal turned to Scott, who was still writing, and to Clawson. "Well, gentlemen, I really appreciated your contribution to this meeting."

"You seemed to have things under control," Clawson said.

"A few words of support now and then, Buck, wouldn't be out of place. And you, Wilbur, what in the world are you writing?"

"I keep accurate records of what we tell the union and what they tell us."

"Look, Wilbur, I don't need a Boswell writing down what I say. And the union can always deny the accuracy of your notes on the grounds that you're biased. I'd rather you took part in the discussion. You can't participate if you're busy scribbling."

"Who's Boswell?" Scott asked.

Breal shrugged this off. "Where does the Jerry and Jim team work?"

"They're both in shipping," Scott said. "They also have super-seniority. That means they have the pick of any job in the plant and are the last two people we can lay off."

"Is there any truth in what they said about dull tools on the production line and that we need more forklifts?" Breal asked Clawson.

"Sometimes it's true, but not often," Clawson said. "But I've heard those speeches for years. They give them to every new man."

"Well, some of their gripes sound legitimate to me. Why don't you start with something simple, like putting floor mats at the punch presses?"

"We don't want to baby those people," Clawson said.

"We're not babying anybody, we're just helping ourselves. You might also want to think about cleaning up the trash around the fire extinguishers and check the guarding on the machines." Breal turned to Scott. "Wilbur, I'd like you to get Sullivan his reserved parking spot and a telephone."

When they left Scott's office, Clawson said, "I'd be very careful with those union guys if I were you. They may not be worth a shit, but they can make your life miserable. It pays to be nice to them."

"I *was* nice. But you might ask yourself what ETI has gained by being nice. We've got high wage rates, high absenteeism, low productivity, and an inspection force twice what it ought to be."

"Yeah, but we've got peace. A strike would really get Lowell pissed. I don't know if you've ever seen the old man really pissed."

"If you'd taken a couple of strikes over the years, you'd have a better plant now."

"Maybe so. But then I'd be out of a job."


It must be an effect of age, of being in spitting distance of the great beyond, this looking back, reviewing, mentally changing the unchangeable. Don't we all think we see our children's lives better than they do? I wonder what Catherine looks like now. A middle-aged woman. Does she have the elegance of her mother? Maybe she's fallen in love with her refrigerator, grown monstrously fat. How beaten by life? And what of her children? Surely she has children. Young men and women now. Whom do they resemble? What are their ambitions? What a mess I've made of things! Did I expect her to crawl back and ask forgiveness? If she did that she would not be my daughter nor her mother's. Is she in Boston—and if not where? It would be nice to find her, spy on her life, watch her go about her day. God! I sound like a jilted lover. I imagine scenes of reconciliation. Tearful reunions, all forgiven (what was there to forgive?). Would she forgive *me?* Would she even deign to see me? Learned to do without me years ago—to lead her own life. Who is this bearded old fart, arms open in welcome? What does he want? Get thee behind me, Lazarus returned from the dead. You threw me out once. Time has chilled my heart. I have no need of you now. Fuck off, old man!

Lowell decided that alternating men and women was the right seating arrangement, and no man could sit next to his wife. At a round table—under the central crystal chandelier at the Algonquin Club, where Lowell had taken Breal for lunch the day of his interview—Lowell was flanked by Tergelen's wife Martine and Susan Breal, Andre next to Susan, and Edna Graham opposite Lowell and between Breal and Tergelen.

As they entered the dining room, Edna told Susan that Dr. Lowell liked to invite new members of his staff and their wives to dinner, "To know them better, I guess." Susan decided that Lowell thought a man's choice of wife revealed much about him, and she was to be on display. Susan wished she were thinner.

"The lobster is excellent," Lowell said after he ordered his Tanqueray martini. "The males are tastier than the females."

"I would have thought that whether a lobster was male or female would only be of interest to another lobster," Susan said. "I'm surprised you can tell them apart."

"Having spent seventy-odd years in the degustation of lobsters, I can assure you that in their kingdom, as in ours, la donna è mobile. Stick with the males."

"After three martinis, I doubt if you can tell a lobster from a clam," Edna said, then ducked her head, apparently surprised at her own words.

Lowell squinted across the table at Edna, shrugged, and did not reply.

When they ordered dinner Susan decided that lobster was the prudent choice, but her husband, who occasionally suffered an allergic reaction to shellfish, ordered steak. "Medium rare," he told the waiter. "No, no," Lowell said. "Don't tell these people how to prepare a steak. Don't say anything. It'll come out exactly the way you like it." Susan concluded that either the chef was clairvoyant or Lowell was into control.

"I understand you're commuting here from Pennsylvania," Martine Tergelen said. "Is this a permanent arrangement?" The woman wore heavy eye makeup and light glossy lipstick; she did not look at Susan head-on but rather turned to the side, giving her a sly appearance as though she possessed some secret information.

"I want to be careful where we move," Susan answered. She was about to go on when Lowell said, "Tell us about yourself, Mrs. Breal. What is your background?"

"I majored in English Lit at Temple University in Philadelphia. That's where George and I met. In retrospect I should have studied something useful—how to hammer a nail or saw a log. Of what use is it to remember, 'I am fire and air; my other elements I give to baser life'?"

"Why, those are Cleopatra's dying words," Lowell said.

"Yes, they are . . . Please call me Susan."

"I went to school to learn a trade," Lowell said, "like your husband, to learn to hammer nails and saw logs. When it comes to the arts I'm self-taught. How much nicer to be immersed in it when you're young."

"It wasn't all that romantic," Susan said while Martine Tergelen regarded her with an estimating eye. "Reading interminable novels, writing silly papers about them, listening to boring lectures. It doesn't increase your faith in culture."

Lowell finished his martini, ordered another, and ordered two bottles of Chambertin when the food arrived. Susan learned that Tergelen had run the company's European operations before coming to the U.S. Though he and his wife were both Belgians, Susan noticed his accent was vaguely Germanic while hers was French. She asked Martine where she was from and, after a profound sidelong glance, the woman said she was from Brussels and Andre from the Flemish city of Ghent. Susan recalled once hearing that the Belgians combined the worst qualities of the French and the Germans. She didn't know what those worst qualities were, but intuited that if she spent much time with Martine Tergelen she would find out. When Lowell spoke, Martine leaned toward him, face rapt and attentive, as though about to receive holy communion.

Susan ate her lobster, found it tough and rubbery despite its maleness (out of curiosity she searched for but could find no evidence of the lobster's gender), noticed that Lowell seemed to have no such problem as he dipped the white meat in drawn butter and devoured it, washing it down with martinis and Chambertin.

"Well, Susan," Lowell said, "do you have the profound knowledge of Shakespeare that I do?" His speech had now grown deliberate.

"I'm certain I don't," Susan said.

Lowell's face lit, eyes bright, playful, a smear of melted butter glistening in his beard. "I'll tell you what," he said, "I'll give you a line and you give me the play."

"I don't think you want to embarrass me, Dr. Lowell," Susan said.

"Try this," Lowell said. "'The graves stood tenantless and the sheeted dead / Did squeak and gibber in the Roman streets.'"

Susan was about to say *Julius Caesar* but then, in a dim recollection, more intuition than memory, said, "*Hamlet.*"

"That's very good," Lowell said, eyes sinking toward the remains of his lobster. He finished his wine, and then peered across the table at Edna Graham. "There you have it, Edna," he said. "A Shakespearian scholar in our midst. What intellectual stimulus can you offer this august company?"

Edna regarded Lowell as if he were an oncoming shark, then said, "It's late. Maybe we'd better go."

"Nay, not so swift, good woman," Lowell said theatrically. "Who's in a rush? Anybody here in a rush?" He scanned the table; no one spoke. "There you are, Edna." He waved an arm as he emoted: "We can go on until the morn in russet mantle clad, walks o'er the dew of yon high eastward hill."

Martine laughed, or rather seemed to be faking a laugh.

"What do you want, John?" Edna said. "I can't quote Shakespeare or say anything brilliant. All I'm good at is taking care of you. That's a big enough job and not an easy one."

Susan liked the way Edna said this, with resignation but also dignity.

Lowell regarded Edna with care, as though she were the object of some experiment he was about to push a notch further. "Recite brillig and the slithy toves, Edna," he said. "They say art is a criticism of life. What deeper criticism than brillig and the slithy toves?"

Edna gave a sad tiny cough, gazed beyond Lowell, eyes round and empty as if she were blind, said nothing.

"The silence of the tomb," Lowell said. "The silence of God. More profound than words. Let me help you out . . . Twas brillig and the slithy toves did gyre and gimble in the wabe, all mimsy . . . all mimsy were . . . Shit. What comes next? Edna, help me out. What comes next?"

No one said anything.

Lowell again scanned the table. "Anyone want dessert?" he asked.

# EIGHT

$B$real took to wearing a wool pullover to work because of the chill February wind that whistled through the cracks between the windows and frames in his office. As Clawson labored to implement the fixes to the microcircuit facility, Breal emphasized that if the operation was to stay fixed, he had to replace Doug Reith. When Clawson finally agreed, Breal prepared a job specification for the qualities he wanted in the new supervisor and gave it to Wilbur Scott. "Let's get a replacement in here and fast," he said to the personnel director. "I'll get right on it," Scott said as he dropped Breal's spec on the sea of papers that littered his desk.

Breal continued his cost reduction activities on the M-90 and kept Lowell apprised of his actions. He found that Lowell sometimes accepted his recommendations without comment, while at other times he became irritated, stared harshly at the air, paced the room, and cursed his subordinates as incompetents over items that Breal considered trivial. Lowell grew excited by degrees: as he dwelt on a subject that displeased him, his voice became progressively louder, his face reddened, and he surged to a crescendo of rage; at that moment he stopped pacing, stood erect as a steel beam, arms rigid at his sides and fingers extended as though his joints no longer functioned, and ranted as if the very survival of ETI were at stake. He subsided in a sudden collapse though a residue of anger remained in a short-tempered abruptness on all subsequent issues.

Much as Breal searched for a pattern, he could find no way to predict how Lowell would react to any given problem, or to the same problem on different days. At any given moment he could not tell which would prevail, madness or reason. Breal came to view Lowell as a kind of unstable nuclear plant where the chain reaction occasionally went berserk and meltdown resulted. He now understood the tendency of his predecessors to send Lowell letters rather than face the uncertainty and violence of his reaction.

At Lowell's suggestion, Breal attended a sales meeting, and listened to bitter complaints over Mühlmann's pricing and lost orders at the original equipment manufacturers. Tergelen shrugged this off, told them to sell harder, and be more aggressive with the OEMs. At dinner, Breal sat next to Fred Standke, the lead salesman at the Chicago sales office, and listened to his warning that Mühlmann was here to stay and ETI management had best take them seriously.

One morning Lowell appeared in Breal's office. "How would you like to meet Victor Cobb, the Silent Killer?" Breal recognized the name of a member of ETI's Board of Directors. As they walked along the executive hallway toward Lowell's office, Lowell waved in passing at the large photograph that hung in the corridor. "The old management team," he said. "They get younger looking all the time."

Victor Cobb was about Lowell's height, also broad-shouldered, trim and very erect. Breal judged Cobb to be in his mid-sixties. Miles had told Breal that Cobb was a retired marine lieutenant general who at one point had commanded all of the corps in the Pacific. Miles commented that, according to rumor, had Cobb been three inches taller he would have been commandant of the entire marine corps. He had a penetrating blue gaze, steel-bottomed, and an unblinking stare.

"Dr. Lowell has been singing your praises since you arrived at the company," Cobb said.

This was the first time Breal had heard that Lowell was pleased with his performance. He managed a weak thank you.

Cobb asked how things were going and Breal gave a hurried summary of his manufacturing initiatives. Cobb's eyes never left Breal as he spoke.

OVER A weekend, Breal and Susan drove his Buick, the United Electric company car he had negotiated as part of his severance package, from Reading to Boston, and dispensed with his rental car. Susan never complained about their furnished apartment and brightened it as best she could. When Breal spoke of moving she answered vaguely. Breal didn't press the question, decided to wait. Susan continued to lunch with Edna Graham. "Edna is decent company," Susan said. "She doesn't get out much and she loves to talk."

"She does? The few times I've seen her, other than a couple of polite remarks, she was as silent as a lampshade."

"That's because you always saw her in the presence of The Great Man. When he's not around she can be a babbling brook. She also smokes Virginia Slims and can pack away three daiquiris at lunch."

"Does she ever talk about the old man?"

"Not really. She thinks he's a genius of sorts, and she did mention that their relations have not always been smooth, but she didn't elaborate."

LOWELL, BREAL and Tergelen sat at the marble table. Frost ferns patterned the windows. The mail net had trapped a letter from ETI's distributor in St. Louis, Crawford Electric, in which he mentioned that he was stocking Mühlmann products. "Two others, one in Houston and the other in San Francisco, are also stocking Mühlmann," Tergelen said in answer to Lowell's question. Breal noticed that Tergelen's vague Germanic accent noticeably thickened as he unburdened himself of this information. "But their *selling* effort is concentrated on ETI."

Lowell paid no attention to Tergelen's last comment. "How long has this been going on?" he asked, voice now a growl.

"A couple of months," Tergelen answered.

"Why was I not told?" Lowell's voice rose in volume. "Why do I have to find out about this by intercepting a letter?"

Tergelen snorted. "I thought we'd be able to convince them to drop Mühlmann and I still believe we can."

"You don't understand, Andre. You don't understand at all!" Lowell's voice, already loud, rose further on the second sentence. "We don't give a damn about these three. What we have to do is show all our other distributors the consequence of taking on Mühlmann. We must demonstrate by action that we will not sit idly by while they smoothly transition from selling ETI to selling Kraut products. We have to terminate every one of our distributors who has taken on Mühlmann, and do it now. And I mean now! Today!"

Tergelen's face had hardened. "By terminating these people," he said, "we give them no choice but to aggressively sell Mühlmann in order to survive. Our largest single account is the Anheuser-Busch brewery in St. Louis. If we discontinue Crawford, he'll actively sell Mühlmann to Anheuser-Busch, something he's not doing now. Right now he only carries Mühlmann on his shelf to answer customer requests, but he doesn't promote their products."

"By God, he still doesn't understand!" Lowell exclaimed. "If we don't cut these people off, every one of our distributors will sooner or later take on Mühlmann and our whole distribution channel will be destroyed. We must eliminate these three—put them out of business if we can—as an object lesson to the others. As for Anheuser-Busch, we can sell to them ourselves."

"All right," Tergelen said, "but you realize that Crawford has been an ETI distributor for more than twenty years."

"I don't care if he's been our distributor for a millennium!" Lowell shouted. "Get rid of him. Now!"

"All right," Tergelen repeated and made a shifting movement with his shoulders, "but you understand that terminating a distributor only because he's taken on a competitive line is against the law and opens ETI to an anti-trust suit."

Breal watched Tergelen. He was pale, mouth drawn into a tight line. He no longer looked at Lowell but spoke to the air. This had been his third rebuttal. Breal wondered why Tergelen would openly disagree with Lowell in a sustained way, why he didn't back off from an argument he could not possibly win. It must be, Breal concluded, that Lowell was treading on what Tergelen considered sacred ground, something that Tergelen had created and was subject to his will alone: ETI's distribution channel.

"Goddamn it, Andre," Lowell exploded, "don't get legalistic with me! Don't wave jack o'lanterns at me! Go find a reason. That's your job. If anyone wants to sue us, let them sue." Lowell paused, then said deliberately, each word as precise as a ball bearing, "Just keep one thing in mind, Andre. I want those distributors terminated by the time the sun goes down tonight."


LOWELL, SITTING at the head of the conference table, Breal, Clawson, Slater, Holloway and Tergelen before him, was taken by a sense of outflow. It shifted form—sales, money, energy, life itself—was trickling like some precious fluid from the company; it seemed a reminder of his own mortality. He visualized the three distributors who had taken on Mühlmann as jagged holes in the ramparts of ETI, blasted out by German artillery. More rounds would be incoming, bent on his annihilation. He scanned the faces before him and experienced a wave of hopelessness.

Where did these men who had the imagination of slugs come from? One who protects our distributors as though they were his harem, and these others—who must be prodded constantly. Go get 'em, Spot! For Christ's sake, Spot, bestir yourself. Sic 'em! The world's a field studded with broken glass. We're under attack, shells exploding around us. They sleep and feed and fornicate and know none of this. Renewal. That's what I need. A new breed. Youthful. Full of piss and vinegar. Not much point in worshiping at the altar of the past. Shed it all like a snakeskin. It's men not machines that win wars. The Roman sword was only eighteen inches long yet it conquered the world. Still—striving to better, oft we mar what's well. This is what I have. Rouse them to battle. To lead means to capture the imagination of those you command. Would Henry the Fifth have made his speech before this crowd?

The faces of the men at the table wore a glaze of wary prudence. Outside, snow fell in leisurely flakes, piling in graceful arcs around the window frames. Breal watched Lowell staring at them all. He sighed inwardly: commit, put his career, his life, in the hands of this eccentric old man? . . . Susan was right: there was no rush.

"When will the integrated circuit for the M-100 be completed?" Lowell directed his question at Slater. The chief engineer turned from Lowell's impatient stare to Holloway.

Holloway adjusted the papers before him, looked around as if he had forgotten something. "We're at least six months away."

Lowell shook his head. "It seems to me I've been asking that question forever, and I always get the same answer— we're six months away. Those must be biblical months, not calendar months. I feel like a man chasing the horizon. Now for the last time and with feeling, when is this damn thing going to be done?"

"This is new technology to us," Holloway said unhappily. "We're designing complicated new features and packing them all into an integrated circuit. Those are major advances, at least in the state of our art, and that takes an amount of time that's not easily predictable." Holloway seemed thinner and paler than Breal remembered and there was a querulous note in his voice as he directed his comments to a phantom above Lowell's head. "It's not possible to invent on schedule," he continued. "I really can't say with certainty that the integrated circuit design will be completed in six months."

"Can you use any consulting help?" Breal asked. "We're right next door to the world's greatest technology center. Is there anyone at MIT who can help?"

"I suspect that integrated circuit design is a bit like sex," Lowell said. "It's a one-man job."

"There may be design tricks," Breal said, "or computer-aided design programs that we're not aware—"

"I have no objection to a consultant," Lowell interrupted. "What I object to is the snail's pace of this program. Your schedule calls for full production in twelve months. That's out of my time frame. At a minimum, we must slice out four months. Do things on a crash basis."

Lowell rose and strode to the other side of the table. Breal saw he was preparing a speech.

"I don't think you people understand," Lowell said. "This is no capricious reduction of schedule I'm talking about. We're under attack by a formidable enemy. Listen. You can hear them hammering at this building. While we come in to work at eight and leave at five, while we go about our tranquil rounds, they're blasting the walls around us, stealing our customers, destroying what it took us half a century to build. Listen. If you hear nothing, you're dead. We're a small beleaguered garrison in hostile country. We must fight back, fight back with the only weapon at our command—technology. This new product, the shortened time frame—these are not the whimsical desires of a capricious boss. These are necessities if we are to beat back and conquer an implacable foe."

Breal had the impression that Lowell expected applause.

"Fortune favors the brave," Lowell continued, his gaze bright and hard. "Do not take the counsel of your fears. Do not underestimate the enemy, but it's just as fatal to overestimate him. Let us show courage. Don't be in awe of the

Germans. We whipped hell out of them in the last war and we can do it again. We only need the will."

Breal wondered whether in this combat Lowell saw himself once again a tank commander, maneuvering through rugged terrain as he sought to put Mühlmann, like the German battalions in the Ardennes, within the deadly circle of his gunsights.

"I'm not Henry the Fifth and this is not Saint Crispin's day, but the battle we're waging is more important to us than Agincourt was to England. I do not exaggerate when I say it's up to you to save ETI. You must carry this message of crisis to your people and insist upon their highest level of effort." Lowell paused and stared at Holloway. "Craig, you've pulled this company up by its bootstraps before. We'll depend on you to do it again."

"I'll do my best," Craig mumbled, his expression that of a man who had just experienced a sharp pain, and he seemed over the fifteen minutes of Lowell's discourse to have grown more haggard.

The meeting next focused on the bread and butter of project management: tooling, test equipment, producibility of the final design. Lowell paid little attention to these proceedings; he busied himself with paperwork and twice left the room for extended periods.

Whem Lowell returned to his office he asked Breal to join him. Back at his desk, Lowell called out, "Miss Krane, check the stock price." Now, evidently in a fine mood, he handed Breal a letter. "Here, take this along to add to your pile of good news this morning. Justice has triumphed again." The letter was from David Ramsey, their labor lawyer. He had won the age discrimination suit.


"Ishmael would like to take you out to dinner," Tom said to his mother over the phone.

"Are you serious?"

"Yeah. Sure. He likes you—thinks you're a good listener."

"Why didn't *he* call?"

"He's afraid you'll say no. It's easier for him if you say it through me instead of to him directly."

"Tell him to come over to the house. I'll cook dinner for us."

Tom was silent for a moment. "I don't think that'll work," he said. "He'll get the impression you're ashamed to be seen in public with a black guy."

"When would he like to see me?"


ISHMAEL PICKED up Catherine the following evening in his cab. Snow was falling, the city in the deep fold of winter. He drove to Roxbury, to a restaurant with half a dozen tables, the room almost full. She looked about: the place resembled any other restaurant, the tablecloths oilskin, the napkins paper. There was an odor of food and spices that she could not place. Scattered on the walls were photographs of black athletes in action: basketball, football, baseball, track and field. "Being a minority can be unsettling," Catherine said after they took the only empty table.

"How do you mean?"

"I'm the only white person in the room."

"Does that bother you?"

"Well, it takes a little getting used to."

"You're probably the first white customer this place has ever had."

"Why did you want to see me, Ishmael? I could almost be your mother."

Ishmael gave a mock frown. "You don't much look like my mother. Why did you accept the invitation?"

"I'm not sure . . . It seemed okay. But you didn't answer my question."

"Most young women are flighty or sizing you up as a husband. I'm not much of a catch." He smiled, a self-deprecating smile. "Maybe it's Oedipal. Who knows what drives any of us? Does it really matter?"

"I think it does," Catherine said. "My choices in men have not been happy. Married twice. Divorced twice. Not a good track record. So whatever drives me does it toward bad choices." She liked the way Ishmael listened: solemn eyes, understanding face. Why was she babbling all this?

"People tend to live their lives in patterns," Ishmael said. "They rarely learn from their mistakes. You're not unique."

"What's your pattern, Ishmael?"

"I think it's still developing. I hope it's not the stubborn pursuit of things that are impossible."

"You're serious about this Dante translation, aren't you?"

"More than I can say. I think the guy had the greatest poetic imagination this world has ever seen. I think maybe I can do him justice in English, though it's very difficult. Many have tried, going back a couple of hundred years. Don't ask me why I think I can do the job better than they. I just think I can." His brows drew together as he said, "I feel an affinity with the man. In some strange way I feel him in me, speaking in English through me." Ishmael gave another self-deprecating smile. "I know it sounds flaky. For all I know, that's how all translators feel."

"Have you ever felt obsessive toward something before, toward some other project?"

Ishmael nodded in appreciation. "For a time I was obsessive about writing poetry. Worked at it every free minute. Even got a couple of poems published in little magazines."

"I'd like to read them," Catherine said.

"Juvenilia," Ishmael said and shrugged. "Then the muse fled. I don't know how it happened, but I'd sit down to write and nothing came. Or it was trivial. I'd find myself reworking the same poem over and over." He shrugged again. "That's when I joined the air force."

Ishmael ordered for them both: fried okra and chicken yassa (whose pepper and chile spice numbed Catherine's tongue), and a shared pecan pie. She recognized the background music because her son Tom played it when he still lived at home—Scott Joplin's rags and cakewalks; Motown: the Supremes, Marvin Gaye and Tammi Terrell. Catherine noticed a worn sign above the entrance: "I've been in sorrow's kitchen and licked the pot clean."

After they left the restaurant, Ishmael drove his cab slowly through the white swirl of snowflakes; he crossed the Charles on the Mass Avenue Bridge and then turned east along Memorial Drive, the lights of Boston across the river flickering constellations.

"Look to your left," Catherine said as the snow let up. "You're next to my father's building."

Ishmael stopped and peered out at the six-story structure. "Old style and a little shabby, but impressive," he said, then looked again. "Is that the statue of a lion at the entrance? It's hard to tell with the snow on it."

"That's a lion all right. I climbed on it as a girl."

"Well, if you're going to have a beast guarding your doorway, it might as well be a lion. They have the loudest voice and sharpest claws in the jungle. That gives them the right to boss around all the other animals."

"Fits right in," Catherine said.

Ishmael stopped in front of Catherine's apartment. "Thanks for seeing me," he said, his face disappearing in the shadows. "You weren't put off by the food or where we ate, were you?"

"No, not at all," Catherine said. She paused a moment, "You have a black thing, Ishmael, don't you?"

"I'm afraid I do."

"Your color doesn't matter to me. It may be hard for you to believe, but it doesn't. I had a great evening . . . I enjoyed your company. . ."

"You know Dante never kissed his great love, Beatrice." He pronounced the name in Italian. "Never even touched her."

"Maybe that's why she was his great love."

"That's very good, Catherine."

"You can call me Kate."

"Good night," Ishmael said. "If you don't mind, I'll stay with Catherine. It has a classical ring that I like."

The taxi did not move until Catherine opened her front door, then Ishmael drove off.

How very different from Kent, Catherine thought. Then she thought of Ishmael's heavy mouth and wished he had kissed her. What would that be like? He had hesitated for a moment. Had he wanted to? Probably was afraid, for the same reason he had asked Tom to invite her to dinner for him.

"Hi, Mom," Michael called from his room.

Catherine answered her son, then plopped on the couch in the living room, and stared at the Indian scatter rug at her feet. Their stop at her father's building reminded her of the letter she'd sent him. He had never answered, but then what had made her think he would?

She noticed a recent issue of the *Globe* on the coffee table, and picked it up to distract herself. As she idly turned the pages, she came across a piece about the Boston Museum of Fine Arts, which had purchased a Childe Hassam painting for a substantial but undisclosed sum, and was having a reception to present it the following Sunday. The trustees would be on hand. The public was welcome. Her father, a trustee, would surely attend. She would recognize him but would he recognize her? If he didn't answer her letter, would he even acknowledge her existence? There was only one way to find out.

"I'VE JUST come from a meeting with the union leadership," Breal said to Lowell.

"Parasites," Lowell said, staring at the papers on his desk. "What they come down to is a mindless litany of more, more, and more again."

Breal thought this a promising beginning. He went on: "Let me tell you one effect the union has that's particularly insidious. Our manufacturing supervisors spend at least a quarter of their time not supervising at all. They're answering grievance filings, or attending grievance hearings, or arbitration meetings. All this over such momentous issues as a supervisor having moved material from A to B instead of asking a union person to do it."

Lowell rose from his desk, walked to the window, and stared moodily out at the river, gray now, reflecting the slate color of the sky. He seemed deflated, spoke in an absent-minded way of the darkling plain the union had made of manufacturing at ETI.

"One thing we can do," Breal said, "is replace Wilbur Scott. He's just not up to the job. A good personnel man can head off most of those problems before they become grievances and a drain on everyone's time."

Lowell turned from the window. "Do you have a particular person in mind?"

"No, but an improvement on Scott shouldn't be difficult to find. With your approval I'll start recruiting—in a confidential way."

"There's virtue in sticking with the devil you know," Lowell observed, then shrugged and said, "hell, go ahead. My Aunt Tillie would be an improvement over Scott. Just let me check out the man you settle on hiring."

# NINE

Breal learned that each salesman submitted a monthly report. These were assembled into a loose-leaf notebook and distributed within the marketing department. Breal asked his secretary to find the notebooks for the last three months. The reports, shoddily written, tended to be self-congratulatory on orders received. Orders lost clustered around original equipment manufacturers and most of the reports named Mühlmann as the winning supplier. A frequent and bitter complaint was price. The salesmen pointed out that application support and service were important to the end-user but mattered little to the large OEMs, most of whom had their own in-house technical staff. One of the salesmen in Chicago observed that your typical OEM would slit his grandmother's throat to save a nickel, but there were more than nickels at stake here. Mühlmann was selling product with performance at least equivalent to ETI at half the price and they were winning order after order.

Breal was summoned to Lowell's office. As he walked through the door Lowell thrust a paper at him. "Read this! It just came in the mail." The letter was addressed to Andre Tergelen and was from Midwest Conveyor Corporation. Breal found it difficult to concentrate as Lowell hovered around him, obviously agitated and impatient for a response. He registered phrases of the letter.

Dear Mr. Tergelen:

I am writing to inform you that, with regret, we have decided not to place our annual blanket order

with Electronic Technologies . . . ETI has served us
well over the years and we appreciate . . . However,
equivalent product, which we have thoroughly tested,
is now available at half the ETI price . . . We cannot,
in our highly competitive business, ignore . . .

"How big an account are they?" Lowell asked as Breal
looked up.

"I'll call in Andre. I would be guessing but he'd know."

When Tergelen entered Lowell thrust the letter at him.
While Tergelen was still reading Lowell repeated the question
he had asked Breal.

"About $400,000 last year," Tergelen said.

"How long have they been an ETI customer?"

"Many years—at least ten."

"Why did we lose the business?"

Breal thought the question was answered in the letter,
but Lowell seemed too agitated to even remember it.

"We'd have to sell our products at half price to get their
order," Tergelen replied.

"No doubt we lost the sale to the Krauts . . . How many
other orders have they taken from us?"

"Some. This is the largest."

Lowell's voice jumped to a shout. "I'm the least informed
person in this whole building! Information is like eggs, the
fresher the better. If I didn't intercept the mail, all I'd ever
get would be rotten eggs!"

Breal decided there was no point in protecting Tergelen.
"This is one OEM order of many that we've lost," Breal said.
"Some small, some large."

"Is this correct?" Lowell asked as he narrowed his eyes at
Tergelen.

"Some orders we win, others we lose," Tergelen said. "Mr.
Breal is taking a catastrophic view of our business."

Lowell strode around his desk, buzzed Miss Krane, asked
her to send in Dick Miles.

"Read this," Lowell said as he thrust the Midwest Conveyor letter at Miles. While Miles was hunched over the letter, Lowell continued, "Dick, do we track OEM sales separately?"

Miles looked up, and eyed Lowell as if he were a dangerous stranger. "No," he answered, "but I'd be glad to assemble that data for you."

"Goddamn!" Lowell exclaimed. "Would it ever occur to any of you to do something like that without my asking?"

"I think you'll find there's been a steady erosion of our OEM business," Breal said. "And all of it to Mühlmann."

Tergelen snorted. "It's easy to complain, Mr. Breal. You were brought in to reduce manufacturing costs so we could lower our prices to compete with the Germans."

"That's a long-term proposition," Breal said. "This problem is now."

"Other companies have low-balled price," Tergelen said. "Then, when their products fail at the end-user and there's no service, the market returns to normal. Besides, I'm sure the Germans are dumping. That's a short term affair. They must be losing their shirt at those prices. The greatest contribution you can make around here, Mr. Breal, is to concern yourself with cost reduction and manufacturing efficiency. That's the best use of your time. Don't worry about marketing."

"The Germans are selling a low cost product that does the job," Breal said. "They've redefined the market. It's a new ball game. The problem is bigger than manufacturing efficiency."

Lowell appeared not to have heard any of this. He paced the room and lectured on the importance of communications for ten minutes. During his speech Breal glanced at Tergelen and Miles: their faces were blank as they stared at the marble table before them. The two men, settled in the same bowed position and with the same vacant look, resembled each other. Breal then noticed that his own mouth was slightly open; it occurred to him that all three of them, seated like patient owls, must at that moment resemble each other.

"Communication," Lowell concluded as he dropped on the couch opposite the three men, "communication is at the heart of management." He laid the Midwest Conveyor letter before him on the table, bent over, and gazed at it. All eyes stared at the paper as though awaiting a revelation. At that moment a drop of bright red blood splashed on the letter.

Breal looked up from the paper. Blood was dripping from Lowell's nose into his beard and onto the table. He jerked a handkerchief from his pocket, dabbing his nose and beard as he ran to his desk and pulled a box of Kleenex from a drawer. He stared at the group with bloodshot eyes. "Would any of you gentlemen care to comment?" His voice had the timbre of someone with a terrible head cold.

Tergelen snorted again and in a noticeable accent said, "When you have chronic shortages of product and are unable to deliver, the customer naturally turns to another supplier. But the fundamental issue is still untouched. The cost of the M-90 is simply too high. In fact, our overall costs are too high. Our sales losses are a direct result of manufacturing problems in-house. That's why you, Mr. Breal, were brought into the company. So I would suggest you concern yourself with *your* problems, the problems you were hired to solve, while I worry about mine."

Lowell again paced the room and for five minutes lectured on the need for cost reduction. He then took the Midwest Conveyor letter from the table and handed it to Tergelen. "See what you can do to win this account back," he said.

As the men filed out of the room, Breal said, "You might want to take care of that nosebleed, sir."

"Not at all," Lowell said. "A nosebleed is like a shear pin or a fuse. When the incompetents around here upset me, I'd rather have a nosebleed than burst an artery in my brain."

LOWELL SAT at his desk, touched a tissue to his nose; the bleeding had stopped, but its very existence now seemed an omen, a foreshadowing of disaster: distributors shifting loyalties, customers defecting. Tergelen placed his faith in the distributors, that they would remain loyal until the new product arrived. But wasn't that naive, wasn't everyone bent on his own self-interest? Lowell wandered into engineering, found Holloway hunched over his breadboard, and reluctantly decided to leave him alone. The old engineer, like the mill of God, ground at one speed: unfortunately, slowly. Instead, Lowell searched out Slater, the chief engineer, and urged him to give Holloway every support, whatever he needed and quickly. When Lowell left, he glanced back at the bent figure of Holloway and again sensed the uncertainty in him. Lowell wondered whether the uncertainty wasn't in himself, in a lack of confidence in his own strength and resourcefulness to beat back the oncoming Huns. He experienced a heaviness in his legs and shoulders, had a sudden sense of his own decline.


AFTER THE meeting Breal found Miles. "What's Andre's problem?" he asked. "Life around here would be a lot simpler if he just acknowledged a problem instead of blaming someone else."

"To understand Andre," Miles said, "you have to understand his background. During the German occupation of Belgium, the SS charged Andre's parents and older sister with spying for the resistance. Andre says that's all nonsense, but under torture they all confessed to being spies and were executed. Andre escaped to Holland where he was sheltered by a friend of the family. The result was an abiding hatred of the Germans. But it also affects how he looks at things and how he reacts to disagreement."

"That's a tragic story, Dick, and I'm sure it's not the sort of experience that builds trust in your fellow man. But how do we live with this guy today?"

"Everyone makes his peace with Andre in his own way," Miles said. "But don't sell him short. Andre is a competent marketing man. He did a good job running ETI's European operation before Dr. Lowell brought him to the U.S. to head up marketing."

"He sure doesn't fit the mold. The marketing men I've known are typically optimistic, outgoing types."

"Andre concentrates on distribution. That's his baby."


CATHERINE'S HEART thumped and her hands turned cold when she recognized him in the crowd. He was shorter than she remembered and she had not imagined him so old. For an instant she experienced the cruelty of time. She held the folded slip of paper in her hand: it gave her comfort. Then she saw Edna Graham beside him, dowdy looking as ever, but heavier, more matronly, more substantial. Catherine stalked them from a distance, turning away when they looked in her direction. He was carrying a hat, a black Homburg, a style he had always favored; in the half-light of memory she recalled that he always put on the hat with a certain solemnity, like a bishop donning a miter. The time is now, she thought, before the speech-making starts, and afterward he might not stay for the reception. She was about to approach when she saw that her father was engaged in conversation with another man. She watched and waited.

After several minutes, he was free. Edna Graham had disappeared. Catherine zigzagged through the crowd, and at last stood before him. "Father?" she said.

He stared at her without comprehension, then his face broke in confusion and he looked away for an instant as though seeking help. "I'm Catherine," she said.

"Yes, you're Catherine," he said. He stared at her. "You still resemble your mother. For an insane moment I thought you *were* your mother."

"I wanted to see you. When you didn't answer my letter, I thought you had no interest. But I decided to find you anyway. I hope I haven't embarrassed you."

"No, no, not at all." His brow drew together. "I never received any letter."

"You have two grandsons," Catherine said. "Fine young men. Whatever you think of me, you might want to know them." She found herself on the verge of tears. "They need you."

Edna Graham appeared beside Lowell. "Look, Edna," he said. "It's Catherine."

"I can see that," Edna said. She did not extend her hand or make any welcoming gesture.

Catherine handed Lowell the paper in her hand. "Here's my address and phone number. Whenever you wish to meet your grandchildren, please call me."

Lowell took the paper, stuffed it in his pocket. "Yes, yes, of course," he said.

The crowd was moving toward the painting. "All trustees in front," a voice called.

"Goodbye, Father. Just seeing you this way has meant a great deal to me. Please call." Catherine turned, and struggled through the oncoming crowd.


THE SCENE with Catherine remained in Lowell's head as an afterimage, clear yet surreal, as though a strobe had flashed. Good Lord, there she was! Appeared like a ghost. Scared the bejesus out of me. Called me father. Haven't been called that in a hundred years. But that's what I am. And grandfather as well. Two grandsons. What courage it must have taken for her to find me, approach me. Old man. Forbidding. "They need you." Not for herself but for her children. Still beautiful. Her life written in her face. Did I really see her face? It seemed to merge with her mother, herself as a girl—all confusion. For an instant I remembered the moment when her mother left, the terrible moment that darkened the world. My daughter. How miraculous! She searched me out at a time when I wished

~ 103 ~

for her. Come to my arms, my beamish lass! All is forgiven. What exactly was there to forgive?

Lowell stared out the limousine window as did Edna Graham, the late February snow piled in dirty mounds along Huntington Avenue, trees skeletal. Neither spoke. As they approached Burlington, fog settled on the city. Lowell touched the paper in his pocket, thought of it as magical, remembered again his daughter's face.

That night Lowell built a great fire, filled a martini glass with Tanqueray, gazed into the flames, and felt the huge house wrap around him like a mausoleum. The thought of Catherine touched him lightly, feathery and alive. He recalled her words, her voice, then remembered other voices, as though he were holding to his ear the shell of the past, listening to the sea of his former life. Scenes long forgotten now returned like old photographs, sepia-colored, hazy, unreal. Edna sat facing away from him, her eyes fixed on the TV screen in the open entertainment cabinet.

Lowell finished the gin, poured another glass. "She mentioned a letter," he said toward the fire. "Did you see a letter?"

Edna continued watching television, and did not reply.

"Did I receive a letter from Catherine?"

"I saw no letter."

Lowell continued to speak toward the fire. "I think I will see Catherine," he said.

Edna, her lips now pursed, again did not reply.

"Did you hear what I said? I'm thinking of seeing Catherine."

Edna rose, switched off the TV, closed the cabinet doors. "What purpose is there in that? You didn't get along then. Why do you think you'll get along now? Why do you want to mess up your life? And why do you want to mess up mine?"

"She has two sons. My grandsons. I want to see how they turned out."

"They must be men in their twenties by now, complete strangers. You might as well stop a couple of people on the street and ask how *they've* turned out. It would be the same thing."

Edna Graham now looked directly at Lowell, her face set, eyes narrowed. "Look at me, John," she said. "I've been with you for twenty-four years. I've taken a great deal of abuse from you but I've never complained. Now I'll draw the line. Let me be blunt. If Catherine comes into this house, I will leave. I will leave the day she walks through the door, and this time you will not be able to coax me back. All of your ridiculous pleading will be useless. Do you understand what I'm saying? Let me say it again. I will leave forever if Catherine comes into this house."

Lowell finished his drink in a long gulp and stood up. "Unarm Eros," he said, "the long day's task is done and we must sleep." He shuffled toward the door.

"Did you hear me, John?" Edna Graham shouted after him. She was breathing thickly, like a wounded animal. "Did you understand what I said? Forget anything you want, but don't forget that!"


I WAIT. What in the name of heaven am I waiting *for?* Should I call, at least let her know that I'm thinking of her? They need you, she said. I can see them sitting before me, my grandsons, eager young men, handsome, I offering sage advice, the wisdom of seventy-three years. But I wait. Not like me to wait. Look at Edna. Goes about her business as though Catherine had never showed up, as if I'd never mentioned her. Would Edna leave? Was that an idle threat? And if she did leave could I get along without her? Can't let Edna run my life. Seize the reins. Pick up the goddamn phone.

Lowell buried himself in ETI, the annual report to shareholders, his speech for the annual shareholders meeting, yet thought again and again of calling Catherine.


BREAL LEARNED from Miles that the spacious corner room on the executive floor, set up with at least a hundred folding chairs and a lectern, was called the Tower, and was used but one day a year. That day had arrived. ETI's annual report was issued on March 10th, and on March 25th the shareholders gathered in the Tower for their annual meeting. Several of the younger secretaries had been recruited by Miss Krane to act as hostesses, seating the guests, handing out copies of the annual report, indicating the location of the restrooms. Victor Cobb, Breal and the other executives of the company sat at a long narrow table in front of the room, packed together like books on a shelf. Breal counted the house at thirty-seven. Clawson, who was seated beside him, leaned over and whispered, "You see that hundred-year-old man, the guy with the white hair and the crutches? His name is Mr. Horsfall and he's been at every annual meeting we've ever had. He always stands up at the end and reads a statement saying what a great guy Lowell is, and how much the shareholders appreciate what he's doing for them."

At ten A.M. Lowell entered the room, strode to the lectern, said good morning, and called the meeting to order. He then read his prepared text; he reviewed the prior year's financial results, said the reduced sales and lower earnings were due to a temporary decline in the factory automation market, increased competitive pressure, and investments in new product development and new facilities. Then, in an assured voice, Lowell forecast an expanding demand for ETI's products, increased sales and earnings, then continued, "At a meeting yesterday, your board of directors voted to leave the annual cash dividend of $1.40 per share unchanged. This action expresses confidence in ETI's solid position in the factory automation field, and in the future of the company."

While Lowell spoke, Breal watched the shareholders: they resembled patients in a doctor's waiting room. Lowell finished, tone upbeat and confident: "In the future we look to *increase* the dividend. Our purpose is to translate company success into material returns to ETI shareholders." There was no applause. Breal figured that the reduced earnings, there for all to see and despite the words of explanation, did not merit approval, nor was the rosy prediction credible.

The white-haired man that Clawson had pointed out to Breal then raised his hand. "Yes, Mr. Horsfall," Lowell said. Horsfall hoisted himself onto his crutches and bent over a sheet of yellow paper. "I would like to take this opportunity," he read in an unsteady high-pitched voice, "to deliver my personal congratulations to Dr. Lowell, who has lead Electronic Technologies Incorporated through thick and thin for forty-three years. His vigor, intellect and judgment are an inspiration to us all." No one applauded and Horsfall sat down.

The price of ETI shares drifted from twenty-four dollars down to twenty dollars over the next two weeks.

The day after the shareholders meeting Lowell invited Breal to lunch. As they left the plant Lowell paused in the pale late March sunshine. "Look," he said with satisfaction, "they're back." Two ducks next to the steps were picking pieces of bread from the grass. Breal thought it must be the guard that tossed the bread to them. Lowell leaned against the flank of the stone lion and watched the ducks. "They come back every spring. I sometimes think they're reincarnations of old friends." At Breal's skeptical look, Lowell said, "If a hundred years ago someone had told you the air would be filled with invisible voices and music and pictures, you would have said he was crazy." As they entered the limousine, Lowell smiled, "It's okay to be from Missouri about my old friends. The Bard said that modest doubt is the beacon of the wise."

"Production planning is a mess," Lowell said to Breal at the table. "Always has been. We either have too much inventory or not enough. And even when we have too much inventory, we never have what the customers want. I'm going to assign production planning and purchasing to you. See if you can put some order in that rat's nest."


ANOTHER SHAREHOLDER meeting over with. Would be good to get out of here for a week. Check on the European operation.

Springtime in Paris. See Cerise. An intelligent whore. More unusual, I suspect, than a whore with a heart of gold. More unusual yet, Cerise actually *enjoys* her work. Can you believe that? No tension in her. Relaxed as a cat. Clients carefully chosen, men of discernment, taste. Hopefully putting aside a nest egg. Still, in France, heard of women turning a trick at sixty. Not at Cerise's prices though.

In the wilderness of a sleepless night, Lowell became aware of the beating of his heart, thought it labored, flagging. He imagined the organ shriveled, like his arms and legs, a mighty effort needed to squeeze along a few drops of blood. He visualized his arteries clogged with a yellowish blubbery substance, his blood struggling through in a thin uncertain filament. Then the rest of him: the plugged drain of his prostate, pocked liver, synapses in his head disconnecting, distant lights blinking out one by one. For a moment, in the wooly dark, he had difficulty breathing, as if an icy weight had descended upon his chest. He turned toward the digital clock on the dresser: 3:31 clicked to 3:32. The present disappearing into the sinkhole of the past. He remembered Catherine's face, which then dissolved into another face, his ex-wife Louella, his Lou, regarding him in the serious way she had, the look she assumed when she was about to say something important. Then it became another look, soft and yielding, the way it was before they made love. The image drifted into view like some miraculous kite. Her face was classic, a Raphael portrait on a round canvas, surrounded by lilacs and camellias and chrysanthemums and violets: the Madonna of the Flowers.

The night drifts on, eternal. Thoughts come and go like blown leaves. Darkness presses against the window. Stroke—that's the worst. Wind up in a wheelchair, mumbling unintelligibly, drooling, in diapers. So dependent you can't even kill yourself. Edna, for Christ's sake, the hemlock. Don't bother holding the glass, I'll sip it through a straw.

Lowell fell into an uneasy sleep and found himself on a vast glacial plain that glittered in moonlight, where a single hole had been dug. The hole was narrow and perfectly rectangular as if machined out of metal. A closed box fashioned of black steel and precisely matching the hole—held by a man at each corner, all four hooded and garbed in black—was carefully positioned above the opening. Lowell watched the scene as if he had died, an observer powerless to act. Then he experienced a strangling sensation, cried out and awoke, the collar of his nightshirt damp with sweat.

At breakfast that morning, Lowell thought his eggs tasted as if they had been fried in motor oil. He ate half, pushed away the plate, stared directly at Edna and said, "I'm going to call Catherine this morning and arrange to see her and my grandsons. See them here, in Lowell House. I would like you to host the meeting. But if you have other plans, don't want to be there, or leave this house, that's your choice."

Edna did not evade Lowell's eyes. "You're a son of a bitch, John. You know that?" Yet while the words were bitter, fear is what Lowell saw in Edna's face.

"Catherine represents no threat to you. She in no way changes our relationship. But I can't allow your paranoia, this childish sibling rivalry you have, to impede me." He pushed aside his coffee. "Stay or leave. It's your choice."

"Wait a minute," Edna said. "Just a damn minute. Things are not that simple." Edna's mouth was drawn tight and Lowell could see the edges of her teeth; he thought of a cornered animal. "I've taken care of you all these years, sacrificed my life, never married, alienated my family, and now you stand there and give me ultimatums. Well, you owe me, John Lowell, as much and more as you would any wife."

"What are you talking about?" Lowell said. "In what way are you being threatened? Why this hysteria?"

Edna was paler than Lowell had ever seen her and she was breathing as if from great exertion. "You may be an intelligent man but you're as sensitive as dog shit," she said, eyes diamond-hard. "Do you think my position is easy? I'm not your wife but I live under your roof, nurse you, attend your social functions, entertain for you, fornicate with you. Those are the jobs of a wife. But that's not what I am . . . What am I then? Have you ever asked yourself that? You parade me around like a pet poodle. Old man can still attract young woman? Is that the idea?"

"What's all this got to do with my daughter and grandsons?"

Edna's eyes shifted from Lowell for an instant, then returned, intense black points. "What's going to happen is absolutely predictable. You're going to get all weepy-eyed over your newfound daughter, your long-lost grandchildren. And you're going to feel guilty over how you've neglected them. Your daughter Kate is a manipulator and she's going to manipulate you. Wheedle money, a car, a house, whatever she wants, out of your tender guilty heart. And before you go to join your ancestors, she'll make sure that whatever is left stays with her. Maybe you'll leave me the silver or the picture of your grandmother, but that's not what I've earned."

So there we have it, clear and simple. The invisible hand. Put money in thy purse. This we can all understand. Would Dr. Freud agree that's the problem? Probably not. More likely pierced by the lance of jealousy rather than greed. I must say, though, this show of anger, this baring of teeth, this unsheathing of claws is more than I thought old Edna capable of. No fury like a woman scorned. Listen to her go on, poor woman, hands trembling like leaves. Must take a world of courage. Spunky girl. Good organizer. I do care for her, you know. You can't live with a woman for twenty-five years and not care for her. She was a good fuck, old Edna. Would do anything. Not too inventive, but eager. Didn't mind a little experimentation. Still willing though it's all mechanical now. Age cannot wither her nor custom stale her infinite variety. Yes, well, not quite so with Edna.

"Let's end this scene," Lowell said. "Our arrangement is straightforward. I pay you well. You travel, meet people, have an interesting life. We've had good times. I'll leave you no less money than I would have if Catherine never existed. You've nothing to fear."

"Put all that in writing," Edna said.

Lowell rose from the breakfast table. "I have a company to run," he said.

Edna got to her feet as well, stood eye to eye with Lowell. "Put it in writing!" she shouted an inch from his face.

She stood there trembling, then her face puckered and contracted like the face of a child. Lowell put his arms around her and sighed inwardly as her body collapsed against his and her tears wet his cheek.

# TEN

Breal, at the kitchen table in his Boston apartment, pored over résumés. "God, what trash you get from a newspaper ad," he said to his wife. "Some of these people have no personnel experience at all. Here's one guy who's had ten jobs in the last seven years. With that track record, why would anybody hire him?" After a while Breal's face brightened. "Now here's a man with no less than a law degree . . . Personnel Officer for the Dedham School District . . . thirty-five years old . . . Take a look at this, Susan. Tell me what you think."

Susan studied the résumé. "You're sure he's not too much of an egghead for ETI? Aren't these industrial characters tougher to deal with than schoolteachers?"

"I suspect it's the other way around. There're smarter people in school unions. I'll interview the guy, see what he looks like. Besides, I'm getting desperate. This is my third ad and I've gone through four interviews."

Breal liked Ron Krakowski as soon as the man walked into Breal's office. A studious-looking individual with metal-rimmed glasses and a strong jaw, Krakowski was frank as to his reason for answering the ad. He had just received his law degree, at night, his salary at the school district was limited and would stay limited forever. He was more marketable now and could command a higher salary. The way to get it was working for industry. Breal asked him to comment on his lack of industrial experience.

"The National Labor Relations Act applies to all unions, whether they're the teamsters, steelworkers, or the Dedham

Teachers Union. What the rank and file do for a living isn't pertinent to the law. I've dealt with some very smart and very tough cookies at the school district. I'm sure I can handle these industrial types."

Breal liked Krakowski more by the minute, the way he looked, and the clarity and precision with which he answered questions.

"What's wrong with the man you've got now?" Krakowski asked.

"He's got a condition that's incurable—he's stupid."

Krakowski hesitated—clearly he had more on his mind—and then said, "I'm told this place is run by an eccentric old gentleman who believes he's always right. There's an axiom that if you find a boss that walks on water, save yourself a lot of grief and have nothing to do with him. I'm also told he's of the 'When in doubt, shout' management school."

"Where did you hear that—about Dr. Lowell?"

"In union circles word gets around."

"I'd be pleased to have you meet the boss," Breal said, "but he's out of the country—in Europe—and will be out for the next week. I'd agree he's a tough guy, but he's fair. Anyway, you'd be working for me, not him."

Krakowski provided Breal with references. Breal called each one: the results were glowing. Everyone, including his adversaries, respected Ron Krakowski.

Lowell telephoned to ask Breal if there was anything new to discuss. Though the overseas line was crackly, Breal chose the opportunity to sell Lowell on Krakowski. Lowell came right to the point. "Does he have any industrial experience?"

Breal hesitated. "Not on his last job," he answered.

"That's not what I asked," Lowell cried. "Since the day he was *born*, has he had any industrial experience?"

"No, but—"

"Then we don't want him," Lowell said. "Anything else?"

Breal was tempted to try again but thought better of it. With Lowell embroiled in the European operation and the phone line unclear, persuading his boss to change his mind was hopeless.

Breal was disheartened. He had thoroughly checked out Krakowski. The man had to be better, much better, than Wilbur Scott.

"If you really like Krakowski and truly believe he's right for the job, why don't you set down your reasons in a letter to The Great Man?" Susan suggested to her husband. "He might like that. I'll bet no one has ever come back and asked him to reconsider a decision."

"The old man gets impatient with letters."

"Write one anyway."

Breal went through three drafts. He spelled out Krakowski's background, alluded to the rules that govern collective bargaining and how they were independent of a specific union, summarized the results of his reference checks and, while he agreed the fit wasn't perfect, he didn't believe this to be a fatal flaw.

"You know," Lowell said to Breal on his return from Paris, while holding his letter, "this is the first time anyone has ever asked me to rethink a decision." He gave Breal an unexpectedly friendly smile. "I don't know whether this man is right for the job, but you must be allowed to make your own mistakes, if indeed this is a mistake. Go ahead and hire him. Heaven knows, he can't be any worse than what we've got now."

When Ron Krakowski came on board, Breal called Wilbur Scott to his office. Scott seemed uneasy as he settled his heavy bottom into the chair beside Breal's desk. Before Breal could speak, Scott plunged into a monologue on union grievance processing and the long hours he was working. He appeared unable to stop.

"Wait, Wilbur," Breal finally interrupted. "Wait. What I want to talk about is your job . . . I'm going to replace you as personnel director." Scott stared at him in a baffled way, mouth ajar; Breal could find no sign of comprehension in his face. "I'm letting you go," Breal said in a flat voice. In all his years in management, Breal had never found an acceptable formula for firing someone. He had finally concluded that no such formula existed and, in order to get it over with quickly, chose the most direct approach, which also turned out to be the most brutal.

Scott finally dropped his eyes. Breal was afraid he might cry. Then Scott, to Breal's surprise, raised his head, his upper lip drawn tight against his teeth, and said, "You never told me my performance was deficient. In no way did you ever let me know that I was doing anything wrong or ask me to improve. Now you're firing me. That isn't fair and it isn't right." In his flash of outrage Scott assumed a dignity that Breal had never seen in him before. "I've never been fired in my life," Scott went on, "and I'm not going to get fired now. I resign. I never did much care for you, Breal." Scott took on a crazed expression. "Let me tell you—you don't know shit about dealing with unions. You've totally and completely fucked up this company's labor relations."

A week later Lowell received a letter from Scott listing his accomplishments and pointing out instances where Breal had undercut him with the union. The letter was astonishingly detailed. Lowell tossed the ten pages at Breal. "Here's some fan mail for you," he said. "It reads like *Gone with the Wind*." He seemed pleased that someone disliked Breal. "The old man must think that's a sign of toughness," Breal later commented to Susan.

Breal called a meeting with the union leadership and introduced Krakowski as the new director of personnel. Breal, seeing Krakowski in action, liked him better than at the interview. He listened, took no notes, and looked the union men in the eye. He had memorized the union contract prior to starting work and answered their questions crisply and with precision.

In the following weeks, Krakowski met with each of the production supervisors and prodded them to settle any differences with their employees quickly, before a grievance was filed. "The worst thing is when a guy thinks he's got a legitimate gripe and he can't get anyone to listen," he told them. He urged Clawson to play a more active role in grievance avoidance. If the supervisor was unsure of his ground, Krakowski asked that he and the shop steward spend a few minutes discussing the matter with Clawson. If that didn't work, Krakowski asked that the supervisor and steward hustle over to his office and seek his input. Only if these informal procedures failed would a grievance be filed.

Krakowski instituted weekly after-hours communications meetings with the union leadership. He invited Clawson and any of the supervisors who were available to attend. All worker concerns, no matter how mundane, were fair game at these meetings. He also met one-on-one with Sullivan and Scadlock to attempt to resolve pending grievances even though this was not part of the formal grievance review process. And feisty Sullivan, all angles and sharp corners, did not succeed in pushing Krakowski around.


LOWELL NOW tracked sales to original equipment manufacturers and noted their steady decline. He knew that in time this would lead to the contraction of his core business. Profitability had fallen and Lowell now saw the dividend in jeopardy and ETI shares—the main repository of his wealth—sliding toward oblivion. He had the sinking impression that he could no more stop that slide than pull a tree up by its roots. He struggled against the feeling that his own aging, his own decline, and that of ETI were linked, both part of the same inexorable destiny. He asked Miss Krane to check the stock price more often, as though he were taking his temperature.

Sometimes Lowell wandered into engineering, and found Craig Holloway puttering around his enormous breadboard. "Why are we still in breadboard?" Lowell once asked.

"Every function has to be right before I commit to silicon," Holloway said. He spoke, head turned away, as if he wanted the words to reach Lowell by some circuitous route. To Lowell it sounded like the voice of grief.

In the passing months Lowell watched Craig Holloway grow thinner, concave, noticed his stammer worsening, as the breadboard swelled in size to a chaotic jumble of wires and components. He seemed to be slowing, as if trudging up a mountain, dwindling as if there was a slow leak somewhere in his life. Yet it had always been so. Hadn't Craig always resembled a man at the edge of defeat? Yes, Lowell had seen this for thirty years. But in the end, somehow—miraculously— a photoelectric design emerged superior to any other. Lowell held this thought, a fragile light, as he and Slater and everyone else waited for the miracle to recur.

Lowell now kept a Mühlmann control in his desk drawer, peered at it several times a day, returned to it like a chipped tooth. He told himself it was to keep focused, stay concentrated on the enemy. But now he associated the small yellow rectangle with some new and deadly virus loosed upon the earth, upon him. Once, as Lowell studied the yellow object, he noticed at its lower edge, in tiny black type, the name of the city of manufacture: Darmstadt, Germany.

He remembered rolling through Darmstadt in *veritas*, the city reduced to a rubble of shattered buildings, only the walls left standing. Out of that devastation had arisen this murderous yellow object. How had that happened? The image of the yellow rectangles now came to him at odd moments, while staring out the window or reading, it shadowed his mind, caused a perpetual throb of anxiety. The world had lost its old logic. He struggled against the thought that he was being pulled along by forces greater than he, a passive spectator in the working of his fate.


"SUSAN, I'M wearing myself to a frazzle," Breal said. "I'm tired of running back and forth to Reading every couple of weeks and fighting the airlines. Then this apartment is too damn small and uncomfortable. We've got to make a decision."

Susan regarded her husband. "This is an important decision for both of us. I'd like to be sure it's right."

"I can't give you any guarantees," Breal said. "I know ETI is bizarre, but that's the hand I was dealt. I can't change that. Let me tell you something. Yesterday I took a production problem to the old man. He looked at me and said, 'What do you think we should we do?' There was a look on his face, sort of vague, confused—I mean he really didn't know what to do—that made me feel awful. I would have done anything to help him."

Susan contemplated her husband for a long moment without speaking. "I can see you're committed," she finally said.

"Committed is the right word," Breal said. "If I'm going to succeed at ETI, I've got to hire my own people. I can't very well ask them to make a commitment to the company if I haven't made one myself." Breal regarded his wife and waited.

After a silence, Susan abruptly shifted her gaze away from her husband and, with a decisive movement of her body, said, "Okay, let's move to Boston."

They decided to look for a condominium on Beacon Hill. Edna Graham accompanied Susan in her search. Susan remarked to Breal that Edna seemed to enjoy dawdling around the converted brownstones where the floors were never quite level and there was a fireplace in the bedroom—and even knew the names of some of the original owners. "Sometimes you'd think she was looking for a place for herself. Anyway, Edna has real estate contacts through her father who, it turns out, was an old business associate of Lowell's. They had a falling out—she didn't say over what—and now they never speak to each other . . . You know, she glances at young men on the street, the way some men surreptitiously watch women. Poor thing. You've got to feel sorry for her."

The two women found a 1,400 square foot condominium on Chestnut Street, near Louisburg Square, in the heart of

Beacon Hill. The apartment was on the fourth floor of a five-story walkup; the living and dining areas faced south, and a small terrace gave out to trees and a garden below. "We'll get plenty of sun," Susan said, "and we can eat outside on summer evenings. Besides, doing all those steps will be good for your heart and good for my waistline."

In June, eight months after her husband joined ETI, Susan Breal sold their house in Pennsylvania, efficiently and brutally reduced their belongings, and moved to Boston.

"I think I can now truly say, welcome to ETI," Lowell said as he came out from behind his desk to shake Breal's hand when he heard the news.

"I don't know why," Breal told his wife, "but I felt real good when he did that."


CATHERINE SCANNED the Great Hall as Lowell mixed their drinks. In memory it was larger yet, cavernous and infinite like a European cathedral. The roaring fire—she recalled it as a gigantic conflagration—was missing. Her glance paused at Lowell's portrait. That's how she remembered him: beardless, round stubborn head like the stone spheres atop those columns that flank an entryway, his gaze a physical weight, his behavior studded with small acts of aggression. Yet now the portrait seemed less forbidding, more open, as if it were listening. Her sons looked around as well, awed, as though transported from Kansas to Oz. She noticed with dismay their ill-fitting suits, Tom's wrists sticking out of a jacket that was a size too small.

"I'm writing a novel," Tom answered in response to Lowell's question, "and I drive a cab nights."

"What's the book about?" Lowell asked.

"It's tough to summarize fiction. It always comes out foolish." He hesitated. "The novel is about my life and the lives of people I've known, all scrambled together in, I hope, an interesting and original way."

Lowell turned to the younger boy. "I couldn't write my way out of a paper bag," Michael said. "But I'm good at math and I like science, so I've opted for engineering . . . Mom tells me you're an engineer."

"Yes, electrical. I went to school in the days before electronics, when motors, generators and power lines were the meat and potatoes of the business . . . What kind of engineering interests you?"

"It would have to be electrical. I'm not much good at mechanical things."

Why, they're like the two sides of me—artistic, scientific—as though I'd been split in two. I daresay the younger one even looks like me. How uncomfortable they must be! Who is this old geezer? A curio: they examine me as if I were sculpted of marble or ivory. Grandfather—returned from the dead to question their lives. How ridiculous! What if *my* grandfather showed up? What have you made of yourself, boy? Account for your life. Well, sir, I should have done better. Safe answer. Who of us should not have done better? No precedent for this, really. What do you say to two young men that you meet for the first time and who are your grandsons?

"You both live at home?" Lowell asked.

"I have an apartment in Boston that I share with another cab driver," Tom said.

Catherine was tempted to speak but held back. Let her sons speak for themselves. She thought of Ishmael. He was a lot more than another cab driver. He invited her to dinner occasionally. Once she suggested a Sunday visit to a Van Ruisdael exhibit at Harvard's Fogg Museum, another time to the Museum of Fine Arts. Ishmael always said no; he seemed to prefer to see her in the dark of night, in his own territory. He had once compared his world to Dante's *Inferno*, and even conjectured that his fascination with Dante could be explained by what he had been born and where he was raised. But Dante's *Inferno*, Catherine had learned, was punishment, eternal punishment. She asked Ishmael for what sin was he being punished. He thought about this, his eyes more solemn than usual, and just shook his head. They would have to talk about that.

"What do you want out of life?" Lowell asked the young men. He noticed that neither was a drinker. The younger boy had asked for a Coke and the older was still nursing his bourbon and water. Better stick with one drink. First impressions matter: wouldn't want them to think grandpa's a rummy. To tell the truth I feel a little shy, as though *I'm* the one being judged. But then wouldn't you, wouldn't anyone, feel that way?

"I'd like my novel to be successful," Tom said. "It needn't be super-successful. Just so I can have enough money to write full time and not have to drive a cab . . . But then you meet a lot of weird people in a cab. Great environment for a novelist."

"I've applied to the best engineering schools," Michael said, "like MIT and Cal Tech. Maybe I can win a scholarship to one of them. My grades are good and so are my SAT scores."

"I'm a trustee at MIT," Lowell said. "I can't get you in, but I can see that your application is on top of the pile."

"I'd rather you didn't do that . . . grandfather," Michael said. "I'd prefer to make it on my own."

By God, he's a proud young man, isn't he? Indeed his mother's son and my grandson.

The Chinese chef/butler appeared and bowed.

"Time for dinner," Lowell said. The group left the Great Hall. Catherine's still slender, he observed, and moves with her mother's easy grace.

As they were being seated for dinner, Catherine thought of her old classmate, Edna Graham, for the first time that evening. Where was she? She had never considered Edna particularly sensitive or discreet. Maybe she had been ordered to disappear for the evening. Yet somehow Catherine thought of Edna as nearby, a lurking presence, somewhere in the shadows.

RON KRAKOWSKI called Breal and told him that Fred Standke, ETI's lead Chicago salesman, was leaving. Worse—Standke was going to work for Mühlmann. Breal hurried to Tergelen's office. For the first time in Breal's experience, Tergelen appeared agitated.

"What reason did he give for leaving?" Breal asked.

"They made him an offer he couldn't refuse."

"Did he tell you what the offer was?"

"It was a thirty-five percent increase in salary plus a sizeable bonus based on sales."

"We don't have a bonus program for our salesmen, do we?"

"No," Tergelen said dismissively. "That's just money down the drain." Suddenly Tergelen leaned back in his chair, put his hands behind his head. He had become the old Tergelen. "Other companies have bought some of our salesmen. That's how things work. We've lost salesmen before and replaced them without a problem. We can do the same with Fred."

Breal did not think replacing Standke was all that easy, but saw no reason to press the point. "What's his job going to be?"

"He'll be in charge of Mühlmann's selling operations in the Midwest."

Breal rushed back to his office and called Standke.

"I was on my way out the door," he said.

"I understand it's for good, that you're going over to the enemy."

"You might look at it that way, but basically I'm a gun for hire, same as you. I've got a wife, two kids in college, and a hefty mortgage . . . Anyhow, besides the money, I think those guys represent more opportunity."

"Why do you say that?"

"As part of the interview, I visited Mühlmann's operations in Germany. They make our production lines look like the village blacksmith. They have more robots in their factory than people. Plus they've got more advanced products."

"Was there anything else?"

Standke hesitated, then said, "It's a general impression. They're sleek and smart and professional." He gave a mirthless laugh. "And they're not weird."

# ELEVEN

"I'd be delighted to have dinner with you, Ishmael," Catherine said on the phone, "but this time I get to choose the place."

Ishmael's voice changed, became wary, remote. "Why? What was wrong with where I took you?"

"Nothing was wrong. But I'd like to take you out of the black world. If we're going to see each other, there's got to be some balance."

Catherine took Ishmael to Ettore's, an Italian restaurant in the North End. She figured that after his years in Italy this would make the smoothest transition. The waiter, an older man, hair combed across a glistening scalp, spoke with a pronounced accent.

"The guy doesn't go in for coffee and cream couples," Ishmael said.

"How do you know that?"

"I can tell. Watch, when he serves my food he'll hold the plate an inch off the table and drop it."

"Try talking to him in Italian. Maybe that'll soften him up."

"Why would I want to soften him up? I don't feel any need to ingratiate myself with him. If he's a racist, he's not alone. Stereotypes make people comfortable, saves them the effort of thinking."

"Do you carry this thing around with you all the time?"

"What thing?"

"This chip. I mean, if you think the other guy is a racist before he's said anything, or done anything, then you behave in a certain way. A way that makes you . . . makes you . . ."

"*Antipatico,* I believe that's the word you're searching for."

"What does it mean?"

"Unlikeable. Sort of obnoxious."

"Well, there you are. *Antipatico,*"

Ishmael smiled, corrected her accent. "I could teach you Italian," he said.

"Don't change the subject," Catherine said. "By behaving *antipatico* you create a self-fulfilling prophecy."

The waiter arrived with their food. He served Catherine with a flick of his wrist so her plate skidded several inches in front of her, then did the same with Ishmael's plate. Ishmael gave Catherine an I-told-you-so look, and shrugged.

"I still think you should have talked to him in Italian," Catherine said.

The couple strolled north on Salem Street toward the pier, past the still-open meat markets and grocery stores, barrels of olives and baccalà ("salt cod," Ishmael explained) on the sidewalk. Catherine took Ishmael's arm; the spring evening was gentle and clear, the light innocent. She could smell the coffee and spice shop as they approached the corner of Parmenter Street.

Ishmael pointed to a building near the corner: free-standing, double-curved concrete vaults sprang like umbrellas from the roof. "Branch of the Boston Public Library," he said. "Can't be all bad. They have a bust of Dante at the entrance."

"All roads lead to Dante," Catherine said. "How's *your* Dante coming along?"

"All roads *do* lead to Dante," Ishmael said. "That's why he's great. Anyway, it's a slow process. Italian is feather-light. English is a lead weight compared to it."

"But every Italian word must have an English equivalent."

"Often more than one. But it isn't just translation I'm after. That's easy. It's conveying the poetic feeling of the Italian in English that's tough." He appeared to reflect on this, debating whether to elaborate.

Catherine saw that Ishmael and Dante had become inextricable, that Dante, though dead six hundred years, had somehow twisted himself into the fabric of Ishmael's being.

"Tell me more about yourself, Catherine. What have you done and what would you like to do?"

And so Catherine, not feeling herself judged, elaborated on her two failed marriages, the loss of her job, her desire to be an attorney, her estrangement from her father. They passed the Old North Church, its slender spire, flood lit, silhouetted against the night sky.

"But you've just seen your father, haven't you?" Ishmael said.

Catherine stopped. "How do you know that?"

Ishmael shrugged. "Tom told me. Maybe he shouldn't have, but the meeting made an impression on him and he wanted to share it with someone. I was handy."

"What kind of impression?"

"From what I gather it was favorable . . . Why are you apprehensive?"

"I think my dad can help Tom. It would be nice if Tom liked him."

"Do you think the old man can help you become a lawyer?"

Catherine turned toward Ishmael. His long face was serious. "He could if he wanted to." She thought further. "Maybe he owes it to me."

"You're a scheming woman, Kate," Ishmael said smiling.

"All women are," Catherine replied. "It comes with the territory, like ovaries."

"Do you know why your parents divorced?" Ishmael asked.

"Their marriage was based on a mutual misunderstanding. She thought he had an artist's sensibility because he quoted poetry, and he considered her a woman of the world because she was a lawyer. In fact, *she* had the poetic soul and *he* was the man of the world."

"Did your parents ever argue?"

"Continually. Mother perceived all her problems in terms of masculine-feminine and fought stubbornly for her rights.

It was this struggle that defined their relationship. I have to say, their incessant arguments had a perverse charm and underneath, despite the surface rancor, I thought there was an undercurrent of love." She considered this a moment then added, "They also disagreed on what was important. Things he considered trivial she took seriously, and things she considered serious he took lightly."

"I imagine when they stopped arguing the real problems began."

"That's true. They stopped arguing after my brother died. Maybe in some way mother blamed my father. But she grew cold, distant. With me as well."

"I gather she left him."

Catherine nodded, was quiet for a moment, then said, "My father wanted to keep captive those he loved. But what he really wanted was impossible. He wanted them to be happy in their captivity."

They walked without speaking for a while, then Catherine said, "What do you want of me, Ishmael? Why are we seeing each other?"

He pondered this. "I'm comfortable with you. I enjoy your company . . . What more is there to say? But if our seeing each other disturbs you, we can forget it."

"I enjoy your company as well, Ishmael. Don't get defensive. Don't let this black thing get in the way. I just think we should be clear and honest with each other."

"Haven't we been that?"

"To a point . . . Will there be physical contact between us?"

"Do you want physical contact?"

"It would be nice," Catherine said. They passed the statue of Paul Revere on horseback—right arm outstretched toward the church tower where he had placed the lanterns—then continued their stroll to the wharf. Darkened gulls on extended wings were gliding toward the sea. Catherine held

Ishmael's arm as the couple gazed across the bay at the lights of Charlestown.


BREAL CONTINUED to read the sales reports and saw the pattern of Mühlmann's attack. They handed out controls, initially gave them away, to stimulate interest. They had started with the large original equipment manufacturers and were now at the second level. They were selling direct to the large OEMs, but Breal knew that in the long term Mühlmann would have to do more. They would have to address the smaller users and the aftermarket. They needed distributors and were signing up second and third tier outlets. Distribution was clearly their weakness. Lowell sensed this and Tergelen knew this as he visited each of ETI's distributors time and again, attempting to keep them loyal, giving them a help-is-on-the-way pitch.

Lowell called Breal and Tergelen into his office and waved a chart. "Look at our sales, for Christ's sake. Down again." He peered at Tergelen. "It's always the Krauts, isn't it?"

"Partially," Tergelen said. "But mostly the economy is weak."

Breal decided that part of his job was to bring honesty to ETI, his relationship with Tergelen be damned. "We're under attack everywhere," he said. "Not only have we lost our largest OEM customer, Midwest Conveyor, but we've lost other important ones, like Signetics Packaging. You might say Midwest Conveyor broke the dike. They tested hell out of Mühlmann's sensors and by deciding to buy Mühlmann they put a stamp of respectability on them. Every OEM is testing their product."

Lowell squinted at Tergelen. "I've directed our salesmen to visit all OEM customers and tell them we're willing to negotiate price," Tergelen said. "That's Mühlmann's main selling point."

"We're losing sales to Mühlmann," Breal said, "but we're also losing people."

"What?" Lowell said.

"Fred Standke was recently hired away by Mühlmann."

"Fred Standke?" Lowell said.

While Tergelen explained, Lowell got to his feet and paced the room. He struck Breal as a man who felt some vital life-giving substance disappearing, not quite certain what, but fearful it could never be retrieved. Then Lowell stopped, looked around, confused, as if sightless. "We've got to hold market share," he finally said, quietly, as if speaking to himself. "When that's lost the company's lost." He turned to Tergelen. "Negotiate price with those OEMs, but if you have to go more than twenty percent below our standard discount, check it out with me first." But Lowell's voice as he said this carried no conviction. He sighed, and added an afterthought, "We don't want to give away the store."


Edna Graham invited Susan Breal to lunch at the Ritz-Carlton. Susan had a glass of chablis with her salad and Boston scrod, while Edna packed away three daiquiris with her halibut.

When they left the restaurant, Edna remarked that it was the first really hot day of the year and suggested they walk across the street and stroll through the Public Garden. She took Susan's arm as they crossed Arlington and entered the park. The tulips were still in bloom, sturdy blocks of red, yellow and white. Edna told her that the year before some lunatic had spent the night lopping the heads off all the tulips in the park. The following morning the plants waved their pitiful decapitated stems while the flowers were shriveling on the ground.

They wandered toward the bridge that led to Charles Street and the Boston Common. The paths were lined with orderly beds of cyclamens, snapdragons, pansies, daffodils, and begonias; children were feeding the ducks in the pond below the bridge; men passed by carrying their jackets over their shoulders. Swan boats filled with small children and elderly couples and propelled by pedaling young men in white t-shirts glided over the pond. The two women paused at the bronze statue of a stooped and humble Edward Everett Hale, and Edna remarked that Lowell loved to quote Hale's famous line from *The Man Without a Country*. "John's a great patriot," she said, "still believes in old-fashioned sentiment."

They crossed Charles Street, meandered through the Common, and finally plopped on a bench. Edna kicked off her shoes, removed a pack of Virginia Slims from her purse, lit up a cigarette, and turned her pale round face toward the sun. On a nearby bench an old woman in a frayed Harvard sweatshirt was feeding morsels of bread to the pigeons. A sprinkler threw a jet of water over the grass.

"You might be interested to know," Edna said, "that John's father was an actor, a Shakespearian actor. He was usually on the road and John was never close to him."

Susan sensed revelation in the air and wasn't up for it; she was drowsy—the wine at lunch, the sudden change to summer, had made her somnolent—and what she really wanted was to go home and nap. But if Edna was in the mood to confide, Susan felt she had no choice but to listen.

"John's mother died in childbirth," Edna continued, "and his father never remarried, though he's supposed to have had many affairs. John was raised by his maternal grandmother who doted on the little tyke and spoiled him rotten. I always thought that's what accounts for his temper tantrums as an adult."

"I see you've put together a Freudian profile on Dr. Lowell," Susan said.

"Well, John's anger is something to behold," Edna said. "It's so awful that it needs explaining." She paused, momentarily distracted by two young males in shorts and wearing Boston University t-shirts jogging by. The joggers disturbed the feeding pigeons and the old woman yelled at them in a foreign language. Edna stared at her with distaste.

"Anyway, John's maternal grandfather owned a shipping fleet that carried bananas from Nicaragua and Guatemala to the East Coast. He was quite wealthy for a while, but then got caught up in market fever and was wiped out in the great crash. He died soon after that and left a big house and some life insurance money. His grandmother was comfortable, but by no means rich. She knew what to hang onto though. In spite of bad times she never let go of that house and the thirty acres around it. John got a Bachelor's and Master's in electrical engineering from MIT. He claims to have taught engineering simultaneously at MIT, Boston University and Northeastern to raise the money for his new company, but that's all bull. It's true he was a teaching assistant at MIT and Northeastern, and a teacher's aide for a while at BU, but the money for the company came from his inheritance. When his grandmother died she left the house plus three hundred thousand dollars to young John."

"What about the doctorate?"

"It's honorary. He was awarded an honorary doctorate by Brookings College after he contributed a million dollars to endow a chair in engineering."

"I don't want to appear critical," Susan said, "but you mean to say that he has everyone call him doctor when it's not even earned?"

"Well, John has a weakness for titles. The guard force always calls him colonel, as though he were the big cheese of some two bit Latin American country. It's semi-legitimate because he was a colonel in the army. Anyway, John was married and had two children, a girl and a boy. The boy died in an automobile accident as a teenager. His ex-wife, a woman named Louella, has grown over the years to wonder-woman proportions. I get nauseous whenever John talks about her. Louella is, depending on the day, a super trial lawyer or, because she dabbled in poetry—had some skinny volume published—a great poetess. Apparently, since John married her, she had to be a combination of Portia and Emily Dickinson."

In the sunstruck afternoon it occurred to Susan that distance idealized all things.

"They were always arguing. I happen to know John's daughter, Catherine—we went to school together—and she complained that her parents fought night and day. They slept in separate rooms. When Louella took off she left a closet full of clothes and anything with the initials LL on it. John didn't touch the room for five years, kept it as a shrine. Then one morning he told me to clear it out, dump everything. He even had the room repainted."

"Maybe he decided it was one of life's errors to sanctify a place."

"John knew me from two sources. My father was an early investor in John's business, so John and his wife were occasional dinner guests at our house. At the divorce proceedings, Catherine chose to stay with her daddy. She and I were classmates at Wellesley and often studied together. Catherine brought me to the house—this was after the divorce—and our middle-aged businessman kept finding reasons to wander into Catherine's room and stare at me. It was embarrassing but flattering too. Whatever I am, Susan, I'm no beauty queen, not now and not then. But I must admit it was flattering that this worldly man who lived in such splendid surroundings was interested in me. But I think now that poor John, smarting from the blow to his ego of the divorce, would have cast a lecherous eye on a brass monkey if it were female and conveniently placed in the house. He offered me a job as a live-in secretary to help him manage the household and his affairs. Naturally, I refused. But he was so persistent, for so long, and so charming about it that I finally agreed. I was twenty-two at the time and he was forty-nine." Nostalgia had crept into Edna's voice, as if recollecting a dream abandoned long ago.

The leaden sun weighed on Susan's face, as did the air, heavy with the scent of growing things. The sprinkler had stopped, water droplets on the blades of grass shown like mercury. The heat and the drone of Edna's voice were making Susan's drowsiness increase. She felt herself sinking into a stupor, experienced a sourceless sorrow. A fly landed on her cheek; she swatted it away and saw Edna's legs stretched out before her, feet toward the sun. Susan's gaze fastened on Edna's toes: they curled inward and each had a knobby protuberance at the second joint; the little toe was particularly misshapen. There was also an outcropping on the side of each foot near the big toe, and all the toes were cramped together as though they had spent a lifetime in the vise of an imperious shoe.

"My father was furious. He saw his daughter as a kept woman. John assured him that he had no such thing in mind, and we really and truly were only talking about secretarial and administrative services. My dad withdrew all of his investment from John's business and has never spoken to him since.

"One day Catherine came home and announced that she had found the man of her dreams. He was a professor of German literature at Wellesley with a real honest-to-god PhD. I knew the man at school and thought him a pompous ass. John took an instant dislike to him.

"My own theory is that Catherine chose a college professor as a prospective husband because of the high premium John sets on academic titles. He bought himself a doctorate and he's always babbling about those romantic early days when he taught here, there and everywhere. Catherine can be pardoned for thinking that a college professor would please Daddy and would be acceptable as his son-in-law. Though I must agree with John that this particular professor was not an inspired choice.

"John can be very brutal when he feels strongly about something. He told Catherine if she married the professor she need not bother returning home. Catherine proceeded to marry the man anyway, and John, true to his word, banished his daughter to the outer darkness and out of his life forever."

"Where is Catherine now?"

A shadow seemed to fall over Edna as she answered. "She lives in Somerville, works as a buyer for some department store. She has two sons, in their late teens or early twenties, and she divorced the professor."

"Dr. Lowell has never seen his grandsons?"

"Never—that is until recently, when Catherine engineered a meeting with John and herself and her boys."

"He agreed to that?"

"Old age. Probably feels the breath of the Grim Reaper. Or maybe he just wanted to see what his grandkids looked like."

"What does Catherine want?"

"Not parental love, I can assure you. No doubt money for herself and her kids."

Hearing the bitterness in Edna's voice, Susan turned toward her. "You're not happy about this, are you?"

"I was going to leave but thought better of it. If Catherine and I are going to do battle over John's soul, my best bet is to stay close to him."

Susan wondered in what role Edna imagined herself: wife? mistress? daughter? "Why do you think a battle is in progress?" She was about to add that people often misread the intentions of others, but held back.

"Because I know Catherine," Edna answered. "Knew her long ago. She's an opportunist. But she also has her father's pride. She must be desperate to do this, and she can go to extremes when desperate. I'll give you an example. When Catherine separated from the professor she was hard up for money. He wouldn't help and she had two small kids and had never worked. Well somehow she found a clandestine outfit that made pornographic movies and for a while made ends meet that way. When she told me about it, she was defiant. Catherine, at least the young Catherine, was something of a rebel. I was appalled. One of the movies was called *Norwegian Nights*. I remember she told me that."

Edna stared at the ground, seemed to lose interest in *Norwegian Nights*, then she turned toward Susan, her eyes and face taking on a hard radiance. "I've dedicated twenty-four years of my life to John Lowell. I'm entitled to something. It just isn't right for someone he hasn't even seen in all that time to show up and make demands. Daughter or not. He may be growing soft, feeling guilty. She could snatch everything." Her hand moved in an odd clawing motion and her face contorted into a grimace of apprehension. "Do you think that's right?" In that moment of Edna's fear, Susan had the impression she had glimpsed Edna's natural face.

Susan wondered whether Edna, in reviewing her past, was finally examining her life, and now felt that by choosing Lowell she had excluded herself from life's feast, had placed herself on the wrong side of the wall so to speak, and only Lowell's wealth remained as consolation. "Maybe it's not as bad as you think," Susan said, feeling obliged to offer a comforting wafer of logic. "Dr. Lowell's judgment is surely sound. After all, he did found a company, and where there was nothing now there's something that gives hundreds of people jobs. You don't bamboozle someone like that easily."

"John is soft in some ways," Edna said, then mused a moment. "He's a worldly success but that doesn't make him a happy man."

Susan felt an obligation to say something profound. "Maybe the character traits that enabled Dr. Lowell to build a successful company were exactly those that destroyed his relationship with his family."

"He may now want to pick up the pieces," Edna said. The tone of her voice caused Susan to turn toward her again: an embittered face stared back. "And where would that leave me? Tossed away like a squeezed lemon, that's where."

Susan saw that fear had bitten into Edna's mind, festered there, and wondered whether she was planning some desperate act to rid herself of Catherine.

A dog tugging at a leash, eyes on the pigeons, pulled past their bench; the birds took flight in a confusion of wings and the old woman shouted and waved her hand. Edna stared at the woman as if she were an enemy. The color of one's thoughts did indeed dye the world.

Susan never told Edna's story to her husband. She had intended to, delayed, then simply put it behind her. It wasn't that she had been sworn to secrecy, because she hadn't. Rather the whole tale was fused with a surreal mixture of bright sun and Edna's toes, and was vaguely unsavory to her. After a while, it just didn't seem to matter.

SUMMER CAME and Holloway remained bent over the same breadboard. The timetable for the M-100 called for production by late fall. In answer to Lowell's skeptical questioning, Slater, the chief engineer, said he was aware that six months was a short time in which to traverse the long and rutted road from Craig's jumbled breadboard to an assembly line product, and he was supporting Craig in every way he could. But as Lowell continued to watch Craig, watched his face shrink onto bone, grow reed-necked, his stammer as well as the bewilderment in his eyes increase, watched his pathetic blinking efforts to move from his monstrous breadboard to a silicon chip, a truth filtered into Lowell's soul. He knew, as certain as a firing squad, that the miracle of a bygone time would never recur. He had a nightmarish feeling of paralysis, of time rushing by, he and ETI in a boat driven by an irresistible wind, heading toward the falls. Lowell cursed himself for a fool, a hostage to his own illusions, for not having understood this from the outset.

Lowell called Breal. "Let's have lunch together. I have an important assignment for you."

At table, Lowell said, "Craig Holloway will never get the integrated circuit done in the lifetime of those now living. I want you to contact every headhunter in Boston. Have them find the best integrated circuit designer in town, in any town, and do it on a crash basis. We'll pay whatever salary. Just have them find the man. And let me check out whoever they recommend."

Breal knew how rare and precious IC designers were and how carefully they were protected by their companies. He stared out the window: two dark figures trudging across the sunstruck avenue seemed charred by the fiery light. Breal had the dead-eyed conviction that he would never find what Lowell wanted. "Yes, sir," he said, and when Lowell ordered a martini Breal decided to have a drink as well.

When they returned from lunch, Breal glanced at the stone lion: even he appeared discouraged.

## TWELVE

Couldn't concentrate. The day interminable. Kept fidgeting, dithering, looking at the clock, thinking ahead to dinner, to being alone with her. Now that she's before me I must confess I still feel nervous. But then wouldn't anyone? Wouldn't you? Man on a date is always jittery. Wants to impress the girl. The girl may be your daughter, but there it is all the same.

"I remembered it differently," Catherine said as she looked around the dining room of the Algonquin Club—at the paintings of hunting scenes on the paneled walls, the great crystal chandelier, the casement windows giving out to the elms on Commonwealth Avenue—"somehow larger, more opulent yet, the way heaven would look."

Beautiful, my daughter, my Catherine, my Kate. More beautiful now that she is touched by life. How nice to be with you, how nice to hear your voice, your wonder over things I no longer see.

"Why did you look for me?" he asked as his eyes brushed hers.

"Why did you agree to see me? The reasons are probably not much different."

Why *had* he agreed to see her? It had taken much courage on both their parts. "The time seemed right," Lowell said. "I'm in my eighth decade of life. Many of the men I knew are dead or dying. It's a chancy business, this growing old." He managed a rueful smile. He wished she would place her hand upon his, tell him he was still young, would live another hundred years. "I've found, looking back, the things I regret are not those that I've done, but those I did not do. I didn't want to make that mistake again."

They ordered cocktails, dinner. "Fill in the gap for me, Catherine. Fill in the missing years."

She told him of her marriages, the importance of her sons, both from her first marriage, her job as a buyer, and now as a women's wear consultant to boutiques that could not afford a full-time buyer.

Lowell experienced a wave of disappointment: twice married, twice divorced. "Do you know why the marriages failed?" he asked.

"I suspect I'm a poor chooser of men. I don't know why. I think I have good judgment in most things, but apparently do badly picking a husband. One was a dishrag, the other a domineering son of a bitch. Opposite poles. I should have seen through them in a week. But it took me forever to sort them out, though all the signals were there at the onset, weak signals maybe but there all the same."

"It must have taken great courage to break away," Lowell said.

"Perhaps so. I never think of it in those terms."

"Are you happy in what you're doing now?"

"No, I'm not." She looked at him carefully, seemed to be studying him as though he were a portrait of himself. Lowell sensed they had come to the subject for which she had struggled to meet with him. Sadly, he was certain, it would have little to do with affection for dear old dad. But wasn't that the way the world worked?

"What would you like to do?" he asked.

"I would like to be an attorney, like mother."

"Nothing wrong with that," he said. At that moment Catherine brushed the hair from her eyes, and in that gesture Lowell saw his ex-wife in his daughter. "By the way, where *is* mother?" He felt apprehension. Surely, if she were dead he would have been told. But by whom?

"She lives in San Diego, married to a retired banker. He's into golf. Spends most of every day with other ex-bankers hitting a little white ball. Life for them is a golf course. Mom complains that she's neglected, but she has activities of her own . . . Arthritis bothers her. She needs a cane to get around."

Lowell recalled his Lou, graceful, a fine dancer. Now on a cane. Had she become a crone, veiny old woman's hands, wrinkles furrowing her lips, face curdled? He remembered her as she was, unchanging, outside of time. She had worn her beauty—worn it as others wore diamond earrings or pearl necklaces. At least she was alive. But what difference did it make? Still, there was some comfort in that. He felt less alone, less mortal. Then Lowell, looking out toward the avenue and into the thickening dusk, recalled a specific moment: Louella had grown tired of setting her hair, ran off and had it permed. She returned home frizzy as a sheep but beautiful all the same, about her a dreamy dazzled aura, her long dress a waterfall of color. She redefined the space through which she moved, caused it to open and expand, become something grander than what it was. Then Eric died. The event that branded time. Things weren't the same after that, their conversations filled with words they did not say. He remembered Lou's suitcase—black leather, chic—accusing and still as she prepared to leave.

"I'm enrolled in a night school law program at Suffolk University," Catherine said.

"That's a long road at a second-rate school," Lowell said, then realized he was being tactless. "I'm sorry, I—"

"That's all right, Father. I don't have much choice. That's the only night school law program in town and the tuition isn't excessive."

Lowell sensed his cue had been given. "Yes, of course," he said, his voice changed, impersonal, as though a stranger had joined them and they were no longer alone. He watched her eyes sink from his. She would never ask directly—he was sure of that. "What about the boys?" he asked.

"We'll manage," she said, her voice now as impersonal as his. "We have before, we will again. Tom, as he told you, has decided to be a novelist. He makes ends meet driving a cab. Michael wants a career in engineering. His grades are good enough for a prestige university but he'll probably wind up at a state school."

Lowell gave a faint nod, then gazed attentively at nothing.

Catherine waited, silence a presence between them. Her father, she knew, though a man of many words, reserved his greatest respect for two words, yes and no, and used them with care. He was being careful now, or was this silence his way of saying no?

So there it is. The invisible hand again. Don't we all want to be loved for ourselves alone? Fat chance. Everyone trying to exploit another. Pay for this, pay for that. Get something in exchange. Life filled with transactions. Worked its way long ago like some permanent stain in the fabric of the world. No need to decide anything now, while she's before me.

"It was nice to see you, Father," Catherine said when they parted, and Lowell thought there was warmth in her voice. But what Lowell most wanted she did not give. He yearned for her to kiss him, to touch her lips to his cheek, and that this had not happened was in the end the cruelest disappointment of the evening.

The meeting with Catherine, the knowledge that Louella was still alive, caused ancient scenes to rise within Lowell, sediment from a roiled pond. As the limousine sped northward, past the lights of Medford and Winchester, he remembered Louella in a trim blue dress that set off her slender frame, about to leave for work, the bedroom window behind her dim silver in the morning light. He angry, her unblinking gaze watching him—clinically, as though he were insane— and this watching drove his rage further, and at that moment perhaps he *was* demented. Then she said in a clear even voice, "John, you cannot push me around, you cannot reduce me to a passive pulp." And she turned and left, proud as an empress, her hair glistening in the light as she passed the window. He was alone with his rage, the silence of the room a deadly vapor. At the very end she said simply, in the same even voice, "I am going to leave you, John." And the words slid like icy shards into his flesh, a wound that would fester forever. She offered no explanation, paid no attention to his cajoling, his attempts at charm, but hastened, tight-lipped and determined, to be gone. Her face took on a special clarity when she uttered those final words; the look only lasted an instant, but he never forgot it.

Other things Louella had said now surfaced: "You have a will to power, John. No doubt had it as a child. But you cannot exercise it over me." "You never learned the art of life and never will." "For you words are instruments of aggression or a means of caress, never mirrors of truth." When she walked out of the house forever, the Great Hall reeked odorlessly of death.

"How did The Great Reunion go?" Edna asked when Lowell returned. "Can I fix you a drink? You look as though you could use one."

They sat in the Great Hall. Lowell took a long swallow of his Tanqueray, stared into a distant time, a remote space, a long-ago summer—in the years when he thought time would not pass for him, only for others—when he and Lou had hiked the Austrian Alps above Gargellen, the sky a luminous gray, fog scurrying by in wraith-like mists. The flowers were butter-yellow and cobalt and salmon-pink—Lou had known the names of all of them. Later, the sky cleared to a miraculous blue, and they made love in sweet-smelling grass in the shadow of the Madrisa. Afterward, as they walked hand in hand, a goat followed them with his eyes while chewing a mouthful of daisies. Some of them stuck out of his mouth giving the goat a festive air and Lou laughed at the sight; then her face, beautiful in the honeyed sunlight, grew suddenly serious as she turned toward him. She contemplated him for a moment, then kissed him impulsively. He thought little of it at the time, but in retrospect it was the happiest moment of his life.

"You haven't answered my question," Edna said. "But let me guess . . . She's hard up for money and wants you to bankroll something. Maybe a business, or some deal for the kids . . . Am I close?"

Lowell did not answer—he was gripped by a cold sadness. What had possessed him to retreat—to back away from offering to help, particularly the younger boy? The words had stayed lodged in his mouth like stones. His thoughts shifted again to Louella. He recalled her bedroom slippers, little pink squirrels beside the bed. Often enough he could not say with certainty what she was talking about. Sometimes he hadn't listened to her at all—her voice like the pleasant sound of running water—and this irritated her endlessly. And for a moment, by some quirk of mind, he thought of her as future, as desire, then remembered that she was long past.

Edna contemplated Lowell with a shrewd stare. "Did you think she wanted to see you out of filial love? Poor John. You're an incurable romantic. Love me for what I am. For a sophisticated man you can be as naive as Snow White."

"Enough, Edna. I don't need parlor psychoanalysis."

Edna's eyes hardened, were now stony and business-like. "Did you agree to give her what she wanted?"

"That's none of your affair," Lowell said as he finished his drink.

"Ah, but it is," Edna said. "We've been through this. Shall I summarize? I've taken care of you for lo these many years, allowed you to play with me, massaged your body, given you pleasure whenever you asked. That entitles me to something."

"Edna, don't make yourself into a concubine. You lead a good life and I've told you I'll provide for you when I'm gone.

That's our arrangement. This is not the moment to negotiate another."

"Catherine may be your daughter, but I hope that doesn't blind you to what she is as a person and what she wants of you."

"Stop nagging, Edna. It doesn't become you."

That night Edna tossed, left her bed, wandered the vast sleeping mansion. She imagined Catherine moving into the house—she displaced like excess furniture—and a giant hand slamming down and stamping CANCELED on all that had gone before. A feral hatred rose in Edna's throat. There must be something she could do. She would find it.

LOWELL DRAGGED Breal to engineering and found Craig Holloway, bent as always over his massive breadboard. Confusion seemed to have spread from Holloway's face to the breadboard itself. Wires were soldered in a drunken web across the array of components. The whole contraption now seemed about as useful as a burned-out light bulb. Craig raised his head. "Good morning," he said, making an effort to smile. Poor Craig. Doing things the way he always had. Alas for all of us: the old ways no longer work. Look at him. Daedalus befogged, lost in his own labyrinth. After they left the department, Breal informed him that another integrated circuit designer candidate was scheduled for later that day.

CATHERINE TOOK Ishmael to the Huntington Theater to see Chekhov's *The Three Sisters*, then to Regina's Pizza. "What a splendid opening," Ishmael said. "'Why do you always wear black? Because I'm in mourning for my life.' It takes a good man to write that."

"Of all the lines in the play," Catherine said, "why were you drawn to those?"

"It must go with my melancholy personality," Ishmael said. "Did you notice I was the only black guy in the place?"

"No, I didn't notice. Nor do I give a damn. And you shouldn't either."

He shrugged. "It's tough to get over the feeling that you're different, and in a way that others find unpleasant. Especially when that's been the experience of a lifetime."

"Ishmael, let's make a pact. I won't talk about my ex-husbands if you don't talk about your victimhood."

"What do you want to talk about?"

"I met again with my father. Just the two of us."

"That must have taken a great deal of courage."

"Mostly on his part. He called me."

"Were you satisfied with the result?"

Catherine shook her head. "No," she said unhappily. "He was cold, distant." And at that instant, she re-experienced an ancient feeling: the hardness of his presence, always faintly critical.

"He was being careful. Probably sensed you wanted something from him."

"I sort of suggested what I wanted. But I could never bring myself to flat-out ask."

"Isn't he a businessman, been that his whole life? Those guys must smell when a request for money is forthcoming. That might account for his keeping his distance. Or maybe he's just a cold guy . . . How did you leave it?"

"We just left. I doubt if we'll ever see each other again."

"Aside from the finances, how did you feel? After all, it's your first meeting alone with your father after a hundred year lapse."

"I haven't gotten over how old he looks. Then I had the impression that in some way he was needy . . . But what did I feel? Apprehension mostly. Maybe I was thinking too much of what *I* needed, like a salesman who badly wants a deal."

"I think you had the wrong perspective on the meeting."

"Should I try again?"

"I think it makes sense. You might start by writing him a note of thanks."

"You know, I wrote him a letter when I first wanted to meet, but he said he never got it. I wonder if that goddamn Edna . . ."

"Who's Edna?"

Catherine explained.

"That complicates things, doesn't it? You've got a rival. You might try writing to him at the office."

As they left the restaurant, it occurred to Catherine that she and Ishmael had become like old friends, and that for whatever reason he would shy away from physical contact. But when they reached her home, on impulse she kissed his cheek and said, "Here, hold me. It'll do us both good." And he did hold her and they held each other for a long moment. Through his thin shirt she felt the warmth of his body, the clean odor of him. Then he kissed her, a long warm chaste kiss.

"That was very nice," he said, then hurried toward his cab.


BREAL HAD learned to read Lowell's moods—if by nothing else than the sound of the old man's voice, had it parsed to the nearest eighth note—and now, at the marble table, he recognized that Lowell's mood was not good.

"Recruiting an integrated circuit specialist isn't going anywhere," Lowell said. "We haven't seen a soul." He glared. "What are you doing about that?"

Breal had provided three search firms with a man specification and each had produced a candidate. He didn't think any of them were worth a damn, but thought it politically prudent for Lowell to interview them. Lowell had dedicated no more than five minutes to each before dismissing him. One man showed up wearing an earring and was pitched out without so much as a handshake. Either Lowell didn't think any of them qualified as "souls" or he had forgotten them entirely.

Breal decided that refreshing Lowell's memory was in his best interest. "I would agree that the three candidates our headhunters sent us weren't worth much," he said. "Why don't I get a couple of New York firms working in parallel, even if it is expensive."

Lowell impatiently shook his head. "You don't understand. We're not talking about money. This is a question of the life and death of the company."

"I DON'T know how to miraculously produce someone," Breal complained to Susan that night.

"Just get every headhunter in the free world working the problem," Susan said. "What else *can* you do?"

"One thing we can both do is pray Craig Holloway succeeds in designing an integrated circuit. Because if the fate of the company depends on a headhunter finding the right guy, we're doomed."

"Christ, and we just moved to Boston," Susan said.

BREAL TRACKED market share. He questioned the ETI salesmen directly and ignored Tergelen. He learned that slowly, in a steady process of erosion, ETI continued to lose share. This was occurring at the OEM level where Tergelen and Lowell lowered price, but could not bring themselves to meet Mühlmann's price. On major orders where, after much agonizing, Lowell did meet their price, Mühlmann went lower yet. In the cases where Tergelen did manage to retain the business, probably as a result of caution on the part of customers, it was at the cost of heavy price concessions. Breal noticed that many OEMs, even when they continued to buy ETI sensors, were buying in smaller quantities than in prior years. He learned that these OEMs were splitting their orders between ETI and Mühlmann, and considered this a prelude to losing their business entirely.

The loss of share was now spilling into the aftermarket. As new OEM equipment went into the field and controls needed replacement, it was now Mühlmann who took the business. Breal continued to read the sales reports. They were now openly bitter. Mühlmann, like some virulent microbe, was implacably eating into the body of their market, and doing it everywhere. Breal realized that for the time being this was masked by a vigorous economy and price increases in the aftermarket, so ETI's sales drop did not reflect the more precipitous decline in market share.

Still, Mühlmann was not all positive. The large OEMs complained of an inadequate number of Mühlmann distributors, their inconvenient location and insufficient stock. For the smaller OEMs, the Mühlmann distributors' lack of product application knowledge was a major deterrent. Breal consoled himself with the thought that as long as ETI kept its own distribution network intact, Mühlmann's penetration would remain limited. That, he saw, was Tergelen's strategy.

Breal and Krakowski hired away a supervisor from Raytheon to be manager of ETI's microcircuit facility. The yield on the M-90 microcircuits continued to improve. Breal commented to Miles that if it weren't for the price concessions the M-90 would now be a real moneymaker. But on reflection, he added, "I guess those are price concessions only from our point of view. What's really happened is that the Germans have redefined the product. We shouldn't be calling those reductions price concessions anymore. Mühlmann's prices are now the way things are."

Miles gestured at the financial charts on his desk. "Whatever they are," he said, "if we're going to stay in business we'd better replace the M-90 with something that's profitable."

By October about half the items on the production schedule had been over-forecasted, and by the end of the year, two-thirds. The economy had turned down.

"There's only one way to react to a recession, Dr. Lowell," Breal said, "and that's quickly. Nobody knows how deep it will go or how long it will last. I would get started now and drop ten percent out of our factory workforce this week."

Lowell was glum as he stared at Breal. "Do what you have to do," he said.

Breal met with the union leaders to announce the layoff. They were not surprised. They had seen the rise in stock levels on the shelves in the warehouse.

Unemployment figures climbed toward ten percent and there were pockets in the Midwest that were over twenty percent. *Business Week* and *Forbes* quoted gloomy economists. As the winter wore on, Breal saw that ETI was being hit harder by the recession than other companies in their industry. He talked with the salesmen and learned that the OEMs, including the smaller ones, were themselves now struggling for orders and looking to cut costs everywhere. Lowell and Tergelen increased their price concessions in an attempt to stem the loss of business.

Breal discussed these issues with Miles and saw before him another worried man. "I've been analyzing our cash flow," Miles said. "Our overall sales are down, almost all of the OEM sales are at a loss, and on top of that customers are stretching out their payments. Receivables are way up. We're coming to a point where we'll have to borrow more money to stay afloat."

"How about eliminating the stock dividend?"

Miles stared at Breal as though he had suggested burning down the building. "I would not make that recommendation to Dr. Lowell," Miles said.

"Sooner or later he'll figure it out for himself," Breal said.

"You don't know what you're asking," Miles said. "Eliminating the dividend would ruin our stock. That's the most precious thing Dr. Lowell has. That's what he lives by."


LOWELL AND Breal hired two integrated circuit designers whose reference checks were ambiguous, and neither of them was completely satisfied with the men. Lowell, looking forlorn, remarked that in striving to do better we often mar what's good—but *something* had to be done.

Slater assigned a section of Craig Holloway's design to each of the new engineers to reduce to silicon chip form, with Craig in charge of the overall integration. In time, both men complained to Slater that Craig continually changed parameters so they didn't have a stable design to work with. And usually Holloway paid no more attention to them than to the potted plants in Slater's office. Slater explained to Breal that Holloway was not an analyst, but an intuitive trial-and-error designer of the Edison inspirational school. When he got the design right—which he had done for years and which had made ETI a world leader in photoelectrics—then it was brilliant. At other times he continued to putter and revise until he hit on the right combination. Breal was not familiar with integrated circuit design, but doubted whether treating it like the composition of poetry would work.

# THIRTEEN

Lowell asked Breal to attend the board meeting.

As Miles was presenting the month's financial results, Cobb—sitting opposite Miles at the elliptical table—fixed the chief financial officer with a blue stare. "We're running out of cash," Cobb interrupted, voice hard and clear. "What's happening?"

Miles gave him an anxious moist glance, and stuttered around an answer. Cobb turned to Tergelen who, brow furrowed, was studying his papers, then to Breal. Breal summarized the Mühlmann onslaught, the reduced sales, the lower prices, all exacerbated by the recession.

"What are we going to do about all that?" Cobb asked.

Breal explained the new product under development.

"That strikes me as an awfully feeble response to a major threat," Cobb said. He pointed an accusatory finger at the financial data. "At this rate, there's no way you can keep paying a dividend." Breal admired Cobb's brutal directness, found that even when he made a simple declarative statement, Cobb's speech had an air of command.

"If we value the price of our shares, Victor," Lowell said, "there's no way we can suspend the dividend. That's a sure sign of a company in trouble. Stopping the dividend, or even reducing it, would cause our stock to plummet. It would also lower our credit rating and make our vendors nervous—they might even ask for COD payment." Lowell decisively wagged his head. "There's no way we can do that."

"Where, then, do we get the money to pay the dividend?" Cobb asked. "It's certainly not being generated within the company. Just look at these numbers."

"We'll borrow the money to tide us over until we get back on our feet," Lowell said, and turned to Miles as if for affirmation. Miles nodded solemnly.

"Borrowing money to hand over to our shareholders just to prop up our stock doesn't strike me as a winning strategy," Cobb said, then pressed on before Lowell could speak. "But whatever we do, it had better be accompanied by a sweeping review of every element of ETI. It isn't only a question of antiquated products. You've got to scrutinize how you design the products, how you make them and how you sell them." Cobb's voice was now clipped, peremptory, his severe expression one of military resolution. Breal imagined the same voice commanding a thousand marines to storm a defended beach. "What I'm saying is that ETI must develop a strategic plan spelling out how it's going to save its business. And the solution will no doubt require radical changes to the company. That's what you have to do if you're going to beat this attack. Change the company."

As Cobb, a man given to cruel truth, spoke, Breal glanced at Lowell. The old man had been staring at the financial statements. Now he raised his head. There were yellow-gray pouches under his eyes and he struck Breal as terribly weary. There was also a pensiveness Breal had never seen before. He wondered whether he was witnessing the cold dawn of awareness, the internalizing of the notion that his company, his business, his life, were under attack in a way that was truly serious, and required a level of response never before demanded of him.

Lowell turned toward Breal, and Breal saw before him a man in dire need of help. "George," Lowell said, "can you draft the plan Victor is talking about?"

"Yes, sir," Breal responded. "I can meet with the department heads and complete the job in the next two weeks."

"Do it then," Lowell said.

After the meeting, Breal asked Miles about Cobb. Miles said that at one point in his military career Cobb had been in charge of weapons procurement for the marine corps, was sent to business school by the navy and had an MBA from Harvard. When he retired from the corps, Cobb became president of a company in Lexington, Massachusetts—Hamilton Aviation—that made pilotless drones. Cobb was a shrewd businessman and the company prospered. Cobb had since retired from Hamilton though he remained on their board. He was also on the board of two companies besides ETI. In his years in business in New England, Cobb had developed a wide network of contacts in the legal and banking communities. Dr. Lowell affectionately referred to him as the silent killer, the name given him by his fellow marine corps officers.

The afternoon of the board meeting Lowell appointed Breal vice president of operations, with manufacturing and engineering reporting to him. He gave Breal an additional option on five thousand shares of ETI stock.

"You don't look overjoyed at the promotion," Susan Breal said to her husband that evening.

"I'm sure I can manage the job," Breal said. "It's managing the boss that I'm worried about."


LOWELL STARED out the window at the late winter afternoon, the stone-gray sky. Cobb was right: to borrow money to hand over to the shareholders wasn't too bright. Lowell repeated the words, *cut the dividend*: they rolled over him like some toxic surf and made him vaguely ill. *Cut the dividend*: the words repeated themselves—they had the finality of an executioner's axe. Then Lowell reached his conclusion; it came to him in the form of an expression Lou had once used: let's not cut off the dog's tail an inch at a time because we don't want to hurt the little fellow. ETI needed every last cent of its cash. *Cut it all.* Lowell stood motionless for a long while, arms crossed, noticing his own ghostly reflection in the glass: he resembled an effigy on a sarcophagus. Yes, cut it all.


LOWELL WANDERED through the plant: failure lay on ETI like a cold damp mist, inhaled by everyone, discouraging everyone. He saw it in the fugitive looks of the engineers, the finance staff, even the women on the assembly lines. The whole place, forty-four years of effort, borne away on a bitter tide. Lowell's thoughts circled around the phrases "strategic plan," "save the company," "radical change." All just words and easy to say. But whatever it was that had to be done, doing it was another matter. He looked about him. The punch presses, molding machines, conveyor lines, even the microcircuit facility, looked ancient, long obsolete. The light itself seemed dimmed and time-worn. The whole place had the rank smell of age and decay, a collapsed pile of ashes. His destiny and ETI locked inexorably. As Lowell gazed at the machines and the workers a barrier rose in his mind, a smooth gray wall, logic and reason trapped behind it. He stared for a long while and thought of nothing.

Breal recommended additional layoffs—in the factory, in finance, even engineering. "We've got to slim down, Dr. Lowell, if we're going to get through this. Make ourselves as lean as possible. I'd also recommend we get rid of the guard force and replace it with an outside service. That'll cut those costs in half."

Lowell stared at Breal. "Absolutely not!" he exclaimed. "I'll buy all your other recommendations, but you underestimate the importance of security and a loyal cadre of guards. Don't touch the guard force!"

Disaster. In the air like a funeral dirge. Empty desks, empty offices, a cemetery silence, production lines not running half the time. The whole business sinking into the quicksand of failure. Asked this man to prepare a strategic plan. Wrong. All wrong. Only I can do that. Where the company goes is my job. Can't be fobbed off. He'll make more recommendations like getting rid of the guards. Old age. Makes you cast about for support. A stick to lean on. Courage. Things are never as bad as you imagine. Screw your courage to the sticking place. The battle is neither forlorn nor empty of hope.

Lowell straightened, felt a surge of energy as he stared down the precipice of momentous change. "Another thing," he said to Breal. "Forget about generating a strategic plan. It's a waste of everybody's time. I know what has to be done. I'll take care of it."


At the annual meeting of shareholders Lowell commented briefly on the recession, remarked in passing on the reduced earnings, explained the suspension of the dividend as a need to direct all available cash to the development of new products and plant modernization, then painted an image of the bright future that lay before ETI. There were no questions of substance, and at the end of the meeting Mr. Horsfall struggled onto his crutches and, in his unsteady high-pitched voice, read from a yellow sheet words of praise for the vision of the chairman.

Lowell watched ETI stock continue its lurching downward slide, his wealth shrinking. The stock dropped from fifteen dollars per share to thirteen in a single day, then drifted down to eleven in the next five days. A quarter of Lowell's wealth was wiped out that week.

Lowell looked out on the vastness of the Great Hall, sipped his Tanqueray, and gazed past where Edna was reading to a corner where the lamplight expired.

What did St. John say? In the beginning was the Word? Renewal, that's the Word. The building is decrepit, badly insulated, the windows lose heat. Probably doubles the heating bill. Ridiculous, really, to manufacture in a multistory building. Haul stuff up and down old freight elevators. Hideously inefficient. The city crept around us, now in the middle of it. Manufacture in the center of a city. Insane. Hadn't really noticed until now. Like grazing cows in Times Square. Big building like that, right on the river, splendid view. Prime property. Must be worth a fortune. Time to act. The native hue of resolution—sicklied o'er with the pale cast of thought.

Catherine. Thomas and Michael. Good names. My grandsons. Why shouldn't I help them, help my own daughter? Wants to be a lawyer like her mother. Nothing wrong with that. So what if she saw me for my help? People act out of complicated motives. Not always sure why they do things. Wanted my help—wanted me. Settle for half a loaf. Home is where, when you go there, they have to take you in. Robert Frost was it?

"What are you thinking about?" Edna asked. "You look like you're staring down a time tunnel."

"I'm trying to figure out how to save ETI. But I can't seem to hold onto a thought. It's like my head is full of scrambling mice. I keep jumping to other things."

"What other things?"

"Catherine. Her sons, my grandsons."

Edna made a chuckling sound. "John, please, spare me. As far as they're concerned you might as well be an ATM machine. Stop this wishful thinking that they will love you for yourself alone . . . What's wrong with ETI. Why does it need saving?"

Lowell explained the Mühlmann threat, the loss of business.

"That sounds a lot more important and worrisome than Catherine and her petty concerns . . . What do you plan to do?"

"I'm not sure. But whatever it is, doing it will be like scaling Everest."

"Can't Victor Cobb help? And Breal seems capable. This isn't something you have to do alone."

"Vision, strength . . . that has to come from me. Others execute. I plan, direct, lead . . ." Lowell finished his gin. He felt his thoughts slow, dissipate, as though a thick greasy substance like motor sludge had spread over his mind. He clutched at the thought of Catherine, then that dissolved as well. He came to his feet, found his movements stiff, robotic. "Sleep," he said. "Time for sleep."


ATTRACTIVE YOUNG men, draped in youth, on the lip of adulthood. They look around, can't get used to the place. Must be baffling, a room this size. Good for them, though. Expand their horizons. Probably think me rich as Croesus, gorged with money. But then they don't know about ETI stock, sliding into the sea. Catherine surprised when I called her, delighted. Edna refused to serve them, asked Wong to bring out the hors d'oeuvres, take the drink orders. She'll get over it. Change in the status quo. Bound to be traumatic. Look at her. A prisoner of war dragged into the enemy camp, glowering at her captors.

"How's the book coming?" Lowell asked Tom.

"I'm into the second draft, rethinking the way it's put together."

"Isn't what the book says more important than the way it's put together?" Lowell asked. Try for a benign expression. The sage grandfather, wise as an old priest.

The young man finished his beer. "I doubt if they're separable." He seemed uncomfortable to be disagreeing. "In fiction execution is all. You can't separate what you say from the way you say it."

"He's his own severest critic," Catherine said.

Lowell turned to his daughter, searched for something to say, noticed her hands. They lay in her lap as if forgotten, not at all graceful, but rather heavy, workmanlike, unadorned by rings. He was moved by them, by their very ordinariness.

"Have *you* read his stuff?" Edna asked Catherine.

Catherine shook her head. "No, and I'm not sure I want to. I'm liable to find myself changed into a witch."

"Where are you attending school?" Lowell asked Michael.

"I'm a freshman in engineering at U Mass," Michael said.

Lowell's brow puckered. "I thought you were going for one of the prestige schools."

"I was," Michael replied and turned toward his mother.

Catherine's face tightened as she said, "He was accepted by MIT but without a scholarship. We couldn't afford it."

No one spoke further. In the silence Catherine's words hung like an inaudible echo. Lowell became aware of the quiet, an oppressive vacuum in the great space around them. He found himself filling the void. "If the cost of tuition is your problem, give it no further thought," he said, startling himself. "I'll pay for that. I'm an MIT alumnus. Nothing would give me greater pleasure than to have my grandson attend the same university I did."

Lowell looked around: all eyes were on him, everyone frozen as though he were a sorcerer. "Do you really mean that?" Michael finally asked.

"Of course I mean that," Lowell said. "I mean everything I say. You can transfer in your sophomore year, start there in the fall."

Catherine, eyes radiant, face a blur of delight, came to him, kissed his cheek. "Thank you so much, Father."

Lowell felt her tears on his skin. "It's nothing," he said, and in a sudden gust of feeling a lump rose in his throat, "absolutely nothing." He would help them, help them all. Flesh of his flesh, blood of his blood. Who else *could* help? Come to my arms, my beamish boys. By God, he would help them all. And this simple thought—that he was responsible for the welfare of his daughter and grandsons, responsible for his own family—came to him as if it were a first wisdom, took root in his heart, and gave him a sense that his life would turn out right.

As they rose for dinner, Lowell had the impression that everything about him was bright and new, as though the world had been cleansed. Then he noticed the glowering Edna, eyelids lowered, as she watched Catherine.


BREAL THOUGHT Lowell looked particularly buoyant as he strode around the office. "Time for renewal," Lowell said.

This was the first time Lowell had mentioned renewal to Breal since his interview a year and a half earlier. Understandably skeptical, Breal wanted to ask, renewal of what, but saw that Lowell needed no prompting. "Let me explain what I mean with a parable," Lowell said. "Do you know how far it is from Cairo to Jerusalem? I'll tell you. It's only two-hundred-and-fifty miles. But when Moses led the Jews out of Egypt it took him forty years to traverse that distance. Even if he had to go twice as far and managed only a couple of miles a day and got lost a few times, he still should have been there in six months. Why do you suppose it took him so long?"

Breal decided his best strategy was to be a disciple at the feet of the master. "Well, now that you mention it, I don't know what took him so long. Maybe, out there in the desert, he just kept getting lost."

"No, George, Moses did not have a navigation problem, he had a philosophical one. The people he led out of Egypt were born slaves, had lived as slaves, and had a slave mentality. Moses understood the great truth that people do not change. He wanted to found a nation with free men. He wandered around for forty years in order for a new generation to come to power, men born to freedom. Those were the guys he wanted to run the show in the promised land."

Breal caught the drift but was not certain, decided to be non-committal. "Moses really thought ahead," he said, rather idiotically he thought.

"The point is not that Moses was good at long-range planning," Lowell said impatiently. "The men we have are locked into old ways of doing things. Routine, like rust, has frozen their minds. They can only conceive of manufacturing in a union shop, running finance the same old way, selling the way they always have." Lowell waved his hands, seemed to be doing away with the past, with forty years of management. "We need new blood, in every function. Look into your old company. Who are the best people there? The least hidebound by big corporation rules. Whom do you know who can make a real contribution? The time has come for renewal!"

"Well, production control needs strengthening. And I do know a good man, a young fellow named Nicholas Fredricks who worked for me at United."

"You know him personally, you say?" Lowell leaned forward on the couch, animated.

"Yes. There's no risk at all. He's good, but he's expensive."

"Go get him," Lowell said. "And don't worry about expense. You can never pay a good man enough."

"If you want to upgrade staff, Dr. Lowell, Dick Miles could use a sharp analytic type under him. I'm talking about someone who understands computer usage and can quickly generate the information you need to manage the company. I know a man who can do that. He used to work for me."

Lowell was beaming, something bright and alert seemed to have leaped up within him. "Bring him in, by God, bring him in! Bring in every good man you know." He rose, paced the room, his face still radiant, and headed for the door. "Those people will have to sit somewhere. Here, come along." He strode out to the Tower. "Except for the one day of the annual meeting, this splendid room might just as well be on Mars. We can surely put it to more productive use. Let's go out tomorrow, you and I, and buy some attractive partitions and furniture to make offices here. We'll hold the annual meeting off campus. This is more important."

They returned to Lowell's office. He looked like a man who had just won a lottery. Breal couldn't imagine what had triggered all that buoyancy, that optimism. But whatever it was, he felt it as a miraculous clearing wind that had blown across an inert and motionless landscape. He decided to act quickly, to head off any change of heart.

"Yes, we'll find handsome and elegant furniture," Lowell went on. "This is a new beginning. A financial analyst to help Miles—an excellent idea. Miles is overworked. We must temper the wind to the shorn lamb." In the last ten minutes he seemed to have shaken off ten years.

Breal located Nicholas Fredricks in Dallas where he ran production control for a computer memory manufacturer, gave him an enthusiastic pitch on ETI, and invited him and his wife to Boston. He contacted his finance specialist at United Electric in Pittsburgh, a man just turned thirty named David Clare, gave him the same pitch, and again concluded by inviting Clare and his wife to Boston.

First Fredricks then Clare visited, both with their wives. Breal had his secretary arrange for a realtor to spend a day exploring the housing options available in the Boston suburbs with each couple. George and Susan Breal took them out to dinner. Breal gave the new prospects a tour of the ETI facilities, then each met with Lowell. "The old man was very charming," Breal told his wife. "In fact, he's a surprisingly good salesman. He went through the history of the company, and told his story about the good old days when he developed products on his kitchen table and traveled to Detroit to get orders. He told them they'd be part of a new era, and waxed poetic about ETI's bright future. I'd have to say he believed it too."

Fredricks was skeptical; he had a good job and his wife was happy in Dallas. He had studied ETI's annual report and was leery of tying up with a no-growth company, especially one that was now losing money; but he valued Breal's judgment and was therefore willing to entertain an offer. Clare voiced the same qualms. After clearing the proposals with Lowell, Breal offered Fredricks and Clare a one-third increase over their present salary, three months' pay as a sign-on bonus, and an option on five thousand shares of ETI stock.

The company would reimburse all moving expenses, provide a generous temporary living allowance during the transition, cover realtor fees, etc. Breal understood the economic incentives needed to persuade people to uproot their lives. It was particularly difficult for Clare since both his and his wife's family lived in Pittsburgh.

Despite the drawbacks, both Fredricks and Clare decided to join ETI. "I'm betting on you, George," Clare said.

EDNA STARED into the dark of her room, saw Catherine rise from her chair, bend toward the seated Lowell, put her arms around him and kiss him—and an unreasoning hatred rose within her. Then she remembered something else, something she had told Susan Breal. The thought resolved itself into a scene: flickering light, she and Lowell the only participants. That night the thought bloomed and blossomed, became a plan, and by morning she was ready, indeed impatient, to act. With a bracing sense of freedom, she felt herself stepping out of her usual role, ready for combat, taking command of her life.

She searched the Yellow Pages, chose Wicklow Investigators and made an appointment for that afternoon. She found the office in an ancient four-story building in a seamy section of the South End. Wicklow, a middle-aged man with a long white face and protruding mud-colored eyes, sat behind a massive wooden desk that was chipped in spots, the top bare except for the sports page of the *Boston Globe* and a worn leather cup containing pencils and pens.

"How long ago was the movie made?" Wicklow asked.

"About twenty years ago," Edna replied.

"Do you know where?"

"Around Boston someplace."

"You say it was called *Norwegian Nights?*"

Edna nodded. The single window faced the brick wall of the adjacent building. The room was lit by overhead fluorescents that gave Wicklow's face a phosphorescent appearance—he looked like a man who had never seen the sun. The place smelled of stale air and damp.

"That's right. I'd like to get a copy."

"These days it's all videos," Wicklow said as though musing to himself. Then he was quiet, focused beyond Edna, apparently deep in thought.

"Maybe it was reissued as a video," Edna said hopefully.

"We'll look around," Wicklow said, suddenly decisive. When he quoted his fee, his eyes sharpened momentarily.

"How long do you think it'll take?" Edna asked.

"Not too long," he said.

# FOURTEEN

Catherine washed the dishes in the minuscule kitchen and Ishmael dried them. Tom had left for his night shift rounds.

"You look troubled," Catherine said. "Sort of absent."

"I've been struggling with the same stanza for a week," Ishmael said. "Just can't get it right."

"Why don't you let it go for a while? Move on. Come back to it later with a fresh eye."

"I tried that. But I keep coming back without wanting to."

"Do you think Dante was as obsessive about writing his poem as you are in translating it?"

"Maybe. But then Dante was a genius." Then, after a meditative pause, Ishmael added, "You know, it's a strange thing, but for me translating Dante is a kind of voyage of discovery. Maybe writing it was the same for him. To read, I mean really read, *The Divine Comedy* is to learn about yourself."

Catherine smiled gently. "What have you learned?"

Ishmael held onto a salad plate, but didn't dry it. He seemed child-like, asked a question for which he was not prepared. "You don't have to answer if you don't want to," Catherine said. "I didn't mean to pry."

"In the first circle of Dante's hell," he said, "you find those spirits who lived lives of apathy, the kind of life most people lead. They care for little and aren't touched by good or evil. They leave no trace of themselves. According to Dante, never having really lived they can never die, so they drag on in a miserable existence just inside the gates of hell. Virgil, Dante's guide, tells him, 'Mercy and justice alike disdain them, / Upon them waste no words, glance and pass by.'" As Ishmael quoted Virgil he finished drying the plate.

"I gather then," Catherine said, "that your fear is ending up in the first circle."

"Wait a minute," Ishmael said, his face taking on a sudden clarity. "Hold on." He ran to his desk, scribbled.

"Don't you have to refer to the Italian?" Catherine asked.

"No," he said, his hand not stopping. "I have that memorized."

Ishmael bent over the papers, back tensed, the bones of his spine rippling the fabric of his t-shirt. Catherine watched: never had she seen such concentration. Ishmael finally looked up.

"Do you want to read it to me?" Catherine asked the triumphant face before her.

"These are the words of Francesca to Dante:

> And she said to me: There is no greater sorrow
> than thinking back upon a happy time
> in misery—and this your teacher knows.
>
> Yet if you long so much to understand
> the first root of our love, then I shall tell
> my tale to you as one who weeps and speaks.
>
> One day, to pass the time, we
> read of Lancelot—how love had overcome him.
> We were alone and suspected nothing.
>
> And time and again that reading led
> our eyes to meet, and made our faces pale,
> and yet one point alone defeated us.
>
> When we had read how the longed-for smile
> was kissed by one who was so true a lover,
> he who never shall be parted from me,
>
> while his body trembled, kissed my mouth."

~ 165 ~

Then Ishmael gazed at Catherine, a look universal, that she had seen on the faces of men many times, some wanted and some not. He took her in his arms, his tongue found her mouth, and he led her out of the kitchen.

"Shall we finish the dishes?" Ishmael asked.

"Let's just lie this way," Catherine said and held him, felt his ribs and pitifully thin body. "What took you so long?" she asked.

"Getting involved means time, emotional investment. Then . . . problems." He sighed. "I've got a mountain to climb. A colossus."

"I see hormones won out over logic," Catherine said.

"Pascal said it more elegantly. 'The heart has reasons which reason knows not.'"

"Sounds like hormones all the same."

Ishmael lay back. "Dante was very responsive to women, you know. He liked to represent his inner life as a female figure. But he also thought women got in the way, made a man aware of his own mortality. He says as much in his *Vita Nuova*: 'Amid a swarm of doubts that came and went, / Some certain women's faces hurried by, / And shrieked to me, "Thou too shall surely die."'"

Ishmael, Catherine decided, was a man condemned to complexity. "You're not Dante," she said. "Why are you identifying so with this guy? You can translate him without becoming him."

Ishmael thought about this. "I suspect all translators get wrapped up in the person they're translating." He was quiet for a moment, and then added, "I feel an enormous affinity for the man. Dante's hell—the way it's hostile to life, cruel, diabolical, always on the offensive—is not unknown to me."

"Ishmael," Catherine said, "You're sliding into the black-white thing."

"You're a smart woman, Kate," he said and turned toward her.

On a hot June morning Nicholas Fredricks, a six footer with red hair and a freckled face that made him look even younger than he was, reported for work. He and his wife quickly found a home in Andover, north of Boston, and in the following month moved from Dallas. Just as quickly, Fredricks discovered problems at ETI. "We make everything," Fredricks said. "There're no make-or-buy decisions. If we can make it, we make it, even though in some cases I know for a fact we can buy parts of at least equal quality lots cheaper."

"See if you can find data that clearly supports a buy decision," Breal said. "If you have a strong case, we'll present it to Dr. Lowell. He's adamant about making rather than buying, but if the result is a big jump in profit, he might come around."

In mid-July, David Clare joined the company as director of financial analysis. He, too, with his wife and two children, moved to Andover. Lowell decided that rather than report to Miles, the company would be better served if Clare reported to Breal. Clare was about five-nine but gave the impression of being shorter. He was solidly packed with muscle and had a habit of bending forward. He had played halfback at Pitt and looked perpetually ready to plow through the defensive line.

Clare interviewed Dick Miles and key people in the accounting department. "Do you know how these people collect receivables?" Clare asked Breal.

"No, I've never looked into it."

"They have the customer mail a check to headquarters, here in Cambridge. By the time the check arrives and somebody gets around to depositing it, at least a week and sometimes more like two weeks go by. Our receivables are around $100,000 a day. If we took a week out of the float, there's lots of money to be saved."

"How do you decrease the float?"

"At United we had lockbox accounts at various banks around the country. The customer sent his check to the bank we designated for him. The bank emptied the lockbox every couple of hours and deposited the checks immediately. The average float was just a couple of days. For ETI we'd need only one centrally located bank, either in Chicago or St. Louis."

"Did you talk to Miles about it?"

"Yes. I also spoke to Continental Bank in Chicago. They'd love to handle a lockbox account for ETI."

"What was Miles' reaction?"

"He said that only Lowell could make that decision."

"Was he willing to approach Lowell on the subject?"

"He was reluctant. He wanted you or me to do it."

"I'll get you an audience with the boss and you can present the case."


BREAL, CLARE and Miles sat at the marble table. "George tells me you have a scheme to reduce the collection time on our receivables," Lowell said to Clare. "That's exactly the kind of innovative thinking I've been searching for around here, the sort of fresh look at the company I was hoping you young people would bring." He then painted a vista of a revitalized ETI populated with youthful innovative thinkers like Clare and Fredricks who would lead the corporation to new heights of achievement. Breal thought this a rather overblown vision based solely on taking a few days out of receivables collection. Apparently Clare had the same feeling.

"This is only a modest proposal," Clare said. He then described the lockbox arrangement.

Lowell nodded approvingly. "Dick, what's your view of this scheme?"

"I think it's an excellent idea," Miles said.

"Let's do it!" Lowell said, rubbing his hands. "The right bank is the First of Chicago."

When Breal, Miles and Clare were in the hall outside of Lowell's office, Clare commented on the choice of bank. "Didn't you tell me, Dick, that Dr. Lowell has a substantial personal loan from the First of Chicago? Isn't there a conflict of interest? I would have chosen the First but after what you told me, I called Continental."

"I think Dr. Lowell has made the decision," Miles said.

"I'll call off Continental," Clare said. "Do you want to approach the First?"

"Why don't we do it together on the speakerphone," Miles said.


LOWELL, TERGELEN, Miles, Breal and Fredricks sat in the dining room of the Algonquin Club by a window that looked out over Commonwealth Avenue. It was a wet August day, but despite the rain an occasional jogger, damp t-shirt hugging his torso, trotted under the elms covering the narrow park that divided the boulevard. As they ate their lunch, Lowell said to Breal and Fredricks, "You gentlemen have several proposals to make on materials management. We're at your disposal."

That morning Breal and Fredricks had discussed the topics they wished to present. Fredricks thought his best case lay in the make-or-buy decision on transformers. He now pulled out of his jacket pocket two oblong shapes, each about the size of a hotel room soap bar, and placed them before him on the table. One was glossier, more finished looking—otherwise the shapes appeared identical. He held up the dull unit. "This is the 8-224 transformer that we manufacture," he said. "Our annual production volume is around 90,000 pieces. Our variable cost—just material and direct labor, without overhead— is $2.83 per unit. Material cost alone on this thing is 59 cents." He held up the second item. "This unit is a standard device made by Jewel Electronics in Taiwan."

Breal noticed a frown settling on Lowell's face, while Miles concentrated on his food, and Tergelen took on a Mona Lisa smile as he turned away from the transformers. This audience reaction was apparently lost on Fredricks. "We've done preliminary tests on the Jewel units," he continued, "including breakdown voltage, temperature, and humidity. To the level we've tested, the Jewel unit is equal to or better than ours. Jewel is a specialized transformer manufacturer. They supply parts to Westinghouse, GE and other major league U.S. customers." Fredricks pointed a decisive finger at the Taiwan unit. "The price of this transformer, in the volume we use, is 56 cents apiece, landed in the U.S., after freight and duty. I'm saying that we can buy this device at less than our material cost, with out-of-pocket savings of better than $200,000 a year." Fredricks looked around the table with the expression of a man clearly convinced of the persuasiveness—the absolute and unarguable persuasiveness—of his case.

Lowell's voice started as a low growl. "George, I thought the ETI policy on subcontracting was clearly understood. I see that it is not." Breal decided that in this circumstance silence was the prudent course and hoped that Fredricks had the good sense to come to the same conclusion. Lowell turned to Fredricks. "Young man, you're apparently not familiar with our policy. Let me state it for you, clearly and unambiguously. *We do not ever wish to subcontract a component we are capable of making ourselves.*" Lowell spoke slowly, deliberately, as if each word were chiseled in rock. "We are in business to manufacture our own products," Lowell continued. "All of them. This bears not only on cost and delivery, but the ability of the company to control its own business."

The freckles on Fredricks' face seemed to darken against his pale skin and his eyes stayed fixed on Lowell. "Sir," he said, "I'm asking that this policy be reevaluated in light of the low cost, reliable components now available from the Far East. I estimate that were we to purchase all of our relays and transformers on the outside, of equivalent quality to units of our own manufacture, we could bring better than half a million dollars a year in increased profit to the bottom line."

"George," Lowell said turning to Breal, "I'm afraid my communication skills are deficient this afternoon. Let me reiterate basic corporate policy." Lowell then went on for five minutes, with heightening agitation, to amplify the statement he had made earlier. As he leaned toward Fredricks to emphasize the point, his bald head glistened in the light from the window as though it were made of marble. He paused and stared at Fredricks. "Is that clear?"

"Yes, sir," Fredricks said as he put the two transformers back in his pocket. Other than a slight flush, his face was now expressionless. Breal debated whether to intercede on his behalf, but decided that at least for now the cause was lost, and his best strategy was to keep his mouth shut and live to do battle another day.

The luncheon was finished in silence. Breal turned his gaze to the window: the overcast sky cast a discouraging light on the street. Neither Breal nor Fredricks chose to present the other items they had prepared.

When they returned to the plant, Breal invited Fredricks to his office and tried to restore some of his enthusiasm. He gave the new man a pitch whose gist was that at ETI it took time to have new ideas accepted.

"Sure," Fredricks said, nodding his head. "Sure. Lots of luck. I'm surprised this guy ever eats out instead of cooking his own food. Anyway, I'm going to stop worrying about make-or-buy and concentrate on getting an efficient production scheduling system in place."

Breal's secretary poked her head into his office. "You're wanted immediately in Dr. Lowell's office. He must be really upset because you can hear him yelling way over here."

Fredricks gave Breal a shrugging half-smile. "Lots of luck," he repeated as Breal hurried out the door.

When Breal arrived in Lowell's office, he found Miles shriveled at the marble table and Lowell pacing the room, a letter in his hand. He thrust the letter at Breal. It was from

Continental Bank and was addressed to David Clare. The mail net had struck again. The phrases that Breal picked out were:

> . . . we regret that you have chosen to place your lockbox business with First of Chicago . . . we understand that in view of the personal banking relationship that exists between your President and the First . . . should you at some point in the future decide . . . Continental Bank stands ready. . .

"Where did anybody get the idea that I suggested the First of Chicago because of any personal banking relationship?" Lowell shouted. "I act solely in the best interests of this corporation. My private affairs never play a part in company decisions. Isn't that right, Dick?"

"Yes, sir," Miles said, "that's right," his expression that of a man facing a cobra.

"How did Continental learn that I had a personal loan from the First of Chicago?" Lowell asked, eyes tightening as he glared at Miles. Silence. "Do you know, Dick?"

"No, sir."

Lowell turned to Breal. "Why is Continental Bank writing to Clare? How did they know we were even *looking* for a lockbox? I thought I had given clear instructions to go with the First of Chicago."

"Yes, sir, you had," Breal replied, struggling for damage control, "and that's what we've done. Prior to our conversation, though, Clare had called Continental to get an estimate of cost, but he made no promises."

Lowell paced the room. "The idea that I would place business with a bank because of some personal bias is ludicrous." He paced some more. "Banking relations are an area of extreme sensitivity. Dick, put out a memo that no one calls a bank—any bank—with regard to company business without my express permission."

When he returned to his office, Breal stood at the window: rain fell in straight gray lines. A woman with no umbrella hurried along the street. He thought about Clare and Fred-ricks. He had no illusions as to why they had joined ETI. He, and to his surprise Lowell, had been persuasive salesmen on the merits and future of the company. But it was economics that closed the deal. These were young men with growing families. They were vulnerable to a pitch on opportunity, but in fact it was the vision of a larger house, a new car, a hap-pier wife, an education nest egg for the children, and a sense that they were moving upward in life that had sold them. The paycheck was a measure of how high they had climbed. By joining ETI they had made a leap upward. Now they had to deal with Lowell. Breal despaired that they would learn to cope. He returned to his desk, noticed that an over-head fluorescent light was flickering and—though the least superstitious of men—Breal took it as an omen of destruction and ruin.

THAT NIGHT Breal decided that a drink before dinner was in order. Susan glanced at her husband. "Let me hear today's episode of the ETI chronicles," she said.

Breal told the story of Fredricks and the transformers.

"Your problem," Susan said, "is that you're questioning fundamental ETI dogma. It seems to me that at ETI, unless you have a death wish, you're best off letting sleeping dogmas lie."

"It's tough to make progress without changing things," Breal said. He then recounted the Continental Bank episode.

Susan thought a minute, shrugged, then remarked, "I sus-pect the closer you get to the truth, the more indignant The Great Man becomes."

"You know," Breal said, "I've been thinking about Tergelen. Here's someone who has seen many men come and go and the pattern is always the same. Initial enthusiasm, Lowell's resistance to change coupled with his erratic behavior, disil-lusionment on both sides, then departure. Tergelen probably gave up trying to change things years ago. He spends his time fluttering around his precious distribution network. Everything else he just waits out, then the inevitable happens. Like you said, what we have here is Mr. Tergelen depending on the relationship between an old dog and new tricks."

LOWELL GAZED out the Algonquin Club window at the steady drizzle, the dead leaves on the avenue. Cobb had decided against a drink and Lowell, reluctantly, demurred as well.

"Nothing is happening," Cobb said. "The company is in the red. Cash is flowing out the door. We're on a path to bankruptcy. What happened to your strategic plan?" Cobb's gaze was steady, hard-eyed. Lowell imagined the terror that gaze must have struck in the heart of many a marine.

Lowell sighed, wished for a martini, searched his mind for a response but found only a void. Now Cobb impatiently shook his head. "The issue is how to save the company. We're not characters in a Greek tragedy. We *can* control our destiny." Cobb stared at Lowell, repeated his previous question. "I thought we were going to produce a strategic plan. What is it?"

In a momentary illumination of cold bright light, as though a strobe had flashed, Lowell saw, simply and directly, the elements of his plan. "It's obvious what has to be done," he said.

"What is that?"

"Three things: bring new products to market, sell our building to raise cash, and get rid of the union. The union's jurisdiction extends only to Massachusetts. We'd have to move manufacturing out of state."

Cobb nodded approval. "Those actions sound proper," he said. "Let's get on with them before it's too late. We need a commitment, a set-jaw commitment to do this. I'll give you the name of a good labor attorney." His voice softened. "Can you do this, John?"

"Of course I can do it," Lowell replied. And Lowell in a shadowy memory recalled asking Craig Holloway the same question many months earlier, when he first stood over Holloway's breadboard. Lowell averted his mind from the thought.

How easy to say these things! An Everest to be scaled. Orders melting away like spring snow. Slippery terrain everywhere, the world without traction. Can you do this, John? No, it wasn't at all clear he could do this. Lowell felt a sudden darkening in his head, as though a cloud had drifted across his mind. He repeated the three elements of his plan. They jumbled in his head.

## FIFTEEN

Based on her LSAT score and the recommendations of her instructors at Suffolk, Catherine was interviewed and accepted at Boston University Law School and started full time in the fall semester—as did Michael at MIT. She felt like a grandmother compared to the men and women around her, decided against dressing down, mirroring the rags the young people wore, and dressed like the decorous old woman she felt herself in their presence. She found the bustle and movement on campus exhilarating though she was largely ignored by the other students. She applied herself to note-taking and homework as if her life depended on it.

Lowell set up a trust fund in her name and another for Michael. The fund paid her tuition and a modest stipend for her rent, food and clothing. Lowell had offered her a larger apartment and a new automobile, both of which she declined. Her son Thomas refused all assistance.

Michael decided that his stipend from Lowell was adequate for him to live in a dorm on campus and, reluctantly, Catherine agreed that if this is what he wanted, she would not object.

Catherine dined with Lowell, either at his home or at the Algonquin Club, every other week and occasionally her sons came as well. She discussed law school with him, and how it engaged virtually all of her time. She grew more comfortable with her father, though his gaze must have recalled an ancient authority, because it made her feel vaguely judged and she was never completely at ease. At one dinner, over coffee, Lowell asked whether she was seeing anyone. Ishmael came to mind and she casually said yes but did not elaborate.

Edna Graham never attended the Algonquin Club dinners, but at Lowell House she was always present, rarely left Lowell and Catherine alone, and never served Catherine. At first Catherine tried to draw Edna into conversation, make of her a friend, but Edna's laconic replies admitted no friendship. Twice Catherine called and invited Edna to lunch, just the two of them. But Edna refused without giving a reason and the nature of her response was to discourage, and discourage absolutely, any further overtures toward friendship. After a while Catherine learned to ignore, though never completely, Edna's icy presence. At times, when Catherine experienced Edna's baleful stare, she wondered what perfidy Edna whispered to Lowell when she, Catherine, was not present. Catherine finally decided that nothing could be done, and adopted a remote and courteous attitude toward Edna and rarely spoke to her. Edna's presence, however, did not seem to bother Lowell, who chatted as though Edna were not there. When he did turn toward her, his comments generally dealt with the meal or household matters, and she answered in a professional way, like an administrative assistant.

Catherine shared her fears about Edna with Tom and Ishmael. Tom said Edna struck him as a frustrated and unfulfilled person, not a Rasputin character. But then he observed that you could never tell from a person's face what he or she is capable of doing. "I once saw a picture of the Boston strangler," he said. "He looked like an ordinary guy."

"Just hope she hasn't read Machiavelli," Ishmael said.

"Did he have something to say about the likes of Edna Graham?" Catherine asked.

"He said that potential enemies must be annihilated. Don't fool with them, just kill them. That was the old Italian's advice."

MILES, RESEMBLING a death row inmate praying for a reprieve from the governor, sat before Lowell. "We're about out of cash," he said. "We have to borrow money."

Lowell stared at him. "Why do I hear this now, when it's a crisis? Why didn't you bring it up a month ago?" But Lowell did not wait for an answer, if indeed there was going to be one. "Going to banks . . . those shylocks will descend on us like locusts, get into our knickers, decide we're a lousy risk. . . ."

"I thought we'd stay away from banks," Miles said, "and borrow from an insurance company."

Lowell's eyes tightened as if he were squinting through a crack. "An insurance company?"

"Yes," Miles said. "They're willing to take more risks."

Lowell finally gave his approval, but remarked that anyone who lends money is a banker no matter what he calls himself.

Miles succeeded in obtaining a loan from New England Mutual. The loan imposed covenants that Clare thought unduly restrictive and he winced at the fifteen percent interest rate. Miles observed that ETI was not in a bargaining position and was lucky to get the money at all. Clare calculated the rate of cash outflow, both to function and service ETI's debt, and told Breal that they had ten months at the outside, if they really tightened their belts, to turn around the company. Breal interpreted the look on Clare's face as that of a man betrayed, one watching the horse on whom he had bet the family farm stumble and fall.

Breal persuaded Lowell to cut back further. In all overhead departments—finance, marketing, administration, even engineering—Breal mercilessly cut heads. And in manufacturing, all functions not directly involved in the fabrication of product were cut. "That's what we have to do if we're going to survive," was his only explanation. The guard force remained untouchable.


A SIMPLE plan. Yes, that's the answer. A plan, simple and sound, that all can understand, rally around. Galvanize the troops. Caesar rousing the Tenth Legion in Gaul, Joan of

Arc leading the French army to victory at Orleans, Napoleon shouting encouragement as he rode five horses to death on the battle lines at Rivoli. Yes, I have the plan . . . but plans are easy. It's execution that's difficult.

Lowell paced the conference room, his direct reports before him, elaborating the three-pronged attack he had given Cobb and that constituted his strategic plan. He tried to exhort the stone faces to supreme effort, spoke of the great battle in which they were engaged, everywhere in the field around them the blue spark and cold clank of sword striking sword. Yet oddly, when it was over—after all the rhetoric—he felt defeated. He looked out the window of his office: under the bleak December sky the river was the color of ashes. He recalled portions of his speech. He had compared his men to the gallant Spartan three hundred who had barred the pass at Thermopylae against the Persian hoards. It now occurred to him that this wasn't the best analogy since the Spartans had all been killed. Now that he thought about it, the whole exhortation had been wrong. He sounded as if he were reading a part. All those dramatic words, the histrionics, without conviction. How do you communicate conviction when you don't have it yourself?

Lowell forced himself to go to engineering. Without success there, nothing mattered. He sought out Craig Holloway and saw by the pucker between his eyes that there was trouble. Craig stared at the pattern on the oscilloscope, rotated a knob. The signal on the screen grew more erratic, the pucker deepened.

"Good morning, Dr. Lowell." Holloway's face resembled those medieval portraits of martyrs.

"Noise problems," Holloway said. "The new engineers modeled sections of the integrated circuit and electrical noise causes the circuit to become erratic."

"How do you solve that?"

"We have to determine where the noise enters, then devise a filter."

"Is this filter on the integrated circuit itself?" Lowell had a sudden vision of disaster: before him a new problem, one beyond solution.

"It has to be on the IC." Holloway appeared apologetic. His timetable, such as it was, had clearly collapsed.

"There're lots of ICs around and they work okay. Why do *we* have this problem?"

"Industrial environment," Holloway said. "Motors, machinery—they create electromagnetic interference. A factory is a tough environment for an IC, especially a complicated one with many functions." He said all this hesitantly—searching for words as if he were speaking a foreign language.

Lowell found Warren Slater, urged him once again to give Holloway all the support he possibly could, hire consultants if necessary. Anything.

As he left engineering, Lowell looked back at the bent Holloway, who now seemed to have a deep resigned sadness about him. He appeared rooted there for ages, like some ancient totem, a now impotent god that one prayed to, hopelessly, for special favors.

Lowell's mood was dark as he headed for Breal's office.

"I think your strategic plan is terrific," Breal said and meant it. As far as *where* ETI manufactured, Breal had intuited the day of his interview that Cambridge was the wrong location. "How shall we proceed?" Breal asked. "Do you want me to approach developers and start exploring the sale of the building?"

Lowell waved away Breal's question. "No, not at all," he said, taking on a tutorial tone. "You have to decide first to whom this property represents the greatest value. That's MIT. We're right next door to them. Buying our land gives them seamless ownership of all property from Mass Avenue all the way to the Longfellow Bridge. If they don't buy the property when we offer it, another fifty to a hundred years will go by before they get another crack at it. Think of MIT as a man who has only one diamond cufflink. The matching cufflink is more valuable to him than to anyone else. We're MIT's other diamond cufflink."

This speech had apparently reinvigorated Lowell. "I'll broach the subject with Tom Stone, the treasurer of the Institute," he said, then turned and left.

Yet as Breal watched Lowell's retreating back, he doubted whether anything would happen. "For the old man to call MIT is equivalent to him launching a nuclear strike," Breal told his wife that evening. "I doubt if he's ready to do that."

"Does he know that ETI is close to disappearing," Susan said, "not with a bang but with a whimper?"

"Some days maybe," Breal shrugged. "Some days maybe not."


A WEEK passed and indeed Breal heard nothing further of Stone or MIT. Breal, desperate as he checked sales and profit figures with Clare (the finance man now openly worried and probably polishing his resume), decided to sidestep the sale of the building and approach Lowell's plan from another direction. "I'd like to contact the labor attorney Cobb recommended and open severance negotiations with the union," Breal said to Lowell.

"All right," Lowell finally said, "you get started with Cobb's lawyer." He paused then brightened, as if recalling something long forgotten. "You do that and I'll call Stone at MIT."

Breal learned that Cobb's labor lawyer was out of the country and would not return for another two weeks. Lowell did not appear unduly disturbed. Breal tried to communicate his own sense of impending disaster, but Lowell stared through him, appeared not to hear. When Breal voiced his frustration to his wife, Susan commented, "Maybe Lowell's a bit like Tutankhamen, the king of denial."

Rather than contacting Stone, Lowell lunched with an old business associate and fellow trustee of the Institute who, according to Lowell, promised action. Another week passed.

Finally, two men from MIT showed up, toured the building, and asked virtually no questions. Another long period of silence followed. When Breal shared with Lowell his impression that the men had visited ETI because they had been directed to, rather than from any conviction that here was an opportunity, Lowell observed that administrative matters didn't generate much excitement in a university. "They'll come around," he said. "It's just that they tend to think in terms of geological epochs rather than days or weeks as you and I do."

Breal, his eye on bottom line losses and the company's shrinking cash reserves as they plowed through the borrowed money, thought that ETI lacked time more than any other resource. After another week, Breal, ever more desperate and feeling himself an onlooker in a theater who could do nothing but watch, told Lowell that he thought silence was MIT's way of saying they had no interest, and ETI had best move along and approach professional real estate developers.

Finally, the trustee called Lowell to say that, with regret, the Institute had decided not to make an offer on the property. Lowell shook his head, disgusted. "Those are supposed to be the deep thinkers of America, yet they can't see value right under their noses. Academics are fools, you know. They think their small world is all of reality."

Breal contacted Ross Associates, the developer whose name Cobb had given him. In a meeting with Lowell, the two Ross people said the value of the property depended on the square footage that could be built on the site. They alluded to environmental issues, parking constraints, zoning limitations, and the need for approval by half a dozen city agencies. Lowell brushed all this aside. He pointed out the window. "That view is the best in New England. I don't see why you can't put a structure on this site equivalent to the Hancock or the Prudential." The Ross people took on the look of patient men listening to someone who understood nothing. They then explained that in the context of the city of Cambridge what Lowell was proposing was not possible. Lowell persisted and the realtors left saying they would think about it, but Breal could see that all their thinking was behind them. "What we have here," Lowell said, "are a couple of small timers. They can't get past their real estate hocus-pocus to see what this place is really worth. Two clowns without imagination."

December was a worse sales month than anticipated. There was no price increase and no year-end influx of orders. Breal cut further, ETI now a skeleton of what it was when he joined the company.

Breal and Krakowski were called to Lowell's office where they shook hands with Stanley Rosenfeld, ETI's labor attorney, a lean graceful man in his late sixties, a spatter of brown spots on his bald head. "That's quite a view," he said, nodding toward Lowell's window, the Charles, and the Boston skyline beyond. The sun, low in the sky, reflected in an orange band off the water and made a golden wall of the western face of the Hancock.

"That view is one of the reasons we're gathered here," Lowell said and explained his plan.

"I trust you gentlemen are certain this is what you want to do," Rosenfeld said as they sat at the marble table. "The law favors the union against the big bad corporation so there are expensive pitfalls every step of the way."

"We have no alternative," Breal said. "We can't be competitive manufacturing in this location—labor rates are too high, we're being suffocated by restrictive work rules, and the place is inefficient—and besides, we want to sell the property."

Lowell then gave a bitter ten-minute harangue on the evils of unionism.

As Rosenfeld listened, he dusted a speck of lint from his trousers. When Lowell was done, Rosenfeld turned to Breal. "Only half the reasons you gave can be used in any union negotiation on plant closing. The wage rates may be too high but, after all, you negotiated them and they're formalized in a contract that you signed. You may find the work rules oppressive, but they're also defined by a contract that you negotiated. We can try to build your case around the value of the property and the inefficiencies of the plant, unrelated to wages or work rules. Here's the approach I would recommend . . ."


ISHMAEL NOW slept over in Catherine's apartment several nights a week. They alternated cooking dinner, and he often read his translations aloud to her.

"Gloomy stuff," she said.

"That's because this is the *Inferno*. The *Paradiso* is a lot brighter."

Once, the apartment manager stopped Catherine to mumble some negative remarks, and told her the other neighbors had commented on Ishmael's presence. Catherine mentioned this to Ishmael. He laughed. "Well, there goes the neighborhood," he said.

Sometimes Tom and Michael came for dinner and they all ate together. Ishmael had become one of the family. They all had their projects: Tom was trying to understand his life and perhaps all of life through his writing, Michael at MIT, she at law school, and Ishmael locked in combat with Dante and the English language. Catherine thought of herself as leading three lives: school, Ishmael, and her father, the last under the venomous eye of Edna Graham. None of these lives intersected, yet one day she sensed they would, and it was at the intersections that problems always arose.


LOWELL AND Breal met with other realtors. Lowell had developed a vision that could not be shaken. He would point out his window, at the Charles and the Boston skyline, and say: "I can picture on this site a lofty tower of a million square feet, more splendid than the Hancock or the Pru, or anything in Manhattan for that matter." The real estate developers patiently told him, after agreeing he had an extraordinary location, that a building of that size was three times larger than any structure ever approved by the city of Cambridge, would create a traffic mess, and would disrupt the scale of all other development along Memorial Drive. When they left, Lowell's comments were always the same: "Small timers. There are many different ways to look at a blackbird. Those clowns just don't have the imagination to see it right."

Breal tried to persuade Lowell to forget about what would be built on the property after ETI left and concentrate on selling at the highest possible price. But Lowell stubbornly held his view, the sale of the building somehow derailed into converting ETI's factory site into a monument.


EDNA GRAHAM heard nothing from Wicklow. When she called, Wicklow said he was working the problem. Edna decided to visit a video store on her own, thought it best to stay out of Boston, and located an outlet in Newton. The porno section was in a separate room marked ADULTS. All the cover photographs resembled each other: women with pneumatic breasts (she thought of her own bust, now flattened to an empty purse), parted tumescent lips, tongues on display, buttocks thrust out, legs apart, hands toying with their sex. It all made Edna a little sick, but excited as well. She forced herself to examine each of the covers. They had titles like *Sex Slaves, Lusty, Party Dolls, Wet Dreams*. She could not find *Norwegian Nights*, nor did she find a face that resembled Catherine.

Edna inquired at the counter. The man punched a computer, and told her *Norwegian Nights* was not in the system. "Any idea when it was made?" he asked.

"Maybe twenty years ago," Edna said.

The man shook his head, gave her a hopeless smile. "Then it must have been a movie. These days it's all video."

"Didn't they transfer the movies onto video?"

"In the beginning, maybe. But the videos these days are a lot more sophisticated than that early stuff."

Edna wondered in what way the carnal act could possibly have become sophisticated. "Any idea how to track down the movie?"

The man shook his head. "It's long gone, Miss. It's not like we're talking *The Birth of a Nation*." He gave her a knowing smile. "We've got a thousand selections. I'm sure you can find one that'll cut you loose."

Edna decided to find a store that had been in business a long time. She went to the Boston Public Library, found on microfilm a Boston telephone directory from twenty years ago, and searched for movie rentals.

# SIXTEEN

The union negotiations took place in the ETI classroom. Demonstration equipment, used to train distributor and customer personnel, lined three of the walls; the windows on the fourth wall looked out over a track of the Boston T and a red brick building beyond. A radiator emitted a hissing sound and a thin stream of vapor escaped, giving the room an overheated damp odor. Patches of grimy late February snow lay on the window ledges.

The desks had been pushed together to form a long conference table in the center of the room. Breal and his negotiating team—Krakowski, Clawson, and Clare—all in shirtsleeves, sat on one side of the table, the six members of the union negotiating committee on the other. In addition to Jerry Sullivan and Jim Scadlock, Breal recognized Lily Malewsky, an overweight lemon-haired woman in her late fifties who worked on the production line; Harry Probska, a compact muscular man with bad skin, in his thirties, who ran a punch press; and Curtis Cornwall, a grizzly emaciated individual with a wispy beard who was a stockroom clerk. They were all dressed in work clothes and had pads and pencils before them. The last member of the union team Breal had never met; he was about fifty, built like a tree stump, with large square workman's hands, and the only member of the union delegation who wore a dress shirt and tie. Beside him was a worn leather briefcase, the name LEON ATLEE printed on a tag hooked to the handle.

"The current union contract expires on May 31st," Breal began, "and we would normally start negotiations on a new contract at the end of March. I've asked to move up our first meeting because I have an announcement to make." Breal then read a statement, prepared by Rosenfeld, announcing that ETI had to make major investments to modernize manufacturing and develop new products; to obtain the funds to do this, the company was considering selling its Memorial Drive property and ceasing all manufacturing operations in Cambridge. Breal, half-way through, looked up: all the union members except Atlee were bent over their pads, intent expressions on their faces, resembling diligent students trying to keep up in their note-taking.

Breal's continued reading the statement, which then listed the other reasons for considering leaving the site, and explained that the company wished to reach a decision with all facts in hand and therefore was giving the union an opportunity to respond. "But let me be clear," Breal concluded, "we've made no decision to move."

There was a long silence as the union members finished their notes. "That's quite a bombshell," said a somber-eyed Atlee. "I'd like to caucus with my people before we proceed further."

The ETI team adjourned to an empty office next door. "Those guys aren't just going to roll over and die," Clawson said. "You're in for a tough fight."

Krakowski agreed. "They may not be brilliant," he said, "but even a dim light concentrated enough can make a bright spot. Those guys can concentrate."

When the ETI team returned to the classroom, Sullivan leaned forward, positively electric, his wiry red hair standing off his head. "First of all," he said, "we want all those phony reasons you just gave us in writing. Second, we're going to want a lot of information, like when did you first start *thinking* about shafting us. Then maybe we'll give you some answers."

He lit a cigarette, took an astonishingly long drag, as if smoke were some life-giving substance.

Breal admired Krakowski's patience as he responded. "Give us a list of what you want and we'll provide you with whatever information we have."

"When do you expect to tell us you've made up your mind?" Sullivan said, blowing the exhaust from his Marlboro toward the management team.

"We won't make a decision until we have your inputs," Breal said, trying to emulate Krakowski's patience. "When can we expect to get your list?"

"We can't say right now," Atlee answered, "but I notice you haven't included wage differences or benefit costs as reasons for moving. Are you saying they don't matter?"

Breal hesitated. He would have to be careful with Atlee. "Well, I'd be less than candid if I said they played no part in our thinking, but they're not the primary reasons for considering relocation."

"The shit you guys hand us and what's really going on are two different things," Sullivan said, a man hard-wired for aggression. "Our job is to find the pony buried under all that manure."

"Shall we set a date for our next meeting?" Krakowski said.


"VICTOR COBB called with what I think is a good idea," Lowell said to Breal. "There's no press coverage at our annual shareholders meeting. We report our sales and earnings in a press release that's picked up as a squib by the *Wall Street Journal*. Lifeless stuff. Gives no insight where the company is heading. My concern is the effect of last year's losses on the price of our shares. The stock has been hovering around eleven for months. Our shares are lightly traded so they can move up quickly on good news, but go down just as fast on bad. ETI's sales and earnings may be down, but we have an aggressive program to turn that around. Victor thought that press coverage at the annual meeting would carry this message into the media and allay investor fears. He cautions that you can't be certain what the press will say, so there's some risk, though he thinks it's worth taking. What's your reaction?"

Breal had no experience with the financial press, but it was clear that Lowell was attracted to the idea. "It's a good idea," Breal said, "assuming they're on our side."

"Good. I've already told Victor to proceed through his contacts to invite the press. Another thing. We're holding the meeting at the State Street Bank building. I'd like tables displaying our products set out along the walls. Also posters spelling out the characteristics and applications for each product. Would you handle that?" Lowell then took a paper from the center of his desk. "Here, read this," he said.

The letter was from a British company wishing to explore the possible purchase of ETI. "I receive one of those a week," Lowell said. "You can't imagine the clowns who are interested in buying this place." He took the letter from Breal's hand, tore it in bits, then let the pieces drift like snowflakes into his trash basket.


THE FOLLOWING morning Krakowski appeared in Breal's office with a copy of the *Cambridge Chronicle*. The front page headline read: "BIG CAMBRIDGE EMPLOYER TO LEAVE TOWN?" Breal scanned the article: the mayor, the city council, the whole city of Cambridge it seemed, were outraged. Breal sought out Lowell who read the article as he sat and waited. Finally Lowell looked up, mouth turned down, obviously disgusted, and delivered his verdict on the First Amendment. "Freedom of the press is a goddamn pain in the ass."

"I'll get the union committee together this afternoon," Breal said. "They have to decide whether they're going to negotiate with us directly or use the press and city council as intermediaries."

Lowell shook his head in a brief decisive motion. "No, no," he said. "No." Breal noticed the old man was becoming increasingly agitated. "No!" Lowell repeated more adamantly. "That's a bad idea." Lowell left his desk, stared at Breal, arms rigid at his sides, fingers extended. "The union will do whatever the union wants to do no matter what you ask. But by asking you show weakness, vulnerability. Don't you understand that?" Breal, feeling like an unsuspecting dove suddenly finding a hawk with unsheathed claws plunging toward it, empathized with Miles, a man who had decided early on that initiative was dangerous. "You must stay aloof in your negotiations," Lowell went on. "You can't modify the union's behavior any more than you can change the weather. There's no point in putting yourself in an inferior position by asking."

Breal, finally able to escape, understood in his soul why his predecessors had preferred to communicate with Lowell by letter. Yet on reflection Breal decided that in this case at least the old man's judgment was right.

When Breal remarked on Lowell's rage to Susan over dinner, she observed that Aristotle considered anger the emotion closest to reason. "I think Aristotle would have had trouble staying philosophical while on the receiving end of Lowell's temper," Breal replied.

LOWELL, HIS beard freshly trimmed and wearing a Burberry raincoat of midnight blue and a black homburg, sat next to Victor Cobb in the Cadillac limousine. They were heading for the State Street Bank and ETI's annual meeting. Breal sat on the jump seat facing them.

"At a minimum, there should be the financial man from the *Boston Globe* and someone from the *Wall Street Journal*," Cobb said, "though we invited at least a dozen others. They've been provided a dossier of company background material as well as copies of the annual report."

It was the 21st of March. As they drove across the Longfellow Bridge toward Boston, Breal looked out at the Charles: the river reflected the bright morning sun in scintillating mirrors of light. He had now been with ETI for two and a half years. Susan was not unhappy in Boston, though she complained that it was difficult to see the children. She mentioned that it was nice of Edna Graham to have invited her to the annual meeting, that she must have gone out of her way to get Lowell's agreement.

Breal studied the rabbinical-looking face before him as the limousine crawled through the stop-and-go traffic on Cambridge Street: Lowell seemed as serene as an old sage. The idea that they were in a race with disaster, that only five or six months remained before their precious cash was gone and bankruptcy resulted, was either a thought Lowell refused to face or he possessed some secret knowledge. But for Breal, worry was now constant, not something he could leave behind like an umbrella, but a part of his skin.

The Cadillac pulled in front of the bank, across the street from the Meridien hotel. It was on Victor Cobb's advice, based on the State Street Bank's location and prestige, that Lowell had chosen it as the site for the annual meeting. Breal had been there two days earlier to inspect the product displays and posters exhibited on tables along the back wall of the auditorium where the meeting would be held.

Breal and the other executives of the company sat behind a long narrow table on a raised platform in the front of the hall. Lowell's place, still empty, was in the center. Breal looked out at the audience, found his wife next to Edna Graham. The other faces, perhaps forty in number, were presumably all shareholders and media people. The meeting was more heavily attended than in prior years.

At ten o'clock Lowell entered the auditorium, impeccably dressed in a charcoal-gray suit as if he too were on exhibit, strode to the lectern, surveyed the house, called the meeting to order, then proceeded to read his speech. Lowell said he was disappointed in last year's results but pointed out that "the factory automation market, because of its robustness and growth potential, was more than ever a bitterly contested battleground." He said that ETI, recognizing this, was increasing its expenditures in order to maintain the company's leadership position and protect long-term profitability. These investments in the future coupled with lower sales had placed the company in a loss position. He listed the actions being taken to counteract the decline in sales and return the company to profitability. Then, in language crafted by ETI's labor attorney, he said the company was considering the sale of its Cambridge property and had opened discussions with its union to obtain their inputs as part of the decision-making process.

As Lowell continued his speech, Dick Miles was following the words in a draft copy he had before him. There was a rustle of paper, amplified by the microphone in front of him, every time Miles turned a page—and twice Lowell frowned at Miles.

Lowell noted that the current year was one of transition during which all the effort of the company was being directed to restoring the earnings pattern of the past. He dwelt on new product development—the lonely image of Craig Holloway bent over his breadboard, the two new engineers trailing him like a pair of ducklings, came to Breal. Lowell concluded by expressing his confidence in the future of ETI. Both Lowell and Miles turned over the last page and looked up in unison. There was no applause, only coughing and shuffling of feet. "I shall now open the meeting to questions," Lowell said.

A young man, who did not strike Breal as a stockholder but rather a security analyst or reporter, stood up. "It's not clear to me why your sales are down," he said. "You say you're in an extremely competitive business, but that's always been the case. Why does that now result in decreased sales? Is there a change in the competitive situation?" The man remained on his feet after asking the question.

"Many factors affect sales," Lowell said, "the economy, the growth of the factory automation market . . . competition . . ." He stopped, looked down at the lectern, then out at the audience. The room grew quiet. Lowell, his mouth slightly open, brow furrowed, continued to stare out at the hall. Breal regarded Lowell: the old man appeared reduced to a wax figure, as though a spell had been cast upon him. The moment lengthened, then lengthened further. Breal had the impression he was watching a film where the projector had stuck on the same frame and would remain there forever. The room grew quieter yet. Everyone watched Lowell as he stood there, motionless as a tree stump. He finally stammered, "All of these factors were negative last year . . ."

The young man, who had been shifting around while Lowell was becalmed, now went on. "I still don't get it," he said. "The economy was recovering."

Lowell looked around in confusion, as if unsure where he was, then his gaze stopped at Tergelen. "I'll ask our marketing vice president to respond," he said.

Tergelen answered in a thick Flemish accent. "In some years competition is more fierce than in others. The past year has been such a time." Then, to Breal's surprise, Tergelen said, "A German company, Mühlmann, is attempting to buy market share in our industry through extreme price concessions. We do not believe their low prices are sustainable. We feel that over the next twelve to eighteen months a more rational equilibrium will be established in the marketplace."

Breal could now spot the reporters: there were six people writing while Tergelen spoke.

"So what you're telling us," the young man said as he took his seat, "is that your sales and earnings are going to stay down this year as well."

Breal glanced at Lowell: he did not look pleased.

Finally, the white-haired man that appeared at every meeting struggled from his chair onto his crutches. "Yes, Mr. Horsfall," Lowell said.

Horsfall bent over a sheet of yellow paper. "I would like to take this opportunity," he said in his unsteady high-pitched voice, "to deliver my personal congratulations to Dr. Lowell, who has led Electronic Technologies through thick and thin for forty-five years. His vigor, intellect and judgment are an inspiration to us all." Breal had the impression that Horsfall would have read the same speech even if ETI were in bankruptcy. "I would now like to lead a round of applause for our chairman." Horsfall put down his paper and, leaning on his crutches, began to clap. There was a ripple of clapping in the audience. Everyone on the platform clapped and Breal noticed that Susan was clapping as well. As the audience filed out, nobody bothered to look at the product displays in the back.

Froze up there for a minute. or was it five minutes— or half an hour? Glass wall, thick, impenetrable. All those faces waiting for me to get through the wall. No idea what I finally said. You have to wonder. One day the wall may be miles thick. Never get through it, ever. Stare out at the world. Mute. Dumb. Behind the wall. Dead.

Lowell decided that to celebrate having put another annual meeting to bed, the board of directors plus Breal should lunch together, and that Edna Graham, Victor Cobb's wife Emily, and Susan Breal should join them. Another woman was present whom Lowell introduced as his daughter Catherine. The woman, black hair, dark eyes under thick black eyebrows, struck Breal as world-weary but still attractive. They walked across the street to the Meridien and dined at Julien's where, in the Louis XIV setting, Lowell cursed the need for annual meetings, cursed the media and unions, and put away four Tanqueray martinis.

Breal noticed that when Lowell made a point, the first reaction he sought was his daughter's. He appeared to cater to her needs more than anyone else's at the table. She addressed him as Father and her eyes shone with a soft light when she spoke to him. Breal also noticed that the closest observer of this interaction was Edna Graham.

The following morning Lowell burst into Breal's office still wearing his hat and coat. He was waving a copy of the *Boston Globe*. "Look at this!" he shouted. "Just look at this!" He had the pages turned to the business section and the headline, "ELECTRONIC TECHNOLOGIES' SALES AND EARNINGS PLUNGE IN FACE OF ECONOMIC RECOVERY." The first lines of text read, "Electronic Technologies, Inc., at its annual meeting of shareholders yesterday, announced a sharp drop in sales and a continuing bottom line loss. The embattled Cambridge firm is under attack by a determined German competitor and is considering the sale of its property . . ."

"Goddamn Cobb," Lowell roared, "he may be good at leading hoards of marines up the beach but he knows nothing about the media. Bad news is meat and potatoes to those people. There's nothing in that article about the positive steps we're taking—new products, improved manufacturing— nothing at all . . . what a stupid thing to invite those people . . . and I couldn't believe that while I was delivering my speech that damned fool Miles was turning pages like the prompter in an opera . . . and why did that idiot Andre bring up the German company?" Suddenly Lowell shot out the door and Breal could hear his voice through the walls, "Miss Krane, check the stock price!"

The stock dropped two points that day and drifted down another point in the next four days to settle out at eight for a total loss of a quarter of its value in a week.


OF THE list of stores renting movies twenty years ago only two had survived and they were both video rentals. The response at both was the same: all the films had been sold or destroyed. But at the second store the moon-faced propri- etor peered at her over bifocals, solemnly, as though she had asked for the original of the Magna Carta, and said he knew a collector who might have something. He called Edna two days later. The collector did indeed have *Norwegian Nights*, considered it a classic of the genre, and was reluctant to part with it.

"Can I borrow it?" Edna asked, heart thumping.

"He's not running a rental service," the man said, "and he's afraid projecting it might damage the film. But he'll sell it to you."

"How much?"

"Two thousand dollars."

"That's crazy!" Edna exclaimed.

"Depends on how badly you want it, lady."

Edna knew she would empty her life savings to obtain the film, and she knew she had communicated her desperation to the video store owner. "I'll pay you a thousand," Edna said, "and not a cent more."

The man never hesitated. "I'm sorry, lady. Two grand is the price."

"Can you transfer it onto video for me?" Edna asked.

"That'll be an extra fifty dollars," the man said.

After she hung up, Edna called the useless Wicklow and fired him.

# SEVENTEEN

Look at them. Alert, wary. They're studying me, trying to see what's behind my eyes. They know what's at stake, be total fools if they didn't. Can he save me? That's what they really want to know. This meeting is an appointment with hope. Save us! We are victims—a curse has wandered blindly around the world and settled on us, the innocent. Can I save them? Can I save myself? It's the same thing.

Lowell stared at Holloway. "One more time—when will the integrated circuit be completed?"

Holloway took on the look of a man seeking divine intervention. "We're still a couple of months away," he said.

"That's a stock answer, Craig," Lowell said. "I get it all the time. Tell me where you stand."

"The integrated circuit is mostly laid out," Holloway said, "but we still have noise problems to solve."

The reply struck Lowell as mechanical. Holloway turned to one of the two new engineers who flanked him. They said nothing nor did Slater or anyone else at the table. There they are, staring at me like a line of tombstones. Those two new men: Rosencrantz and Guildenstern. Who hired them? Nothing more terrible than ignorance in action. The room leprous with broken promises. A speech. Rouse them to battle. Henry the Fifth. Agincourt. We few, we happy few. Shit! Toothless words, like whistling past a graveyard.

Lowell scanned the faces at the conference table, sensed hopelessness. Do they really understand? Even if they did, were they capable of beating back the Germans? Look at them. As alike as a pack of Dalmatians. Waiting for me to cry "fetch!" They couldn't beat back a couple of flies. Lowell roused himself, concentrated on Holloway—as if by incantation he would make the old engineer stronger, smarter, fiercer—then, exhausted, left the room. He had an urge to flee, spend a week in the field, question ETI customers, the sales staff. Time well spent.

Lowell toyed with an emery board, touched up a fingernail, as he said to Breal and Tergelen, "In these troubled times it's important to hear firsthand what our customers think. Let's the three of us venture out and see how bad things really are."

Both men unenthusiastically nodded agreement.


At the end of March a subpoena was served on Lowell directing him to appear seven days later before the Cambridge city council, "to give evidence of what you know relating to the possible relocation of your company from Cambridge." It was the view of Stanley Rosenfeld, ETI's labor attorney, that nothing in the Cambridge city ordinances regulated the comings and goings of businesses, and Lowell did not have to appear if he did not want to. Lowell, much relieved, signed a letter, prepared by Rosenfeld, stating that since the company was conferring with its union on this matter, he deemed it inappropriate to debate publicly issues which were the subject of these sensitive negotiations.

The day after Lowell's aborted appearance, Krakowski handed Breal that morning's *Cambridge Chronicle*. The headline read: ETI TELLS CITY COUNCIL "DROP DEAD." The accompanying article said that ETI had defied a council subpoena ordering the company's chief executive officer to appear before it, and the council voted to take the company to superior court to enforce the order.

"We're supposed to leave on our field office tour this Sunday," Breal said to Lowell. "Do you still want to do that in light of this mess?" He nodded toward the newspaper on the marble table.

"Of one thing we can be certain," Lowell said, "and that's the law's delay. Rosenfeld can keep this tied up in litigation for months if we want him to. In the meanwhile we've got to run our business. Let's travel."

Breal chose not to disagree; and Lowell seemed cheered by the prospect of getting out of the office. But Breal was certain there would be no resolution with the union until the Cambridge city council was eliminated as a factor in the negotiations, and the only way to do that was to meet with them. He could not find the courage to suggest that to Lowell who, after all, would have to personally take the onslaught of the council and do it in a public forum. In due time, Breal felt, Lowell would reach the same conclusion, but meanwhile their precious hoard of cash was disappearing like water into a sandy beach. Productivity at the plant had declined after the first union meeting and was now declining further. Absenteeism had risen. Losses were increasing. Extinction was only months away.

"We're going to meet with Aubrey Vaughan, the owner of Imperial Electric. He's our largest distributor in Pennsylvania," Ken Kruger, the ETI lead salesman for the territory said to Lowell, Breal and Tergelen as his Buick Century company car headed down the Schuylkill Expressway toward King of Prussia.

"How are their sales holding up?" Lowell asked. His voice was flat and he sounded tired; he had struck Breal as fatigued from the moment they left Boston. It occurred to him that maybe Lowell's fatigue was induced by apprehension at what he might learn.

"Weak," Kruger answered. "Overall, ETI sales are down twenty percent. Original Equipment Manufacturer sales are down about twice that. It's the aftermarket that keeps us going."

"Is all the loss to the Germans?" Breal asked.

"Yes," Kruger answered. "Mühlmann is concentrating on the big OEMs and pretty much ignoring the small fry, but the large OEMs account for a lot of our business. We met with every OEM in the territory trying to keep them all ETI, but even the midsize ones are using or testing Mühlmann products. If Mühlmann had good distribution, with competent applications salesmen, we'd be dead."

The Buick pulled into the parking lot of a gray windowless concrete slab building. High on the wall, printed in massive black letters, were the words IMPERIAL ELECTRIC; next to the name was a shield outlined in black and within it a rampant yellow lion on a field of blue. The colors looked as if they had been brighter in the past.

Vaughan, the owner, a large top-heavy man with crewcut gray hair, resembled a shot-put thrower in middle-age. He gave Tergelen a big hello and seemed genuinely pleased to meet Lowell and Breal. Turning to Lowell, Vaughan said, "You probably don't remember me, Dr. Lowell, but I met you once years ago when you were visiting with my dad."

"Why, yes," Lowell said looking up at Vaughan without recognition, "as a matter of fact you very much resemble your father."

The group sat around Vaughan's desk on which were scattered letters, invoices, trade publications, and electronic parts.

"How's business?" Lowell asked.

"It stinks," Vaughan said. "What I mean is ETI business stinks. OEM sales are off at least forty percent."

"That's because . . . ?" Lowell said in an absent voice.

Breal attributed the ridiculousness of the remark to fatigue.

Vaughan stared at Lowell. "If *you* don't know why, then you're in bigger trouble than I thought. Mühlmann is eating your lunch. They've got a superior product at a much lower price. That's a tough combination to beat."

"Andre," Lowell said, "tell Mr. Vaughan about the new products we're bringing along."

Tergelen explained the features of the M-100. "When will it be available?" Vaughan asked.

"In three months," Lowell said.

"What will the price be?"

Breal, who had winced at Lowell's reply, hastened to speak first. "We haven't reached a decision on price," he said, "but you can be sure it'll be competitive."

"You guys had better hustle," Vaughan said. "Right now, it's only caution and inertia that keeps any of the OEMs buying ETI. If it weren't for aftermarket sales, you'd really be in the soup."

"Hang in there." Breal said. "Help is on the way . . . Is there anything we can do to make your job easier?"

"Well, your new products always give us fits. I hope this one is really checked out before you put it on the market. The last thing we need now is an unreliable new product. That would ruin us all."

"I can assure you that won't happen," Breal said. He paused and then asked, "Has Mühlmann approached you to be their distributor?"

Vaughan folded his arms across his chest, and sighed. "Yes, they have. Actually it was an old ETI man that showed up." He rummaged around his desk, found a bright yellow business card. "Fred Standke. He's got a good pitch, but I told him no thanks. We've been with ETI for thirty-five years. You've had your problems—my dad has a bagful of ETI war stories—but you pulled out okay. I'm betting you'll pull out okay again."

The group then traveled to Cleveland and Atlanta prior to going on to Chicago, Houston and Los Angeles. The message was the same everywhere: OEM sales were down twenty-five to fifty percent.

As they headed through the Atlanta terminal to their gate, Lowell was shuffling his feet as he walked. He had two martinis on the flight to Chicago and slept most of the way. They were met at O'Hare, where a steady rain was falling, by Len

Buncher, a stubby melon-faced man who had replaced Fred Standke as the area's lead salesman. On the trip in his Buick Century to their hotel in Oakbrook, Buncher's responses to Breal's questions were more pessimistic than Ken Kruger's in Philadelphia or those they had heard in Cleveland and Atlanta.

"Fred Standke has high credibility here," Buncher said. "He's doing a number on us with the OEMs."

The following morning, a wet gray light hung over the city as the group drove to Cicero. They sat in the conference room of Pac-Tec, an important OEM and user of ETI controls, with Tom Hanson, the president of the company.

"Right now, we're splitting our orders for photoelectrics between ETI and Mühlmann," said Hanson, a man in his fifties with a cool, remote manner. "We tested Mühlmann and they performed very well, better than ETI. But we're careful. Only after those German units have proven themselves in the field will we switch all our business to Mühlmann. We'd be fools not to. If those controls can do the job and are a lot cheaper, then we have to use them. This is a cutthroat business. A single packaging machine can have up to a hundred photoelectrics. If we saved twenty dollars a unit, that's two thousand dollars saved on each machine, and that's a lot of money."

"I think it's self-evident," Lowell said, "that the Mühlmann price is not sustainable. If they make inroads into the U.S. market, they'll gradually increase price. In the long run you'll have the worst of all worlds—high price and poor service." Lowell's voice was hoarse.

Hanson glanced down at the business cards before him, leaned back in his chair. "Mr. Lowell," he said, "I'm afraid that's not my reading on the Germans. Experience tells us that when they penetrate a market, they keep prices competitive and emphasize service in order to hold market share and discourage competition. If you believe otherwise you're kidding yourself, and you're going to get hurt a lot worse than you have been already."

THE WEATHER had cleared and early spring sunshine glinted off the wet pavement as the group rolled down the Eisenhower Expressway to their next appointment, their distributor Standard Electric on the west side of Chicago. Lowell sneezed twice, and said he felt a cold coming on. They met with the president, a man with the stern gaze of a hanging judge.

"You guys had better get your ass in gear before we lose the whole market," he said.

"What do you need to turn this situation around?" Lowell asked, blowing his nose.

"If you gentlemen don't know what we need, then lord help us all . . . We need new, high-performance products at a low price. Make them smaller, smarter and cheaper. That's it."

Lowell turned toward Breal—he seemed to be seeking protection. Breal gave him his "help is on the way" speech, to which the man—apparently unimpressed—responded, "You'd better hurry."

Lowell left Standard Electric like a refugee from a plague. He sneezed again and then said, "I'm going to peel off this formation and head back home. You gentlemen proceed on to Houston."

"We'll go back with you," Breal said. "I think we've got the picture."

"No, no," Lowell said. "This is very useful. I'm sure I can make it back to Boston alone. You go on."

Lowell caught an evening flight to Logan. Tergelen commented that Lowell looked awful. "Hearing what we heard would make anybody sick," Breal said.

The story in Houston was much the same as in the other cities. On Friday night, a tired Breal checked into the Valley Hilton on Ventura Boulevard in Encino where ETI's Los

Angeles office was located. An urgent message to call Warren Slater was waiting for him at the desk.

"Craig Holloway had a heart attack," Slater said.

"How bad is it?"

"I've no way of knowing, but it can't be good. He's in the intensive care unit at Mass General and no one can talk to him or see him, not even his family."

"There goes the ball game," Tergelen said when Breal gave him the news. "Craig's the only creative engineer down there." He thought a moment, then his face brightened. "Listen, there's a man we meet at trade shows. Works for a competitor, Opticon. His name is Emil Rostov and he's responsible for their new designs. He's an émigré and his English isn't the best, but he's a very smart cookie."

"Is he unhappy at Opticon?"

"I think so. Opticon was just acquired by a conglomerate. He mentioned that he doesn't like big companies—too much bureaucracy, like Russia . . . I don't know if he'd be interested in ETI, though."

"Jesus, Andre, why didn't you bring up this guy before? Craig's been in trouble for at least a year."

Tergelen shook his head. "Craig *always* looks like he's in trouble. He's looked that way for thirty years." He wagged a finger at Breal. "I'll tell you this. Craig *is* ETI. He's designed the best photoelectrics in the world. Without him, there'd be no company. I still believe if he ever recovers from his heart attack he'll succeed."

"He can't handle the technology change," Breal said.

Tergelen stubbornly shook his head again. "There's nobody in the world who can design electronic controls like Craig."

"Well, he's run out of time."

On Sunday morning, Lowell called Breal at home. "How was the rest of the trip?" His voice was terribly nasal.

"No different than the portion you were on." Breal saw no point in dwelling on how awful things were, particularly to a sick John Lowell. "How are you feeling, sir?" he asked.

"To paraphrase Sam Goldwyn—terrific, but improving. I really called to talk about Craig. Without the M-100 we're dead, and Craig is the key to the M-100. Now he's gone, and there's no telling for how long or for that matter what he'll be like when he returns . . . What are we going to do about him?"

"I talked to Tergelen," Breal said. "There's a Russian engineer who's the number one designer at Opticon. Tergelen knows him from trade shows, says he's a very impressive guy though his English isn't too swift."

"I don't care if he's an Eskimo and speaks Esperanto. Bring him in. Let's take a look."

"Andre isn't sure he'd be interested in ETI," Breal said.

"At the right price, everyone is interested. We're talking about the life and death of the company. We're not going to haggle."


THE FOLLOWING Wednesday, when Breal arrived in the office, Krakowski handed him that morning's Cambridge *Tab*. It carried the headline "ETI ZONED OUT." Breal slumped in his chair as he read the accompanying article. The city council had voted to rezone the ETI property for low-income housing. The rezoning would not affect the company's current manufacturing, but it would severely limit the type of buyer they could sell to were they to move.

At nine-thirty that morning, Lowell, still wearing his hat and blowing his nose, came into Breal's office. "The ducks are back," he said with a satisfied smile. "Take a peek. They're out in front, near the steps."

Breal showed Lowell the article. They immediately called Rosenfeld and met with him that afternoon.

"Can they do this?" Lowell asked; his eyes were bloodshot and the skin around his nostrils was red. He strode around the room, stopped at his desk, took a tissue, blew his nose, then continued. "Can they arbitrarily change the established use of our property, something that's been well-settled for half a century, to something as ridiculous as this?"

"These people—" Rosenfeld began, but Lowell interrupted, "These fools are using their authority as all small men use power—to be arbitrary and vindictive." Lowell looked out the window: the trees along the Charles were still leafless but there was a spatter of sailboats on the river. "What do we do now?" he asked.

"We can fight these people in the courts over rezoning and surely win," Rosenfeld said, "but it may take years, or at least months. My advice is to appear at the next council meeting and answer their questions as best you can."

"All right then," Lowell said. He waved theatrically. "I shall appear dressed in rags and genuflect, a supplicant in the dock."

## EIGHTEEN

Look at the size of this place, will you. Must be larger than Notre Dame. Post-and-lintel architecture. Ancient Greece. Recall the classical past—always a safe bet. The majesty of government. Makes you feel diminished. That's the idea, isn't it? Councilors up on a dais, black high-backed chairs, we below, petitioners. Eight councilors plus the mayor. Nine, a venerable number—planets, Supreme Court, muses, lives. Seal of the city. *Cantabrigia*. Latin for Cambridge, wouldn't you say? Using Latin always good, lends *gravitas*. Founded 1630. Couple of oddballs, misfits from the old country. Didn't know they were founding *Cantabrigia*, future home of Harvard, MIT, ETI. Supposed to start at five. Nobody in a hurry though, wander in like strolling players at the opening of an Italian opera. American flag to the left, Massachusetts flag to the right . . . Ahh, here's the mayor—dandy of a man: hair, mustache, features, arranged impeccably as if he were a bust of himself. *Homo bureaucraticus*. Raps his gavel, fifty minutes late. Insolence of office. Everyone rise, face the American flag, pledge allegiance. A prudent course. Who can fault you for that? Patriotism, the last refuge of scoundrels. What's this? Everyone remain standing. A moment of silent meditation. Can't hurt. Dear God . . . no atheists in a foxhole.

"I understand that a representative of Electronic Technologies is present this evening to address the council," the mayor said. "If so, please rise and state your name and residence."

Breal watched from the audience in the vast council hall and found great dignity, even grandeur, in the lonely figure of the old man, perfectly erect, without notes, facing the council.

"My company has been accused of many things in this chamber," Lowell said. "Of being unfeeling, mean-spirited, and disloyal to the city in which we have resided for the past forty-five years. That we plan to leave the Cambridge employees who have served us faithfully without jobs or support of any kind. It is my intention this evening to inform you as best I can of the cloud that hangs over our company and the actions we must take if we are to survive."

Breal found Lowell's voice clear and resonant, all traces of the nasal quality of the previous week gone. The mayor, long slim fingers joined, listened. Lowell sketched the competitive struggle in which ETI was now engaged, and the absolute necessity for the company to restructure itself in a far-reaching and radical fashion if it were going to continue to exist. "Never, even in the early, precarious days, was the thread that held us so slender."

Lowell went on to summarize the state of ETI's negotiation with the union, then stopped. Breal waited for more, and as the moment lengthened experienced a twang of fright—the episode of the annual meeting was about to be repeated: Lowell would collapse in confusion. But the old man rallied, stumbled through the first sentence, then the motor purred smoothly. "This council is concerned over the fate of the four hundred hourly employees of ETI. I can assure you that we are as well. The council wishes to preserve the jobs of these citizens of Cambridge. That is our desire as well. However, undoubtedly with the most noble of intentions and without malice, you have embarked upon a course that will destroy our company and all the employment it now provides." Lowell's voice now took on the fervor of an Old Testament prophet. "By rezoning the property so that its sale at anything approaching its real value is foreclosed, then so will be the funds we need to rebuild our enterprise and we shall be undone. And so shall all the people we employ and their families, as well as the subcontractors and vendors who depend on us."

Lowell paused; Breal guessed that Lowell's real estate vision was forthcoming. "We sit at the base of the Longfellow Bridge, the very gateway to the city. Can we not imagine a structure in this setting of grander design than the ETI factory? Would not the city of Cambridge benefit through increased tax revenues and employment by placing a more substantial construction at that location? We are not at odds. The interests of the city coincide with the needs of ETI. It is to our mutual advantage to develop this riverfront location, which is not only unique to Cambridge but to all of Boston, to its highest use. We are engaged in discussions with real estate entrepreneurs, asking that they consider the development of a landmark structure comprising office space and possibly condominiums. We ask them to translate into reality what we believe represents a magnificent one-time opportunity to gain the very best for this location.

"Let me now state a personal conviction," Lowell continued, his voice once again taking on a biblical fervor. "I believe it is within the power of government to do great harm but not great good, whatever its intentions. When the government tampers with the free market and the mobility of business, it puts both the economy and society in jeopardy. Free enterprise is a messy affair in which many good and innocent people sometimes get hurt. But, imperfect as it may be, it is superior to any other economic system yet devised." Breal thought Lowell delivered this closing statement with great sincerity, though he wasn't sure how susceptible the council was to a pitch on free enterprise since the mayor was a socialist.

In responding to questions put to him by the councilors, Lowell said, "No decision will be reached until the discussions with our union are concluded. I believe it is a disservice to the employees and to the company to allow our dialogue with the union—which is fragile, delicate and highly confidential—to become part of a public debate. I urge you to allow us to settle our affairs with our union employees in negotiation between the concerned parties."

Jerry Sullivan followed Lowell. Through a flurry of "you knows," Breal filtered out that "ETI's weak, inefficient management" was the problem, not the Germans, and all this talk about considering the union input was just a charade, and the company had made up its mind to move long ago. Breal had difficulty following the fractured syntax of Sullivan's argument and he noted with relief that the councilors did as well, because the mayor finally cut him off. Sullivan's answers to questions, some from councilors clearly sympathetic to him, were equally rambling, as he loudly accused ETI of lying and deceit, but never offered proof or examples.

The mayor closed the hearing by saying, "I would like to thank you, Dr. Lowell, for opening the lines of communication with the council and appearing before us to most eloquently present your company's situation. We wish you luck in your battle with the Germans. I might point out that we have a sister city program with Heidelberg. If this can be of any benefit to you, please do not hesitate to ask."

"I believe zoning the property for a maximum size office and condominium structure would be of greater immediate benefit, Mr. Mayor," replied Lowell.


WHEN BREAL returned home, Susan asked, "How did the showdown at the OK corral go?"

"The old man did good," Breal said. "As a matter of fact, he did great. I didn't think the crazy little guy had it in him."

"Great men rise to the occasion," Susan said.

"That may be, but let me tell you, this great man has faults that make him tough to live with."

"Agrippa, Caesar's favorite general, said the gods always give great spirits flaws to keep them on a human level."

Next morning the *Cambridge Express* carried the headline: DRAMATIC APPEAL BY ETI CHAIRMAN WINS COUNCIL SYMPATHY. The article summarized Lowell's speech and ended with a quote from the mayor: "I think they've always wanted to be just a quiet, solid, industrial citizen."

That same morning Breal asked Slater, "How's Craig doing?" as he added his signature to a get-well card for Holloway.

"He's out of intensive care, but they want to keep him in the hospital for another week. Anyway, even after he goes home, we won't see him for something like three months, and then only part time." Slater said all this in a defeated voice, a man who had faithfully watered and tended a plant that never flowered.


BREAL, SLATER, Lowell and Emil Rostov sat at the marble table. "Tell me about your background, Mr. Rostov," Lowell said.

"I have bachelor's and master's degrees in electrical engineering from Moscow University and a second master's in electrical engineering from University of Pittsburgh. I came to United States eight years ago and joined Opticon."

"What type of engineering work have you done there?"

"I am primarily designer and problem solver," Rostov said. "I designed entire line of polarized controls for Opticon, and they are now leader in field. I try to design always keeping production in mind. Easy to design product in vacuum, but more difficult to design product simple to produce. I have just finished design and test of photoelectric control built around custom integrated circuit. This is not easy to do. Control will soon go into pilot production."

"Are there any secrets for the newcomer?" Lowell asked.

"My approach is to design on computer, then do complete circuit simulation on computer before committing to silicon."

"What are the problems you run into with an integrated circuit design?" Breal asked.

Rostov described how to avoid parasitic oscillations on the chip, how to separate power and signal sections to avoid crosstalk, how to minimize the amount of silicon used, thereby increasing yield and reducing cost. He mentioned problems hidden within problems, causing Breal to think of the design as a kind of Russian doll where discovering one problem revealed another, and then another, of steadily diminishing size, until the last problem was found.

Rostov's speech was even, unhurried, and, Breal observed, efficient. His presentation was direct and logical, devoid of trivia. As he spoke, there was an orderly accumulation of detail which had a mesmerizing effect, so as his discourse proceeded all questions of credibility melted away and you believed Emil Rostov.

Throughout Rostov's lecture Lowell never took his eyes off him. Breal had learned that Lowell in his own remarks was a generalist, but he particularly appreciated a subordinate, like Craig Holloway, with a passion for detail. Of the two forms of power, organizational power and knowledge power, Lowell appreciated the latter and was always respectful of it.

"Are you familiar with Mühlmann?" Lowell asked.

"Yes, I know them," Rostov said. "They make excellent products and are formidable competitor."

"Can they be beaten?"

"Mühlmann's products are very good," Rostov said, "but they are not perfect. They can be beaten, but with considerable effort."

"We need an outstanding technical man to lead the battle against them," Lowell said. He contemplated Rostov for a moment. "What will it take to persuade you to join ETI?"

"Three things," Rostov said. "Interesting projects, good title, and more pay."

Lowell leaned back on his couch. "Developing sensors superior to Mühlmann has to be the most interesting and challenging controls project in the country. . . . What is your current salary and title?"

Rostov named a figure and gave his title as director, photoelectric engineering.

"Mr. Rostov," Lowell said, "I am prepared to offer you a salary fifty percent higher than you are currently making, a sign-on bonus of twenty thousand dollars when you report for work here, an option on five thousand shares of ETI stock at their market value on the day you join the company—and I might add that our stock is an extraordinary value now—and the title vice president, technology, reporting to Mr. Slater. Would that be acceptable?"

For the first time, Rostov hesitated. He seemed to be measuring Lowell, his seriousness, his intent, searching for some catch in the offer. "That's most generous. Don't you want to check references?"

"No, I don't," Lowell said. "I've been hiring people for fifty years, Mr. Rostov, and I have learned to trust my intuition . . . How say you?"

Rostov hesitated again, then said, "Let me repeat, Dr. Lowell, you have been most generous. However, I would like your offer in writing and discuss it with my family. This will not take long. I will give you answer two days after I receive your letter."

THAT AFTERNOON, Lowell received a copy from the mayor of a letter he had sent to the members of the Cambridge city council. Lowell forwarded it to Breal, circling the following paragraphs in red:

> I was especially impressed with the attitude of Dr. Lowell. I believe that he is sincerely trying to balance the needs of all parties concerned while addressing the difficult challenge now facing his company.

My recommendation to the Council is that ETI and the Brotherhood of Electrical and Electronic Workers be left to settle the issues which confront them without assistance from the Council. And further, that the order to down-zone ETI's Memorial Drive property be shelved until further notice.

I believe that ETI, after forty-five years of doing business in our city, deserves such support and assistance as we can provide.

Now, more realtors visited ETI, patiently listened to Lowell's vision, told him in various ways why they thought it was wrongheaded, then left and were never heard from again. Breal, desperate, decided to try a frontal assault on Lowell's fantasy. "We have to shift our ground," he said. "Let's not concern ourselves with what these people build. We'll contact a dozen of the larger Boston developers, tell them we're only interested in a cash deal, and ask for a written proposal within fifteen days. When we get an offer, we shop it around. What I'm suggesting is a kind of quiet auction."

"Hell, let's do it," Lowell said. "I'm sick of telling these people how grand the view is. I'm also getting the impression that none of those clowns have two dimes to rub together. They're all looking to make a killing with someone else's money. Go ahead, George. Proceed fearlessly. I sense the planets aligning in our favor. Just keep me informed."

Lowell gazed at Breal, seemed to have more to say but was having difficulty locating the thought. Breal waited. "I've been thinking, George," he finally said, "I used to go to Europe twice a year to check on the incompetents that run that operation. I can't remember the last time I went. When we've put this union nonsense behind us and sold the building and have everything moved, let's go see what those clowns are up to." On that basis, Breal didn't think they would see Europe anytime soon, if ever. "I'll show you my old haunts on the

Left Bank. Take your wife along. There's no harm combining business with a little play."

When Breal left, Lowell recalled the trip to Europe when he had cajoled Lou into visiting Patton's grave—in the American cemetery at Hamm, in Luxembourg—and had openly wept as he stared at the simple cross. Lou was astonished. "Why, you loved the man," she said. "Yes, I suppose I did," he said. "I still see him, standing very tall, chin and chest out, surveying a battlefield, his helmet all burnished and lacquered, reflecting the sun. He looked like Alexander the Great, Caesar and Napoleon all rolled into one." He continued to stare at the grave. "That was a chosen time . . . I remember when we finally crossed the Rhine, on a pontoon bridge at Oppenheim. Half-way across Patton stopped, and standing on the edge of the bridge, urinated into the river. He had waited a long time for that." Lou was not impressed. "It must have been standard practice," she said. "Churchill did the same."

As they were leaving, past row on row of Third Army dead, the wind tugging at her dress, Lou asked, "Why didn't they bury him in Arlington?"

"His widow wanted him buried with his men," Lowell said, "where they had fought together. Patton believed that the boundaries of a nation's greatness are marked by the graves of its soldiers."

Lou had liked that.


"I WOULD like to show you something," Edna said to Lowell. They were seated in the Great Hall; Lowell, martini before him, was browsing through the *Wall Street Journal*. Edna opened the entertainment cabinet, clicked on the TV and VCR. "There's a video I would like you to watch."

"What is it? I'm not in the mood for a movie."

"This will interest you."

Edna inserted the cartridge, started the machine. The film was grainy, over-colored, but clear enough.

"I've skipped the titles and preliminaries," Edna said. "Here's the heart of the matter."

Two women enter a well-furnished living room, one tall, blond, the other smaller, dark, rather timid, the tall one older.

"Daphne, darling Daphne," says the blond. "Here, let me help you." The camera follows her hands unbuttoning the back of Daphne's dress, fingers long, slender, nail polish deep red. She pushes off the shoulder straps of Daphne's slip then holds her from the back, eyes closed, hands cupping Daphne's breasts. Then she licks Daphne's shoulder, eyes still closed, and helps her out of her slip.

Lowell peered at the screen. The younger woman appeared vaguely familiar. "What in the world is this?" he said.

"Keep watching," Edna said, "particularly the dark-haired one. See if you can figure out who she is."

"What are you talking about?"

"Just watch, please."

"Are you sure this is all right, Ingrid?" Daphne asks as she helps Ingrid unhook her bra.

"Oh, yes," Ingrid says. "Oh, yes." Her movements now take on urgency.

Ingrid strips off her own clothes and the two naked women hold each other, Ingrid's hands pressing Daphne's buttocks toward her, her own hips rotating in a grinding motion.

Lowell stared. "I don't know what's got into you, Edna, but I have no interest in watching a pornographic movie."

"I don't either," Edna said. "We're not watching this to enjoy ourselves. I'm only asking you to identify the younger woman. Then I'll switch it off."

Daphne lies on the couch, eyes closed, Ingrid kneeling on the rug beside her. Ingrid's tongue, circling around Daphne's nipple, fills the screen. The camera pans to Ingrid's hand as it caresses Daphne's sex. She lifts one leg over the back of the couch as she says, "You have such clever hands."

Lowell watched, both repelled and mesmerized, as though he were watching surgery. "I've had about all of this I can stand," Lowell said. "Just tell me what it is you're trying to prove, then turn the damn thing off."

"John, I wouldn't subject you to this if I didn't think it was important."

The camera is now focused on Daphne's face, head back, eyes closed, mouth slightly open, moaning in soft cries.

Lowell edged forward: the feeling of familiarity had increased, accompanied by a throb of foreboding.

The camera shifts to Ingrid's tongue lapping Daphne's inner thigh, below the dark of her pubic hair. "This is so beautiful," Daphne whispers, and she caresses the back of Ingrid's neck.

Ingrid's face is now buried in Daphne's sex while her hand moves busily between her own legs. Both of Daphne's hands press Ingrid's blond head into her and her moans grow louder.

The focus is again on Daphne's face, head thrown back, eyes closed, mouth now wide open, emitting cries that swell to a crescendo.

Then Daphne's eyes open, her face grows composed. "What can I do to give you pleasure, Ingrid?" she asks. Lowell's heart gave a murderous throb. Much younger, face rounder, but there she was. Unmistakable.

Edna had stopped watching the screen, her eyes fixed on Lowell. Now she relaxed, smiled.

"Turn it off!" Lowell cried. "Turn the goddamn thing off!"

"Don't you want to see your daughter do her complete repertoire?" Edna said. "A man comes in soon. Name of Giovanni. They make a charming threesome."

Lowell felt a pulse beating in his temple, mouth dry.

Edna turned away from the stricken Lowell and switched off the TV, just as Ingrid was guiding Daphne in giving her pleasure.

"I'm sorry to subject you to this," Edna said, now smiling with a forlorn sweetness. "Your beloved Shakespeare would tell you I must be cruel only to be kind."

"Where did you get it?" Lowell asked.

"A video store."

"How did you know it even existed?"

"Catherine once mentioned it to me, defiantly as I recall."

"When was it made?"

"What's the difference? You've always said people never change."

Lowell pushed away his martini and peered hard at Edna: she was suddenly unfamiliar, as if he were seeing her for the first time: glittering eyes in a round face, she appeared depraved. He shuffled from the Great Hall.

"It's called *Norwegian Nights*," Edna called after him.

# NINETEEN

The two negotiating teams sat opposite one another in the classroom. The room was warm, smelled of dead cigarettes. Someone had opened a window. Periodically a train clattered by. Breal sneezed twice; the hay fever season was in full swing. "The purpose of this meeting," he said, "is to review your counter-proposal letter."

Krakowski read a portion of the union letter aloud, and then said, "You address the issue of our selling the building by saying this is the wrong time to sell, that real estate values in this area are skyrocketing and will at least double in the next five years. Is this view based on professional opinion?"

"There's more building going on around here every day," Sullivan said. "This area is hot. You'll get more if you hang on."

"But is there any professional opinion behind your statement?" Krakowski persisted.

"Does the company have data showing that now *is* the best time to sell?" Atlee countered.

"All this misses the point," Breal said impatiently. The roof of his mouth itched from allergy; he had taken an antihistamine that morning but to no effect. "We need the money now, not at some vague point in the future. Maybe we *can* get more money for the building later. But it won't do us much good if the company has been wiped out."

"The next section of your letter deals with manufacturing," Krakowski said, and read on. "ETI has been in business in Cambridge for forty-five years. Over this time it has produced products that are untouchable in the electronics world. Clearly, this is a good reason why the company should remain in Cambridge. Under the leadership of Dr. Lowell and the employees, both the union and the management of the company were able to manufacture products we can all be proud of."

While Krakowski was reading, Lily Malewsky was cleaning the fingernails of her right hand with the fingernails of her left; Curtis Cornwall was slouched deep in his chair, eyes closed, a lascivious smile on his face, as if he were in some mental whorehouse; a delicate wreath of smoke curled from Sullivan's cigarette. On the ETI side, Breal tapped a finger on the table.

"With the company growing its business because of the above-mentioned," Krakowski read, "the employees find it incomprehensible that the company would consider a move. It seems to us, with this winning combination, that ETI should stay where it is and continue to be a winner with the labor force in this plant." The union team had lapsed into total impassivity as Krakowski finished his reading.

Breal rubbed his nose and cleared his throat. "Gentlemen," he said, "maybe there's something profound here that I'm missing, but it seems to me that the union and ETI are talking about two different companies. We've been steadily laying off people and losing money. That doesn't sound like a company that's quote growing its business." Breal looked at Sullivan. "You were at the presentation Dr. Lowell gave to the Cambridge city council. He didn't say we had a winning combination. He said we were pinned to the wall and a bulldozer was rumbling toward us from Germany with Attila the Hun at the wheel."

"It's not very complicated, Mr. Breal," Scadlock said. "We think your problem is lousy management."

Harry Probska gazed at Breal, "We don't have all the equipment or tools we need," he said. "We're missing tools."

"Do you get involved in buying tools, Mr. Breal?" Sullivan said.

Clawson shifted into a semblance of alertness. "We buy the tools we need," he said. "A bigger problem is people stealing tools."

"Not having tools is very inefficient," Probska doggedly continued. "It keeps everybody standing around."

Breal sighed, blew his nose as Krakowski took up the struggle. "We've told you that a major reason this plant is inefficient is because it's multistory. Your attack on the quality of management fails to address that issue."

Cornwall's eyes opened. "You ought to look into power factor adjustment to save on your electric bills," he said and smiled, teeth crooked little tombstones, then relapsed into his comatose state.

"Take your head out of the sand," Sullivan said to Breal, the words punctuated by puffs of smoke. "You guys haven't really looked at making this building efficient. How about zone heating or alternate fuel switching?" he asked on a triumphant note. "Have you ever investigated those?"

Probska had been staring at Breal, eyebrows drawn together, then said, "I don't understand why, if you've got to sell the building, you don't just go ahead and sell it—then we all move back in when a new building is put up."

"Good lord, man," Breal said, all patience gone, replaced by a surprising anger, "office space around here rents for thirty dollars a square foot. If we tried to do manufacturing in space that expensive, we'd go broke in no time. We can't afford to spend more than a tenth of that for manufacturing."

The group then reviewed the union responses to the remaining reasons given by ETI for considering the move. There were a few concessions, but Breal found them no more imaginative or constructive than the responses to the sale of the property. When they left the meeting, Breal sighed in exasperation and then said to Clare, "God, what a bunch of losers!"

"Look at it this way, George," Clare said, "if those people could grasp what was happening to ETI and propose creative solutions, then they wouldn't be here. They'd be in other lines of work, not sweating at a punch press, or stuffing components into printed circuit boards, or loading boxes on a shipping dock."

THE ETI negotiating team plus Tergelen and Miles met in the executive conference room with Lowell. Miss Krane was there since Rosenfeld had insisted that minutes be taken. Breal projected a series of charts listing the reasons given by the company for considering the move of manufacturing, the union position on each point, and the company response. Clare presented an analysis of the financial benefits of the move, demonstrating that these far outweighed the gains to be obtained by remaining in Cambridge and accepting the few concessions offered by the union. Then Breal, looking directly at Lowell, said, "It's our recommendation that the company terminate its manufacturing operations in Cambridge and proceed to sell the Memorial Drive building."

"We're knee-deep in blood and have no alternative but to go forward," Lowell said. "Let's take all necessary action to get out of here."

"The next job is to negotiate severance," Breal said. An hour later Breal announced the company's decision to move to the union.

THREE DAYS later, when Breal arrived at work, he found the letters FJL spray-painted in black on the glass of the entry door to the building, directly below the ETI logo. Worse, the letters were also sprayed on both flanks of the stone lion. "What the hell is going on?" Breal exclaimed to the guard. The guard calmly replied that he didn't know, that the letters were already there when he started his shift, but thought it had something to do with the union. In any case, he had filed a report.

Breal hurried over to the shipping area, found Scadlock. The union steward was wearing a button about a thumb length in diameter pinned to his shirt, the letters FJL in black on a yellow background. "What's that you're wearing?" Breal said, motioning toward the button.

"It's a morale booster," Scadlock said.

"What does it mean?"

"The letters stand for Fuck John Lowell."

"That's goddamn infantile!" Breal said in disgust.

"I know," Scadlock replied, "but it makes everybody in the shop feel better. It's kind of a theme for our severance negotiations."

"You guys can wear any buttons you want, but you can't screw up company property," Breal said, struggling to control himself. "You can't spray-paint letters around the place, like on the lion. That was fucking dumb. If we catch anybody scrawling graffiti, he's fired. Right then and there. We'll talk about it afterwards. Pass that on to Sullivan."

Breal hustled around and found the plant maintenance supervisor. "Get that spray paint off the lion and the front door," Breal ordered. "Right now!"

"It's bigger than the lion and the door," the man said. "Have you seen the production area?"

"Get started in the front before Lowell comes in."

Breal entered the factory. FJL buttons had blossomed everywhere. People wore them on their clothing and stuck them in front of their workstations. The letters were also sprayed in blue and red and orange on the windows and, silhouetted against the light, gave the place a party atmosphere. It seemed to Breal that the cloud of dejection and resentment that had hung over the workers since the phaseout decision had lifted, and everyone in the shop that morning was bright and cheerful.

Breal found Clawson in his office. "Where in the world were your supervisors while those windows were being sprayed?" Clawson, who looked exhausted though it was early morning, said he had no idea. His phone rang, he listened, said "right away," and hung up. "Lowell wants us both in his office. Right now." Clawson left a chink of space between the last two words. Breal sighed—the maintenance man had not cleaned the lion and the door in time.

"What's the meaning of those letters sprayed on the lion?" Lowell howled.

Breal saw real pain in Lowell's face, as if his own body had been vandalized. He searched for the response least likely to cause a meltdown. "This will amuse you, sir," he said. "They stand for Fuck John Lowell."

"We are not amused!" thundered Lowell. He then launched into an anti-vandalism tirade that Breal thought could be heard across the river. After a while Lowell reduced the volume and said, "I understand those sons of bitches are frustrated. So am I. Nor do I feel personally insulted. No man is insulted unless he feels himself insulted. But this is anarchy, a loss of all discipline. The next thing you know, those madmen will dismantle the assembly lines. Are those letters anywhere else?"

"They're on the windows in the factory," Breal said. He was about to mention the buttons when the storm broke with renewed vigor.

"Get this cleaned up right now!" Lowell shouted. He paced the room. "I want an investigation launched. I want to find who's responsible for this and fire him. This is not a court of law and we don't have to *prove* anything. If you *think* you know who painted the lion and the windows, fire the bastard. Fire him now! Let's not get picky over justice. And George, issue a letter to the union this morning. I want the company position on this madness a matter of record."

Breal then raised the question of the buttons. Lowell continued to pace. "I can't do much about their damn buttons or anything else those idiots choose to wear on their clothing.

But nothing goes on company property. Do you gentlemen understand that? Nothing!" Lowell glared at the men before him. "This place is coming apart. We have to get out of here and fast."

Breal wrote the letter to the union and showed it to Stanley Rosenfeld; the attorney suggested it be toned down.

"This reads like it was written by Little Red Riding Hood," Lowell grumbled. "Lawyers be damned," he growled, and beefed up the letter.

At the next negotiating session, all of the union committee sported FJL buttons. Sullivan greeted the ETI team with a chipper, "Good morning, good morning." The one female member of the union team, lemon hair freshly dyed and done up in an elaborate garden, wore radish-colored blush, blood-red lipstick, and seemed ready to party. Everyone was in excellent spirits. Absolutely nothing was accomplished. Breal found he despised them all.


CATHERINE SAT in her living room and stared at the Indian scatter rug at her feet.

"You look like you should be dressed in black," Ishmael said. "In mourning for your life."

"I lost my father," Catherine said. "Again."

"What do you mean?"

"He wrote me a letter. He doesn't want to see me. Ever. Or the boys either."

"Jesus. Did he say why?"

"Sort of. He said there are some things you do in life, no matter how young you are at the time, that reveal your character. I've revealed a sleazy side so egregious—sleazy and egregious were his words—that he could never condone it in a child of his."

"What in heaven is he talking about?"

"I wouldn't have any idea except that he addressed the letter to Daphne."

"Who's Daphne?"

"It took me a while to figure it out, then I remembered." Catherine heaved a long sigh, a deep indrawing and expulsion of breath. "Right after my first divorce I was desperate—and I mean really desperate—for money. I had two small children and my ex-husband was not making his child support payments. Anyway, I met a fellow who introduced me to a movie producer. He made pornographic movies and offered me a job. Talk about sleaze—now *he* was sleazy. It was disgusting work but it paid very well. I made three flicks, then gave it up. Daphne was a character I played in one of the films."

Ishmael stared at her, threw back his head and laughed, a clear marveling laugh; he came over and hugged her. "Well good for you, Catherine. That must have taken a bundle of courage."

"Actually, it's a lot more work than you might imagine. And there's nothing sexy about it."

"Well, that's hardly enough of a sin to consign you to the second circle . . . that must have been, when, twenty years ago?"

"Something like that. At the time, I thought I was a maverick, that I was above such things as sleaze or degradation. I wasn't. Each performance was a little death."

"How did the old man find out about it?"

"You get one guess."

"How did *she* know?"

"I must have mentioned it to her years ago, when we were friends."

"But he had to have more than her word . . ."

"She must have found a copy of the film. You've got to hand it to her. This isn't deathless stuff. It surely took lots of work to track it down."

"She was super-motivated." Ishmael, now beside her, took her hand. "What now?" he asked gently.

"My dad said he would continue to pay my law school tuition and keep the stipend going. He'll also pay for Michael's schooling, all the way to a PhD if that's what Michael wants. And he'll help Tom should he need help. But he doesn't want any direct communication between us. He gave me the name of his attorney. Any request would have to go through him."

"The guy is a nut. He should have heard your side of the story."

"Well, seeing your daughter perform unnatural acts . . . it must get to a man."

"Anyway, he wasn't vindictive."

"I'll have to tell the boys," she said miserably.

"YOU MEAN you were a porn star?" Michael said, eyes open wide.

"No, I wasn't a star. I made three dumb movies and they disappeared without a trace."

"That must have taken an awful lot of guts," Tom said.

"I suppose so," Catherine said. "The guts of desperation, I'd have to say."

"By God, Mom, you're okay," Tom said.

"They say you're only as sick as your secrets," Ishmael said. "So I'd say you're pretty healthy."

Catherine was astonished. She had dreaded this moment of awful confession, afraid that the men in her life would all be disgusted, want nothing more to do with her. Instead they were all proud. It made her weep.

"I THINK we've found something," Fredricks said. "We were looking at old textile mills up in New Hampshire that you could have for next to nothing, but they're like this place— multistory, big leaky windows, and expensive to rework. Then Cobb's friend on the Manchester planning commission told us there's a K-Mart on the outskirts of the city that's closing down and the owners are looking to lease the place. We're talking about a hundred thousand square feet on a single floor, well lit, no windows so it's energy efficient, good heating and air conditioning, and a monster parking lot. We were impressed."

"When will the place be vacated?"

"They moved out this week. The place should be empty now."

Breal drove to Manchester with Clawson and Fredricks. The building was set back some two hundred feet from the street; in front was a parking lot capable of holding at least a thousand cars. The interior was empty except for some stray boxes and debris. Breal scanned the vast empty space, brown-tiled floor, beige walls, all lit by row on row of fluorescent lights. "This is one hell of a place," he said and turned to Clawson. "What do you think, Buck?"

"I think it's terrific," Clawson said. "All those lights—perfect for electronic assembly." He pointed downward. "You can see from where some of the tiles are missing that the floor is cement, so it should be able to handle all of our machinery except for the punch presses and molding machines. We'd build reinforced concrete foundations for those." He then indicated several discoloration marks on the ceiling. "The roof needs a little help."

Two days later, Lowell, Breal and Clawson drove north in the Cadillac limousine. Lowell squinted through the June sunshine at the ten acres of parking. "This should be adequate," he said. Breal had asked that the building be swept clean of all remnants of the department store. Inside, they stared across a floor space greater than two football fields side by side, spotless and gleaming under the lights. "I think if you look carefully," Breal said, "you can see the curvature of the earth."

"Now this is what I had in mind," Lowell said. "By God, this is exactly what I had in mind. What do you think of this place, Buck?"

"I think it's perfect."

"How much are they asking?"

"Three dollars a square foot," Breal said, "with us picking up all insurance, taxes, and maintenance costs."

"See if you can get the place for two-fifty with an option to buy," Lowell said. "When the city expands in this direction, this property will be worth a fortune. It's large enough for a hotel or shopping complex. Only a question of time." Lowell looked around further. "We could never live with those tenement-ivory walls. What we need here is a light blue, a sweet blue." As they left, Lowell added, "In your negotiations, George, see if you can get them to throw in a new roof."

Breal, Fredricks and Clare concluded a twenty year lease at two dollars and sixty cents a square foot with an option to buy the thirteen acre site, exercisable at any time, for five million dollars. The owner balked at a new roof, but did agree to patch the existing one.

Lowell asked that a floor plan be laid out and presented to him within a week.

WITH LOWELL at the head of the table, the engineering progress meeting convened in the executive conference room. "It has to be redone," Rostov said. "Mr. Holloway's design not conceived for integrated circuit. Circuit layouts are useless. It will not work and must be redone."

"The perfect is the enemy of the good, Mr. Rostov," Lowell said. "Can Craig's design be modified so it does the job, albeit less than optimally?"

"More time will be spent redoing Mr. Holloway's design than with new one. I have started new design. It will be completed and guaranteed to work in six months."

Breal, who now had an ever-present vision of himself trudging across a parched desert, his water supply dwindling, said, "We don't have six months. Can it be done in two?"

"Possibly," he said, "but only if no problems."

"It seems a terrible shame to throw out everything Craig has done," Tergelen said.

"Basic circuit concept will be retained," Rostov said.

"Do you concur with Emil's position?" Breal asked Slater.

Slater made a futile gesture. "Emil and I have gone through this in detail. He's convinced me that Craig was on the wrong track. Not much of Craig's design is salvageable, except for the basic circuit concepts."

"How can we be sure that the design will be done in a couple of months and that it will work when finished?" Tergelen asked.

"It took nine months at Opticon," Rostov said, "but I have learned much since then. Opticon chip now in pilot production."

"When the design is completed, what will we have compared to the Krauts?" Lowell asked.

"We will have product superior to Mühlmann and Opticon," Rostov said. "It will have more functions and greater sensitivity and therefore longer range. All in a package about same size as Mühlmann and at about same cost. Also easy future expansion to perform other functions."

Why am I betting my company on this man? The thought came to Lowell with stark, cold clarity. But then, he told himself, betting on people was what he had always done. Only now . . . He contemplated the Russian: high intelligent forehead, alert eyes—he could be an Einstein or a brilliant idiot. Lowell felt his intuition slipping. He tried to concentrate on the group before him, sensed a barrier rising; then from the formless swirl in his head images coalesced: his daughter's naked breasts, buttocks, closed eyes, open mouth. The other woman's hands. Much as he tried to push them from his mind, these grainy over-colored images always returned. At odd moments, at night or in his office or now, before these men, the shameful scenes replayed themselves, in slow motion, frame by frame, a moist tangle of female bodies. He thought that writing the letter that once again banished his daughter—a letter written in ten minutes of icy rage after two days of brooding—would exorcize the images, but it did not. All that happened was that rage and shame were replaced by sorrow, as though he were grieving the death of someone dear. He felt hollow, as though his insides had been emptied, then despair, a low-lying cloud of gloom that never lifted, a consciousness of failure and loss. Time, he told himself, would dim the scenes and the heartache as it dimmed everything else. Yet he knew there were some disappointments that could rise in you like molten iron, harden, and last as long as life itself.

Lowell looked around the table at the faces staring back, puzzled it seemed, waiting. How long had he sat mute and dumb before them? He groped through the confusion in his mind, turned to Rostov. "We'll help you in any way we can," he stammered. "Don't be afraid to ask. Whatever you need we'll get for you."

Rostov bowed his head in an old world gesture.

LATE THAT afternoon Lowell called Breal to his office and handed him a single sheet of paper. It was Clawson's letter of resignation. There was no date set for leaving; the letter said that Clawson would stay on to complete the move of manufacturing, then retire.

"Let's get Buck in here and see what this is all about," Lowell said. "He's never done this before."

Clawson did not look at either Lowell or Breal as he settled into a chair at the marble table. Lowell held Clawson's letter. "If I knew you were a short-timer, Buck, I would never have hired you. How long have you been with ETI?"

"Forty years this October," Clawson replied.

"You're still a young man, Buck. Why do you want to leave?"

"I'll be sixty-three next month," Clawson said. "I own a couple of acres of land on Moosehead Lake in northern Maine. I'm having a house built there, a big A-frame, and that's where Edith and I want to settle. I'll be doing the interior finishing myself." He looked up. "I'm well fixed, thanks to you, Dr. Lowell, and now I'd like to relax and enjoy things. The wife and me have talked about it a lot. I'll help you move and help you break in a new man, but in the next three to six months I'd like to leave."

"God, Buck, you'll go crazy in your cabin in the woods," Lowell said. "How about working part time, say, three days a week?"

Breal noticed a dew of perspiration on Clawson's forehead. "That's very kind of you, Dr. Lowell," he said, "but then I wouldn't be doing a very good job at ETI or a very good job at home. It's too far to commute, so I'd have to leave Edith alone up there two or three nights a week. Thanks for the offer but I think a clean break is best." Breal admired Clawson's courage. After forty years of conditioning, it must be hard to say no to Lowell.

After Clawson left, Lowell scratched his head, seemed to be wondering where everyone's life had gone, including his own. "Where do we go from here?" he asked Breal.

"I like Buck," Breal said. "But there's a man for every season and I question whether Buck is now the right man to lead manufacturing. He likes to spend his time in the machine shop, or fooling with the punch presses. He's uncomfortable with the technology of the M-90 and he's totally at sea when it comes to integrated circuits. I suspect he knows that and that's why he's chosen to leave. Frankly, Dr. Lowell, I don't view Clawson's leaving as a problem. It's an opportunity."

"How are we going to capitalize on this opportunity?" Lowell asked with an ironic smile.

"The best manufacturing man I ever knew was a guy at United Electric named Frank Norrie. He's in his late forties and he's spent his entire working life at United so I don't know if we can induce him to leave, but it's worth a shot."

"Well, the factory floor is where profits are made or lost," Lowell said. "It's easier to recruit a PhD physicist than a good manufacturing man. You can't pay an individual like that too much." He rose and walked to the window. Breal joined him. It was evening. The river seemed to be washing the light of the setting sun and all of ETI's past out to sea.

"ETI won't be the same with Clawson gone," Lowell said. He contemplated the jagged outline of Boston now silhouetted against the darkening sky. The dome of the State House reflected the last trace of daylight. Lights were coming on in the Hancock and the Pru. "It certainly is a magnificent view," he said. "Let's enjoy it while we can. Soon enough it too will be gone."

# TWENTY

Clawson and Fredricks laid out the Manchester plant. Lowell reviewed the plan, made changes, then visited the building and drew chalk marks on the floor where he wanted the machinery and production lines located. Lowell thought the area that Fredricks had designated for his operation was in the wrong place and changed its location too. "I know I've pushed them against the punch presses," Lowell said, "but putting them anywhere else gets in the way of the production layout. We'll insulate the walls so the noise doesn't get through." He also determined the size and arrangement of the cafeteria, the color of the walls, the placement of the company name and logo on the building.

Breal and Clare prepared a letter asking for bids on the company's Memorial Drive property. They sent the letter to fifteen developers, including those that had already visited ETI. Breal, in response to the numerous requests to inspect the site, assigned Clare to deal with the stream of developers who passed through the building. Clare insisted on a written proposal; there was no interest on the part of ETI in meetings or special propositions. "Just put your price on paper," he said, "and keep our objective in mind: all cash up front and no involvement."

The first letters were disappointing. One proposed a partnership with ETI. Another wanted a guarantee that ETI would return to the building as an anchor tenant, locating their headquarters there. Still another wanted ETI to take part in lobbying activities with the Cambridge authorities and made his price contingent on the floor area approved by the city. "These guys just don't listen," Clare said. They finally received a letter that caught their attention. The offer was for $13,750,000, all cash, payable at closing—ninety days after both parties signed the purchase and sale agreement.

At Breal's suggestion that they open negotiations with the bidder, Lowell said, "Let's wait until we have all the offers before we talk to anyone. I think we can do better."

The next day Breal, fatigue and allergies dragging at him, said to Lowell, "We've reached an agreement with the union on severance payments. Stanley Rosenfeld is drawing up the final document and negotiating the language with the union attorney."

"What's the bottom line?"

"The total cost of the severance package is $1.1 million."

"That's superb, George. A million dollars to get rid of those idiots isn't a high price." Lowell then gave Breal a fatherly smile. "You look worn down," he said. "Why so sad?"

On Breal's mind was the severance package hit on cash flow and the need to sell the building quickly before ETI's bank account ran dry. But he said, "Dealing with the union, hour after hour . . . It's a depressing exercise."

"St. Francis said we know only what we have suffered." Breal could find no response to this, but Lowell apparently was not expecting one since he continued, "Here's something to cheer you up. In recognition of the successful completion of the union negotiations, I'm going to bestow upon you as a bonus ten thousand shares of ETI stock. However, to keep you motivated, we'll award you those shares at the rate of two thousand a year. Of course, should you at some point conclude that you can no longer stand us and decide to leave, you forfeit any bonus shares forthcoming. Miles is arranging for the first two thousand shares to be delivered to you this week. Congratulations!" Lowell shook Breal's hand.

"We still have a long way to go," Breal said. "The building isn't sold yet. Then we've got to transfer manufacturing, train a new work force, find a new headquarters building and move, finish development of the M-100 and put it into production . . . We've just begun to fight, Dr. Lowell."

As he said this, Breal recalled that he had spoken almost the identical words to his wife the previous evening. He also said, "While we're doing all this Mühlmann isn't just sitting there. They're developing newer products, better production techniques and, by the way, cutting deeper into our market."

Susan had looked at him in her contemplative way and said, "Is all this really worthwhile? I mean, there's no guarantee any of this is going to be successful and you might kill yourself along the way."

"I've got an obligation to the people I've brought in and I've got an obligation to myself." Then with an upwelling of emotion that surprised him, Breal said, "And I've got an obligation to the old man."


Lowell WANDERED into engineering, and found Emil Rostov, the unlikely person on whom all else depended. Rostov was peering at a computer screen.

"No point duplicating Mühlmann product," Rostov said. "I met with Tergelen, salesmen, customers, and developed specifications for radical new product. Must leapfrog Mühlmann and be superior to Opticon. That is what I am working on."

"I don't see any circuit layout or breadboard," Lowell said sourly.

"Not needed," Rostov said. He pointed to the screen. "Product design and performance evaluated on computer."

"Do you need any help? Consultant support. Anything."

"Need high-speed computer. We can buy time on machine next door at MIT."

Lowell stared at the lines and curves on the screen: it could be the Rosetta stone or senseless doodling. Does this man know what he's doing? Can I trust him? *Can I trust anyone?* All men are subject to sudden lapses of judgment, of reason. Probably more so when young. Look at Catherine, for Christ's sake, look at my daughter. Raised her well. Gave her life's best. Patrician mother. Sunk to the actions of a common whore. Who could have imagined that? Could you—of your own daughter? Can't tell when madness will strike, sink the company. Stay alert. Watch for the small signs. For danger.

The highest bid for the building was $14.6 million, all cash, from a company called Norwood Properties. Breal was impatient to accept it. "Not so fast, George," Lowell said, rubbing his hands like a banker. "This is just the start of negotiations. No man's first offer is his best offer, even on a competitive bid."

Breal and Clare met with Ted Carey, the president of Norwood. Carey, a man in his forties with an aristocratic manner, was handsome and slight. He was accompanied by his partner, a round-faced man with small shrewd eyes named Dean Stratis who resembled a young Buck Clawson. Breal voiced dissatisfaction with Carey's price. Carey, in the most reasonable and persuasive voice Breal had ever heard, listed the costs to develop the property, the marginal nature of his return given the risks he was taking, and would not budge. Stratis, in a disgusted tone, said that, if anything, their bid was already out of line, and if it were his decision alone, he would never have gone that high. Breal decided that the two developers acted as a good cop/bad cop team.

"Do we have a deal?" Carey asked.

"It looks that way," Breal said. "Let's get started on a purchase and sale sgreement and see if any snags develop."

Breal called the real estate attorney recommended by Cobb. "Have you guys talked to the Rodneys?" the attorney asked. "They're real high rollers."

"Who are they?"

"A Boston real estate outfit owned by twin brothers, Bob and Bruce Rodney."

The Rodneys toured the building, grumbled over the short time to prepare a bid, then came up with an offer of

$15.4 million, all cash. Breal urged Lowell to close the deal. "No, no," Lowell said, resembling a Vegas gambler on a roll. "Go back to the first guy. Hell, you never know. See if he'll up his offer." Ted Carey, it developed, was off on a yacht race in the Bahamas and would not be back for several days. Breal spoke with Dean Stratis. "We've got a higher offer," he said. "Do you want to reconsider your bid?"

"I thought we had a deal," Stratis grumbled. Breal did not answer, waited for more. "How much is the offer?" Stratis finally asked. Breal gave him the number.

"Hang loose for a couple of days until Ted comes back," said Stratis in an irritated voice.

Two days later, at nine in the morning, a tan Ted Carey and Dean Stratis sat with Breal and Clare in ETI's conference room. Carey placed a set of computer printouts before him. "Where do we stand?" he asked.

"After we talked, I received a firm offer of $15.4 million, all cash, but we're open to a higher bid."

Carey leafed through his printouts. He reminded Breal of a movie actor, the one who always got the girl. "We're prepared to offer you $16 million, all cash, for the property," he said. His face paled through his tan as he named the price. "And that's our last and final offer." He stood up.

"When can we have it in writing?" Breal asked.

"Today, after lunch," Carey said.

The offer from Norwood Properties was trapped by the mail net at three-thirty that afternoon. Lowell clapped his hand over the letter. "By God, $16 million! Now we're getting somewhere, George."

"I don't think we're going to do any better," Breal said.

"You never know," Lowell said, his eyes bright with mercantile fervor. "Don't forget, we're conducting an auction. As long as the tote board keeps rising, there's no point in closing the bidding. Go back to the other guy. See what he says."

Breal called one of the Rodney brothers, gave him the Norwood price, and asked, "Do you want to rethink your bid?" Rodney, in a petulant voice, said that ETI already had his best offer, and hung up the phone.

"Congratulations!" Lowell said to Breal. "You've found the peak."

Five days later, ETI issued a press release announcing the sale of the company's Cambridge property: the transaction would close in forty-five days and would result in a one-time after-tax gain of $10,400,000, or $5.70 per share. Breal sent up a prayer of thanks to the god of real estate, whoever he or she was, who had smiled upon him. He commented to his wife that Lowell had the prime attributes of a successful negotiator: patience and stubbornness.


FRANK NORRIE started work as vice president of manufacturing, replacing Clawson, right after the July fourth holiday, in time for the manufacturing move. The plant was moved piecemeal, a production line at a time. The move of the punch presses and molding machines required special rigging equipment to place the heavy pieces on oversized eighteen-wheel flatbed trucks for transport to New Hampshire, then to unload and position the machines on previously prepared reinforced concrete slabs which reached down to bedrock. Clawson supervised emplacement of the machines.


LOWELL, UNABLE to sleep, stared into the graveyard darkness of his room, listened to the creaking of the house, the night wind through leaves and branches, found something malignant in the sounds, then thought he heard the howling of wolves. Randomly, he traversed the bits and pieces of his life—they seemed the life of someone else—but ETI, the future, were hidden behind an impenetrable white fog. In the morning he scrutinized his face, found it had a corpse-like pallor, skin a wilted leaf, gray, bushy old man's eyebrows. He stared at himself like an invalid, thought he had grown thinner overnight; it occurred to him that his life had shrunk together with his body. Edna wanted to trim his beard—she said it was looking like an unpruned bush—but he told her no with a venom that surprised him. At odd moments he thought of Catherine, saw her before him in a soft light, as if lit by an inner glow. But this image morphed into scenes from the film; these had settled in some vital inner chamber of his mind, taken on the imprecise reality of a nightmare and could not be excised. Surely she had reasons, but you forget reasons: facts are what matter. As he sat in the Great Hall, it seemed to have grown vaster—he regarded the walls around him as though they were an unfamiliar landscape. Isn't trust the foundation of love? When that's gone what's left? An icy mass of mistrust, of all things and all men, came down and covered him like a bell. Stay alert, he told himself, watch for the small signs, for danger. He couldn't sleep.


"WHAT'S THIS letter about?" Lowell asked, thrusting a sheet of paper toward Breal. The tone of Lowell's voice told him that he knew perfectly well what the letter was about and didn't like it.

The letter was from the U.S. Trust Company, the bank that carried ETI's revolving credit account, and was addressed to David Clare. It said that, with regret, they could not provide an answer to Mr. Clare's question on the remaining debt capacity of the company without detailed study and analysis of the firm's current financial statements. It was signed by a Ms. Jessica Fine, Vice President, Corporate Credit.

"Who authorized Clare to ask the bank that question?" a tight-faced Lowell asked.

Breal's heart contracted as he sensed the storm about to break. He had learned that once the heavy winds started to blow his best strategy was to adopt an even, rational tone and ride out the gale as best he could. In his most reasonable voice, Breal answered, "As head of financial analysis, I'm sure

Clare considered it within his authority to approach the bank without asking anyone."

"I thought I said no one contacts a bank without my prior approval. Anyway, why is he asking the question?" Lowell's face, hardened to granite, now seemed unreal.

"Dr. Lowell, I can certainly conjecture," Breal said in the same tone as his previous answer, deciding to ignore the problem of prior approval, "but I suggest we invite Clare into your office and simply ask him."

Lowell, expression unchanged, strode to the phone, buzzed Miss Krane, and asked her to send in Miles and Clare.

As Lowell paced the room, Clare and Miles huddled over the letter lying before them on the marble table. "We won't receive the cash for the sale of the building for another month," Clare explained, "but we've got severance payments and bills for the preparation of the Manchester plant due now. In a nutshell, we're running out of cash, but now it's only a short-term problem. So I was trying to establish how much short-term borrowing capacity we have left to tide us over until the building sale is closed."

As Clare spoke, Lowell continued to pace the room, head down. It was not clear he had heard anything Clare said. He now pointed to the letter, finger trembling like a compass needle. "Who signed it?"

"Jessica Fine," Clare said. "She's in charge of our account at U.S. Trust."

"We've always dealt with bank presidents," Lowell growled. "Why are we now dealing with girls?"

"She's a vice president," Clare said.

"You don't understand!" Lowell shouted; he scooped the letter from the table and waved it at Clare. "*Everyone* in a bank is a vice president, including the tellers." He strode around the room, crumpled the letter. "Banking relations are extraordinarily sensitive. You haven't spent your life dealing with bankers the way I have. They're a very nervous bunch. The reason they're nervous is that they know very little about anything, and the thing they know least about is money." He continued his pacing. "You can't ask those people anything because they don't know anything. When you ask them a question you only increase their anxiety. You can only *tell* bankers, you can't ask. By asking the bank what our borrowing capacity is, you've caused them to question the solvency of our enterprise. The letter says they want to examine our financial statements. They would descend on us like a plague of locusts and far from allowing us to borrow more money, they'd question the wisdom of the loans they've already made."

"Yes, sir, I understand," Clare said, his face grim and shoulders tensed as though preparing to smash through the defensive line.

"I wonder if you really do understand," Lowell said, then proceeded to repeat his speech with a new set of words. This time his speech was longer and louder, and Breal found it rambling. "Given the sensitive nature of banking relations, only someone experienced in dealing with those clowns can speak to them. Dick Miles is the treasurer of this corporation. Why didn't *he* call the bank?" Neither Miles nor Clare answered. Lowell started pacing again, frowned. "I'm not certain that I've successfully communicated to you the gravity of this matter. The leveraging of the assets of ETI through prudent borrowing is an important part of the financial strategy of this corporation. By asking that question, Mr. Clare, what you have done is compromise one of the cornerstones of our business."

Clare said nothing, but by the set of his face and body Breal had the feeling that Clare was undergoing an internal struggle: deciding whether to quit the employ of ETI now by telling the madman before him to go fuck himself—or wait until later.

Lowell finished with, "I hope this is clear to you gentlemen. As for this letter . . ." he crushed the crumpled paper into a ball and dumped it in the trash, "just forget it."

In the corridor, Clare shook his head and said to Breal, his voice hoarse, that he had taken care to tell Jessica Fine that his request was informal and that a phone call reply would suffice. "How could she possibly know that the son of a bitch that runs this place is nuts and that an innocent letter asking for information would cause the roof to collapse? By the way, I *did* ask Miles to contact the bank and he asked me to handle it. Also, after all that bullshit, we still have a cash flow problem."

"Let's lie low for a couple of days, then I'll approach the old man," Breal said.

"We can't wait much longer. We have a creditor problem now. But I really don't give a shit anymore. Let the place collapse. Screw it." Clare turned and left.

Breal found Miles and asked why Lowell had borne down so hard on Clare. Miles thought the whole incident deplorable, said he admired Clare and thought his intelligence and energy an asset to the company. "But that's exactly the point," Breal said. "Clare is an intelligent man and Lowell surely knows that. Now if Clare is told something once, he understands it. If he's told the same thing twice, for emphasis, then he understands it very well. But if he's told the same thing a third time, then something more than the thing itself is being communicated. Is there some encrypted message here? Is the old man trying to condition Clare not to take any initiative? Maybe initiative by these young people frightens him in some way."

"I think you're reading too much into this," Miles said.

"Then why did the old man repeat the same speech three times?"

"For emphasis, possibly. Or maybe each time he finished he didn't quite remember what he'd said before, so he thought he had to repeat it."

Breal left Miles' office, and decided to practice Management-by-Wandering-Around. He drifted down to engineering, waved hello to Slater in his office, and passed Craig

Holloway who was slumped in his chair, a black shade over his eyes, apparently asleep. Now that Craig was back from his heart attack, he took naps midmorning and midafternoon. He did not seem disturbed that he was no longer responsible for the M-100 design. Slater had given him a long-term assignment on which he puttered. A different Craig Holloway had returned, one with the serenity of a Trappist monk, and when he moved, he did so carefully, with a sad deliberateness, as if guarding against a fall. He seemed covered with a layer of dust.

Breal stopped to say hello to Emil Rostov. The engineer showed him the final package for the M-100, the integrated circuit control. Breal held it in his hand: rectangular, slightly smaller than the Mühlmann control, the ETI logo on the side, silver and red against the black plastic.

"Well, Emil," Breal said, "on this little fellow rides the future of ETI. If it doesn't work, none of us will be working."

"Don't worry, George," Rostov said. "Control will work perfectly."

Breal gazed down at the unit: the most advanced photo-electric device in the world. He sent up a plea that somewhere in Germany there wasn't someone gazing at a similar control, bright yellow in color, and thinking the same thing. "Our future is in your hands," Breal said, and meant every blessed word. Rostov bowed gravely.


At the end of that week Breal sat at the marble table. "What I'm saying, Dr. Lowell, is that we have a short-term cash flow problem. The sale of the building doesn't close for almost another month. In the meantime, we have union severance payments to make and extraordinary bills for work on the new plant in Manchester. We've got to borrow money, but since this is a short-term affair, I thought the simplest thing to do was increase our existing line of credit."

"Sure, that's okay."

"But to do that we have to meet with the U.S. Trust people. Do you want to participate in the meeting?"

"No, not at all. You and Dick can do that. Take them to lunch at the Algonquin Club. Bankers love a square meal."

"Any particular counsel on strategy?"

"The best approach," Lowell said, "is to find out what our borrowing capacity is and borrow to that limit."

Breal stared at Lowell. "Sir, are you sure that's what you want us to do?"

"Certainly. Why do you ask?"

"Well, perhaps the circumstances are different, but earlier in the week you emphasized to Clare that it was against company policy to ask for that kind of information from the banks."

Lowell wrinkled his brow—he looked like a man searching for an object in a cluttered attic—and finally said, "Of course the circumstances are different, it's a question of level. At your level that kind of inquiry is appropriate, but not at Clare's."

As Breal rose to leave, Lowell said, "I want to be sure those manufacturing types get off on the right foot. Let's you and I visit Manchester this coming Monday to see how the plant is shaping up."


When Lowell and Breal arrived at the Manchester plant, they were met by Frank Norrie and Buck Clawson. Lowell had insisted that Clawson accompany them on the plant tour. The largest portion of the floor space was devoted to the production lines, while the rest had been partitioned off to form a warehouse, the microcircuit facility, the cafeteria, offices, and an enclosed space for Nicholas Fredricks' production control department. The punch presses and injection molding machines were located in the corner of the building adjoining Fredricks' area. The assembly lines were in operation and several of the Cambridge supervisors were instructing the women on the line. The plant, partitioned off and populated with rows of women seated at moving conveyor belts, now seemed to Breal less immense.

Lowell's first comment was that the light over the production lines was inadequate. Breal had to agree: the operators were bent close and squinting over the small circuit boards and miniature parts before them. "We've already ordered high intensity fluorescents," Norrie said. "If there's still not enough light, we'll go to spot illumination."

At the end of a line, Lowell stopped to watch a woman place the cover on an M-90 and tighten the three screws that held it in place. The woman was a dark-haired Latina with heavy eye makeup, dark patches of rouge, and outsized earrings. He watched her for almost a full minute, and then asked, "Why is that girl using a handheld screwdriver?"

"We've had problems getting the air compressor installed," Clawson said. "It should be in place by tomorrow, then we'll switch to air-driven tools."

Lowell decided he would like a cup of coffee. On the way to the cafeteria, he commented to Breal that the woman with the screwdriver was quite attractive.

"Don't you think she was sort of cheap looking?" Breal asked.

Lowell thought about this. "Yes, I suppose so," he said, "but that's all right."

When the three were seated at a table, Lowell commented on the bright colors of the room and the cheery atmosphere. Breal found the bright yellows and reds a bit too cheery, but didn't give it much thought. He shifted his thinking to the remark he had made to Susan the previous evening: it remained to be seen whether out of this move, the result of so much struggle, would emerge a tough competitive ETI, and whether it would emerge fast enough. As they drank their coffee, Breal contemplated the bearded man before him: he had come a long way, accepting change that initially he'd thought him incapable of even considering.

Breal prayed that some crazy decision, made in a moment of madness, would not undo everything.

As they approached the machine shop, the thud of the punch presses and the whack of the molding machines grew louder, and Breal could smell the machine oil. The machines had been scrubbed and given a fresh coat of paint before being installed and now seemed less ancient than they had in Cambridge—but their noise had not diminished. The workers wore ear protection against the incessant pounding.

Production control had offices for Fredricks, his managers and senior staff, but the majority of the people sat at desks in an open space. The party entered, passed through one door, then a second, then into the department. Fredricks greeted the group as they entered. Once inside, Lowell stopped, hesitated, then turned and frowned at the door. "Was that second door in the building plan I approved?" Breal felt a twang in his stomach as he recognized the growl-like note in Lowell's voice.

"No, sir," Fredricks said, "but that door leads out to the punch presses so whenever anybody would go out or come in, the racket from the machines would disturb my people. I had the second door put in to cut down on the noise."

"You had no approval whatsoever to put in that door!" Lowell's voice had leaped in volume. His body grew more erect, arms rigid at his sides, fingers extended. "I want that door taken down!" he exploded. "I want that door down *now!*" The people at their desks flinched and peered at Lowell. The room was absolutely silent. Heads appeared in the doorways to the offices, looked out, and then disappeared. Lowell seemed oblivious to anyone there. "Buck! Get a screwdriver and take that door down. Right now. While I stand here. I mean the hinges off. Everything!"

Clawson scurried out and returned with a long-barreled, yellow-handled screwdriver. Breal watched him open the door, place a chair under the hinges and, with surprising agility, scramble onto the chair and attack the screws holding the top hinge. Breal thought it would be easier if Clawson first removed the door and then the hinges, but decided he really didn't give a damn how he did it. Lowell, arms still rigid at his sides, watched Clawson. "If everyone decided to redesign his department according to his own taste, this place would look like the tower of Babel," he snarled.

"It was only a small change, sir," Fredricks said, freckles carrot-colored against the pallor of his face.

"That's in the eye of the beholder," Lowell grumbled while continuing to watch Clawson. "To me a change is a change is a change."

Breal tugged Fredricks' sleeve. "Don't say anything!" he hissed in an urgent whisper, and Fredricks, his expression defiant, bit his lip and kept quiet. The people in the room returned to their papers, and from time to time peeked up at Lowell and the massive Clawson atop the chair.

"What do you want me to do with the door?" Clawson asked when he finished.

"Get rid of it," Lowell said.


THAT EVENING, Breal recounted the door incident to his wife. "It takes a terribly insecure man to do something like that," Susan said. "You should feel sorry for him."

"The only people I feel sorry for are poor Fredricks and his troops, who'll now be tormented by the whomping of those presses every time somebody opens the door. More important, I'm worried about Fredricks getting totally disgusted and leaving. He called me this morning and made noises in that direction. Then Clare is upset and talking about leaving. I'd be dead without those two guys."

"I wouldn't worry," Susan said. "They're both trapped in economic bondage the way we are."

The morning following the door incident, Breal was summoned to Lowell's office and found Miles and Clare already there. As they sat at the table, papers before them, Lowell paced the room; the anger of the previous day appeared to have stayed with him, now a steady dull rage. "Look at those losses, for heaven's sake. It's worse than last quarter."

"Revenues are down further," Clare said. "OEM sales are killing us. All of our sales to OEMs are now at special prices, so we lose money on every OEM order. Productivity in Cambridge last quarter was unbelievably bad. Our rework and scrap costs were thirty percent higher than normal. Absenteeism was a phenomenal twenty percent."

"Another quarter like this and we'll be a penny stock," Lowell said. "Another two quarters and we'll be in receivership."

Breal decided that sharing the thoughts that were now comforting him was in order. "I think we can see daylight," he said, and waited for the inevitable question.

Lowell glared at Breal. "What inspires you to this Candide-like view of our business?"

"Well, we've sold the building. That'll give us an influx of cash in a couple of weeks and allow us to finish our restructuring moves. Then the $5.70 per share gain from the sale will certainly dress up the income statement. We've finally ripped manufacturing out of Cambridge and have an excellent low-cost plant in Manchester coming on stream. Rostov's integrated circuit is finished and we're committing it to silicon this month. Assuming it passes reliability testing, market introduction isn't far away. Last month was a trough. After that, all of this effort will pay off."

Lowell sat down on the couch. "Those best-laid plans had better work out, George, for all of our sakes." Then, after a rueful smile, "But especially for mine."

When they left Lowell's office, Clare turned to Breal and said, "You know, there's an awful lot that can screw up that rosy scenario of yours."

"I know," Breal replied. "And the guy who can really screw it up isn't in Germany but short, bald, and right here."

"You got it."

# TWENTY-ONE

All of us have it. Think of it as an internal map. Where we have been, where we are going. Sometimes I feel a membrane, soft, diaphanous, the color of egg white, interposing itself between me and the world. The map is blurred, pieces gone. I stare at myself in the glass: old age, a ship's silted wreckage—confusion lodged in the eyes. The trick is to concentrate. Forget the map. Tend to the details. God is in the details. I stare deeper into the glass, squint: eyes unsound. Beard hides the sinking jowls, hair growing in tufts from unlikely places. We all preside over our own dissolution. If you don't like your face at seventy-five, you have only yourself to blame. Easy wisdom. Little aphorisms to live by. I imagine myself being ferried across a river—a small, crowded boat, the night dark, moonless, everyone draped in an identical black cape, the only sounds the creak of oarlocks and the plash of oars—each of us holds a coin in his mouth to pay for the passage. Who said there is nothing serious in mortality? Macbeth, was it? All is but toys. The wine of life is drawn. The sere and the yellow leaf. Cerise. It would be good to see Cerise. Paris. Thoughts come and go like fireflies. Chunks of time disappear without a trace as though never lived. One morning I will not wake up. Concentrate. Stay alert to the small signs. The details.

THROUGH EARLY October, David Clare bent his efforts toward finding a headquarters building. Breal urged him to spend every waking hour on the project. Clare contacted three real estate brokers and inspected some fifty vacant buildings within the circle of Route 495 inward toward Boston. Lowell and Breal visited Clare's best choices. Lowell looked around one entryway, then frowned when he was told the building shared the lobby with other occupants. "The old man doesn't want to mix with aliens," Clare said. "That'll scrub most of the buildings around." Other structures caused Lowell to shake his head before the group had even stepped inside. "Architecture is in a sorry state," he said.

After they left the fifth candidate, Lowell said in the car, "I've had enough. What we have to do is buy a piece of land and design and build our own headquarters. An elegant building with our name and logo across the front. A structure worthy of ETI." He leaned back in his seat; the day of traveling and trudging around buildings had tired him. "Yes," he said in an absentminded way, "that's the ticket. Design and build our own headquarters."

A desperate Breal debated whether to air the harsh reality to a weary Lowell, and decided to wait. Norwood Properties intended to tear down the Cambridge building after the structure was vacated. ETI was renting back the building on a month-to-month basis until it moved headquarters—in effect paying interest on a $16 million dollar loan—the outflow at least three times the cost of office space. Money was disappearing like soda pop sucked through a straw. ETI had to move, and quickly. In Breal's office, Clare voiced the same thought. "The business is in deep yogurt. You've got to get the old man to drop this roll-your-own crap. We can't afford to screw around and custom-build our headquarters."

That night Breal lamented his fate to Susan. "I think you're drowning in two feet of water," she said. "What we have here is a man with an Edifice complex. He wants to build a monument to himself and his company. He probably visualizes the place standing alone on the horizon, bathed in a golden light like the Emerald City in the Wizard of Oz.

You have to see the building the way he does—as Lowell's last erection."

Breal raised his eyes heavenward. "Susan, what are you trying to tell me?"

"I'm saying that you *know* what he wants: a building all his very own, possibly with a magnificent lobby, and a long facade on which you can emblazon the company name and logo. It would also be nice if it were on a hill. As he sat in his office he would have the feeling that he was commanding a ship, steering it to safety through U-boat infested waters. Anyway, that's the idea. Turn your bird dog Clare loose on finding a building something like that. Then, if you could arrange to have The Great Man stumble onto it, as though he'd found it himself, that would be ideal."

The next morning Breal went into Lowell's office to obtain a signature and found him bent over the elliptical table, a sheet of drafting paper taped to the surface, a perspective view of a building taking shape on it. Lowell was animated as he pointed out the virtues of his design. When Breal left, he hurried in a panic to Clare's office. "We've got to locate an acceptable building and fast. Lowell is busily designing his own. If he gets much further along, pride in his own creation is going to keep him from considering anything else." Breal then broached Susan's idea and implored Clare to hurry.

The following Monday, Clare came into Breal's office obviously pleased. "I spent the weekend looking for your building. I think I've found it. It's got everything you wanted—a super lobby two stories high with an enormous domed skylight, a big deal entrance, space for our name and logo in front—it's all there. It's even on top of a hill, not a big hill, but a hill."

"Where is it?"

"That's the best part. It's right off Route 128 in Burlington. Isn't that where the old man lives? He won't have a big commute to get to work. The building is sixty thousand square feet, about what we need. We'd take the whole thing. No aliens."

Breal found his first view of the building promising. It stood at the top of a rise and was sided with brown pebbled slabs, causing it to blend into its wooded surroundings. The structure was three stories high, the windows half the height of each floor and wrapped around the entire perimeter, each pane separated from the next by thin aluminum mullions. It did indeed look like an ocean liner about to set sail. The grounds had newly planted trees, shrubs and sod. The entry-way and lobby were all Clare had said. The interior of the three floors was an empty shell to be laid out, and walls constructed to suit the tenant.

"How do we get the old man to look at it?" Breal asked. "He's buried in his own design."

"I've got a plan," Clare said. "You don't even have to think about it."

The next day Lowell strode into Breal's office still wearing his hat. "I just found our building," he said. "Get your coat. Let's go look at it right now."

On the way, Lowell said, "You and your team were asleep at the switch on this one, George. My chauffeur found the place."

LOWELL SAID he planned to be actively involved in the layout of the headquarters building. As Breal and Clare completed the negotiation of the lease, Breal wondered what Lowell had in mind. Clare had located an interior designer named Pamela Brewster who had consulted on other buildings in the area. She was a long-boned woman in her late-thirties, stick figure, plain-faced, with an animated manner.

Brewster interviewed Lowell, and then prepared a floor plan which she submitted to him. He told Breal with evident satisfaction that she had caught the sense of openness that he wanted, particularly in the entryway. The lobby was cylindrical in shape; a curved staircase on either side of the entrance led to a second floor mezzanine. She suggested an imposing cylindrical desk for the guard who manned the lobby. This, she said, would accent the regal look of the staircases. She placed shrubbery and plants near the stairways to complement the great splash of sunlight that fell from the glass dome that capped the lobby. Lowell reserved the southwest corner on the executive floor for himself and made his office a duplicate of the one in Cambridge.

Lowell poured over the choices of carpeting, interior colors, and venetian blinds. He came in each morning with a new thought and asked for Pam Brewster first thing. He wanted a slate floor in the entryway and, to Breal's dismay, dragged him off during a freak November snowstorm to visit a slate quarry in Vermont. Lowell was particularly fussy about the company name and logo on the face of the building: he changed the size of the lettering and position of the logo three times before he was satisfied. Lowell wanted two flagpoles in front, one for the American flag and the other to fly the ETI flag. "I've never worked this closely with the chief executive before," said a puzzled Pam Brewster to Breal.

Musing aloud, Lowell said to Breal, "I wonder how Leo would look beside the entrance."

"Leo?"

"The lion," Lowell said impatiently.

Breal decided that a question was more prudent than a direct statement. "Don't you think, sir, that it would clash with a modern building?"

Lowell didn't answer, but the next day he ordered Clawson to have the statue hauled to Lowell House. He had a concrete slab poured beside the driveway, beyond the thicket of trees, and there the lion was carefully set down, facing toward the approaching world.

Lowell laid out the striping in the parking lot, assigned reserved spaces for each of the executives and senior staff, and specified thirty visitor spots "for customers." "All those visitor spots are crazy," Clare said. "We never have customers visit headquarters. We get our business by having our salesmen visit them. Now we're going to have the best parking spots—those right in front of the building—vacant forever."

"Well, David," Breal said, "we have to decide which causes are worth fighting for. I don't think it's worth going to the mat over visitor parking spots. I've got to say, though, the building has certainly kept the old man occupied. I've never seen him so busy."

"It's not being busy that matters, it's what you're busy at."

Lowell visited the site every day. He complained to Breal of shoddy workmanship and asked him to speak to the superintendent. When the flagpoles were installed, he grumbled that they weren't straight and had Breal bring the workmen back to straighten them while Lowell supervised. Breal emphasized to Lowell the need for haste, the need to move. Lowell nodded agreement but continued to nitpick every detail.

Headquarters was moved over an unseasonably warm President's Day weekend. Lowell arranged each piece of furniture in his office and the executive conference room to be identical to its position in Cambridge. In the corridor outside his office, Lowell hung the large photograph of the old ETI management team.

The Tuesday following the holiday was an unpacking day as desks, chairs, tables, filing cabinets, engineering equipment, model shop machinery, and computers were put in place, and everyone settled down to work. Breal walked around the building and felt a buoyancy in the air. He commented to Clare that people probably sensed a new beginning, in attractive new offices, and were happy to be a part of it.

"We're out of Cambridge and that murderous rent," Clare said, "and there's plenty of money in the bank from the sale of the building. We've got a new lease on life. Everybody must feel it. I sure do."

Breal was pleased. He had succeeded in isolating Clare from Lowell, at least for a while.

At nine o'clock in the morning of the following day the fire alarm went off. Gongs sounded all over the building. Employees wandered out into the parking lot as three trucks from the Burlington Fire Department, making a great racket, arrived. It was a sunny morning and the outing took on a holiday spirit; people chatted and laughed while drinking coffee and asking where the fire was. Breal found the fire chief: there was no fire. A technician was welding pieces of steel to make a pad for a lathe and the smoke from his welding torch had triggered the smoke detector.

As Breal spoke with the fire chief, he saw the black Cadillac limousine ease through the crowd and into its reserved parking space. The chauffeur leaped out to open the door, but Lowell was already out of the car. Breal hastened over to Lowell and was about to explain when Lowell, scanning the throng in the parking lot, exclaimed, "What in the name of heaven is going on?"

As Breal described the circumstance of the false alarm to Lowell, the fire trucks, lights flashing, drove away.

"False alarm," Breal announced. "Everybody back to work." The people straggled back into the building.

Thirty minutes later Breal was summoned to Lowell's office. "There's no way we can live with the productivity loss I saw when I drove up this morning," Lowell said, mouth tight, and handed Breal a letter. "I've written this for your signature." Breal read the single paragraph as Lowell stared out at the parking lot. The letter directed that in the event the fire alarm sounded, all personnel in the building shall first call Breal's office to determine whether there truly is a fire. Only after receiving his approval could they evacuate the building.

The right approach, Breal decided, was to buy time; there was then the possibility that since the letter was written in haste, Lowell might think better of it. "Why don't I take the letter with me," Breal said. "I'd like to study it before signing."

"There's nothing to study. The letter is only three sentences long."

Breal adopted his even tone. "Dr. Lowell, I value your judgment on matters of business and matters of life"—Lowell peered at him with narrowed eyes—"but I have some problems with this letter. First, there's no way for me, sitting in my office, to know when a fire alarm goes off whether there really is a fire or not. But if I did know, and was willing to stay in my office while the building was burning, the first person that called might reach me, but the next would get a busy signal. Second, these new office buildings contain huge quantities of plastic. For instance, the rug in the corridors is all nylon. Plastic burns fast and hot, so the building needs to be evacuated quickly or people may be trapped."

"What do you suggest then?" Lowell asked. "The situation now is intolerable."

"The false alarm was triggered by a welding torch in the engineering model shop. Since this place is armed with smoke detectors, I'll make arrangements for smoke-producing activities, such as welding and brazing, to be done in a special area where there is no danger of triggering the alarm."

"All right," Lowell said; his face appeared to sag—wrinkled and weary, a grandfather's face—and with a small gesture he dismissed the problem.

In late February, one month prior to the annual meeting, Lowell promoted Breal to executive vice president and made him a member of the board of directors. Now all department heads, including Tergelen, reported to him. Concurrent with his appointment, Lowell presented Breal with an added bonus of ten thousand shares of ETI stock, payable at the rate of two thousand shares per year, and an option on an additional fifteen thousand shares.

Victor Cobb wrote Breal a letter of congratulations and gave him a firm handshake of welcome at Breal's first board meeting. Lowell commented that anyone who could get rid of a union and sell the Cambridge building for sixteen million dollars deserved a seat on ETI's board. Breal fumbled through some words of gratitude saying that Lowell's faith in him would not be misplaced. Miles congratulated him after the meeting. Tergelen said nothing.

One morning Lowell appeared in Breal's office still wearing his hat and coat, and dragged him out to the parking lot. On the way, Lowell said, "After the annual meeting let's get out of here. Go to Europe—see what those clowns are up to. Spend a week in Paris. Take your wife. We've all earned a little R&R."

Lowell led Breal to the edge of the parking lot. They stood in the slanting March sunshine and Lowell pointed across the cars to the building. "Look at the facade," he said. "Some people leave their blinds open and others pull them shut. The effect is to make the line of windows look like a mouth with missing teeth. I want this place to be at its most attractive for the shareholders meeting, but those randomly open and shut blinds give the place a ratty appearance. I'd like you to ask everyone to keep their blinds drawn. They can adjust the amount of light they get by changing the angle of the slats. That's the virtue of venetian blinds."

Breal placed the subject on the same level as the fire alarm memorandum. This time, however, he dutifully issued a window blinds directive and refused to hear any complaints.

The annual meeting was held in the classroom, a replica of the one in Cambridge. Lowell made it a point to observe that the modern surroundings were but one reflection of the profound changes the company had undergone. He was very bullish. Earnings for the prior year were $4.21 per share, the proceeds from the sale of the building canceling out the losses from operations. Lowell in his speech summarized what had been accomplished, then set forth a vision of a new, competitive ETI emerging to restore the earnings pattern of the past. He waved the M-100 control at the assembled group and said that the unit was now in production and being enthusiastically received by ETI's customers. This, Breal knew, was only partially true. The unit was indeed in production but, because of ETI's record of premature product releases, was being received with caution by ETI's customers and distributors alike. The audience did not appear moved by Lowell's vision. After all, he had presented a similar picture the previous year and, after the one-shot gain from the building sale was subtracted out, the operating losses were there for all to see. At the end of Lowell's speech there was no applause, and even Mr. Horsfall was restrained in his praise for the chairman. Yet—Lowell later observed—somebody out there had faith because the stock edged up to nine.

# TWENTY-TWO

The two couples—Lowell and Edna Graham, and George and Susan Breal—left Boston on a Sunday evening. On board the United flight, Lowell immediately complained of a draft, and the stewardess, a young black-haired woman with a smile that caused even Susan to turn her head, adjusted the ventilation. Once in the air, she brought Lowell the martini, very dry, he had ordered, and then a second. Lowell's gaze followed her as she moved about the first class cabin. Finally he told Edna that he was going to skip dinner, loosened his seat belt, slumped against a pillow, and slept the rest of the flight.

They arrived at Charles de Gaulle airport at eleven Paris time on a gray drizzly morning. Edna looked out the window, complained about the weather, and kept smoothing her dress (of a color that could not be named), rumpled from her night on the plane. Susan observed to her husband that Edna always wore her clothes with a certain awkwardness, as though they were lent to her and would have to be returned in immaculate condition. "She doesn't look too keen on this trip," Breal remarked. Lowell received a last dazzling smile from the stewardess as he left the plane.

The group was met by Roland Lemec, ETI's head of European operations. Lemec, the wind dislodging the hair combed across his shiny scalp, glided around the party like a reptile while loading their bags into his Peugeot wagon, then headed onto the autoroute du Nord toward the city.

"When did you say you were last in Paris?" Edna asked Susan.

"The last time I saw Paris," Susan said, "my heart was a lot younger and gayer than it is now. It was about ten years ago. George tagged a vacation onto a European business trip and he and I spent a week here. Looking back, it's all a blur of museums, monuments, churches, restaurants, and rude people."

When they arrived at their hotel, the Bristol, on the Rue du Faubourg St. Honoré, Lowell said, "I'd like a shower and a nap. Why don't we meet in the lobby at four, do a little sightseeing, then have dinner."

When they met in the afternoon, the weather had cleared and a refreshed Lowell decided they would drive to the Left Bank, stroll along the Boulevard Saint-Michel, then stop at a cafe for an aperitif before dinner. In the Latin Quarter, Lowell pointed out the Hotel du Grand Condé where he had stayed on first arriving in Paris as a young man, the Sorbonne where he had attended the Cours de Civilisation and the tenement where he had roomed on the Rue St.-Julien-le-Pauvre, behind the Church of St.-Séverin. Edna walked beside him, a shawl like a cowl around her head.

"He makes the same pilgrimage every time he comes to Paris," Susan overheard Lemec say to Breal.

They passed two women, heavily made up, tight skirts at mid-thigh, one with pewter-colored hair, chatting with each other in an animated way.

"This place is full of whores," Edna said. "They seem to spend an awful lot of time yakking with each other. You wonder what on earth they have to say."

"I would guess they're having a tart to tart talk," Susan said.

Lowell glanced at her and smiled appreciatively.

They stopped at a café, and since the April evening was chilly and still damp, they sat indoors where Lowell ordered Dubonnet for all. The tour seemed to have put him in a reverie and he sipped his drink in silence. They walked to the Tour d'Argent for dinner. An elevator took them to the third floor dining room. Lemec had arranged for a window table that overlooked the Seine and the rear quarter of Notre Dame; the church was illuminated to a ghostly pallor by floodlights, and the flying buttresses that supported the walls appeared to rise from the river like the tentacles of a giant sea creature holding the structure in its grip. Periodically, a *bateau-mouche*—only sparsely filled with tourists—and which Edna claimed wasn't much smaller than the ferryboats that cruised between New Bedford and Martha's Vineyard, steamed down the river and illuminated the buildings on either side with broad beams of white light.

"What a ghastly thing to do," Lowell said, sipping his first martini. "You can't find the charm of Paris by lighting it as though it were a patient on an operating table. Anyone who thinks he's seeing Paris by the light of those boats is being badly misled."

Lowell insisted that everyone try the pressed duck, the specialty of the house, and chose a Châteauneuf-du-Pape to accompany the meal. He stared at the great cathedral beyond the window, seemed lost in some private musing, and said little throughout the dinner. He did grumble that the pressed duck wasn't what it used to be. Susan, who thought the duck looked as if it had died in the previous century and found it as tasty as canvas, commented to her husband that the dining room, with its dark wood paneling, heavy burgundy-colored drapes and glittering chandeliers, was a lot more impressive than the food.

When they returned to the Bristol, Susan said to Breal, "You know, George, I can't sleep now and it's useless for me to try. It may be ten o'clock at night here, but it's only four in the afternoon in Boston and that's what my body rhythms tell me. Why don't you rest while I take a walk. I'm sure the streets in this neighborhood are safe."

"Well, move briskly. At this hour someone might take you for a streetwalker."

"That's very flattering, George. I take that as a compliment."

Susan was about to leave the hotel when she saw a short man with a pearl-white beard crossing the lobby. "Dr. Lowell?" she called.

"Why, Susan . . . I was about to have a drink as an antidote to jet lag. Would you care to join me?"

"I was going to take a walk for the same reason. It's a pleasant night. Can I induce you to take a stroll?"

"You can induce me to do anything," Lowell said. "I'm sure a walk will do me more good than a drink."

On leaving the Bristol they turned east on the Faubourg St. Honoré, toward the presidential palace. "You know, I lived in Paris as a young man and studied here," Lowell said. He seemed to have forgotten that he had evoked those times during their walk in the Latin Quarter that afternoon. He went on to describe the Sorbonne as if he were describing a fragment of heaven, and then added, "There was a young lady I was quite serious with at the time."

"It must have been a delightful experience," Susan said. "To be a student in Paris, young and in love . . . It's difficult to ask for more." It occurred to her that the only real paradise was the one you have lost.

"It was a wonderful time," Lowell said. "I learned a great deal about the world and much about myself. In a way I grew up here, and whenever I visit there's always a sense of homecoming." He didn't speak for a while—he seemed to be in the midst of some internal debate—until he finally said, "The stewardess on the plane reminded me of my daughter."

"When did you last see her?"

"We had a falling out some twenty years ago and I hadn't seen her in all that time, then we reconciled. She has two sons . . . I must confess, it was a great pleasure to see her and meet my grandsons. They're fine young men. All three were rather hard-up financially and I did agree to help them. Then I learned of something." He went on to explain. "That act was so unworthy of a daughter of mine, I was so repulsed, that I decided again to have nothing to do with her. And, of course, not seeing her it would be awkward to see her children." He spoke of the event as a closed chapter.

Susan recalled staring at Edna's deformed toes as they sat in the Public Garden on a hot June day, and easily guessed how Lowell had learned of his daughter's past. There was, she had to concede, a tactical advantage to considering oneself the wronged party. And of course in war one did not feel sorry for the enemy. But at that moment, in the cool Paris night, Susan's heart went out to the proud old man beside her and she decided to ignore Edna's fears.

"But that must have occurred many years ago," Susan said.

"Does that make a difference? People do not change their nature. It occurred. That's what matters."

"Your daughter was young and no doubt in desperate need of money. She was too proud to ask you. Surely she's a different person now. People *do* change, you know, they mature, develop better judgment. How bad could she be having raised, as you yourself said, two fine young men?"

Lowell stared at the ground as they walked, and Susan was not sure he was listening but continued anyway.

"Dr. Lowell, why deny yourself the pleasure of your daughter's company, and that of your grandchildren, over something that happened decades ago? I spent a week last month visiting with our oldest daughter in Pennsylvania. She has two children, a boy and a girl. There's a sense of continuity and satisfaction that you feel in seeing your children raising children of their own, that some racial destiny is being fulfilled. That's very gratifying and can be gotten in no other way. It gives me a sense of peace and rightness, that while my life may have had its disappointments this most important part has turned out well. Also, as I get older, I find the circle of my friends narrowing, and all that really matters, and the greatest pleasure, comes from my family. Why deny yourself that when it's in your power to have it?"

"You didn't see the film," Lowell said. "I could never look at her in the same way after that. In fact, it would be difficult to look at her at all. I would keep seeing that movie."

They walked past the Rue d'Aguesseau and could see St. Michael's English church on their left. Susan was about to comment further, when she sensed a displacement in Lowell's attention. He was looking at a woman ahead of them who was leaning against a wall near a streetlamp. The light was insufficient for Susan to tell her age, but she saw the woman was dark-haired, had excellent legs, and looked expensive.

"*Bonsoir,*" the woman said and nodded encouragingly.

"*Bonsoir,*" Lowell said. The woman took a step away from the wall and Lowell shook his head.

"*Dommage,*" the woman said and returned to her station.

"If you're tempted, Dr. Lowell," Susan said, "I have no problem leaving."

"No, no," Lowell answered smiling. "'Tis one thing to be tempted, another thing to fall. You know, the French say that love is serious while sex is frivolous. Americans believe it's the other way around. I think the French are right. We make too much of these transient encounters."

They arrived at the intersection of the Faubourg St. Honoré and the Rue Royale. To their left was the Madeleine, its columned Roman facade dark and forbidding though floodlit, and to their right the lights and obelisk of the Place de la Concorde. "Shall we walk toward those lights before returning?" Susan asked.

Lowell gestured toward the square. "That's the . . ." he said, "that's the . . ."

Susan glanced at the old man. "The Place de la Concorde?" she suggested.

On returning to the Faubourg St. Honoré, they could see down the street the woman at the wall, dimly lit by the lamp. Approaching, Susan noticed that there was now something different yet familiar about her. A moment later, Lowell exclaimed under his breath, "Good Lord!" and quickened his step. Then Susan saw why.

"Edna, what are you doing here?" Lowell said.

"I couldn't sleep so I came out for some fresh air. Is anything wrong?" By the jauntiness of her tone, Susan knew that Edna had been drinking. She was also wearing makeup, something Susan had never seen before, her smile painted, whore-like.

"It isn't safe outside, alone at this hour," Lowell said.

"Oh, I don't know," Edna chirped mischievously, arching an eyebrow. "First one man then another tried to pick me up. Unfortunately, neither of them spoke English." She gave an abrupt and unexpected laugh. "Too bad because the second was quite attractive."

"Why don't we try to get some sleep," Lowell said and, head down, hastened toward the Bristol. Edna hesitated for a moment, shrugged and then followed.

It was clear to Susan that Edna was not at all displeased that Lowell had found her outside, and probably stationed herself by the streetlamp to wait for him.


WHILE LOWELL and Breal attended business meetings, Susan and Edna spent the following morning strolling along the Champs-Elysées, through the Tuileries where children were playing soccer, then on to the Louvre. When they tired of the paintings, they wandered in the sunshine across the Pont Neuf to the Île de la Cité and Notre Dame, and discovered that one could climb to the top, which they did along with a hundred other tourists. Susan thought the view of Paris— shimmering and floating below them, the pale gray basilica of Sacré Coeur to the north—magnificent—but the high rise buildings to the west reminded her of Manhattan and destroyed some of the city's magic.

The pair crossed to the Left Bank, to a small side street restaurant where the menu was handwritten in purple ink, and where they had lunch and killed a carafe of house white wine. Then they rested in the Luxembourg Garden. Taking in the sunshine, they sat on the great veranda, in front of the maple trees and the white marble statues of the ancient queens of France. They gazed past the encircling stone balustrade to the children sailing model boats in the octagonal pool and the Senate building beyond. Edna pulled a pack of Gitanes from her purse, took a cigarette from the compact blue box, and as she lit up commented that French cigarettes had a lot more sock than American and they never gave you smoker's cough.

"You know," Edna said, "John is going to spend the evening with a whore." She said this after taking a long drag on her Gitane and in the most casual way.

Susan didn't know how to respond. "How do you know that?" she asked.

"It's a ritual whenever he comes to Paris. It's the job of the European manager—in the old days Tergelen and now Lemec—to procure the girl . . . petite, brunette and about thirty-five are the specifications . . . preferably someone cheap. John has a weakness for cheap women. As a matter of fact he married one."

Susan's brow pulled together. "I thought his wife was something of a blue blood."

"That was his first wife. I'm talking about his second." Edna took another drag on her Gitane, inhaled French style, and Susan leaned back, gazed at two teenagers throwing a Frisbee, and resigned herself to hearing the story of Lowell's second marriage.

"This happened about fifteen years ago," Edna said. "There was a girl that worked in the plant, on the production line, an Italian girl named Fiorella Manzini. The name means Little Flower, and that's what they tell me she was. John is really a business recluse, you know; he rarely leaves his office. But once he spotted the girl, he toured the plant every day and sometimes twice a day."

"How old was she?"

"Middle twenties, something like that. He got her address from personnel and sent her flowers. She lived with her family in the North End and they said they'd kill John if his intentions weren't honorable. He invited her to Lowell House, but her family said she wasn't going to set foot in the place without a wedding ring. I'm sure they had their eyes glued on John's money."

"How did he get to talk to her?"

"He would ask the employee relations man to call her to personnel on some dumb excuse or other. When she went everyone knew where she was going, and they'd yell, 'Make him pay for it, Fio!' That upset her because I understand she rather liked John. He can be a very charming character when he wants to be. Sometimes he took her out to dinner but she had to be home by ten. Everyone in the North End must have been impressed when that big Cadillac limo rolled up to her house. This went on for months. I, of course, was long gone. But John, when he wants something, particularly something he can't or shouldn't have, becomes a man obsessed. After the years we had been together, he just let me walk out the door. The son of a bitch even offered to carry my suitcase." At the last sentence, Edna dropped her unemotional tone, turned to Susan, eyes wide, and said, "Can you believe that?

"John was looking haggard. He was impossible to deal with. I'm sure everyone at the plant was praying for him to marry the girl so he would stop being such a pain in the ass. Finally, I guess he just couldn't stand it anymore. She wanted a big church wedding but he convinced her that a little private ceremony would do fine. She agreed on the condition that for their honeymoon they take a Caribbean cruise. I guess it's something she'd always wanted to do. So they were married and the Italians had a party after the ceremony, and everybody got drunk and danced and sang songs and welcomed John to the family. Knowing John, I'm sure he didn't enjoy that party much. I suppose it never occurred to him that cheap women come from cheap families. Anyway, John finally got to wrap his arms around the Little Flower."

Susan gazed out at the world before her: on the pool, the children's boats floated like innocent thoughts; in the stillness of the afternoon the scene took on the serenity of an impressionist painting, incongruent with the tale of obsession and betrayal Edna was relating. "How long did it last?" Susan asked.

Edna lit another Gitane. "Not too long. As a matter of fact it's probably the shortest marriage on record. They flew to Puerto Rico and picked up a cruise ship in San Juan. The marriage lasted three days. When they got to St. Croix she left the boat and took a plane back to the North End. I don't know how they found out about it, but the *Herald-Examiner* ran a headline, BOSTON GIRL JILTS ELDERLY TYCOON ON HONEYMOON IN VIRGIN ISLANDS."

"Why did she leave?"

"Nobody knows, but there are lots of theories. Some say John threw a tantrum with little Fio—he can do that, you know, and the first time you see a John Lowell tantrum it can be quite a shock—and she told him to fuck off." Susan had never before heard Edna use a real obscenity, and she said it in the most matter-of-fact way; for the first time in Edna's narrative Susan perceived the depth and bitterness of Edna's feelings. "But there are other theories, a lot less nice. Anyway, John had the marriage annulled, but it cost him plenty."

"What happened to the girl?"

"I don't know. She went back to her Italian neighborhood and disappeared."

"How did he coax you back?"

"John courted me for a year after the breakup. He said it was an aberration, a midlife crisis, and he'd gotten it out of his system. He was his most charming self—sent me gifts, thoughtful little surprises—and I was lonely. My whole life had been wrapped around John. Going back was the easiest thing to do." Susan pictured the two of them, like a long-married couple who'd had a temporary falling out, comfortably resuming their previous life, like dropping their feet into old house slippers. "But the old goat still has his Paris ritual," Edna went on, "and he knows that I know. He also knows that I'm not going to do anything about it. I don't view it as seriously as I used to. If John wants to spend a debauched evening in Paris, then what the hell. At the age of seventy-six, how much harm can it do?

"I pulled out of Lemec that John has been seeing the same whore for the last ten years." Edna uttered this in a dispassionate voice, yet her tone had subtly altered; and when Susan glanced at her, she found Edna's face pinched and pink blotches had appeared on her cheeks. Pity for the poor woman beside her rose in Susan and she had an urge to embrace her. She saw that the wrongs inflicted on Edna were incurable wounds that would throb forever, that whatever love Edna may have felt for Lowell had long ago withered. She wondered whether all those who had loved Lowell had suffered the same fate, had their love destroyed by his lack of understanding of the nature of affection and what it asked of the recipient.

"John is a creature of habit," Edna said. "When he gets comfortable with something he doesn't change easily."


LOWELL HANDED the taxi driver the card with the Rue Massenet address that Lemec provided him on every trip. Cerise's mother, Mme. Poulaine, opened the door, welcomed him, said her daughter was dressing, led him to the *salon* and offered him a drink. Lowell relaxed on the sofa, sipped a Dubonnet, once again admired the Louis XVI furniture, and felt the touch of a vanished world. He experienced the sense of peace this apartment always gave him, enjoyed its classic look, its restrained elegance. He chatted with Mme. Poulaine; she spoke slowly, never corrected his French.

A tiny chime sounded and a smiling Mme. Poulaine said he could go upstairs. Cerise greeted him at the top of the stairs, lights dim. She wore a body-hugging deep blue gown, slit down the front from mid-thigh. Her black hair was cut short, emphasizing the bones of her face and the shape and size of her eyes. Lowell kissed her cheek and the warmth and fragrance of her body caused a wave of relaxation to pass over him. She led him to her room, fixed him a drink while he leaned back in a bergère easy chair of blue velvet. The room, carpeted in deep burgundy, carried a delicate scent, a light perfume he experienced nowhere else. He gazed at the king-sized bed against a draped wall—the drape, he knew, could be drawn to reveal a mirror which extended the full length of the bed—the two chairs with lyre-shaped backs, the chiffonier, the corner cupboard and the book cabinet, all decorated in gilt and porcelain with rosettes, ovoli, entwined ribbons, gadroons, satyrs, and nymphs. The lamps were arranged so the lighting was a subtle interplay of light and dark shadows.

"We have not seen each other in a long while, my dear John," Cerise said as she handed him a martini. "How have you been?" Her accent was British/French.

"My company has had its difficulties," Lowell said. "Very great difficulties that have taken all of my time." He made a small gesture, sighed. "And all of my energy as well."

Cerise sat on one of the lyre-backed chairs, sipped a Campari, her naked legs now on display as the slit in her gown opened. Lowell had to admit, Cerise had splendid legs She contemplated him for a long moment. "Have you ever thought of selling it?" she asked.

"Selling what?"

"Your company. The source of all your frustration."

Lowell admired Cerise's pragmatic wisdom: he had always found her a shrewd observer of events. Lowell sipped his martini—as if by magic, Cerise always got his drink right. "The company has been my whole life," he said. "How do you sell your life?"

"You have the soul of a poet, John," she said with a light laugh. "You see your life so harshly. Your company is but one part of it. There surely are other parts. Perhaps it is time to emphasize those."

Cerise smiled, a wide glamorous smile. She had a broad, full mouth, superb teeth. But now, as Lowell adjusted to the dim light, he saw that the years were beginning to show on her. The smile had revealed wear around her eyes, and two hard lines that makeup couldn't hide were now incised around her mouth.

Cerise's last remark caused Lowell to think of his trustee-ships, at MIT and the Museum of Fine Arts, then of young Michael and Tom, and finally, with a sudden pulse of sorrow, of Catherine. There were other parts to his life. But sell ETI? That was unthinkable.

Lowell gently shook his head. Work was everything to a man. Without it there was nothing. Money meant little. Command was everything. He could not explain this to Cerise. He said, "My family has only caused me disappointment and pain. I am best staying away from it." Yet as he said this, Lowell was aware of the lack of conviction in his voice. He sensed that he was fishing for something—but not sure what. Perhaps hope. He was pleased when Cerise asked, "How have they hurt you?"

Lowell, hesitantly, unburdened himself of the weight that had oppressed him since he had written the letter to Catherine. He had spoken of it yesterday evening with Susan Breal and here he was, repeating it again.

"Why, my dear John," Cerise said, truly astonished. "You have banished your daughter over a silly indiscretion that happened a thousand years ago? The indiscretion of a desperate young mother trying to provide for her children? For that you are denying yourself the pleasure of your grandsons? *Mon cher, Jean*, your pride, *votre orgueil*, how misplaced it is!"

Cerise's words reached some secret part of him, as though she had found a crack through which his soul could be touched. He once again thought of the film: it had grown unclear, blurred like the memory of a nightmare. Then he remembered his daughter's face when she had magically appeared before him at the Museum of Fine Arts, and in the same recollection he remembered Lou—the two most important women in his life, radiant as jewels. What a mess he had made of things!

"Would you like another drink?" Cerise asked. "Or perhaps you would like to relax in bed."

"Let's not make love, *chérie*," Lowell said. "At least not yet. Let's just sit and talk. And yes, I would like another drink."

And so Cerise mixed Lowell another drink, and they sat and chatted like old lovers who had become friends. Lowell, surprising himself, emotion thickening his voice, told Cerise how much he loved his daughter and his grandsons and how, though he knew it was late, he wanted to shelter them from the hard edges of life, shield them from the random disasters visited upon the world. He thought he was babbling like a lunatic but went on anyway.

## TWENTY-THREE

Dick Miles was seated at the marble table, papers before him, when Breal entered Lowell's office. Lowell turned from the window, which no longer looked out across the Charles to the Boston skyline but to a parking lot, a line of high tension wires, and a wooded area beyond. Since their return from Europe, Lowell had been in good spirits. Breal thought Lowell must feel as he did because things were going better. Profitability had crept over breakeven after the move to New Hampshire and was increasing as the efficiency of the plant improved. The M-100 was in full production and sales of the unit were rising. The financial community must have sensed this improvement in ETI's fortunes for the stock edged up to eleven.

"Have you read this article?" Lowell asked Breal, pointing to the *Wall Street Journal*. The headline dealt with salesmen's compensation.

"No, sir," Breal said, "but I can scan it quickly right now."

"Let me give you the gist," Lowell said, perching himself on the arm of the couch. "This consulting company claims that salesmen should receive at least a quarter of their income via incentive compensation . . . We don't compensate our sales people that way, do we?"

"No, we don't. Our sales force is on straight salary."

"I believe ours is the proper philosophy. Don't you agree?"

"Well, there are alternative perspectives on the issue, as that article no doubt argues."

"I'd be willing to debate that with you," Lowell said, smiling benignly at Breal. "You take the devil's advocate position."

Miles gathered up his papers and stood up. "If you don't need me anymore, sir . . ."

"No, no," Lowell said, "why don't you stay and support George. He'll need all the help he can get." Lowell seemed in a playful mood.

"My view," Lowell stated, "is that a salesman is a professional, like an engineer or a finance man. He has an assignment and is expected to carry it out. None of these other functions are given a special reward for doing the job they're paid to do in the first place. Why should a salesman be treated differently?"

"Well, in an ideal world you would be absolutely right," Breal said, assuming his devil's advocate role. "But a salesman is the least supervised individual in a company. He spends much of his day alone in a car fighting traffic. He deals with people who, in general, consider him a nuisance and a waste of time and just want to be rid of him. He's in a constant struggle to get other people's attention. It's a lonely, frustrating job. Since his boss can't be there to check whether he's giving a hundred percent, and since good excuses are always available, a reasonable approach is to make a portion of a salesman's salary depend on results. In that way excuses no longer matter. If he doesn't perform he gets paid less, and the absence of supervisory motivation is compensated by economic motivation." Breal thought he had presented a reasonable case, but noticed that Lowell was frowning.

"Motivation lies within oneself," Lowell said. He rose from the couch. "As a young engineer and entrepreneur, I worked sixteen-hour days to found this company because success was important to me. What a man accomplishes depends on the demon within. If a man does not have the will to succeed, then setting a bushel of money before him will not create it."

"But wasn't your desire to succeed an ambition for the economic reward success would bring?" Breal looked at Lowell's face and decided this would be his last rebuttal.

"Ambition?" Lowell cried, "fling away ambition! By that sin fell the angels. We're not talking about that at all. I founded this company out of the urge to create a great enterprise, to make a difference in an indifferent world, and you speak to me of ambition. I don't think you understand the nature of entrepreneurship and the single-mindedness of purpose that lies behind it." Lowell glared at Breal, his face tense and suspicious. "Why are you disagreeing with me? Why have you chosen to be defensive and negative?"

"You asked me to be, Dr. Lowell. You asked that I play devil's advocate. The issue was salesmen's compensation."

Breal, who felt a heat-seeking missile bearing down on him, was about to point to the *Wall Street Journal* article when Lowell thundered, "I asked you to do no such thing! I have no interest in silly debating games."

"Perhaps I misunderstood," Breal said.

Throughout this exchange, Miles had pushed himself to the side, a man who hoped to be forgotten. Now, in a stealthy gesture, he took his papers in hand and came to his feet.

"Where are *you* going?" Lowell exclaimed.

"I believe, sir, that our business is concluded," Miles said.

"Did I ask George to be a devil's advocate?"

And Breal, with a sinking heart, watched Miles, loyal as a golden retriever, answer, "No, sir, you did not."


NIGHT IS the worst time. The feeling that some essential part of me is dissolving in the dark, disappearing in a fine mist like vapor from a pond. I ask what happened today? Whom did I see? What questions did I ask and what were the answers? Like peering into a strange room: incoherent voices, senseless movement. I hesitate to think back. Chunks of time vanish without a trace as though never lived. What happened to peaceful sleep? Wilt thou upon the high and giddy mast seal up the ship-boy's eyes . . . How does that go? Look it up. Things have grown oddly foreign—my shoes, ties, shirts, my own face—newly seen. Like lifting the trunk of a strange automobile and viewing its contents. The house is growing foreign: walls in odd places, doors disappearing. The world shifting, out of balance. My voice. Sometimes I listen to my own voice, its timbre, quality, and hear it for the first time. Alone, I speak aloud, hold discourse with the incorporeal air. Often chilled. Need more clothes now. Stumbling into the mists of old age, memory an empty attic. Catherine. That film: a melted ooze of female bodies. But the face, the face was Catherine. Another Catherine, someone I've never known. Does she still exist? Who told me to forgive? Cerise? The Breal woman? Forgive what exactly? When you think about it, Catherine is the granddaughter of an actor, has an actor's blood. She may have taken a wrong turning—this wasn't exactly *Antony and Cleopatra* or *Saint Joan*—but it was acting all the same. Edna, poor Edna. Sees it as a battle for my heart, or is it my purse? Sleep, knits up the ravel'd sleeve. Where is sleep? . . . Did you ever think of the inside of your head as a room? I think of mine that way, a room lit by a dying fire, me staring into the flickering dark. Catherine. I've been waiting for her like some tireless watcher at a window, a foolish fond old man. Go off with Catherine. Pitiful old Lear, a man defeated by age. Cordelia. Come, let's away to prison. We two alone will sing like birds i' the cage. When thou dost ask my blessing, I'll kneel down. And ask of thee forgiveness. . . . What's the rest of it? Not many useful thoughts occur in the middle of the night.

THE M-100 had gone into full production with surprisingly few difficulties. Breal credited Rostov and Frank Norrie for this success. They respected each other and worked well together. Norrie tracked every failed production unit, insisted on knowing the source of failure that very day, and immediately took corrective action. He and Rostov dealt with problems by phone, calling each other at home nights and weekends, communicating this sense of urgency and responsibility to the manufacturing engineers, the inspectors, the women on the production lines. As the product proved itself trouble-free in the field, the initial caution of ETI's distributors and customers was turning to enthusiasm and sales were accelerating.

Lowell now made it a point to attend Breal's engineering progress meetings. As Breal watched Lowell take a seat on the window side of the conference table, next to Tergelen, he took comfort in the fact that the next generation of new products—built, like the M-100, around custom integrated circuits—was moving along well. Rostov had made the difference. He and Clare had developed a niche market strategy, searching for markets less heavily populated with competitors. They had identified four niche markets and new products were under development in each. The first product Rostov termed an intrinsically safe control, a unit which stored so little energy within itself that it could never, even if inadvertently short-circuited, generate a spark and ignite a combustible mixture around it. The product would have great appeal to certain customers and could command a high price, but its cost to manufacture was no greater than a standard unit so it would boost the company's profitability. Mühlmann had no such product nor was it clear that they were even interested in these specialty markets.

The other participants stirred as Lowell took his seat; they all sat straighter, appeared more alert. "We have the intrinsically safe unit in computer simulation," Warren Slater was saying, "and it works great but we can't apply for Underwriters Laboratory approval until we have the packaged control to send them for testing, and those guys usually dawdle around for a couple of months."

"What's the bottom line?" Breal interrupted.

"I'd say we're a year away from full production," Slater concluded.

Lowell, who had been fidgeting through Slater's presentation, now came to his feet. "What's happened to the fire in engineering? We don't *have* a year. When I started this company—" Breal saw the Detroit story coming. He looked around the table: there was no change in expression, just the usual wary watchfulness. "—I would go to Detroit, get an order, Craig would design the product and we'd build it and ship it in a week. I'd like to know why it now takes a year to go from design to production." He turned to Tergelen. "Andre, do you understand why it should take a year to bring this product to market?"

"No, not at all," Tergelen said.

"Time is the one commodity we don't have," Lowell said. "We can throw money at this project. We can throw manpower. But not time."

Breal decided, reluctantly, that for his own protection he had best come to the aid of his chief engineer. "I share your sense of urgency, Dr. Lowell," he said, "but we're developing a control that's designed specifically for operation in hazardous environments. We've got to be absolutely certain it'll do that flawlessly before we put it in the field. It wouldn't do to blow up a petroleum refinery or cause a mine explosion."

"I applaud your caution," Lowell said. "I'm not saying do not test. I'm not saying damn the torpedoes full speed ahead. I am mindful of liability and I'm aware that prudence is the better part of valor. But I do not, as you gentlemen do, equate these things with time. I want to see this product in full production by the end of the year so we can feature it in the annual report. What is today's date?"

"May 28th," Breal said.

"That gives us . . . how long?" Lowell's brow wrinkled as he performed the calculation.

Breal decided not to help; a distant memory came to him: his father staring into his bourbon said, apropos of nothing, "The Sioux do not have a word for time."

"Seven months," Lowell concluded. "Slater, modify your chart to telescope this affair into seven months."

Lowell turned to Tergelen. "Andre, this is the most exciting new product we've introduced in years. I want the sales brochure to contain elegant graphics and be of the highest quality."

When the meeting adjourned, Lowell beckoned Breal to his office. "You may think I'm being unreasonable, George," he said, "and perhaps I am. But show me a man who is willing to listen to reason and I'll show you a lousy manager. Technology may be more sophisticated now than it was forty years ago when I was selling in Detroit, but I can't believe what took us a week then must take a year now. What we have here is a hardening of the engineering arteries."

"We'll do what we can to put the intrinsically safe control into production by the end of the year," Breal said, "but I doubt whether we can push Slater to get *everything* done on a crash basis."

"In that case," Lowell said, speaking carefully now, each word as precise as a blade, "we had better get ourselves someone who can."

In the succeeding weeks Lowell's emphasis in Breal's meetings never varied: he hammered at time. When Lowell appeared, Slater took on the frightened look of a man facing an armed intruder. Breal doubted whether Lowell understood the nature of the new products or their level of sophistication. He confused the function of one device with another, and his knowledge was superficial and prone to error. In truth, Breal did not consider Lowell's emphasis on time all bad, but it had an obsessive mindless quality that swept away all judgment and made it dangerous.

One morning Warren Slater stood at the door to Breal's office. He appeared thinner. "I've upped my jogging miles," he said, answering a question that had not been asked. "It helps me deal with this place." He entered the office, shut the door. "George," he said, "I don't know how much longer

I can handle the old man. He comes down to my office every day. 'When is this going to get done?' is his favorite question. He asks me that every twenty-four hours." Slater's voice took on a querulous tone. "Isn't there some way you can get this guy off my back?"

CATHERINE SAT opposite Lowell at the Algonquin Club. Miss Krane had called to make the appointment, as if it were a business meeting. He appeared to have difficulty starting the conversation. He sipped his martini, gaze drifting to the window and the traffic on Commonwealth Avenue, the world on the gray edge of evening. He had aged more than she would have anticipated in the year since she had last seen him. Then there was disorder in small things: his beard was ragged and, astonishingly, his shirt cuff was frayed. He spoke of the weather, the cold spring, though she remembered it as unusually warm. He said his business was improving, yet when he said this he appeared morose. His voice had taken on a robotic quality. He seemed a man who had lost something, yet not sure himself what it was.

"I'm grateful, Father, that you continue to pay for my schooling, for Michael's and the rest," Catherine said. "I'm starting my senior year this fall. It's hard work, especially since I've been away from school so long, but I'm into the rhythm of it now and I like law. Maybe it appeals to some basic sense of order that I have, or maybe it's mother's influence, I don't know, but I do enjoy it. It was the right thing for me to do. It would have been impossible without you. I'm deeply grateful." He nodded, seemed pleased, though she had the impression it was less with what she was saying than that she had taken the burden of conversation on herself. "I'm sorry I've done things that hurt you, Father," she finally said.

"Everyone does foolish things sometimes," Lowell said, eyes drifting away. "There's no need for me to punish you over it. And there's no need to punish myself."

"Is there anything I can do for you?"

"I would like to see you and I would like to see my grandsons."

"We would all like that."

Lowell took a long swallow of his drink. "Strange things are happening to me, Kate. I have a feeling of impending disaster, though I can't say where this feeling comes from, or what form disaster will take or when it will strike." He stared at his martini glass, then gave her a brittle smile. Gloom seemed to have seeped into his soul and lodged there—a man preparing for his own funeral.

"Those fears sometimes come to all of us," Catherine said. "It'll pass." She put her hand on his and was surprised at how cold it was.

Lowell turned his hand, held hers. "I doubt it'll pass," he said, "but I do know that while I can I'd like to spend time with you and your children."

"We would like nothing better. And the boys, who have never really known a father, admire you so much."

Lowell squeezed her hand, let go and looked away, and Catherine thought his eyes blurred. "Tell me," he finally said, now looking directly at her, "is there anything else I should know? I suppose I'm talking about skeletons in the closet . . . It's best that I know. I'll not be angry. I want to be certain there are no further surprises."

"I'm engaged to be married," Catherine said and experienced a twinge of guilt, as if she had confessed a crime—the last time she had told him this, well over a quarter century ago, a distant echo in her mind.

Lowell's face slackened, went blank, then he rallied. "I should congratulate you," he said. "Who's the lucky man?"

"He drives a cab by day and is translating Dante's *Divine Comedy* into English the rest of the time." Catherine felt a need to say more but held back, not certain why. She again touched her father's hand. "I think you would like him," she said, not at all sure that he would.

"You were always drawn to scholarly men," Lowell said. "A taxi driver scholar. The ones I've talked to were usually philosophers . . . When will you be married?"

"We haven't set a date."

"Can I meet the man?"

"Certainly," Catherine said, and felt in the pit of her stomach the twang of an ancient apprehension.

"I'll arrange a dinner at Lowell House."

That night, at home, Catherine asked herself why she had shied away from telling her father that Ishmael was black. She now realized that she no longer thought of him as black. He was just Ishmael, a caring loving man who himself needed care and love. To say he was black must have struck her as wrong, as though she were warning her father, confessing some sin. Yet perhaps in a sense she *had* warned him. For when he asked for hidden skeletons she had immediately brought up marriage and that meant Ishmael.

# TWENTY-FOUR

Mid-June, summer was approaching but the ducks had not appeared at the new headquarters building. Breal toyed with the idea of somehow finding a pair of ducks and having them hang around the doorstep for Lowell to discover. "How do you locate a pair of ducks and bring them to Burlington and have them stay put?" he asked Susan. "And who would I assign to do something as bizarre as that?"

"Well, in light of Lowell's views on the true nature of the ducks, how about personnel?"

Lowell never mentioned the missing ducks to Breal. He imagined Lowell hesitating when he came in, looking about, sensing that something was now missing and the round of the seasons not complete, then going to his office with the vague hope that perhaps tomorrow would set things right. Breal wondered whether Lowell also missed the sight of his stone lion when he came in to work, then he remembered that the lion was guarding the entrance to Lowell House and the old man saw him morning and evening.

Breal spoke to key members of the sales force. Ken Kruger, their lead salesman in Pennsylvania, was more than happy to share his good news. "We were so glad to see that M-100 that we just gobbled it up and we've been pushing hell out of it ever since. In fact, it's now gotten the attention of the OEMs who'd switched to Mühlmann. They've all ordered trial quantities." Then, eyes bright, he finished, "We're getting the market back. We'll beat shit out of those Krauts yet." In general, Breal heard more of the same: the salesmen were upbeat about the launch of the M-100 and said the distributors, who were starved for new product, were overjoyed. The price of the unit was the same as its Mühlmann counterpart.

Breal wandered past the potted plants and into Warren Slater's office. "You're not going to hound me about schedule, are you?" Slater said. He had acquired a belligerency that Breal had never seen in him before.

"No," Breal said, "it hadn't occurred to me. Why? Has the old man been bugging you?"

"I have the feeling he lives here," Slater said. "This guy is relentless. He asks the same questions every day. I don't know if he's trying to trip me up or what. Anyway, my wife says I ought to look for another job. Nothing is worth this kind of aggravation."

Breal could see that Lowell's impatience had worked its way like a plumber's snake into Slater's psyche. Two weeks later Slater quit. He said goodbye to everyone except Lowell and left. Breal, with Lowell's approval, appointed Emil Rostov vice president of engineering.

LOWELL, COBB, Breal, Tergelen, Miles and Miss Krane sat at the elliptical table for the board meeting. Every board member with the exception of Lowell had brought a folder of papers. Lowell asked Miles, as treasurer, to report on the financial results for the last quarter.

As Miles compared sales and profit for the second quarter with the same period in the prior year, Lowell yawned, gazing off toward some distant space. "Things have definitely improved," Cobb said as Miles concluded.

"Not nearly enough," Lowell said. "George, give General Cobb a rundown on where we stand in new product development."

Breal went through the status of each new product and when production start was scheduled.

"You must understand, Victor," Lowell said, "that what we have here is a curious new phenomenon, namely that time matters very little or not at all. It's certainly a far cry from the old days when we built and delivered in a week. I'm told the effect is due to the complexity of modern technology. I don't believe any of it. What we have here is complacency. Nobody is motivated to get the job done quickly or well. Think back to the war, Victor, to our war. In the space of four short years, from scratch, we designed and built the atomic bomb, fighters and bombers of remarkable performance, radars of every description, thousands of liberty ships, tanks, armament of every type. In this weak piping time of peace we can do none of this."

"There were also infinite resources," Cobb said mildly.

"We don't lack for money," Lowell said. "What we lack is commitment and fire."

These words seemed to have refreshed Lowell, who now struck Breal as completely alert and focused. Lowell turned to Tergelen. "Andre, tell General Cobb how we plan to launch our new products."

Tergelen handed out copies of a brochure. "This is typical of the literature we're now using to introduce our products," he said.

Cobb leafed through it. Lowell had chosen the colors and designed the cover layout. "This is an impressive selling document," Cobb said.

Lowell squinted at the cover of the brochure. He held the booklet at arm's length and squinted again. "It's off center," he said. "I specifically centered the logo on the page. The titles and photographs are all shifted to the right."

Breal studied his copy and under close scrutiny he could indeed discern that the printing on the page was slightly off center.

"The printer must have made an error," Tergelen said.

"Ours is the more grievous fault," Lowell said, voice rising. Breal wondered whether Lowell had sufficient control to avoid a meltdown in front of Cobb. "We must look to ourselves, not the printer. I can't be everywhere at once. I designed the cover page—very precisely I might add—and this is what comes of it. Didn't the printer submit a proof copy?"

"I never saw it," Tergelen said.

"We can live with this, John, can't we?" Cobb said equably.

"You don't understand," Lowell said to Cobb. Breal saw in the tightness of his mouth and the rigidity of his neck, the effort Lowell was making to hold himself in check. "This brochure describes a device which is unique to the industry. If the brochure is slovenly in its presentation, what does that say about the article we're selling? Or for that matter about the company that sells it." He turned to Tergelen. "How many of these have we printed and where are they?"

"Fifty thousand pieces," Tergelen said.

Cobb watched Lowell as the old man picked up the brochure, held the cover at arm's length, squinted at it once again, and said in a decisive voice, "I can't live with this. No, I can't live with this at all." He jabbed the brochure toward Tergelen. "I want you to retrieve all copies and destroy them. Point out the deficiencies of his work to the printer and have him redo the order at no cost to us." He glared at Tergelen. "There's a penalty for sloppy work and the printer must pay that penalty or forego any further business with ETI. Is that clear?"

"Yes," Tergelen said.

Lowell's face was now less tense and Breal relaxed: the old man would not become unstrung. "In business as in love, it's the little things that matter," Lowell said to Cobb. "We must strike a small blow for perfection. We can't lower our standards of excellence, particularly for a product as unique as this." Cobb did not reply.

The meeting ended with Lowell in good spirits. Everyone gathered up his papers. "Well, Victor," Lowell said, "give my best to . . ." He paused, frowned, and stared before him in a dim way.

Cobb waited to learn who he was to give Lowell's best to. "To Emily?" he finally ventured.

"Why, of course, to Emily." Lowell raised his hands, palms upward. "I'm in the springtime of my senility," he said, smiling.

THAT EVENING, Breal summarized the brochure incident to his wife.

"That's interesting," Susan said, "because it ties in with something Edna told me at lunch today. She says The Great Man's behavior has grown bizarre. He's always gotten irritated when little things were out of kilter, but now she says it's much worse. He'll throw a major tantrum over some trivial thing. He used to watch the news every evening and curse the commentators as pompous asses or clowns. Now he doesn't even bother to turn on the TV. Instead, he has a couple of extra shots of gin and stares at the walls. Edna mentioned one particularly odd thing. They were sitting in the Great Hall and she left to go to the bathroom. When she got back Lowell wanted to know why she'd left the house. She said she hadn't gone out. How could she? She'd only been gone for a few minutes. But he insisted that she'd been gone for at least an hour and had left the house. Then he got upset that she would contradict him."

"Maybe he was just tired."

"There are other things. For example, he stalks her like a house detective—into the kitchen, her bedroom, wherever— and seems disappointed that he hasn't caught her doing something wrong. Or he interrogates her for an hour on some trivial point. Or he complains about the house—the bathroom floor, dust on the furniture, tarnished silver, dirty windows—even though Edna swears the place is immaculate."

"What did Edna think was the problem?"

"She didn't elaborate. But Edna has a deeper problem than Lowell's odd behavior. He's seeing his daughter again. Apparently she's engaged to be married."

"Why does that bother Edna?"

"I always thought Edna's dislike of the daughter was a kind of sibling rivalry. But now she's afraid the fiancé is a Rasputin-like character who'll somehow manipulate the old man through the daughter. From Edna's perspective, Lowell owes her, owes her a lot."

"Edna Graham, this is Ishmael Carter," Catherine said.

Edna stared at Ishmael, then gave him a celestial smile and a "How are you?" She ushered the couple into the Great Hall where Lowell rose to greet them. He paused, and peered at Ishmael longer than Edna did. Catherine made the introductions. Edna took drink orders. "How do you do, Mr. Carter," Lowell said.

"Call me Ishmael, as Herman Melville would say."

"I understand you're a scholar, Mr. Carter," Lowell said, "a scholar of . . ." Lowell's brow puckered.

"I'm tryin' to translate Mr. Dante, Mr. Dante Alighieri, into our native language," Ishmael said.

Catherine turned to Ishmael in astonishment. He had adopted a thick Negro accent.

"Aren't there already many such translations?" Lowell asked.

"Well, yessuh, there are, but none of them is worth a damn."

Lowell's brow puckered again as he stared at Ishmael, apparently baffled about how to go on. At that moment Edna arrived with a tray of smoked salmon on crackers.

"What in the world are you doing?" Catherine hissed at Ishmael.

"What you talkin' 'bout girl?"

"You know damn well what I'm talking about. You sound like Uncle Tom."

"The man expects a stereotype. I don't want to disappoint him."

~ 290 ~

"He doesn't expect any such thing. Now stop it!"

"I want him to see me as a black man. Completely. Not a white man in a black skin."

"Just be yourself, Ishmael. Forget this black/white crap."

"I've never read Dante," Lowell said. "But I understand the Italians at least place him at the level of Shakespeare. What is he about?"

Catherine watched her father: he appeared wary but genuinely interested.

Ishmael regarded Lowell, seemed to be weighing how to continue. "*The Divine Comedy* is about fundamentals," he said. "What is sin? How shall we live together? It's a journey. From darkness to light, from evil to virtue, from error to truth."

Edna gaped at Ishmael as he spoke, as if he were an alien creature recovered from an archeological dig and mysteriously come to life.

Catherine felt her body relax—she hadn't realized how tense she had been—as Ishmael's black accent lightened through this small discourse.

The Chinese butler arrived with their drinks. Lowell tasted his martini, took an hors d'oeuvre. "And how does your Mr. Dante define sin?" he asked with a smile.

"Sin is hurting others," Ishmael replied, "as well as hurting yourself."

"And what happens to these sinners?" Lowell asked.

Catherine was pleased that Ishmael chose to ignore the irony in her father's half-smile. "They wind up in hell," Ishmael said. "Dante's hell is a rough place and it's forever. No one is rehabilitated. It's where you suffer alone, where you always blame others for being there."

"It doesn't sound all that different from this world," Lowell said.

"Perhaps that's why I was drawn to it," Ishmael said, the Negro accent completely gone.

"It doesn't sound like much of a comedy," Edna said.

Ishmael turned to Edna, seemed to assess her as though she were an applicant at a job interview, and then smiled at her, an unexpectedly gentle smile. "In medieval times," he said, "—and you have to remember that Dante wrote at the beginning of the fourteenth century—any poetry that began in fear, but ended happily was called a comedy."

"What makes it great?" Lowell asked.

Ishmael thought a moment. "Probably the enormity of its conception and how perfectly it's worked out. Dante reflected on life on earth. But he also reflected on death, which according to him has its own life. The whole universe is contained in *The Divine Comedy*. Dante, a very conscious poet, recognized this. In the *Paradiso*, toward the end, he says, *'il poema sacro al quale ha posto mano cielo e terra.'* The sacred poem to which both heaven and earth have set their hand."

Catherine liked the way he quoted the Italian, easily, without making a big deal of it.

The Chinese servant appeared in the doorway. "Dinner is ready," Edna said.

Lowell, over his baked halibut, asked, "What do you do, ah . . ."

"Ishmael," he supplied.

"Yes, what do you do, Ishmael?"

"I drive a taxi. You can think of me as an entrepreneur. I'm one of the few taxi drivers in Boston who own their own cab."

"How did you get interested in Dante?" Lowell asked.

Ishmael went through his year at U Mass, his military service in Italy, his discovery of Florence.

"How far along are you in the translation?"

"I'm about through with Hell and ready to move on to Purgatory. After that Paradise. That's the toughest."

"Hell seems like more fun than Paradise," Edna said.

"Not Dante's hell," Ishmael said.

"He sounds very different from Shakespeare," Lowell observed.

"Not really. Dante's whole life seemed predestined, as though he were fated to write *The Divine Comedy*. Shakespeare's career also has that aspect, at least in the perspective of his last plays." Ishmael thought a moment. "Maybe that's what a great poet is. Someone who can live through all the common human experiences consciously, and in the end transmute the whole sequence into art."

"WELL, THERE you are," Edna said after Catherine and Ishmael had left. "Catherine is always full of surprises, not all of them pleasant."

"He's no fool, I'll say that for him," Lowell said.

"There must be a hundred thousand eligible white men around. Why would she pick a black taxi driver?"

"What's your answer?" Lowell asked.

"Because she has lousy judgment. In everything."

"THAT WASN'T so bad, was it?" Catherine said in the cab.

"I kind of liked the old man," Ishmael said. "A little slow on the draw sometimes but his instincts seemed good. That pad he lives in. Reminded me of Xanadu in *Citizen Kane*."

"I think you made a good impression on him."

"Was that important to you?"

"Yes, it was. I wanted him to like you . . . When you started that Stepin Fetchit imitation, you had me worried."

"I was trying to make the point that accents don't define the man. But you're right. It was a foolish thing to do."

"What did you think of Edna?"

"Well, she didn't *look* like Iago, but then Iago is in the soul, not necessarily obvious."

"She's a scheming bitch."

"I don't know. I think she's just scared. She thinks she's got dibs on the old man. Daughter or no, you're a latecomer. She's put in a lot of years. Must have been tough. She doesn't want the payoff snatched from under her at the last minute. Defeat from the jaws of victory, so to speak."

"There's no way my dad would leave Edna his wealth."

"That doesn't keep her from hoping, and getting nasty with anyone that gets in the way."

SO THERE he was, my future son-in-law. Sounded like an escapee from a cotton field for a while. No idea what to make of him. Introduce him to the trustees at MIT or at the museum. "Like you to meet my son-in-law, Ishmael Carter." Could put a turban on his head, introduce him as an African potentate. Don't think Ishmael would go for that. Definitely no fool, though. High Shakespearian forehead. Hard to understand the world, isn't it? Keeps shifting around. Out of kilter, disordered. But then maybe you don't have to understand. Life doesn't necessarily take the shortest distance between two points. If this man is smart and good and they love each other and get on well . . . All the same, it takes a lot of getting used to. Things just won't stand still, will they?

LOWELL CONTINUED to spend time in engineering. He told Breal that he wanted to personally monitor engineering headway because of its paramount importance to the company. In the past this monitoring had consisted of badgering Warren Slater on his slow progress. The rate of progress under Rostov had increased considerably. Rostov did not give his designers free rein as Slater had. There was far less trial and error designing under him. The engineers and technicians respected his judgment and liked the firm direction he provided. He got rid of people he considered marginal and hired replacements from his old company. He conducted an after-hours course for his engineers and persuaded Breal to purchase computer-aided design terminals and modern machine tools for his engineering model shop. Breal gave Rostov whatever he asked for.

Rostov always appeared pleased to see Lowell when he showed up in the laboratory. He took pains to explain to him what they were doing and, whenever possible, to demonstrate functioning hardware as opposed to paper designs. His answers to Lowell's questions were well-organized, detailed. The times when Breal accompanied Lowell on his tour of engineering, Lowell, on leaving, always commented favorably on Rostov's performance and had a satisfied look, as though he had just spent time with a particularly talented chiropractor or masseur.

Lowell caught the flu that fall and was out of the office for two weeks, but called Breal every day, sometimes two or three times, his voice stuffy and hoarse, asking if anything was new. When Lowell returned to the office, he was pale and irritable. On his second day back he suffered a massive nosebleed, and decided to throw out his shear pin and fuse theory and have the faulty blood vessel cauterized. He only worked mornings, on the annual report and his speech for the shareholders meeting. He dozed often and had difficulty concentrating.

Sales and profitability continued to improve. The M-100 had halted then reversed Mühlmann's erosion of ETI's market share, but the major profit improvement was the result of the niche market strategy. Mühlmann introduced some follow-on products, but their additional features were not perceived as major advances and their effect in the marketplace was minimal. Yet Breal continued to worry about Mühlmann. The threat lingered in the air like the odor of a fire long after water has extinguished it.

The year-end quarterly report to shareholders signaled an upturn in ETI's fortunes. The stock rose to fourteen then sixteen. Lowell was pleased, but less so than Breal would have expected. "Our stock should be trading at forty," he said to Breal's astonishment. "No foresight. Those clown investors can't see past the next quarter."

Lowell spent weeks, draft after draft, on his annual meeting speech. Breal did not think Lowell had ever fully recovered from the flu and he didn't look well. He easily lost the thread of a discussion, and was cranky.

One day he found Breal and dragged him off on a tour of the building, something he had never done in Cambridge. They wandered into engineering where Lowell made the observation that there were cardboard boxes everywhere—mostly there, but also in marketing and finance. He noted that they were of varying sizes, some open and some shut, some piled on other boxes, others sitting alone. "They make the place look like a trash heap," Lowell said. "I want you to get rid of those boxes, George."

"We do not have boxes because we are fond of cardboard," Rostov said to Breal. "They are cheap storage and fit nicely under workbenches. Besides, what does it matter? We are only ones here. Things here are to be convenient for us."

Lowell gave Breal no peace on this. Finally, Breal chose to use the upcoming shareholder's meeting as an excuse to attack the boxes. He wrote a memorandum to all department heads, read it with disgust and signed it.


THE ANNUAL meeting was scheduled to start at ten in the morning. At nine-thirty, Victor Cobb appeared in Lowell's office—Lowell was seated on the couch staring at the speech in his hand. They chatted for a few moments and Cobb congratulated Lowell on ETI's much improved financial results. Lowell had scotched any talk of inviting the press. "Good news will out, Victor," he said. "In this computerized age, it's no longer possible to hide your light, or absence thereof, under a barrel." Lowell asked Cobb to excuse him as he wanted to make a last-minute review of his speech.

Lowell rose from the couch, laid the paper down, went into his private bathroom. When he came out, he looked for the paper, searching the marble table, his desk, the chairs, on the floor . . . it seemed he had been searching for an hour. He felt perspiration on his face, panic rising in his throat; he felt himself imprisoned beneath a lid of ice. "Miss Krane!" he shouted. "I seem to have mislaid my speech." They both searched, and Miss Krane found it atop a pile of papers on the elliptical table near the entrance to Lowell's bathroom.

After Miss Krane left, Lowell stared at the document, double-spaced, all caps. He leafed through the pages: was this his speech? He turned to the first page. The bold-faced heading read, ADDRESS TO SHAREHOLDERS. He told himself to be calm and read the words. What was all this? What was he saying? It was familiar but only vaguely. His speech resembled an old book, read many years ago and now only dimly remembered. After what seemed like hours of reading, he came to the conclusion:

"We have been through a period of transition and emerged a tougher, leaner, stronger company. We have a seasoned management team in place, able to deal effectively with increasingly complex markets and sophisticated technology. I have never felt more bullish about ETI's prospects. We look forward to a bright future of increasing sales and earnings."

Lowell turned through the ten pages of text. The speech seemed to rattle on forever, tiresome, dull as dirt. Were all those words really needed? Did anyone care *what* he said? Speeches, annual reports: trivial victories, trivial defeats, of no more consequence than the struggles of ants. He took off his glasses, slid them into the inside left breast pocket of his jacket.

Miss Krane poked her head in the door. "It's five to ten, Dr. Lowell."

He nodded toward her, rose from the couch, stopped at the window. He stared out at the parked cars, the high-tension wires, the leafless trees, the iron-colored sky. All these forms glared back at him, brutally, as if carved by a savage hand. He focused on the trees and heard the sound of rushing wind. The outside world appeared to be dislocating inward, toward the building.

He gripped the pages with both hands and headed toward the meeting room. He felt he was trudging through a space that had thickened, that yielded only reluctantly, as though the air itself had solidified. He found he was shuffling his feet and quickened his step. He strode through the doorway; on the raised platform was a long narrow table at which sat all of his vice presidents and Victor Cobb. To the left was the lectern, its height adjusted for him that morning by Miss Krane. He managed the step onto the platform, arrived at the lectern, placed the papers before him, peered out at the faces; they looked back: alert, waiting, somehow hostile. He heard again the great black flood of wind. He found Edna: she was smiling toward him, unworried. It gave him a sense of tranquility, like still water, comforting, understanding. He experienced an instant of panic as he groped in his left breast pocket, then found his glasses, put them on, positioned the pages, clutched the lectern with both hands, and began his speech.

# TWENTY-FIVE

Throughout the spring, sales of the M-100 continued to climb and so did the unit's profitability. Reliability in the field was excellent. Many OEMs who had defected to Mühlmann were returning to ETI despite Mühlmann's further reductions in price. The OEMs viewed the M-100 as a superior product and preferred a domestic supplier with an extensive distribution and service network. Finally, Mühlmann was simply being outsold.

LOWELL CONTINUED to invite Catherine and Ishmael for dinner, sometimes with Tom and Michael. After a while he came to think of them as a group that naturally fit together. If there was any tension among them, he could not discern it.

Lowell, to his own surprise, came to enjoy Ishmael's company most of all. Lowell found him a good listener whose comments were always incisive—his knowledge was wide-ranging. He was always respectful to Edna Graham, drew her into conversation, and often complimented her on something she was wearing. Lowell could see Edna thaw toward Ishmael, and several times he even made her laugh.

Ishmael once asked Lowell if he would be interested in accompanying him around Boston as he went about his taxi rounds, to see the city from a different perspective. Lowell accepted the invitation, enjoyed Ishmael's effortless driving, and marveled at the way, without hesitation, he went unerringly to some obscure address a passenger had given him.

Lowell discovered the sweet music of the words, "Take me to the airport," admired how shrewdly Ishmael assessed the traffic, sometimes taking the Callahan Tunnel, other times working his way around to the Mystic River Bridge and the capillary system of streets that led to Logan. Ishmael took Lowell to lunch at a soul food restaurant in Roxbury, and ordered blackened catfish for him. Lowell found it delicious and settled for beer instead of gin.

Ishmael continued to invite Lowell on his taxi rounds and Lowell willingly accepted. One morning, as they drove along the north shore, Lowell—gazing past the ribbon of beach, past the foaming breakers to the great sea beyond, ocean and sky meeting in an indistinct haze—experienced a peace he had not known for years, here in a taxi with this new and improbable friend.

On a sunny June morning, Catherine received her Doctor of Jurisprudence from Boston University. Lowell, Ishmael, Edna, Tom and Michael attended the general graduation ceremony at Nickerson Field, then the presentation of the degree at the law school. Edna had reluctantly agreed to come along after some coaxing by Lowell. Michael took his mother's photograph, she in cap and gown, then a picture of Ishmael hugging her, then a photo of the whole group including Edna. Catherine, cheeks flushed, thanked her father time after time, told him again and again how grateful she was. Lowell mumbled something, felt pride and joy choke his voice: he loved his daughter. In fact, he loved them all. In the presence of these people, Lowell found himself relaxing, bathed in a family warmth he had never known.

The following month Michael suggested they go to a Red Sox game; and so the whole group, on a Sunday afternoon, ate hot dogs, drank beer and watched Boston pummel the New York Yankees. It was the first time in his life that Lowell had ever attended a baseball game. His grandson Michael explained the nuances of the game and the physics of pitching and batting. Lowell watched the boy's face as he spoke and saw the adult he would eventually become: grave, studious, analytic, not troubled by life's ironies or puzzled by the unfathomable disasters visited upon the world. Lowell listened to the young man's disquisition on baseball, did not follow it at all, and was completely at peace.

"WHAT'S THIS letter, Craig?" Lowell asked as Holloway took a chair at the marble table.

"I think it's self-explanatory, sir," Holloway answered, stumbling over "explanatory."

"I still think of you as a bright-eyed young engineer. I can't imagine you sitting at home. We'd be pleased to keep you on, say on a three-day-week basis. You'd be able to ease into your retirement gradually and we'd have the benefit of your technical judgment."

"That's very generous of you, Dr. Lowell," Holloway replied. "Something like that hadn't occurred to me. But considering it now, I'd have to say no."

"I'm sure you can make a far more substantial contribution than those new engineers we've been hiring."

"That's just the point," Holloway said. "I can't. I watched Emil Rostov zip through that integrated circuit design. It was depressing. I knew for a long time that integrated circuits were the way to go. I spent nights reading up on the subject, but all that happened was that I got sleepy. It took me weeks to do things he finished in a day. The way I design is not the way it's done anymore. Now it's all mathematical modeling and computer simulation. Then sensor technology is going digital and that's just not my cup of tea."

"You make yourself sound old, Craig," Lowell said.

"I don't think of myself as being old physically, but I feel old relative to my work. Anyway, since my heart attack Rosemary has been urging me to retire."

"In that case, I see that I can't possibly convince you to stay. Women sooner or later get their way. They've learned to use a powerful force of nature—erosion."

Holloway rose to leave.

"Everyone is leaving," Lowell said. "Buck Clawson is gone . . . you're leaving . . . I don't recognize many of the faces I now see in the halls."

"Isn't that the way it should be?" Holloway said.


LOWELL AND Victor Cobb sat at a secluded table in the Algonquin Club. "What's on your mind, Victor?" Lowell asked as he took a sip of his first martini.

"I've received a feeler from a banker with regard to a company that's interested in buying ETI."

"Is that all?" Lowell laughed. "I get one of those a week."

"This is different," Cobb said. "It's a German company and very well heeled. Those people can afford to pay an excellent price. You must understand, John, that the mark is now very strong. What we may think of as a high price is a bargain to the Germans. There's something else. The tax laws are changing. This is the last year for special treatment of capital gains. Next year, all gains, whether capital or short-term, will be treated as ordinary income."

"You sound like a real advocate," Lowell said.

"In all honesty, I am," Cobb replied. "I'm not exactly a poor ex-soldier, fading away, but a part of my wealth is in ETI stock. This is an opportunity to cash out at a sizeable gain, and more importantly, because it may never happen again, keep almost all of it."

"Who's the company?"

"Mühlmann, your German competitor. The proposition was brought to me by an investment banker friend in Boston."

Lowell shifted in his chair, and peered into his martini glass. "Was a price mentioned?"

"No. At this stage they're only trying to find out whether we're interested. By the way, there's no question here of a hostile takeover. This would be a friendly transaction. If we have no interest, they'll just click their heels and leave."

Lowell toyed with his glass. "Things are looking up at ETI," he said. "We're on our way to a record year. The stock has been edging up—it's now over eighteen. Whatever the company is worth today, it'll be worth a lot more in a year or two."

Cobb repeated his capital gains argument. "You may sell for more, but you'll keep less," he concluded. "The opportunity is now."

When Lowell did not respond, Cobb continued. "There are other things, John. We're not getting any younger. Isn't it time for you to consider cashing in your chips at ETI and using the money to advance interests that are important to you? You've spoken of endowing a chair in the humanities at MIT. You've mentioned establishing a scholarship fund to assist able young men train for a military career. You can be useful to America and achieve satisfaction beyond anything you can attain at ETI."

"This isn't only stock we're talking about selling," Lowell said as he rotated his glass.

"I understand that, and I thought carefully before deciding to discuss it with you." Cobb waited as Lowell finished his drink. "You've had years of achievement. You've revitalized ETI. Why repeat yourself? Why not move on and in the time remaining to you, accomplish those lasting things that will complete your life?"

Lowell stared into his empty glass as if his future were written there. "I've known men who sold their company. Some deluded themselves that they would stay on because they had done such a splendid job creating and building the enterprise, but of course they never did. Some fooled with government service. Others just cultivated their garden or wound up in a retirement community, a gulag for the old and

~ 303 ~

useless. You might say, well, they had the money to console them, but they were not happy men. They had been turned into capons, rich capons to be sure, but capons nevertheless. Many would gladly return the money to be in command again. No, money did not buy them contentment."

"They may not have had your range of interests."

Lowell sighed, had a sudden sense of the dreariness of the world. "I think it proper," he said, "that we hold a board meeting to discuss this. What's at issue is not only the personal gain you and I stand to make, but our responsibility toward the shareholders. Let's do this by the book. Anyway, I'd like to sleep on it. We've gotten hundreds of these feelers over the years. There will always be another."

"But there may never be another tax window," Cobb said.


THE BOARD sat at the table. "We have received an approach for the purchase of ETI," Lowell said. "We wish to decide whether to proceed further or drop the matter." He then asked Cobb to report what he knew to the group.

After Cobb's presentation, Tergelen snorted through his nose. "You said the company was Mühlmann?" Breal was surprised at the intensity in Tergelen's voice.

"Yes," Cobb said, a questioning look on his face.

"The reason why Mühlmann would want to buy ETI is certainly clear enough," Tergelen said.

"What is that?" Cobb asked, his face now blank and hard.

"Let me first say what the reasons are not," Tergelen said, answering in Lowell's direction. "It can't be for ETI's technology. We may have a slight edge now, but they'll leapfrog us in a year or two. They certainly don't want us for our manufacturing facilities, which are probably laughable compared to theirs. Then what? They want to buy ETI for the one thing they cannot duplicate—our distribution channel."

"Suppose that's true," Cobb shrugged with impatience, "how does that change this discussion?"

Tergelen now faced Cobb directly. "We can achieve far greater gains, Mr. Cobb, not by selling the company, but by doing ourselves what Mühlmann wants to do. What I'm proposing is that we push other products, not necessarily of our manufacture, through that same channel. There are excellent companies in Europe and Japan, with fine competitive products, who do not sell in the U.S. because they don't have the distribution. We can do that for them, using the ETI label, and make a substantial profit in the bargain." Breal glanced at Cobb and Lowell as Tergelen made his proposal: Cobb's face was set, expressionless; Lowell was frowning as he stared at Tergelen.

"How long have you been with ETI, Andre?" Cobb asked.

"Thirty years. Why does that matter?"

"And how long have you been head of marketing?"

"About twenty."

"It seems to me that you've had plenty of opportunity to leverage ETI's distribution channel. If you haven't done so by now, it's reasonable to question your ability to do so in the future." Cobb's voice had taken on a hard edge; Breal thought of a military commander addressing an obtuse subordinate. Breal didn't think the idea a bad one, though it was awfully late in the day to consider it now.

"Andre," Lowell said, "that's not what we're talking about at all. We have a straightforward question before us. Do we proceed further toward the possible sale of the company or not? Let's not burden this deliberation with new marketing ideas."

Cobb turned toward Lowell and said, "The decision before us obviously depends on price. I suggest we ask George here to research the premiums over market that are being paid for acquisitions. Also, the multiple of earnings that's being paid. Oh, one more thing." Cobb turned to Miles. "Since this is the last year of taxation at the low capital gains rate, at what increase over a price obtained this year would we have to sell the company next year to realize the same after-tax gain?"

"That may take some time," Miles replied.

"Think of it as an exam," Cobb said in the same voice he had used earlier with Tergelen, "and you have to turn in your paper in two days."

Lowell's brow wrinkled. "It's more complicated than that. My shares are forty percent of all the shares outstanding. They were accumulated over almost half a century and are far more valuable than the shares some speculator bought in Las Vegas yesterday."

Breal didn't understand this logic at all, and as he looked across at Cobb he could see the general didn't understand it either. Lowell must have sensed the puzzlement around the table for he added, "My shares represent control. Without my shares, there's no purchase of ETI. That's worth a premium."

"What did you have in mind?" Cobb asked, a suddenly wary salesman before a capricious and unreasonable customer.

Lowell peered into the distance, did not speak or budge; he seemed frozen in place as if some sorcerer had touched him; the moment lengthened. Breal had an urge to shake him as if he were a stopped clock. Finally, Lowell said, "Today is . . . ?"

"Tuesday," Cobb replied in a relieved voice.

"Let's plan on meeting here next Monday morning at ten," Lowell said. "We'll review these analyses. I'll have my answer as well."

When they left the meeting, Breal invited Tergelen to his office. "It's clear that you're opposed to this, Andre," Breal said, "but let me appeal to your enlightened self-interest. This sale would make you rich, or at least very well off. Why are you opposed to it?"

"I'm quite comfortable," Tergelen said. "I can't eat any more than I do, our house is perfectly adequate, our children are grown and doing well, and I'm reasonably secure financially. What benefit will more money bring me? Mr. Breal, you have done many remarkable things, things I didn't believe possible under Dr. Lowell. But I have done one remarkable thing—over many years I've constructed ETI's distribution network. I inherited something feeble, and piece by piece I've pruned and strengthened it until now it's a powerful selling machine. I don't want to see it taken over by anyone, but especially not the Germans."

Breal waited a moment before replying. The sale of ETI was his opportunity—the only one that had come along in his lifetime and the only one that might ever come along—for him to become rich. Lowell had been generous to him, and any reasonable premium over market would put well over a million dollars in his pocket. "I don't share your aversion to wealth. Also, the Germans will need a local management team to run the company. What better than the one that's successfully competing with them now? We would only be working for a different boss." Breal knew this to be a weak argument; his experience at United Electric had taught him that. Still, it had a certain logical appeal and, despite his experience, made good sense.

"That's naive thinking, Mr. Breal. Mühlmann will not make the huge investment needed to purchase this company, then disappear while we continue to run it. No, you will be replaced by a German manager, someone they trust. He in turn will replace the rest of ETI's management with a team congenial to him. We may be wealthy but we'll be out of work. The question for you, Mr. Breal, is why do you want to give up all that you have slaved for over the past five years, especially now that it's amounting to something?"

"The reason is very straightforward, Andre. It's money."

"I'm afraid you and I just don't understand each other," Tergelen said.


BREAL FOUND Clare, swore him to secrecy, and asked him to do the research that Cobb had suggested. Clare seemed very pleased with the assignment.

That evening Breal gave his wife a summary of the board meeting. She did not appear overjoyed. "It sounds like United Electric revisited," she said. "You'll be back on the street."

"But we'll have a million dollars to keep us warm."

"You'll still be on the street."

"You sound like Tergelen. That's exactly what he said. But he also has a special dislike for the Germans."

"Didn't you tell me that as a young man his family was tortured, then executed by the Nazis? That must have given him a fair amount of exposure to the darker side of the German character."

"It was difficult to argue with a man who has an aversion to getting rich, however."

"I doubt if that's his point. He has an aversion to getting rich if the price he has to pay is losing control of everything he's worked for. To put it another way, he thinks trading power for money is a bad bargain."

"Well, there's no point in deciding how we'll spend the money," Breal said, "because I don't think it'll happen, either because the old man will get cold feet or because he'll set an unrealistic price and a lot of crazy conditions."

SOMETIMES I feel as if I'm leading someone else's life. House a museum filled with the relics of another person's years: clothes, rooms, furniture—unfamiliar. Even your handwriting changed, crabbed. In bed at night, breathing, not you but a stranger. Memory shrinking to the size of a nut. Faces around you curiously vacant. Sometimes they whisper as though at a funeral. Cabinets oddly locked, doors without handles. The simple act of living, exhausts all your energies. The plash of fountains from the mouths of stone lions—where was that? Paris? Rome? When were you there and with whom?

Lowell filled a martini glass with Tanqueray. The Great Hall seemed haunted, about it an odor of damp and concrete, tomb-like. Edna Graham sat in the stuffed chair opposite him. "I heard you walking around last night," she said.

"I was lying awake," Lowell said, "trying to remember Henry the Fourth's soliloquy on sleep. At the beginning of it he says, 'How many thousands of my poorest subjects are at this hour asleep! O sleep, O gentle sleep, Nature's soft nurse, how have I frighted thee . . .' But there's a lot more to it, so I went downstairs to the library, and looked it up. When I had it straight, I returned to bed, but when I reached my room it was all gone. I went back to the library and got it straight again, then, back in bed, it had disappeared once more. I gave up." As he said this, Lowell saw himself—in an unreal yet precise way, as if it were an out of body experience—replacing the book on the shelf so it was perfectly aligned with all the others; this had given him a sense of peace and satisfaction and at last he was able to sleep.

"Those things happen," Edna said. "It was very late and you were tired."

"I imagine my brain shriveling, rattling around in my skull like a loose marble." Lowell drank his gin. "I'm thinking of selling the company," he said.

"It's about time," Edna said.

"That's what Victor Cobb said . . . Why do you feel that way?"

"That place used to be a source of pleasure for you. Now you return home irritated and depressed. You're not sleeping well. I don't mean only last night. Often, very late, I hear you wandering about. It's ETI that's troubling you."

"ETI is doing well," he said.

"Maybe that's the problem. Maybe you're happiest when the company is in crisis."

"That's a good piece of insight, Edna."

"I'm not as foolish as you think."

"It's not out of frustration that I'm considering selling ETI."

"What is it then?"

After a long while, he said, "The last time I saw my father, he was a shrunken old man. I asked him if he was working, and he said no, he'd given up the stage. I asked him why and he answered, 'It's very simple, Johnny. I can't remember my lines.'" Lowell was silent for a moment as he recalled his father in the last years—mellowed and varnished like an old violin—then went on, "Something like that is happening to me. Some defining part of me is disappearing, fading like old ink. I don't know what it is and maybe I don't want to know, but I think that in a year or two I may not have the faculty to sell the company. Then, in due time, the trustees of my estate, Victor Cobb and Dick Miles, will sell it. They may know many small things but I know one big thing: how much ETI is really worth. They'll sell it at a bargain price because they don't have the vision to comprehend the great treasure that ETI is. So you see I'm considering selling the company because I can sell it better than anyone else. And the time remaining for me to do that may soon be over."

"I think you're being unduly morbid," Edna said, "but whatever your reason, I agree it's the right thing for you to do."

Lowell again recalled his father: face perplexed and weary, a man for whom life had exhausted all of its surprises, for whom existence had become a burden; the old man had said, "Here I am, on the garbage heap of old age. But it's funny, inside this ruined old body I still feel like the same person." He smiled ruefully, as if he were the butt of some cosmic joke, a man who had never liked the mention of death.

"I HAVE performed the analysis you requested," Dick Miles said to the ETI board. "The answer is this: because of the changing tax law, whatever price you receive for your stock this year, it must be thirty percent higher next year, and forty-five percent higher the year after to break even with this year."

"Those are telling numbers," Cobb said. "Let me see if I have it straight. We're now in July. If we wait five months, until January, to close a deal, then the price must jump thirty percent for us to take the same amount of money to the bank. Is that correct?" Cobb looked at Miles.

"Yes, that's correct," Miles answered.

Breal did indeed find the numbers telling and was gratified to see Lowell scrawling them on a yellow notepad. He then reported on the outcome of his assignment. "Here are the results and my conclusion." Breal handed out a chart. "The average multiple of earnings paid was 18. Our estimated earnings for this year are $2.50 per share. The product of these two numbers yields a sales price for ETI of $45 a share. A price arrived at as a multiple of asset value gives the same answer: $45 per share. Lastly, applying the average premium paid over market yields $35 a share. Using three different approaches, then, we get two estimates of ETI's value at $45 per share and one estimate at $35."

Lowell tossed aside Breal's chart. "I have no interest in these numbers. They're the hobgoblins of small minds." Lowell came to his feet. "It seems to me that a multiple of earnings is the fairest measure of worth. The question is—what earnings?" He turned to Breal. "What did you say this year's estimate was?"

"$2.50 a share."

"What would you forecast those earnings to be over the next couple of years?"

Breal consulted his notes. "$2.91 next year and $3.69 the year after."

"Calculate what the sales price would be in *those* years," Lowell said.

Breal did the multiplication and gave the answer. "The sales price would go up to $52 per share next year and $66 the year following."

Lowell nodded with satisfaction. "That's more like it. Those prices give you a far better sense of the worth of the company than anything you said earlier."

"Those numbers are debatable, aren't they John?" Cobb said. "They're based on a best case scenario."

Lowell felt confusion rising within him, Breal's numbers jumbling in his head. He turned to the men at the table: they seemed without importance, as if they were trees. Then Lowell stared out the window. The scene appeared chaotic, distorted like a Van Gogh landscape. "I have to think about this further," he said abruptly. "Thank you, gentlemen."


THERE'S A storm in my head, a tempest that drowns out reason. Blow winds and crack your cheeks! rage! blow! . . . Concentrate. In the name of heaven, concentrate. Tough to keep a complicated thought together. Pieces are there—momentarily, like a beacon flashing through a gale, they come together, then blast apart. Chaos loosed upon the world. Keep things simple. What were all those numbers? They are to ETI what a cat's shadow is to a cat. ETI can't be reduced to sterile figures. Memory comes and goes—a will of its own. Shipwreck. Must see beyond the numbers, the words, to the cold beating heart.


"FOR HEAVEN'S sake, it's two o'clock in the morning," Edna said. "Why are you wandering around the house?"

"I had a nightmare and couldn't get back to sleep," Lowell said. "I thought I'd make myself a cup of warm milk."

"What did you dream?"

"I dreamt that the head of my penis had been torn off. I was holding the head in my hand trying to reattach it to the stump, but I couldn't. For some reason it was no longer possible. When I awoke, the dream seemed to go on—life and the dream mixed—and I held myself like a child."

"Here, sit in the library and rest," Edna Graham said. "I'll bring you a tray with warm milk and some toast."

Where is sleep? Try to read. *The Iliad.* Loved it as a boy. Greatest story ever told. Glorious prose. The Greek ships and "the broad oars that smote the wine-dark sea," and Ajax the mighty who struck his foes to the ground "and loud their armor rang," and Patroclus, beloved friend of Achilles, who "crashed upon the earth and darkness filled his eyes." Is that how it happens: darkness fills your eyes? How would Homer know? How would anybody know?

"I'M THINKING of selling my company." Lowell said as he sat in Ishmael's cab and they waited their turn in a taxi stand line.

"You don't seem enthusiastic about it, Dr. Lowell," Ishmael said.

"Well, it's a little like dying. It's difficult to be enthusiastic about it."

"Then why sell? Stay with it. Take what satisfaction you can."

Lowell repeated the argument he had given Edna.

Ishmael moved his cab up, thought a moment. "I don't know if you're right or not. About your health, I mean. But being in charge no doubt keeps you alert. Before you think about selling, you might want to ask yourself what you'll do afterwards. And will it give you the same satisfaction the company does."

"Nothing will give me the satisfaction the company does."

"Then don't sell."

Why he only cares about me, Lowell thought. He doesn't give a damn whether I sell or not. The idea astonished him, reinforced the fondness he felt for the man beside him.

Ishmael's cab was approaching the front of the line. Lowell said, as though speaking to himself, "I no longer recognize half the people in the place. I wander through engineering and feel insubstantial, irrelevant. Sometimes, in meetings, the discussions—it's like they were talking in some kind of patois. I'm an anachronism, Ishmael, that's what I am . . . Ripeness is all. The time is ripe to give it up but, you know, I can't bring myself to do it."

Ishmael turned toward Lowell. "It's what's on the other side that troubles you. It's foggy, unknown. But if you concentrate, as Dante would tell you, 'Little by little vision starts picking out / shapes that were hidden in the misty air.' " Ishmael put his hand on Lowell's arm. "We'll help you. You won't be alone. It'll be okay on the other side."

Lowell looked at the face before him and realized that for some time he had forgotten that Ishmael was black. He had become a friend, a young but surprisingly wise friend. But he was more than that. Lowell sometimes had the feeling, as he did now, that he was speaking to the son he never had, who had died before he had a chance to live.

"Do you really mean that?" Lowell asked.

"Yes, I do, Dr. Lowell. I'll help you and I know Catherine will. I love your daughter and I care a great deal about you."

Lowell felt a desire to embrace this man.

The cab was at the front of the line, and an attractive black woman got in and gave Ishmael an address in Newton.

"Of course," Ishmael said, "I may love your daughter but I still appreciate other women."

Lowell laughed, felt a great burden lifting from him. "So do we all," he said.


THAT NIGHT Lowell called Victor Cobb. "Let's do this," he said. "Have your banker friend tell those people that ETI is interested. The price is $70 a share for my block and $60 a share for the rest. And we have no interest in negotiations. It's a take it or leave it proposition."

"I suggest we seek legal advice," Cobb said. "Two price levels may be dangerous. The lawyers may know of some approach to get your premium without risking stockholder suits. Why don't I contact Sherman & Frye to get their counsel?

If anything comes of this, we'll have to bring our attorneys into the picture anyway."

"Don't do that, Victor," Lowell said. "Just send them the two tier offer. Let's not give the lawyers a chance to screw things up."

"Shall we see if there are other interested parties?" Cobb asked. "Auctions typically yield the best price."

"Absolutely not!" Lowell cried. "We'll not put ETI on the block like a head of cattle."

# TWENTY-SIX

Chris Grattan, a senior partner at Sherman & Frye, had once played center for Penn State, and the width of his shoulders and bull neck recalled those distant years. Miles told Breal that though Lowell considered Grattan a worrywart, it was always Grattan he consulted on any serious legal issue. Grattan had flown into Boston on the shuttle from New York that morning, and now he, Lowell, Cobb, Miles and Breal sat at the marble table.

"There is no way, John," Grattan said, shaking his bear-like head, "that you can be paid an amount for your shares in excess of the offer to the rest of the shareholders. That would leave you open to a plethora of stockholder suits. But there are other ways to get your premium. We can put together a package—a long-term consulting agreement, travel allowance, other perks—that would in aggregate come close to the premium you're asking."

"That's ridiculous," Lowell said. "I can sell my land and I can sell my ox for any price I can persuade a buyer to pay. Why not my shares in ETI?"

"Because you're not uncoupled from the rest of the stockholders," Grattan explained. "In the sale of the company, you're their agent as well as a shareholder. You can't be perceived as having negotiated a better deal for yourself than for the others."

"Jack-o'-lanterns," Lowell said. "Those are jack-o'-lanterns you're waving at me."

"I can only tell you, John, what prior case law has demonstrated," Grattan said. "You can then make your own judgment. But I can assure you of one thing—a series of stockholder suits would quickly eat up in legal fees any premium you receive. They would also inconvenience you considerably."

"It would be awkward to modify the offer now," Cobb said, "after it's been transmitted."

"There'll be a fair amount of negotiation," Grattan said, "with plenty of opportunity to modify the offer and substitute the perks I just mentioned—should John agree to do that."

"The Mühlmann people will be here in a couple of days," Breal said. "Are there any specific actions you recommend we take?"

"Yes," Grattan said. "Bring an investment banking house into the picture. They'll serve as your intermediary in negotiations."

"I've worked successfully with Lehman, Roth here in Boston," Cobb said.

"Do you know them?" Lowell asked Grattan.

"I've never dealt with them directly, but they have a good reputation in New York banking circles."

"That's equivalent to one whore praising another," Lowell said. "All right, if those parasites are necessary, I suppose giving the business to a Boston firm is the proper thing to do."


MÜHLMANN SENT a contingent that met with ETI's board and then were dinner guests at Lowell House. Lowell and Edna sat at opposite ends of the table and hosted the evening.

"How did things go with the rapacious Huns?" Susan asked her husband when he returned home. "How did The Great Man perform?"

"He did very well. I must say, he has a way of rising to the occasion."

"It must be his actor ancestry," Susan said.

"He probably has a good adrenalin pump. That helps too. The Mühlmann people did say that if this deal goes through, they would retain the present management team and keep the old man on as chairman—to benefit from his wisdom and counsel, they said."

"You mean you would still work for Lowell?"

"No. The way I get it, Lowell's title would really mean chairman emeritus. He would be a consultant, reporting to Mr. Big in Darmstadt. I suspect it's a gesture aimed at Lowell's vanity and he'd never hear from them. I'd report to Mühlmann's head of U.S. operations."

"Do you think this is going to happen?"

"If I were to bet, I'd say no."

THE FOLLOWING morning, Breal asked Lowell his view of the previous day's events. Lowell grunted a non-committal reply. Breal couldn't resist saying, "I thought their proposal to keep you on as chairman was an interesting one."

"Let me tell you something, George," Lowell said. "There's a clown, a real clown, in one of Shakespeare's plays that says something like, 'to say nothing, to be nothing, and to know nothing is to be a great part of your title.' I think that nicely sums up what they're proposing."

"THEIR LAST offer is $45 a share for all shares, regardless of who owns them or for how long," Cobb said to the ETI board.

"I've been thinking of Chris Grattan's warning," Lowell said. "He's a shrewd lawyer and I take his advice seriously. He said that two tiers of pricing for the stock is risky and recommended I get my premium some other way. All right then, let's modify our proposal. Let's ask for $60 a share for all shares plus the benefits for me that I've spelled out in this chart. Those benefits plus $60 a share for all shares and stock options is what I propose on a take-it-or-leave-it basis." No one at the table objected.

When Breal returned to his office, he calculated the dollar value of Lowell's package. It resulted in a premium of eleven percent over the other shareholders. Lowell's business instincts, Breal concluded, were still intact.

A week later ETI received a response from Mühlmann on the Lowell issues: most of the employment contract terms for Lowell were acceptable, retention of Lowell's present office was not only acceptable but desirable, and they would provide Lowell with a transportation allowance of $50,000 a year to use as he saw fit. But Roth also conveyed the message that while Mühlmann thought ETI a fine company, $60 per share—which amounted to an aggregate price of $120 million—was hopelessly out of line and Roth should discuss this with their client.

VICTOR COBB sat alone with Lowell at the marble table, door closed. "They've been most generous with you, John," Cobb said. "I asked for this meeting to speak frankly with you about the sale of ETI, and to do this as a friend, a concerned party, and a director of the company." Lowell turned an uneasy face toward Cobb. "First I'd like to discuss price. All the analyses we've done result in a value for the company well under $60 per share."

"That's at current earnings," Lowell retorted. "If you look at projected earnings, in a couple of years you easily exceed my $60 asking price."

"Your numbers are conjectural," Cobb said. "Plus—and it's a big plus—this is the last year of preferential treatment for capital gains. If you persist in the $60 per share number"—Cobb looked around, found a pad, scratched some figures"—you'll need to obtain $87 a share in two years. That, you'll agree, is farfetched. But the earnings projections are farfetched. They're unreasonably success-oriented. You're a strong-minded man, John. People tell you, more than most bosses, what they think you want to hear, not necessarily what they believe."

"What are you trying to say, Victor?"

"I'm the only outside director on your board. The other three depend on you for their livelihood and so are cautious in giving you their views. Our relationship is different. I can and must tell you clearly and candidly what I believe. This is not easy for me to say, but I feel it's in the best interest of all of us that it be said. It's time for you to relinquish leadership of this enterprise. You've done a splendid job leading ETI for half a century, a long time in the affairs of men. Two of your finest attributes are grit and perseverance, but these strengths are now weaknesses because they keep you from accepting the change that must be made. You now have the opportunity to step down in a fashion that provides maximum financial gain as well as a comfortable transition. This opportunity will almost certainly never recur."

Lowell had felt confusion rising within him for days, the clarity of his earlier decision growing chaotic. He looked up. "You're right, Victor," he said, "this is an opportunity, and that's why we're talking to those clowns at all. On the one hand, I recognize this and want to get the best price I can. On the other hand, I feel I can still contribute to ETI." Lowell paused, searched for the thought that had plagued him through much of the previous night. "I know myself better than you think. I know that my memory is not what it used to be and that I tire more easily than I did in the past. But I've seen just about every business situation and I know the answers that work . . ." Lowell stopped, felt himself floundering, confusion now a surging wave, then started again. "It's a silly thing to say, but on the one hand I want a high price and on the other I still want to keep ETI." Lowell had a bewildered expression as he said this, smiled foolishly.

Cobb shook his head. "Whether you have one or the other depends on the price you set. In the last three years you've performed a miracle, in my view the final kick of a great marathon runner. This work has now culminated in a unique opportunity, but one that's limited in time. You can't have both the money and ETI. You have to choose. But as things stand now, you *have* chosen. You're ostensibly going through the motions of selling the company. But by setting the price so high you've in effect said no, but you'll be able to blame the shortsightedness of the Germans and not yourself when the deal falls through."

"That's a dizzying flight of pop psychoanalysis, Victor," Lowell said.

"I'm saying let's put this negotiation on a realistic basis. It's bootless to ask for $60 a share, a premium more than three times the market price. That will never happen. Let's drop the price to $55 and see what they come back with. They have, in giving you most of the perks you asked for, agreed to a ten percent premium for you. Now let's address the whole deal realistically. I'm asking your permission to lower the price to $55 a share."

Lowell looked up at Cobb: he seemed a man lost in a cavern. A drop of spittle glistened in his beard; he needed a haircut, and looked tired and rumpled in a way that Cobb had never seen.

"Let me sleep on it," Lowell said. "I'll give you my answer in the morning."

A few minutes after Cobb left, Andre Tergelen appeared in Lowell's office. "I would like to speak with you about the sale of ETI," he said, "not in my official capacity but as a colleague. Mr. Cobb is not a disinterested party in this affair," Tergelen said. "He has much to gain financially from this transaction and nothing to lose. But you—and in a modest way I also—stand to lose the company. No amount of money will compensate for that loss. All of Mühlmann's talk of benefitting from your wisdom and counsel is a sham. Yes, you will have a consulting contract, but you will never be consulted by anyone. Yes, you will have the title of chairman,

but it's only a sop to your vanity and is hollow and mean-
ingless. You will be chairman of nothing. You will sit here,
isolated in this room, unable to give orders to anyone other
than your secretary. There will be no meetings to attend, no
annual report to prepare, no board of directors, nothing. For
you ETI will cease to exist. Cobb cares nothing about this.
He emphasizes changes in the tax law to give you a false
sense of urgency. The fundamental issue here has nothing to
do with taxes. The question is—do you wish to trade your
testicles for a bag of gold? That, Dr. Lowell, is the issue. Cobb
doesn't understand this."

"Why are you so concerned over my welfare?" Lowell
asked, eyes tightened. "What about you? You'll be both rich
and have ETI. I take these people at their word when they
say they won't change management."

"Dr. Lowell, believe me, I know these people far better
than you or Cobb. Their word means nothing. As for me, I
would never work for those animals."

"You were badly traumatized by your wartime experience, Andre. War does not bring out the best in people."

"But why are we only talking to Mühlmann? Why sell
to the first bidder who comes along? There's time. Why not
ask for bids from an American company? You may well get a
higher price. You will never know unless you ask."

After Tergelen left, Lowell realized with a shock that
each time he looked out the window the scene appeared
unfamiliar, as if he were a traveler in a passing train.


THAT NIGHT he dreamt that his teeth were embedded in a
crag of stone, and workmen—armed with small hammers
and cunning chisel-like instruments—chipped at the rock as
they tried to loosen then dislodge his teeth. He awoke with
a splitting headache, tongue like burlap, and shuffled to the
kitchen; he switched on the light and found himself in the

library. It was two-thirty in the morning. Edna Graham found him there at three, slowly articulating Henry the Fourth's soliloquy on sleep. "The line I keep forgetting," he said, "is this: 'O gentle sleep, Nature's soft nurse, how have I frighted thee, that thou no more will weigh my eyelids down?' It just disappears, like the shred of a dream."

As he lay in bed, Lowell recalled again the trip to Europe with Lou when he had stood over the simple cross that marked Patton's grave. In the dark of the night, Lowell nodded toward his fallen hero: he had died at the right time, when his triumphs were fresh, before he turned into a caricature of himself.

The recollection of that scene brought forth another, when the past had been the present, when they had visited Switzerland and rowed on Lake Lucerne and Lou's face was reflected in the water like a lily on a pond. They kissed and her mouth tasted of toothpaste. He had said something witty and she laughed—a clear high-pitched laugh. Then they visited the Lion of Lucerne. The great lion, carved into the living rock of the cliff, a spear plunged into his flank, lay dying. Lou commented that Mark Twain had called it the most mournful and moving piece of stone in the world. Lowell turned in his bed: why was he thinking any of this?

THE FOLLOWING morning Lowell telephoned Cobb. "Victor, I don't think it benefits negotiations to have them proceed with unseemly haste. The Krauts may not like our price, but let them stew over it a while. Since price is what we're after, why don't we do what Breal did for the building? Let's, on a discreet basis, see if an American company is interested at $60 a share. The Mule-whatever people may consider our price too steep, but others might not."

"I thought you were violently opposed to an auction," Cobb said.

"I've changed my mind."

"Well, John, if that's what you want, Lehman, Roth can stall the negotiations with Mühlmann while they look for bids from other companies."

Lowell derived satisfaction from the note of irritation in Cobb's voice.


IN TWO weeks, word came back from the American companies that Lehman, Roth had contacted. "Everyone considered your price way out of line," the LR man said.

"Did you show them our sales and earnings projections?" Lowell asked.

"Absolutely. One man responded by saying that he didn't believe the earnings projections of his own company, so why should he believe anyone else's. Another fellow said your projections weren't at all credible based on past years of low-growth performance. The general impression was that if you can get an offer in the $40–$45 per share range, jump at it before the other guy changes his mind."


THE NEGOTIATIONS with Mühlmann stagnated and there were long intervals of silence. Mühlmann invited Lowell, and whomever of his staff he wished, to visit Darmstadt. Perhaps, they said, it would facilitate matters if Dr. Lowell obtained a firsthand impression of Mühlmann and the dimensions of the company. They understood that ETI represented Dr. Lowell's life's work, and his wish that it would continue in competent and sensitive hands. Lowell declined the invitation. "What good would eating wiener schnitzel and drinking beer with those clowns do?"

Lowell continued to cruise the streets of Boston with Ishmael. He listened to the Dante scholar as he counseled patience; Ishmael reassured Lowell that the other guy was eager and time was on his side. Lowell relaxed, watched the streets of Boston, Chelsea, and Revere roll by, and felt protected.

Lowell moved on price, slowly, reluctantly, with rock-like patience, a dollar per share at a time, over the period of a month. The final agreed-to number was $52 per share, all cash.

"The word I get back," Breal said to his wife, "is that the Germans consider the old man the wiliest fox they've ever done business with. He got one hell of a price . . . well over twice market, more than twenty times earnings, and almost four times the book value of the company."

"They must have really lusted after the place," Susan said. "What happens now?"

"The next step is a board of directors meeting. Lehman, Roth and our lawyers are supposed to present us with the case for accepting the Mühlmann offer. The board then votes on the merger and makes a recommendation to the shareholders."

"Isn't that something of a ritualistic ceremony?" she asked. "I mean, isn't it a foregone conclusion what they're going to recommend and how the board is going to vote?"

"Like they say, it's not over until it's over. There's still plenty of room for cold feet."

# TWENTY-SEVEN

The meeting was held in ETI's executive conference room. In addition to the ETI board and Miss Krane, three spare steno pads before her, there were the Lehman, Roth account executive and two assistants, plus Chris Grattan and two associates from Sherman & Frye. Everyone had a neat pile of documents before him. The lower ranking individuals had the greater masses of paper.

"Gentlemen," Grattan started, "we are here to consider whether it is in the best interests of ETI's stockholders to accept a $52 per share offer for all the common stock of the company. Our investment banker has data to present in this regard."

The LR man handed out copies of a spiral-bound notebook and proceeded to go through the book page by page. In the end, he observed, the Mühlmann offer of $52 per share was most attractive. It was manifest that ETI was worth a good deal more to Mühlmann than to anyone else because of synergy considerations.

"So, gentlemen," the LR man concluded, "Lehman, Roth is prepared to write an opinion letter to your shareholders summarizing the analyses we have made and representing that the Mühlmann price is a fair one." He looked around the room; there were no comments.

"To proceed," Chris Grattan said, "we need a vote of the ETI board of directors accepting or rejecting this merger agreement."

"Let's get on with it," Lowell said. "I vote yes."

"Allow me to poll the board in alphabetical order," Grattan said. "Breal?"

"Yes."

"Cobb?"

"Yes."

"Lowell?"

"Yes."

"Miles?"

"Yes."

"Tergelen?"

"No."

Everyone, including Miss Krane, stared at Tergelen. "Did you say no?" Grattan asked.

"That's correct. I said no."

Lowell stared at Tergelen as if he were not a person at all but some new and inexplicable phenomenon, like the conference table bursting into flame, then exclaimed, *"Why?"* His cry seemed directed more to the heavens than to Tergelen.

"My understanding, Dr. Lowell, is that I don't have to give a reason."

"Like hell you don't!" Cobb exploded. "There's over a hundred million dollars on the table you're saying no to. You've *got* to give a reason!"

Tergelen stared through Cobb without speaking, his face pale and expressionless except for a tightness around his mouth.

"Is it because the buyer is German?" Cobb asked.

No response.

"Look, Tergelen," Cobb said, staring bullet-eyed at the marketing man, "I can understand why you don't like the Krauts. But we're not talking personal animosity here. This is a straight business proposition. You're being asked as a director of ETI whether this deal is in the best interests of the stockholders or not. You're not being asked to vote for the fucking Germans in a popularity contest. Knowing all that you know about the company, is this a good deal for Mr.

and Mrs. Shareholder or not? That's all you're being asked to decide. And, I might add, the shareholders are heavily represented around this table."

"Mr. Cobb, you cannot browbeat me into changing my vote," Tergelen said, his face paler yet.

"But surely, Mr. Tergelen," the LR executive said, "you have some rational reason for opposing this merger."

"We can always sell the company," Tergelen replied. "I see no reason to plunge into this sale now."

"Let's stop right here," Lowell said. "Miss Krane, strike this past conversation from the minutes. Andre, let's you and I have a private talk."

When they left, Cobb said, "That's one crazy son of a bitch," leaving a sliver of space between each of the words. No one disagreed.

They returned twenty minutes later. "Do we need the vote of the board to be unanimous?" Lowell asked, his face dark.

"It's desirable," Grattan replied, "but not essential. Only a two-thirds majority is necessary."

"Let's poll the board one more time, then," Lowell said.

The vote was four to one in favor of merger.

"Can Tergelen screw things up?" Cobb asked. He spoke as though Tergelen were no longer in the room.

"I don't see how," Grattan said, and the LR man concurred.


THE FOLLOWING day, a joint press release—crafted by the Mühlmann and ETI attorneys and reviewed by the management of both companies—announcing the acquisition was issued. Simultaneously, Lowell put out a one page statement that was posted on the bulletin boards in the cafeteria of the company's Burlington headquarters and the New Hampshire plant, and stuffed that Friday in the paycheck envelopes of all employees. This letter had also been approved by Mühlmann.

The offer that went out to the stockholders of ETI was a long and complex document, but the operative statements were few and were spelled out on the top page. The headline read: "OFFER TO PURCHASE FOR CASH ALL SHARES OF COMMON STOCK OF ELECTRONIC TECHNOLOGIES INCORPORATED BY MÜHLMANN OF AMERICA, A WHOLLY OWNED SUBSIDIARY OF MÜHLMANN AG OF DARMSTADT, GERMANY, AT $52 PER SHARE." This was followed by the statement: "The Board of Directors of Electronic Technologies Incorporated has determined that the offer is fair and in the best interests of the shareholders of the company, has approved the merger, and recommends that the stockholders accept the offer."

On the advice of Chris Grattan, Lowell did not fire Tergelen. "It would be viewed by the courts as retaliation," he said, "and put in question his independence as a director."

In the ensuing weeks, which were a limbo period as the ETI shareholders tendered their stock, Andre Tergelen became a pariah within the company. No one spoke to him; his people avoided him except for the strictest necessities. He came to the office less often, and then finally didn't show up at all.

Krakowski wondered whether Tergelen would resort to one last malevolent act. Clare thought a full-page ad in the *Wall Street Journal* opposing the offer would be an interesting though expensive move. Breal thought Tergelen might send a letter to all the shareholders stating his position, whatever that was, assuming he could get his hands on a stockholders list. But Tergelen did none of these things. On the day the offer expired, he delivered a brief letter of resignation to Lowell, cleared out his desk, and took home his personal effects. He did not say goodbye to anyone other than his secretary. Breal wandered into his office, shook Andre's limp hand, and wished him luck. Tergelen was growing a beard; it was still in the early stages and made him look disreputable. Clare wondered whether Tergelen had tendered his shares.

Krakowski remarked that Andre may be crazy but he wasn't stupid.

During the limbo period, Lowell cruised the streets with Ishmael. He learned that Ishmael admired the churches of Boston—Trinity Church in Copley Square, St. Paul's in Brookline, St. Stephens in Cohasset, the First Unitarian in Newton—and as they drove by he pointed out their uniqueness and sources of beauty. Lowell found that Ishmael's aesthetic judgments coincided with his own, adding to his feeling of comradeship with the man. "They're not starved like the churches in Italy," Ishmael said. "Many of those are shut down, even very beautiful ones, abandoned because there's no money to keep them up. They're just a roost for birds now. A terrible pity."

Look where we are. Watertown. A scrim of snow covers the monuments. Not a place but a distant sorrow. Mt. Auburn cemetery. Always avoided the spot. A cross weighs down his head. Lou's idea. Flowers in perpetuity. Her idea too. Poor Eric. Death lay on him like an untimely frost upon the sweetest flower of all the field. Killed twice. Impact broke his neck, a shard of glass punctured his carotid artery. See him through a swirl of mist—a young man as he was when he died, an island in time. Forever young. Forever lost. Grandmother said that when you died, your soul became a star in the sky. Where was Eric's star? And where would mine be? And what did it matter?

Lowell often invited Breal to lunch. As he put away martinis, Lowell recounted stories of the early days at ETI. He repeated himself more frequently now. Once he told Breal the same story each day for three consecutive days. Yet his face had now acquired a look of wisdom, of invulnerability, as though life could no longer harm him.

Lowell also spoke with affection of his friend Victor Cobb. The story goes that at Annapolis, Cobb never asked a question of his instructors, yet he finished third in his class. He was also the star of the wrestling team; he was quick to discover and exploit his opponents' weaknesses and he never grunted the way other wrestlers did. It was his wrestling teammates who dubbed him the silent killer. In the war in the Pacific, Cobb led successful marine attacks at Guadalcanal, Kwajalein, and Saipan. He was possessed of great physical courage. He was a marine corps first lieutenant at the start of the war and a full colonel at the end. Eventually, he commanded all marine corps operations in the Pacific. But there was no war then and it was a lot less fun, or so Lowell claimed. He also said that Cobb was sorry he had already retired from the corps when Vietnam rolled around.

At one luncheon invitation, when Breal arrived in Lowell's office, he was seated on his couch, a pile of folders stacked on the marble table before him. "This might interest you, George," he said. "I'm going through my files trying to clear out fifty years of debris. You should do that every fifty years, you know, whether you need to or not." Lowell set aside one paper then another. Letters no doubt written by men whose gravestones had long ago tilted in the icy winters and thawing ground of the New England seasons. Lowell handled the papers with the reverence of old family photographs, a man replaying the tape of his life. He threw nothing out. As Lowell turned over these old memos, reports, financial statements, so important at the time, he seemed to become part of them, to give off an odor of decay and sadness—the melancholy scent of time past, lost days. Then Lowell said, said it to the documents before him, "It's difficult, you know, to get up in the morning and have no place to go."

Breal thought of one platitude then another, but Lowell never looked up nor did he appear to expect a response. Seller's remorse, Breal decided, but had the impression there was much more, that before him was a man from whom some essential part had been removed—a kidney or a lung—with only an airless hollow left inside.

Lowell invited the Cobbs and the Breals to dinner at Lowell House prior to the close. As Breal and Susan pulled into the driveway, Breal saw the old stone lion at his lonely vigil beside the asphalt. It struck him as the most mournful sight he had ever seen.

"It's okay," Susan commented by way of consolation. "The Romans said that sculpture had the power to influence the world. They thought stone was immortal, so the power of a stone figure would survive forever. Maybe they were right."

But Breal did not hear Susan's observation. As he parked his car, the image of the old lion in the dying twilight stayed with him and pushed aside all else.

Before dinner, Lowell put away three martinis and rambled on about the lack of vision in American industry. Not much was said of the acquisition. Breal found the evening a desultory affair. The Monet, the candelabra and silver, all glittering, now struck Breal as loot from a sacked city, the spoils of ancient victories. Lowell gave the Breals a tour of the house—George Breal's third—and in doing this seemed to take on a weary nobility. He paused at the portrait of his grandmother, called her a saint and dropped into a reverie. The portrait, Breal now saw, resembled Lowell's daughter. At the photograph of Lowell and his tank, Cobb pointed to the figure of Patton and said, "That's the best goddamned marine the army ever had."

"It's tough to know by what scale to judge a life," Susan said to her husband when they left.

Breal signed a two-year employment contract with Mühl-mann at the same rate of pay he received at ETI, but with considerable incentive compensation based on performance. He received $2 million in cash for his ETI bonus shares and stock options, and would keep almost all of it even after federal and state taxes. Breal decided to invest the money for the time being in U.S. Treasury securities. He and Susan did not celebrate nor did they speak of the change in their finances with their children. Susan commented that she didn't feel any more secure now than before they had the money. Breal had to admit he felt the same. He briefly wondered why, with all that money in the bank, he was working at all, but could not bring himself to think too deeply on the subject.

The day after the close, Dick Miles handed Breal his resignation. "This'll save you the trouble of letting me go," he said. "A subsidiary company doesn't need a treasurer." Breal was relieved.

All of the men Breal had brought in—Clare, Fredricks, Krakowski, Norrie, Rostov—made a substantial sum as a result of the stock options they had been granted. As far as Breal knew, some of the men took their wives out to dinner, but there were no big celebrations.

After the close, one of the first things Breal did was have the second door in the Manchester plant—in the corridor that led from Fredricks' production control area to the punch presses—reinstalled. He also modified the parking lot in front of the headquarters building to eliminate the reserved parking spaces. He told all hands, "If you want a good parking spot, all you have to do is get to work early." He replaced the guard at the front desk with an attractive receptionist, the remaining guards with an outside security service, and he hired a new head of marketing.

Breal was tempted to pitch the photograph of Lowell and his ancient management team. Yet he found something both tender and quaint in the picture: a window on time past, a much older reality. The figures reminded him of the apostles at the last supper. Breal finally decided to leave it, a record of an earlier perhaps more innocent ETI. It gave the place a sense of tradition, like a portrait of the Founding Fathers.

A technology transfer program between ETI and the Mühlmann laboratories in Darmstadt was put in place. The first project was for ETI to tailor Mühlmann's design for a "smart" sensor, which contained a built-in microprocessor to manipulate information, for the U.S. market. Emil Rostov met with Mühlmann's head of research and development and they formulated the program together. Rostov was enthusiastic.

Mühlmann jettisoned their U.S. distributors for sensor products and switched to the ETI network. The two product lines complemented each other, and where they competed the customer decided which was preferable. The distributors were delighted with the arrangement. Mühlmann became the dominant U.S. supplier of sensors to the factory automation market.

ETI's European operation was merged with that of Mühlmann, and Roland Lemec was fired.

# TWENTY-EIGHT

Catherine passed the bar on her first try. Cobb offered to help her obtain a position as an associate in one of the larger Boston law firms. Instead, with Ishmael's encouragement, she accepted a job as a public defender in the Suffolk County district attorney's office. She took only women's cases, frequently those of desperate black women accused of prostitution, drug-related crime, theft, or vagrancy. She derived great satisfaction from this work, though the pay was mediocre. She often counseled with Ishmael on her cases and found his advice down-to-earth, commonsensical.

Ishmael's translation of Dante's *Inferno* was published by the Empire Press, the text illustrated with William Blake's 1824–1827 watercolors. Astonishingly, the book became a best seller. "Sets a new poetic standard," "whirling linguistic momentum," "speaks poignantly to the modern reader," "sheer drama," "seethes with passion," "for everyman," were phrases the critics used. The work was an alternate selection of the Book of the Month Club, went through six printings in hardcover and was issued in paperback. In an article on Ishmael, the *New York Times* wrote, "Who would have predicted that a fourteenth-century Italian poem freighted with medieval notions of sin and retribution would achieve bestsellerdom at the end of the twentieth century? And who would have imagined that this miracle of translation would be accomplished by a Boston cab driver?"

Ishmael was wary of compliments, avoided interviews and lectures, and resisted being lionized by the black community.

He sought shelter in Catherine and bent his efforts to completing his translation of Dante's *Purgatory* and *Paradise*. Lowell remarked that he had known from their first meeting that Ishmael Carter was a genius, Dante improbably reincarnated in modern America.

Tom's novel, *Homecoming*, wandered through the publishing world for a year, then was picked up by a small press in Philadelphia. While the book was not a financial success, it did receive excellent reviews. Tom adapted the novel for the theater and the play was produced in Boston to good notices. Tom decided to devote himself completely to drama, stubbornly refused Lowell's offer of financial assistance, and continued to drive a cab, saying it was a superb source of material.

Michael graduated magna cum laude from MIT with a BS in electrical engineering, and was accepted into the school's computer science PhD program. On one occasion, Lowell, seated in his chair with folded hands like some placid household god, listened to his grandson explain that parallel processing computers were the wave of the future. Lowell nodded sagely and agreed that this was undoubtedly true.

Evenings, Lowell and Edna sat in the Great Hall. Sometimes they watched television. Other times Edna read while Lowell drank his martinis, pondered the eternal mystery of things, and often fell asleep in his chair.


IT WAS a dazzling fall day, the air crisp and clear, and the elms along Commonwealth Avenue in brilliant color. As the guests entered the Algonquin Club, no one could resist commenting on the weather.

Catherine wore a traditional ball gown in silk-faced satin, while Edna was clad in a floor-sweeping all silk A-line. Catherine had a garland of Queen Anne's lace in her hair, while Edna wore a crown of Chantilly lace spangled with pearls and a pearl necklace. Breal had never seen Edna with jewelry or makeup. She usually wore black or gray, but now, dressed in white, her features accented, she appeared youthful and full of spirit. Lowell, attired in an Oxford gray cutaway, silk ascot tie with winged collar, and striped trousers, freshly barbered, seemed a bit confused, but looked very distinguished. Ishmael was similarly dressed: he appeared shy and vulnerable and also a bit confused.

Ishmael's parents were there along with his brother and sister. Lowell welcomed them and told them that Ishmael was a brilliant man. They smiled and nodded, though they never seemed completely at ease.

Buck Clawson was there, as big as ever but looking tanned and fit. He was adding additional touches to his A-frame house on Moosehead Lake and wanted to get the job done before the start of the long Maine winter. His wife, a thin gray-haired woman whom Breal had never met before, shifted position and disappeared behind Clawson as he spoke. Craig Holloway attended with his wife Rosemary. They held hands, seemed as happy and innocent as Hansel and Gretel. Craig told Breal that he was now a consultant to the Museum of Science in Boston on their technology exhibits. Dick Miles and his wife also attended, both tanned from two weeks in Nassau. Breal had imagined Mrs. Miles as a dour New England matron, but instead she was a diminutive bubbly woman with bright, intelligent eyes.

Lowell's best man was Victor Cobb, and Susan Breal was Edna's matron of honor. Tom was Ishmael's best man and Catherine chose a law school classmate as her matron of honor. A string trio of bearded young men played in a corner of the private hall. Lowell introduced Breal to Gordon Barrett, an MIT fundraiser, then disappeared to chat with other guests. Barrett told Breal of their plan to raise a hundred million dollars for the Institute. "It's called The Millennium Fund," Barrett said. "John's idea."

"Does he ever yell at people?" Breal asked, smiling.

Barrett looked puzzled. "You must be thinking of someone else," he said. "John Lowell? He's the sweetest of men. Honey wouldn't melt in his mouth."

Edna pushed back her veil, regarded herself critically in the glass. She had refused Catherine's offer to help with her makeup and had gone to a professional instead. She thought the result made her look whore-like, then decided that was all right. How strange! A change in clothes and hairstyle, the application of lipstick, eyeliner and blush, and she had become another person. She saw herself as fluid, without sharp edges, like a watercolor, yet she felt perfect: hair, clothes, face and body. She adjusted her crown, was surprised at the loveliness of her hands, freshly manicured, smooth and innocent. Lowell had once told her that for the ancient Egyptians exactitude was symbolized by a feather that served as a weight on scales used for the weighing of souls. What would she place in balance against her soul? A hummingbird perhaps. Suddenly she liked herself, decided she had an instinct for life. She had not wanted the double wedding, had wanted the triumph all to herself. But Lowell had been so insistent— something about starting his family afresh—that she had to agree. But she would not agree to she and Catherine wearing the same gown, something else Lowell had wanted, and she had insisted on different bouquets and separate wedding cakes. The honeymoon together, alas, was not negotiable. Lowell would hear of nothing else.

Edna prepared to enter the hall. She dropped her veil, regarded herself again, dress, pearls and crown, all white, and now saw herself as infinitely untouched, radiating a virginal aura. Then she thought of her past life—lonely as a hermit is what she had been—and then she thought of Lowell, her groom. And where love should be, she found only an empty hollow. Suddenly she felt ashamed. Then she thought of her life to come: Lowell ever more confused, more demanding, and on and on, while she grew wizened, stale like old bread, inexorably drifting into a heartbreaking twilight. In the glare of this sudden vision, a sense of irretrievable loss sprang up and took possession of her.

Lowell came toward her and as she lifted her eyes toward him, she felt a lump rise in her throat—as when she was a child, forced to go to church, her mother shook her like a rag doll for moving about in the pew. Lowell smiled at her, a reassuring smile, yet she saw it as needy and experienced an instant of tenderness. He took her elbow as though to steer her through dangerous terrain and they entered the hall. She felt herself moving slowly through a large still space. They advanced down the aisle, Catherine and Ishmael behind them. She clutched her bouquet, had the feeling that a lighthouse had turned in its great round and now momentarily shone upon her. Faces, indistinguishable one from another, smiled at her, and she heard soft admiring murmurs. Improbably she wanted to cry. Lowell's grip on her arm tightened: they had stopped before the improvised altar. The ceremony was about to begin.

In the double ceremony, Catherine carried a hand bouquet of lilies of the valley, while Edna's bouquet was white cattleya orchids and caladium leaves. Both Lowell and Ishmael wore a single matching flower in their lapel. Breal thought the couples very handsome as they walked down the aisle as the trio played a muted version of the "Bridal Chorus" from *Lohengrin*. Both couples were very solemn as they exchanged their marriage vows.

At the reception after the ceremony, Lowell, a martini in hand, found Breal and thanked him for all he had done for ETI. He introduced Breal to his friends, MIT and Museum of Fine Arts people mostly, and commented that, like Lincoln, it had taken him a long time to find a good general. "In my case, about forty years," he said. "Why did it take me so long? I guess I was just plain stupid." He put an arm around Breal as he said this, the only paternal gesture he had ever made toward him. Lowell gave the same speech a moment later when introducing Breal to another group. This time he added, "I think there was an element of providence. When I had reached the limits of frustration and despair and wondered how I would go on, why the good Lord sent me George Breal." He introduced Breal to Gordon Barrett a second time.

Breal and Susan stood in line at the buffet and chose Irish smoked salmon, a cucumber mousse, and something which the French server said was carbonnades flamandes, a Flemish beef stew made with ale. Breal watched Lowell while he circulated, holding a fresh martini, and accepting congratulations. "You know," Breal said to Susan, emotion hoarsening his voice. "I really love the little shit." "Of course you do," she replied. The trio played "We've Only Just Begun," "Just in Time," and a spirited rendition of "Yes Sir, That's My Baby." Susan contemplated the two brides: for a moment they were back to back, an unlikely Janus head.

The Breals sat at the head table together with Victor and Emily Cobb. Everyone except the newlywed couples rose as Victor Cobb raised his glass of champagne to toast the health and happiness of the two brides and grooms. Cobb then read Chapter 13 from First Corinthians, substituting the word love for the word charity. The room was still as he read, and Breal— at the words, the scene, and Cobb's obvious sincerity—again felt emotion rise within him. He turned towards Susan: she had tears in her eyes. Then Ishmael recited from memory the words of Dante, then offered his translation, which finished: "And I shall sing of that second kingdom / wherein the human spirit is made clean, / becoming worthy to ascend to heaven."

The wedding cakes were both three-tiered affairs in white, one with yellow accents and the other trimmed in pale blue. At the top of one was a vial holding two cattleya orchids—the other topped with lilies of the valley. Lowell held his hand over Edna's as she cut the first two pieces of cake and Ishmael and Catherine did the same. Each groom offered his bride a bite of the first slice and she offered him a bite of the second.

The two couples were honeymooning together in Italy. Ishmael would show them around his beloved Florence, birthplace of Dante, then to Ravenna, to visit the resting place of the great man. Ishmael, when he spoke of this, seemed to be speaking of a departed friend, and the least he could do was pay his respects at graveside.

When the two couples ducked into the Cadillac to leave, Lowell tripped over the sill. Edna caught him, then straightened him in his seat. The couples waved and smiled at the crowd—though Susan later commented to Breal that Edna's smile seemed a bit forced—as the limousine pulled away from the curb and into the traffic on Commonwealth Avenue.